The Stuff You Fail To Notice

A Novel By

Annie Cook

ISBN:978-1-917601-07-8

www.Anniecookwriter.com

Other Novels by Annie Cook:

THE TEAPOT COTTAGE SERIES

No Small Change (#1)

The Power Of Notes And Spells (#2)

When It's Meant To Happen (#3)

Ruin Reins and Redemption (#4)

~ * ~

A Moral Swerve

Thicker Than Water

~ * ~

About The Author

www.anniecookwriter.com

Annie Cook is a writer of women's contemporary fiction, and literary fiction. She has self-published five novels so far, in the Teapot Cottage Series, and has also written a number of 'filler' novels as stand-alone works that link by adding different dimensions to some of the characters in the TC series. Annie is originally from New Zealand but divides her time between the UK and her home in Southern Italy.

To my Aunty Beryl Greenhalgh.

You understood betrayal all too well,
yet you rose so elegantly and beautifully above it.
You were an inspiration to me;
in that, and in everything else.

Rest in peace, darling. This one's for you.

Acknowledgements

Several people have helped me bring this book to life.

Kerry Purvis, my biggest champion, best friend, and husband of 28 years; you are the unfailing rock who takes care of me when I'm so absorbed that I forget to do it myself. Tea, toast and kiwi marmite are a winning combination. Keep it up!

Beryl Greenhalgh (deceased); you showed me, many moons ago, how important dignity is in the face of unbearable heartbreak, and how well a strong woman can recover. You were a spectacular influence in my life more than sixty years. Thank you for all that you were, to me and to so many others.

The gorgeous shiny diamonds in my life; Yvonne Raymond, Katherine McDiarmid, Dawn Walter, Keren Cook, Laura Toop, and Jean and Trevor Jones; thank you for your unfailing support, frontline cheering and promoting. Your belief in me and my work means everything.

Aisha Jamil, my brave Graphic Designer; thank you for having the patience of a saint while I've nitpicked over details. I know I sometimes drove you bonkers, but you're still here.

Gwen Morrison and the team at Publish Nation; thanks for all the work you so calmly and professionally do, in making this book accessible.

To my fans and readers across the world; thanks for hanging with me, I'm so very glad you're here!

Chapter One

The over-warm and poorly ventilated bus, with its steamed-up windows and slightly dour driver, finally arrived in Torley town. Minty Cartwright gratefully got off it, stretched, yawned, and looked wearily around her. It was such a relief to finally be here. The train journey from Bristol to Carlisle had been long, and then she'd had to take a bus to Torley. Thankfully, she hadn't had to wait for very long at the uncovered stop outside the station. The Lake District weather was notoriously unpredictable, especially in early November. It had been closing in quickly as she'd got off the train and she hadn't thought to bring an umbrella. She berated herself for having walked past the tall tub in the hallway at home, crammed with brollies of all colours and sizes, without even really seeing it.

It's normal enough to tune out to what's right in front of you, I suppose, when you see it every day and don't need it. But how annoying, that I didn't even think to grab one on my way out. Probably 'peri,' messing with my head as usual.

She made a mental note to try and find an umbrella in Torley town, if there wasn't one at Teapot Cottage, but she'd check first. There wasn't much point in getting another to add to the dozen or so that were already sitting at home, if she didn't have to. It was why they had so many, she supposed. They always seemed to be going somewhere without one, buying one to use when they got caught short, then adding it to the collection when they got home again. They were all guilty of it; herself, her husband Leo, and their kids; Belle and Ethan.

It had been a huge relief to finally get off a very tatty train. Minty had muttered to herself more than once, on her long and protracted journey, about how poor the rail services were nowadays, with their endless delays and grimy carriages with ripped upholstery and unwashed windows. Most of the bigger stations had a general air of scruffiness too, with suspect 'spillages' congealing in corners, overflowing bins, and dirty little mice hopping all over the tracks, but the smaller stations were even worse. They were marginally cleaner, in most cases, but automation had replaced the need for a human presence at far too many. It left them with a distinct air of abandonment, as if nobody really cared anymore. It always felt a little spooky, and vaguely dystopian, especially when she happened to be the only person there. The presence of CCTV was only vaguely reassuring.

At one time, when she was younger, the rail network had been amazing. Train travel was exciting, back then. She could have gone virtually anywhere, and she often travelled to all kinds of weird and wonderful places. She seldom had to worry about a train being dirty, delayed or cancelled, and she could certainly make a trip without feeling like she might need to sell one of her kidneys for the price of the fare!

How times had changed. Not only were most services unreliable these days; the ticket prices were nothing short of astronomical too. It annoyed her a lot, that she could have had a full week by a pool somewhere in sunny Spain (albeit with a 'cheapie' airline and a basic three-star hotel) for less than the eye-watering cost of her return train fare within her home country. No wonder commuters felt ripped off for their simple need to get from A to B, and even that wasn't as simple or straightforward as it used to be, for many.

Thanks to years of rail network privatisation, hundreds of little towns had lost their train stations, and Torley had been one of them. Some fool, somewhere in high office, had declared that the smaller stations weren't 'viable' anymore for the all-important stakeholders to get their lovely profits from. Lines all over the country had been systematically torn up, and railway stations closed or demolished. It sent a sad message to the people in those places, that their needs were no longer important.

It all made most people think twice about going on holiday by train anymore but for Minty it had still been preferable to driving all this way – even with the inconvenience of having to 'bus-it' from Carlisle city.

On its arrival into Torley, the bus had stopped in front of a florist shop called Heavenly Blooms. The shop's riotous sign was painted in striped and spotty multi-coloured lettering, and littered with flowers in impossible colours and shapes. It had a distinct sixties-style, flower-power vibe; funky and cheerful, and Minty was faintly amused to see that the local undertaker, Frost Funeral Services, was conveniently situated right next-door. That had a smaller and far more discreet sign, lettered in simple gold-on-black, as if it were making a quiet but important statement of refusal to be intimidated or outclassed by the florist shop's overt brashness.

Like all the other little shops that lined the High Street, these two were made of local stone and finished with multi-paned windows set into bay-shaped sills. One or two panes, in different bays, had the dimpled glass of 'yesteryear.' The overall effect was quaint, cheerful and welcoming. All of the shops seemed to be independently owned and run, too. There wasn't a single chain-store sign in evidence, which immediately made Minty feel as if she'd stepped back in time. If it weren't for the cars that lined the curbs on both sides of the street, she wouldn't have known what century she was in!

She was keen to find a taxi and get up to Teapot Cottage as quickly as she could. As the bus had rumbled its way here from Carlisle, the early-November sky had taken on a slightly over-brilliant metallic hue, behind the darkening clouds that now hung like an oppressive shroud above the town. It would be sensible to get to the cottage and get settled before the incoming storm unleashed its fury across the Torley valley.

Sadly, although her mind was focussed on that, Minty's body had other ideas. As she stepped away from the bus, she instantly started feeling wobbly and lightheaded, and she realised that she needed to eat something – and quickly – if she didn't want to collapse in the street!

She'd left home at the crack of dawn, without having any breakfast, and the train journey from Bristol Temple Meads to Carlisle, via Manchester Piccadilly, had been ridiculously long. It had also been hampered by a delayed connection. She hadn't fancied anything from the uninspiring selection of food on offer, at the station kiosks or on the train, and she was hungry enough now to 'eat a scabby horse and go back for the rider,' as her grandfather used to say.

The sudden, dire need for sustenance sent her scurrying down a little road called Amble Walk, just off the High Street. She found a lovely traditional café called Ye Olde Torley Tea Shoppe, and decided that a cup of coffee and a sticky bun would probably be enough to save her from passing out.

Despite the fact that it was still around seven weeks until December, the café already had a naked Christmas tree propped up just inside the window. It was still waiting to be decorated, and it looked a little forlorn, in its abandoned state – much like Minty was feeling, herself. Christmas was racing towards her like a freight train she couldn't jump clear of, but she couldn't bring herself to think about it yet. To her current scrambled frame of mind, it would be the best of blessings if someone cancelled the so-called 'festive season' altogether. This year, for the Cartwright/McLeod family at least, it promised to be a monumental shambles.

A woman quickly came across and introduced herself as Peg Tripper, the owner of the café. She grinned and nodded when Minty remarked on the starkness of the tree.

'Ah, yes,' she explained. 'My husband Eric popped in here on a rare visit, a few days ago, so I got him to drag the tree down from the loft for me. I'll chuck a few baubles on it in a couple of weeks, when folk start feeling a bit more festive. I can get those down myself, but the tree's a bloody nuisance to haul down from up there. I took the chance for some help when it came, but the poor thing does look a bit sad, I'll grant you.'

She responded to Minty's question about where to find a taxi, with a rueful shake of her head.

'I'm sorry, love. There's no taxi stand here, I'm afraid. There's no demand for it, but there is a service. I'll call our local cabbie Adam Driver for you, when you've finished your coffee. It should only take him a few minutes to get here. Where are you headed?'

She smiled broadly when Minty told her she was headed for Teapot Cottage. Apparently Peg was a good friend of the owner, Mrs Raven.

'Ah, you'll have a nice quiet time up there,' she said with a wink. 'It's a very special, cosy little place. And you're welcome back here love, whenever you want, for more coffee and cake, or something a bit more hearty.'

She offered to sell Minty a wedge of spinach and sweetcorn quiche and a take-away pot of vegetable soup, suggesting she could reheat it for her dinner a bit later on. Minty hadn't even thought about an evening meal for her first night, and she didn't have the energy or the enthusiasm to go trailing round the town's little supermarket that was visible through the café windows. Quiche and soup seemed like an excellent idea, so she readily agreed.

A taxi came to collect her, just as she was finishing her snack, and it only took a couple of minutes to whisk her from the town to Teapot Cottage. She found the key under the rosebush pot next to the front door, right where the owner Mrs Raven had said it would be.

As the heavy wooden door swung open, on its quiet, well-oiled hinges, she was greeted by a surprising sense of warmth. A rush of gratitude hit her but, just as she crossed the threshold, her mobile phone rang. Her stomach plummeted, when she saw the caller ID.

Clutching both her holdall and her bag of dinner with one hand, and pressing the phone's 'decline' button with the other,

Minty stretched her right leg out behind her to close the front door. Terminating the call was the wisest choice for now. It would only be another nasty one, like all the others, from the one person in the world she never wanted to hear from, ever again; 'Bloody' Fiona Winterson – the woman she used to love with all her heart.

She fought back the rising tide of fury that threatened to swamp her, and actively resisted the urge to throw the phone to the floor and stamp on it.

For God's sake, you crazy bitch, give me a break! I haven't even made it through the freakin' door here yet!

She closed her eyes and did her fail-safe 'one-minute remedy.' She took three deep breaths; in, to the count of six, hold for six, and out to the count of six. After those, and a quick roll of her shoulders, she'd calmed down again, and managed to put the call out of her mind – for now at least.

She dropped her heavy holdall to the floor, put the little paper carrier-bag of quiche and soup onto the coffee table, and shrugged out of her backpack. She turned to look out through one of the picture windows of Teapot Cottage, and took a sharp intake of breath. The view extended right across the Torley valley, and it was *stunning*. Dramatic and tranquil, it instantly soothed her.

Feeling overwhelmed by the desire to escape for a while from everything that had been dragging her down, back in Bristol, Minty had acted on instinct and done a quick internet search for holiday houses. Teapot Cottage had popped up, and she'd immediately given in to an overriding compulsion to book it straight away, drop everything in her life without even bothering to question the sanity of doing it, and rush blindly to its front door. Impulsivity wasn't in her nature but, for whatever reason, the pull to come here and hole up for a while had been impossible to resist.

She was relieved and delighted, therefore, to find that the cottage was every bit as beautiful as the website showed it to be, and happily just as remote. It was exactly as described; a quiet, tucked away house, nestled into a quiet corner of a small farm on the edge of Torley; a Lake District 'working' town. It was a farming community; not on the tourist trail at all, and that suited Minty just fine. As a God-sent bolthole, where she could catch her breath and ignore the outside world for three weeks, this little place was perfect.

She'd come up from Bristol by train because she wanted to feel like she was embarking on a real adventure; not just jumping into her car and 'running away from home' because things were difficult. That felt too convenient; like a cop-out. So did the prospect of having a car at the ready that would make it so much easier to 'wimp out' and head home again too early, before she'd really given herself enough time to process everything that had happened in the past couple of weeks. She wanted to feel like she was on a voyage of discovery because, in essence, that's what this journey needed to be. A much-needed chance to reflect, get her scrambled thoughts back on an even keel, and find a new way forward from her blown-apart life; it all needed to start right now.

That includes getting a handle on these stupid phone calls from Bloody Fiona, who has no damn right to be angry at all, about anything!

Minty took another couple of deep breaths, and looked around her. She decided that Peg Tripper had been right; there *was* a real cosiness about Teapot Cottage. It *did* feel special; more like someone's much-loved permanent home, instead of the average typically soulless holiday let.

She pinched herself a little when she wandered upstairs and saw the beds with their brightly patterned, patchwork-crocheted bedspreads and their plump and enticing pillows. They looked *so* homely and inviting! The cosy little bathroom tucked between the two bedrooms, with its dove-grey walls and luxurious fluffy pink towels, felt warm and welcoming too.

Oh, this place is gorgeous! I'll be very cosy and happy here. I think the only problem I'm going to have is not wanting to leave, at the end!

Back downstairs in the lovely brick-walled kitchen, she grinned at the bright red Aga. She quickly set about filling the kettle and setting it onto one of the hotplates to boil, to make a pot of tea. The little Aga was an older version of the black one she had at home. She loved them; they always felt comforting, and this one lent a lot of character to the charming little space. The big, traditional old wooden drying rack above it had what looked like a couple of Keily-printed tea towels hanging off it. Set against the opposite wall was an old Welsh dresser, heavily crammed with crockery and serving dishes, and a dining table and chairs claimed the space in between.

She was delighted to find that Mrs Raven had thoughtfully provided a few provisions. There were some items in the fridge, and a loaf of home-made bread wrapped in another pretty tea towel sitting on the bench. A welcome note with a smiley face on it sat propped up against a very nice-looking bottle of cabernet sauvignon, on the kitchen table.

Okay, so there's milk, eggs, bacon, butter, cheese, bread and wine! How lovely, to walk in and find all this! Quiche and soup for supper then, and scrambled eggs for breakfast! That's not a bad start, is it?

Minty didn't eat meat, so she could probably give back the bacon, with gentle thanks, but everything else on offer was very welcome. She decided to take her cup of tea to one of the two generously padded curved window seats that sat in front of Teapot Cottage's living room windows. She tried to concentrate on the wonderful view of Torley Valley, instead of dwelling on Bloody Fiona's latest telephone 'missile' that had hit her as she was walking through the door. She hadn't answered it this time, which was a 'first,' and therefore a good step forward, but she knew it wouldn't be the last call that came.

Clearly, hightailing it north for the last three weeks of her month's leave of absence, in an attempt to pull her scrambled head together without major distraction, was not going to be as easy as she'd hoped. The plan was still in danger of serious derailment but, to be fair, that was largely her own fault. She could certainly fix it, and stay on track. All she needed to do was stop answering her phone, and listening to Bloody Fiona's bitchy, rambling rants.

As much as she knew she shouldn't give in and answer the calls from her ex-best friend, the urge to do so was irresistible; almost as if she felt on some level that she actually deserved to be shouted at. She didn't of course, but could she say no? No. Not yet, but Fiona's constant barrage of abuse still had her fuming, nonetheless.

She'd been fuming a lot in recent weeks, which wasn't like her at all. Normally, she was quite easy-going. She didn't suffer fools for more than a split second, but she was pretty good at keeping her blood pressure where it should be, and not getting too upset by stressful situations or by the people who caused them. Rarely did she ever lose her cool and feel like throttling someone.

Walking away was usually the easiest and absolutely *always* the more dignified choice. But, in the space of twenty days, nineteen hours and sixteen minutes, everything – and it really was *everything* – had turned completely on its head. Minty's life now looked and felt more like an ash-filled nuclear winter, than the sun-filled 'picnic in the park' of just a few weeks ago.

And it wasn't just her life that was undergoing a sea change. Minty truly felt that she *herself* was changing. Despite her best efforts, she wasn't quite able to connect anymore with the chilled, laid-back person she'd been just prior to finding out, in the course of an accidental conversation she arguably shouldn't have been having in the first place, that her husband Leo – the erstwhile love of her life but now officially the Biggest Asshole of the Century – was having an affair with her best friend Fiona, and had been for two and a half years.

Minty's 'chilled' vibe had all but disintegrated, along with her marriage and the longest and most important friendship of her life. She was now, more or less, a seething mess of murderous intent.

Oh, and let's not forget about my questionably stable hormones, which are probably fuelling all this fury and confusion raging around in my head!

Minty was officially in 'peri'; that delightful pre-menopausal place where she was teetering on a hormonal cliff edge, dealing with all kinds of random and unpredictable emotions and bodily quirks and bangs. Most of the time, she felt as if she were suspended, in the weirdest, unfamiliar psychological state; of continually bracing herself without really knowing what for. She sensed a storm, rumbling in the distance. As low-key as it was right now, she had a horrible feeling that behind the gentle rumbles, a full-force, hormone-stripping hurricane was on its way to turn her inside out.

Timing was everything. But it was such a cringeworthy stereotype, wasn't it? Mid-life Marriage Meltdown colliding ever-so-sharply at the intersection with 'The Change Of Life'? It seemed to happen with monotonous regularity. She knew far too many women who had suffered from the exact same set of circumstances – the worst that life could throw at them, all at once.

'Okay, here you go; how about *this* for a laugh? Your husband's shagging your best mate. Yeeha! Oh, and just for the joy of it, now that we've popped you onto *that* rollercoaster, let's also chuck some haywire hormones at you too. Wassamatta? Not enough hot flushes and bouts of weeping? Palms and feet not sweaty enough? Need a few more homicidal mood swings? Well, let's dial things up a bit then, shall we? Let's turn your top lip into Sherwood Forest, litter your chest with pretty little pimples, pop out a couple of random varicose veins, drench you in a few really nice night-sweats, and wehey! Strap yourself in good and tight, sweetheart, because the ride's about to start.'

Yes, the timing was a bitch. Minty's journey towards the menopause had subtly started, at the precise point where the *rest* of her life had imploded without warning, in the course of a random meeting in Sainsbury's supermarket, with a woman called Margie Bluett. Margie was a long-remembered, much-feared high-school bully that Minty had never wanted to see again, after the torment of her school days had ended. But, unhappily, Margie had chosen Bristol University too, after leaving college in Cheltenham, so the two women did occasionally see one another around town. They usually managed to avoid any meaningful contact but, that day in the supermarket, they had more or less collided in the coffee aisle and the awkwardness of manoeuvring trolleys around one another, without some kind of nod to one another's presence, was plainly ridiculous.

After a superficial exchange about the weather, and the local authority's relentless persistence in trying to close down the local library, Margie had casually enquired how Minty was doing, in the aftermath of Fiona Winterson having run off with her husband.

The incredulous look on Minty's face had been enough to move Margie, by now grown up and far more compassionate and caring, to tears of embarrassment over her detonating clanger. She'd been nearly hysterical with panic and regret, that she'd been the one to spill the beans and blow Minty's world apart. To give her some credit, she hadn't even tried to backtrack, bleat all manner of inane excuses, and pretend to have made some kind of terrible mistake. Margie Bluett *spectacularly* blew it but, to be fair to her, she'd owned it, and she'd tried to do her best to mitigate the damage.

Minty had politely and distantly declined Margie's kind and genuine offer of a cup of tea and solace at the supermarket's corner cafe. She'd stumbled home, with white noise hissing in her head, and spent the evening ruminating on everything Margie had reluctantly spilled forth after being pressed into finishing what she'd started. 'You have to put the full stop at the end of the sentence, Margie. It's unfair, and far too cruel, not to finish what you started to say.'

Margie had promptly dragged her over to one cold corner of the supermarket, where they managed to wedge themselves between two semi-deserted freezers. In the course of that miserable and only half-private conversation, it transpired that

Bloody Fiona had been bragging about her long-time bedding of Leo, and how he 'already had his bags packed,' to leave his oblivious wife! It had all come out one night in the Black Horse pub, when the two women had met for one or five drinks too many, which they apparently did quite often.

Why didn't I know they did that? Where the hell was her loyalty to me? She was supposed to be my best friend, yet she regularly meets for drinks with a woman who tormented me horribly for years when we were at school?

The conversation had ended with Margie biting her bottom lip and apologising yet again. She'd added how sorry she was for having bullied Minty relentlessly at school, too. 'My home life was a terrible mess, back then, Minty, and I wasn't handling it well at all. It's no excuse for being a horrid little bitch, and taking it out on you, but please believe me when I say I'm truly sorry for everything I did.'

Margie's apology for *that* had helped, more than she could have known, but it didn't ease the shock of all the other stuff she'd said. Slowly but sadly, as Minty started trying to wrap her head as best she could around the multiple forms of betrayal, certain things had started falling into place. Leo's sudden and increasingly more frequent 'work' absences, particularly on Friday nights when they usually went out somewhere together instead, now began to make more sense. Only now did she make the connection between those and the fact that she could never get hold of Fiona either, to arrange to meet *her* for dinner, a drink, or a movie instead, when Leo let her down.

Other changed behaviours that had only ever vaguely puzzled her also began to take on a different meaning, like Leo fussing more than usual over buying a new shirt, suddenly taking more care with his previously unkempt appearance, insisting that Minty buy him a nose-hair trimmer, of all things, and getting straight into the shower when he got home after working late, even before he'd kissed her hello. Stupidly, naively, she'd thought the stupid fool was making more of an effort for *her!*

The acceptance that Leo had been playing away finally hit home at around the same time as Minty's third rum and coke. It amazed and angered her that she hadn't even been the slightest bit suspicious, in the whole two and a half years he'd been doing it, with the kind of predictable 'textbook' behaviour that had sailed straight over her head. She'd trusted him, like she thought she could and should. That's what good marriages were based on, wasn't it? Trust? Clearly that trust, that quality it never occurred to her to doubt, had made her as blind as a bat to what was going on right under her nose.

Some people might have described Minty's unexpected conversation with Margie Bluett as unfortunate. Others would have said it was one of the luckiest she would ever have in her whole life. The jury in the court of Minty's mind was still out but, somewhere in the deepest part of her consciousness, she knew that finding out about Leo and Fiona really had been the best thing for her – however much it hurt.

She'd confronted Leo in the kitchen that very night, as soon as he'd walked in from work, and to her utter dismay he hadn't even tried to deny the affair. He'd come clean, and admitted it, knowing that the game was up. He'd told her everything, rounding off with a whiny, peculiarly desperate-sounding 'Oh, come *on*, Mints! You know we haven't been happy for a long time now!'

'*Really?* Haven't we? Well, that's news to me, Leo! I've been happy, actually. Patently ignorant, it seems, but still happy enough after twenty-two years of marriage to not want to blow it all apart. You know? Still feeling like two children and more than two decades of history together is worth more than a roll in the hay with someone else?'

'There's none so blind as those who will not see,' Leo had muttered in response and, in that instant flash of clarity, Minty had understood that there wasn't much more to be said; only to ask him if he wouldn't mind leaving please, and finding somewhere else to stay, before she gave into her overriding impulse to run him through with the sharpest kitchen carving knife in the block on the kitchen bench.

She had then left the room, run herself a hot bath, poured an entire three-kilo bag of lavender-scented salt crystals into it and lay in it for a good hour, until well after she'd heard the front door slam behind her cheating bastard of a husband, and the water had gone stone cold. For the first few seconds after Leo had left, she hadn't known whether to laugh or cry but, predictably, tears had won the toss.

God, what a cliché! It was almost as cringe-worthy as the exec who runs off with his bloody secretary! If Leo had had a secretary, she mused, maybe the lying, two-faced toe-rag would have run off with *her* years ago. The wife's best friend, she supposed, was the next best handy choice.

Men want it all on tap, don't they? Minimum effort, maximum gain?

To Leo, being able to take advantage of something offered on a plate was undoubtedly a lot easier than actively having to chase a short skirt. That wasn't really his style. He'd never been much of a flirt; in fact, he was lazy to a fault, regarding most matters of the heart. He barely remembered roses on Valentine's Day, or to book a table in a restaurant on their wedding anniversary. Minty was always the one to do that.

Bloody Fiona must have made it easy for him, to indulge in a little extra-marital folly. Except it wasn't just a *little extra*, was it? It was two and a half bloody years' worth.

No man was a paragon of virtue, it was fair to say, but Minty had always imagined that Leo had some scruples; at least a few more than all the other cheating cesspool-scum who managed to make laughing stocks and clichés out of their own and their families' lives. What a crushing disappointment it was then, to find that Leonard McLeod, 'man of three lions' (his middle name was Carleon – *yes, really! What the hell were his parents thinking*?), was no better than any other selfish prick who couldn't say no to a bit of stray sex when it was dangled in front of him.

Telling the kids had been painful. She hadn't trusted Leo to do it with any degree of sensitivity, so she'd contacted their nineteen-year-old son Ethan and their twenty-year-old daughter Belle, set up a group call, and told them herself. They'd been incredulous at first, when she'd given them the news, thinking she was winding them up. It had taken some convincing, to assure them that she wasn't, and when she'd finally let her tears get the better of her (again), Belle had cried too, and Ethan had been furious with his father.

The turning point she'd arrived at had been decimating and painful in the extreme. But the ever-capable, rational, solution-focussed Minty (who was still wandering around somewhere inside the outwardly barely-functioning basket-case version) instinctively knew that the demolition of her marriage was the starting point for something else and probably, in the end, the start of something better. She also knew that her future would be a lot clearer after the dust finally settled on two roundly written-off relationships.

If she was to follow her own typical approach to life, all she really had to do was breathe, let the emotional juggernaut take its course, and see where it came to a stop. However, as the saying goes, hell hath no greater fury than a woman scorned, and it was pretty damned hard to suffer being scorned not only by your husband of twenty-two years but also by your best friend; the woman you'd loved trusted for almost double that length of time! That particular double-whammy, of being betrayed by the two people who knew more about you than everyone else in your life put together, pretty much puts paid to the lofty ideal of maintaining a dignified silence, doesn't it?

Reserved response? *Erm, no.*

If there was ever a situation where the straightening of one's spine and shoulders, the folding of one's hands in one's lap, and the simple continuance of breathing and smiling serenely while waiting for the fallout to end was warranted, this wasn't it.

Vengeance had risen like a phoenix from the ashes. For the first time in Minty's typically laid-back life, she had truly felt vindictive and vicious. Revenge became an impulse she couldn't resist, and to hell with serving it cold! The wave of white-hot fury was one she rode with relish.

After Leo had slunk away like a sly fox into the night, she had got herself out of the bath, dried herself off, moisturised herself to the hilt with the most expensive body lotion she had in the bathroom cupboard, put a full face of makeup on, and stepped into the best dress in her wardrobe. Then she'd poured herself another hefty rum and coke, put a Metallica CD on the stereo at full, house-shaking volume, and got to work.

All in all, it had turned out to be quite a busy night.

Leo's left-behind clothes had been meticulously and beautifully butchered, with one sleeve artfully hacked off each shirt, and one leg roughly 'sawn' off each pair of jeans, trousers and shorts. His expensive, prized 'McLeod tartan' kilt that only ever came out on special occasions (he'd worn it for their wedding) had been reduced to a mini-skirt of obscene proportions. The horizontal tartan lines had helped a lot with keeping the scissors straight.

Every t-shirt had been slashed straight up the middle, jumpers were unravelled, the toes had been lopped off every single sock and – with particularly satisfying viciousness – Minty had cut the crotch out of every pair of underwear and sleep shorts. By the time she was finished with her Grandma Clara's heavy old long-blade dressmaker's scissors she had blisters on the thumb and all four fingers of her stiff right hand and had needed another equally stiff rum and coke to help restore the circulation.

Leo had answered her invitation the following morning, to collect the rest of his clothing from the front lawn, after it had spent a full night under a mysteriously 'faulty' garden sprinkler. He'd found a forlorn, sodden pile of tattered scraps that even the local rag merchant might struggle to accept.

Seventeen pairs of his trainers, boots and shoes had ended up on the catering-size barbecue on the back patio, flaring deliciously with the benefit of a few fire-lighter cubes tucked into the toes, to help them on their way. Minty had watched with unbridled glee as they'd ended up looking like most of the steaks Leo had ever cooked there. The blackened, melded pile had then been hosed down and placed in a soggy cardboard box, the bottom of which had been carefully constructed to fall out as soon as he'd tried to lift it.

Well before he'd set off to John Lewis, to try and replace what he could, Minty had logged on to the internet banking and cleared out the joint account (including the overdraft facility), and she'd cancelled all the shared credit cards. Left with seventy-three pence, Leo wasn't even able to buy a reel of cotton to sew up a single pair of boxers. Still, Minty reasoned, maybe Bloody Fiona had a needle and some cotton she could let him have, or maybe the silly bitch would even sew his crotches back together.

Welcome to the realities of domestic bliss, you shitty little hag.

Leo's prized Honda Gold Wing now had two full tins of treacle sitting in its tank, and his fishing rods had all been snapped in half.

Less than forty-eight hours after his admission of adultery (including two full sleepless nights where she'd had plenty of time to consider all the options), she had also put the house on the market; well-priced for a quick sale, despite his outraged protests that it was worth tens of thousands more. He was absolutely right, of course, but Minty wouldn't have listened if her life had depended on it. The contemptible Leonard Carleon McLeod had given up his right to be heard on any matter at all, by his wronged wife. That ship had well and truly left the harbour, and would never be invited back to port. With any luck it would be roundly torpedoed somewhere out in the ocean of infidelity.

By the time Leo's lazy, lard-arsed solicitor got around to doing anything to try and force Minty to raise the price of the house or change the status quo in any other way that might have benefitted his cheating, two-faced client, the place would be sold and she'd have moved on. Besides, she would have flicked it off for fifty quid, if that had been the only way to guarantee that Bloody Fiona didn't get her hands on it, and she'd have dealt with any resulting court case on her own terms. Getting to move into Minty's home was never going to be on the cards for the shameful Fiona Winterson. Having liberally helped herself to Minty's husband, that would have to be enough for the greedy cow.

Two and a half *years*? Yes, the bastard really *had* been looking her in the eye and lying through his teeth for that long. Well, in the cold light of day, it was at *least* that long, wasn't it? Even bare-faced liars, when caught red-handed, will try to minimise what they've done in the hope of some reprieve. So it wouldn't be at all surprising if she'd been lying in bed every night with the cheating pig for much longer than just the two and a half years she knew about. What made it all the more likely was the fact that she hadn't been able to get a straight answer out of him, about whether Bloody Fiona had been his only indiscretion, or simply the unfortunate one of his extra-marital adventures that actually came to light. And if Fiona herself knew the answer to that question, she certainly wasn't saying.

'What good would it do to know that?' Fiona had asked, in whingeing tones, in the middle of one of the many heated calls she'd made to Minty in the aftermath of revelations. Odd, how Fiona – the lying duplicitous mistress – somehow felt justified in randomly ringing Minty (the best friend she'd royally shit on) to pick a fight!

Clearly, I never knew that two-faced bitch as well as I thought I did.

Yes. Night after night for however long (who would *ever* really know?), when he'd climbed into bed with his wife, Leonard Carleon McLeod had been thinking about – and no doubt actively preferring to be – shagging someone else. Bloody Fiona Winterson; Minty's hitherto best friend and confidante.

They'd been friends since they were five. They'd been the maid and the matron of honour at one another's weddings. Minty had got married first, incredibly young, fresh-faced, still working towards her medical career, and hopeful for a bright future with her newly-qualified architect husband. Had Fiona already been coveting Leo way back then, twenty-two years ago? She had ended up rather acrimoniously divorced after five turbulent years of marriage to a man who bored her silly, but Minty and Leo's marriage seemed stronger. Until it wasn't, of course, which was obviously well before Minty had become aware of the fact.

Bloody Fiona was Godmother to Belle too, and that didn't make things any easier. Belle was living on the other side of the city with her lovely boyfriend Tim. At twenty, she probably wasn't going to need a Godmother to take charge of raising her, should her parents suddenly tumble off the mortal perch, but the two had been close for all of Belle's young life. However, once Fiona's true colours had come to light, Belle had made it plain where her loyalties lay, and had already vowed to do the kind of unspeakable things to her that Minty didn't know her gentle sweet child even had the capacity to imagine. She had even gone as far as offering to 'help hide the body,' with a coldness and rage in her voice that Minty hadn't even realised she was capable of.

Being betrayed by her beloved Godmother with her father was something the shocked, angry and broken-hearted Belle would overcome in due course. She was nothing, if not resilient. But right now, with the news so horribly fresh, she was still struggling hard to get to grips with it. She was, quite understandably, refusing to speak to Leo at all. He and Fiona had smashed her heart to pieces. She'd adored them both, and their bare-faced betrayal was a bitter pill to swallow.

Ethan was currently sharing a flat with a few friends over in Swindon, where he was working through his final year of an electronics apprenticeship. Minty was grateful that he was far enough away to feel less of a direct impact of the bust-up of his parents' marriage. He wasn't finding much to say to his father either, but he texted Minty most days, to check on her and see if she needed anything. Bless him, at nineteen he was already shaping up to be a caring, considerate man, who clearly had more respect for his mother than his own father did!

Leo had said very little to any of them, since the split. He'd wisely kept a very low profile. As time slid by, he was no doubt starting to count the cost of his folly, and Minty was pretty sure that he would now be starting to realise exactly what he'd thrown away.

For God's sake! Could he not have talked to me about how he was feeling, at some point over the past few years, if he was that unhappy? Why would he let it get to this? Why would he throw away everything we've built together, simply to avoid a confrontation?

If he really was miserable enough to want out, Minty would have let him go. Didn't he know *that* much about her at least, after two decades; that she wouldn't stand in his way if he was desperate to call time on their marriage? Would that conversation have been any more painful than what they were all faced with now?

Clearly, Leo hadn't been man enough, or respectful enough, to openly declare that he'd *had* enough, and simply leave. That would have allowed Minty, Belle and Ethan to at least have some dignity. Instead, the fool had sneaked around and had a long-term affair! By doing it with Minty's best friend and their daughter's Godmother, he'd lost the trust and respect of his family, friends and colleagues. Once they'd all heard about exactly what he'd been up to, and with whom, the fall-out was felt far and wide. *Everyone* was reeling from the shock.

Leo had gambled with his family, his home, his credibility, and at least some of his social standing, and he'd lost. Even Henry, his best friend and staunchest ally since their school days, had been sick to his stomach about it. He'd said, in a touchingly kind and compassionate call to Minty, that he hoped Fiona would prove to be worth such massive loss. He'd added that he wasn't going to hold his breath for the proof of it. It was interesting, Minty reflected, how Leo's best buddy had contacted *her* first, to offer his condolences and support.

‘Oh for heaven’s sake,’ Leo had said with an almost casual shrug, as she was asking him to leave and quietly mentioning carving knives; ‘Can’t you understand, Mints? Fiona and I, we just fell in love! It’s as simple as that. We didn’t intend for it to happen. It just did!’

Funny how that little word ‘sorry’ never cropped up anywhere, not then and not since, not even from Bloody Fiona, from whom Minty had expected and deserved at least that.

Fiona appeared to be astonishingly unrepentant; probably relieved that everything was finally out in the open, and no doubt glorying in the ‘spoils.’ She now had Leo, the shirtless, shoeless, kiltless, crotchless wonder, all to herself. What a catch! Lucky lady? Maybe she’d prove to be, once the dust settled. But, as the saying went, a man who leaves his wife and moves in with his mistress simply creates a vacancy. How long might it be before the smug, self-satisfied Fiona ended up as the cheated-on partner herself?

Fiona had flown into a rage when she’d found out what Minty had done to Leo’s wardrobe. She was on the phone within the hour, moaning at Minty in her whining voice.

‘What did you have to do that for, you vindictive cow? All he’s got is what he was allowed to pack into a tiny overnight bag! How is he supposed to go to work, with no decent clothes to wear and no money to get what he needs? That’s so bloody unfair, Minty! Can you imagine how embarrassed he was, at John Lewis, when his cards were all declined? That was pretty mean of you. Why do you have to be such a bitch about everything? He’s going to take you to court over this, you know that don’t you? It’s wilful damage, and financial abuse.’

The bag he was *‘allowed’* to pack? Is *that* what he’d told her?

Minty had been too incredulous to answer her former friend. She’d simply cut the call off instead. Fiona had probably just assumed her laid-back, easy-going erstwhile pal Minty-moo would just roll over and say; ‘oh okay, go on then mate, help yourself to my husband. Tickle my tummy before you go. That's fine. Here, now that I think about it, why not have the house as well?'

Certainly, nobody had expected an instant morph into a savage, vindictive wronged wife. Once, not so long ago, Minty wouldn't have believed *herself* capable of such viciousness. But that was then and this was now and *everything* had changed.

The most ridiculous thing of all, apart from Bloody Fiona's weird penchant for picking up her phone and trying to start a fight every other day with Minty, was Leo's incredulous reaction to the fact that his wife and his children literally couldn't bear the sight or sound of him. But how could the man have been stupid enough to imagine he could throw a bomb at his entire family, watch it go off, and not feel the fall-out from the blast? What else could he realistically have expected, but for the doors to stay firmly closed against him?

It seemed to Minty that both her husband and her best friend had taken leave of their senses. That had to be it. They'd clearly lost the plot, because sane and rational people didn't shit where everyone they were supposed to love slept, and then expect them all to be alright about it. Nobody in their right mind really thought that way, did they?

The phone rang again, and Minty dragged her eyes away from the view of Torley valley. She was relieved to recognise the caller ID as the estate agent's. This was a call that *might* be vaguely helpful.

'Hello, this is Dr Cartwright.'

'Minty, hi! It's Maya Saunders from 'On the Move.' Great news – we've had an offer on your house and it's for just five thousand less than the asking price! Youngish professional couple, three kids, no chain, mortgage firmly in place, but five thousand less is the absolute most they can stretch to. They really, really want the place, Minty! They're excited about it, but they've admitted the offer maxes them out.'

The agent paused, briefly. 'Look, I'm sure we can get more, in fact I *know* we can. We could even end up with a bidding war on your place, as it's so well priced! But, for what it's worth, I think these people are genuine. I know the house hasn't long been on the market, and the price means you're bound to get more interest, so you might want to turn it down. I wouldn't blame you if you wanted to hold out, of course, but for a loss of just five thousand, for a straightforward sale, what d'you think? Get it done and dusted quickly, maybe?'

Minty's heart lurched. An offer! And a fairly respectable one too. Wow! It meant things were moving in the right direction, just as she needed them to. Only five thousand less than what she wanted was manageable, considering it would be less of a hit after she'd split it with Leo.

The house was definitely worth the asking price, considerably more in fact, but Minty had been hoping hard for this very outcome – a quick sale – and there was a certain savage amusement at the notion that Leo would get a lot less than what he'd been banking on, even though she would too. Not that that mattered; although she had more money than her husband did, it had always meant a lot less to Minty than it did to him.

She closed her eyes, took a deep breath, let it out slowly on the count of three, and jumped.

'Oh, you know what, Maya? That's fine. Tell them yes, if they can complete quickly.'

The agent didn't press her again to reconsider. She didn't tell her she was bonkers for taking the first low offer. What she did say was that she saw no reason to wonder if the sale might fall over. That was encouraging. In any case, someone once said that the first viable offer you get is usually the *best* offer you'll get, and maybe that was right. Did Minty really want to put that to the test and take her chances, with buyers who were part of chains that could drag on for months and still collapse at any moment, when there was someone already waiting in the wings waving the nearest equivalent to hard cash?

No. Not really. Not in an already-deflated housing market. That could prove to be very unwise. Several people had already viewed the house but despite it being priced to sell quickly, most viewers had been part of a chain, and of course none of those could guarantee selling their own houses first. Minty and Leo's house was a dream house, and a lot of people were just dreamers.

What the hell! Let's just get it done.

So there was another thing to successfully tick off the list, in walking away from her sack-of-shit husband.

They'd worked hard over the past two decades, to get the mortgage paid off, and they'd made various alterations, additions and improvements over the years. It should have been their home until retirement and beyond, but things could never again be what they were, and it was time to be realistic. Selling the house meant that Minty would have a decent amount of money left to start afresh with. She wouldn't have much trouble getting another mortgage in her sole name if she needed one, especially since her earnings had always been a lot higher than Leo's anyway.

She also had at least another twenty years of working life left, if she chose to go that long. Under those circumstances, paying off another mortgage didn't look like being too much of a stretch, especially if she was a little more modest in the choice of her next house, and that wasn't going to be a problem. Her list of 'homely' wants and needs had never been as long as Leo's.

Her financial stake in the marital home had been greater as well. She and Leo had paid more or less equally into the mortgage and alterations but she'd paid the hefty initial deposit herself, from the inheritance she'd got from her grandmother. Leo hadn't a bean to his name when they'd fallen in love with the place.

Under those circumstances, a fifty-fifty split wasn't what most solicitors would call strictly fair, but Minty was prepared to offer Leo half, in the interests of keeping things civil. Having selected and paid for most of the furniture, though, she intended to keep every last stick of it. There was a lot of money invested in that too.

Let's see if he's prepared to try and haggle over beds and bloody sofas! If he really wants half of the walnut dining table and chairs he loves so much, he can have it. I can easily use his chainsaw in the garage – the one I forgot to vandalise – and give him exactly half of whatever he feels he has to have.

She would dispense with the marital bed though, which she hadn't been able to bring herself to sleep in since Leo's affair had come to light. She planned to set the bed out on the front lawn, all made up with Leo's favourite (and very expensive) bedding set, and pour petrol over it and set it alight. No doubt the fire service would turn up and tell her off, and she might be sent a bill for wasting their time (even though it would be someone else who would call them), but it would be worth it, especially if she could give the local paper the head's up that something interesting was occurring at the bottom end of the very secluded Coronet Grove in the upper-crust suburb of Midtown. She smirked at the thought of the little domestic scene ending up on the local rag's front page, complete with Leo and Fiona's full names and occupations and a photo of the burning bed.

Her own reputation would survive that minor domestic scandal. Minty was confident of that. A & E Consultants didn't tend to lose their jobs over something so banal as an ugly public marriage split. Leo had more to lose, in terms of social standing, as the lying scheming adulterer. It wouldn't compromise his career as an architect, of course, but his peers – especially his female ones – might start to treat him as what he was; a man without much of a moral compass. He might not be as readily invited by his bosses (two of whom were female) to speak at construction conferences and seminars next year, and his colleagues might not include him in their Thursday night after-work drinkies for a while. He would feel a certain degree of shame and be out of his comfort zone. Minty thought she might even forward the bill from the fire service on to him and Fiona. He was living with her now, of course.

Belle had found that out, after turning up at Fiona's to throw her Godmother's 18th birthday gift back in her face – a gold locket with a photo of Fiona holding Belle when she was a newborn baby. In a few short hours, a previously cherished piece of jewellery had become a worthless piece of trash that symbolised nothing more than betrayal, to Belle.

'She was already shagging Dad when she gave me that necklace, Mum. That's so sick I can hardly believe it. I'm done with her. She's Ground Zero to me.'

Minty was sad that Belle had felt compelled to give the necklace back, but she admired her daughter for her loyalty, and her moral sense of right and wrong. Two days after learning that her father had taken up residence in what Belle had started referring to as 'the whorehouse,' Belle had driven the little red rag-top Fiat he'd bought her for her eighteenth birthday round to Bloody Fiona's and thrown the keys in her face, telling her to shove them straight up his arse, since she was clearly so familiar with it. Belle, bless her, was now cheerfully taking the bus to work each morning and walking home on the days when it wasn't raining.

In hurling her keys in Fiona's face, Belle had managed to cut the woman's cheek a tiny bit. Minty waited for news that the police had been over to Belle's, to question her about what had amounted to a common assault, but nothing came. Fiona had obviously thought better of reporting her goddaughter to the police, not that Minty suspected for one second that the stupid, selfish woman would even imagine – let alone concede – that she'd deserved what she'd got and more besides.

Minty had already decided she would buy Belle a new car from the proceeds of the sale of the house. A Mini, maybe. A fun little convertible something-or-other for the next summer. As well as making her daughter smile again and giving her back the independence she was used to, it would neatly shave something off the profit Leo and Bloody Fiona might expect to get from the sale of the matrimonial property, even though it meant she'd take an equal hit herself.

Come to think of it, Ethan could probably use a car too, after he'd passed his test. Minty and Leo could at least bankroll the lessons, as a starting point, before the 'spoils' were divvied up. Leo wouldn't *dare* challenge that.

A text pinged back from the estate agent to say that the sale of the house had been agreed, subject to contract. So; it appeared to be time for Minty to go house-hunting again, this time with the luxury of only having herself to please. It wouldn't matter anymore, if a place she might fall in love with didn't have a garage or a workshop. It wouldn't matter if there wasn't a spare cupboard for golf clubs.

Ah, the golf clubs! She grinned a little, at the memory of deliberately laying the full set of Leo's much-loved golf clubs outside on the back patio picnic table, neatly side by side, in the pouring rain. They'd gone spectacularly rusty. His outrage over that had been rather comical, and entirely disproportionate in Minty's opinion, to the fact that she'd bought them for him anyway as a gift to mark their twentieth wedding anniversary.

What a joke. The bastard was already sleeping with Fiona, then. Bloody Fiona; who'd organised the catering and baked the cake for the party! She'd even wrapped the golf clubs on Minty's behalf, in their lovely leather bag, and put an emerald-green bow around them, as the symbolic colour that represented twenty years of marriage. She'd gone shopping with Minty to help her pick out a gorgeous emerald-coloured dress for the event, too. It was exactly the right colour for her anniversary, but it was also a perfect hue for her honey-coloured skin and dark hair. She'd been surprised to see that when she first tried it on, tears had sprung to Fiona's eyes. Supposedly, it was because Minty had looked so beautiful. But, thinking back to it now, was that the real reason? Or was it instead the fact that the man Fiona was sneaking around with, behind her best friend's back, was about to celebrate twenty years with that friend, and that Fiona was squarely on the sidelines? A mistress is still a mistress. A wife is a lot more substantial - until she isn't, of course.

Sometimes Minty wondered if Fiona had some weird kind of dissociative disorder, where the one decent part of her psyche remained completely oblivious to what all the other, meaner parts were doing or thinking. But, she decided, that was being unreasonably kind. The woman was a two-faced adulteress, and nothing more. How Minty could have missed seeing that self-serving side of her, for the forty-one straight years they'd both been looking one another in the eye, was beyond her own comprehension.

Do we see only what we want to see? If so, how hard do we have to try, to ignore what we prefer not to notice? Did I always know what she was capable of, and did I simply choose to ignore it? Perhaps it wasn't a conscious choice at all. Maybe I was genuinely unaware of her selfishness, and lack of empathy. Maybe I've just been arrogant, or complacent, in assuming she'd never hurt me or step in and steal what was mine. I don't know what to think anymore, but it's going to drive me mad if I keep on picking at the scab of all this. I have to find a way to stop.

Fiona had lost little time in launching her landslide of complaints. The stupidest was moaning that her two high-society gossip magazines hadn't been delivered to her house as expected. Minty had set the subscriptions up as a birthday gift, but she'd decided to have them redirected to herself instead so she could flip through their inane, irrelevant content about people who didn't matter (in her humble opinion) before taking them into work to leave in the waiting area.

Fiona had been highly indignant. 'I can't believe your cheek! You took back my birthday present? What an Indian giver! Jesus, Minty! I would never do something like that to you!'

No, thought Minty. *You'd just take my husband instead. You'd just break up my family. Slightly worse than stopping a couple of vacuous, pointless publications, I believe. How about I find a way to blow <u>your</u> world to smithereens? Then you might just have a scrap of a reason to bawl from that high horse you're sitting on, but – umm – I don't think so.*

She hadn't said the words. She didn't want to fan the flames of Fiona's fury. She'd simply let the stupid slag run out of steam, before quietly clicking off her phone. That had become the easiest way of dealing with the calls.

The subject of Fiona's last harassment call had been Leo's mail, and the fact that Minty hadn't made any effort to redirect it. 'Honestly, Minty! He's been to the house *again* today, to try and pick up his post, and it's clear you're not there. You could at least have sent it on, couldn't you, before you changed the locks and buggered off somewhere without telling anyone? Would that have been too much to ask? Why be so mean? Where the hell are you, anyway?'

Wouldn't you like to know! I'm a long way from you, and that's where I'll be staying, at least until you stop whipping yourself into a rage so you can call me, in a pathetic effort to try and make yourself feel better about what you did.

Fiona clearly hadn't thought much about how hard she was making it, for Minty to ever forgive her for what she'd done. She either didn't care about the meaning of forty-one years of friendship, or she was extraordinarily short-sighted about what the damage really amounted to.

Love sometimes did strange things to people, Minty did know that. But a friendship spanning more than four decades had been wiped off the map of her life, as if it had never existed. Even if Fiona didn't feel it herself, couldn't she understand the pain she kept inflicting? The woman had won the 'prize' for God's sake! Minty was the torn-and-bleeding loser, while Fiona had swiped the spoils.

Why wasn't that enough? Why was the stupid cow still hell-bent on haranguing her over the silliest things, many of which had little if anything to do with her anyway? Did she not understand that the pain, the details, the minutiae of a marriage break-up was strictly a matter for the pair involved; that nobody else was entitled to have a front-row seat to it all, even when they'd served as the catalyst?

Fiona seemed to lack the common human decency or respect to back off and let Minty recover from the brutal shock of such a deep betrayal; to lick her wounds in her own private space, and try to heal. The terrible woman didn't have sufficient dignity to allow Minty to have a little of her own.

I know that her persecution of me is driven by her guilty conscience. It must be close to unbearable, and the only way she can deflect it, in an attempt to make herself feel less wretched, is to keep haranguing me. It's 'my fault' that Leo had no clothes or money, and his kids won't speak to him. It's 'my fault,' that he can't get access to his mail. But any idiot with half an internet-focussed brain cell can go online and work through the simple process of redirecting mail to themselves at a different address, can't they?

The fact that neither Leo nor Fiona could manage to do it was a complete mystery to Minty.

Everything was her fault. Fiona knew it wasn't, but the only way she could live with herself was to pretend that it was. She even went as far as blaming Minty for the fact that she'd 'had to' rescue Leo by paying quite a few thousand pounds for the new clothes he'd picked out at John Lewis and couldn't then pay for at the counter. It seemed that saying 'no' was a missing part of Fiona Winterson's vocabulary on every level; just like that other word; 'sorry.'

For Minty, losing her marriage was only part of her grief. The loss of a lifetime of trust in a friendship that had been everything to her since she was a little girl was decimating too. If losing a marriage felt like losing an arm, then Minty had officially lost two. Time would help heal the wounds, and no doubt these notions of amputation would one day fade enough for her to feel close to whole again, but it would take a fair chunk of time to recover from losing two of the most important relationships of her life.

Luckily, time was one thing she did have. A month's leave of absence from work, with roughly three weeks left, should be enough for her to at least start to work out how to move forward.

An hour into her stay in this gorgeous little cottage, with its womb-like atmosphere of protection and solitude, she already felt like she just might be in the perfect place to do it.

Chapter Two

Leo McLeod was snuffling in his sleep. Fiona looked across at him from her side of the bed and felt a quick spike of irritation. He sounded like a small puppy that gently creaked and rumbled to itself, as if it was sniffing something interesting and talking to itself as best it could, while it slept. Normally she found his little sleep-sounds quite endearing but all she really wanted this morning was for him to shut the hell up so she could get some sleep herself.

To be fair, he wasn't particularly noisy; not like her ex-husband George, who used to 'pop' in his sleep, like a woodpecker bashing its beak on a tree trunk all night long. That used to drive her crazy. Leo sounded more like a baby; like his daughter (her gorgeous god-daughter, Belle) used to sound when she was asleep in her cot, twenty years ago. As a baby, Belle was indescribably beautiful; utter perfection, but her vulnerability and innocence were truly terrifying to Fiona, who used to watch her sleeping, with a mixture of awe and fear.

But there was nothing vulnerable or innocent about Leo. Here was a guy who actually defied moral logic. After managing to disembowel his family by admitting to having a close-to-home long-time mistress, and then moving in with her before the steam had even left the shit of his words, he was sleeping *just* like a baby. Who in their right mind could do that?

Fiona wasn't sure what it really said, about a man who could destroy his wife and children's trust but she was pretty sure it wasn't anything good. As a ruthless (and seemingly conscienceless) breaker of hearts that were supposed to matter to him, Leo McLeod would never go down in the annals of history as a fine, upstanding man.

But who am I to judge? I'm even worse, aren't I? I'm the bloody mistress! I helped myself to another woman's husband, and as if that wasn't bad enough, that woman was my best friend for forty-one years. Well done, me!

Yet another fuck-up. Yet another push of the self-destruct button. Yet *another* wrecked relationship that once meant everything; not just to herself, but to the family she'd destroyed. It was what she was best at – her one true talent – alienating the most important people in her life. She might not be too clever at a lot of other things, but she certainly excelled at breaking hearts. In that respect, she was a perfect match for Leo.

Minty, her lover's wife and erstwhile closest friend, would probably never speak to her again, and neither would the treasured Belle, or Minty and Leo's sweet son Ethan, or anyone else even vaguely connected to their family. The true cost of Fiona's selfish indulgence was already starting to make itself felt but, as per usual, she simply did the *other* thing she was really good at, and scuttled back into her sturdy little shell of denial. It didn't have a door but, if it did, she'd have slammed it shut and sealed the edges so she'd never have to open it again.

She reached across to Leo, and gave him a gentle shove. Maybe if she moved him, he might go quiet.

It didn't work. He carried on regardless, snuffling away. She decided now that he actually sounded more like a baby *pig* than his 'as-was' baby daughter.

She tutted and rolled her eyes at the bedside clock that told her it was twenty past five. It was the stupidest time of a workday morning to be lying awake; too late to feasibly get back to a sleep of any quality, and too early to get up and do anything meaningful. Her irritability was so extreme that she wouldn't have a clue what to do with herself even if she *did* get out of bed!

She turned onto her back and tried to figure out why Leo's simple act of being asleep was annoying her so much this morning. In the grey half-dawn that was slowly staking its claim on the waning night, she finally allowed herself to admit that it might've had something to do with him showing up on her doorstep unannounced, three weeks ago, on a night when she wasn't supposed to be seeing him. He'd just stood there, with a small suitcase at his feet, looking hapless and helpless, and decidedly sheepish to boot.

That was more than she'd bargained for, and it hadn't been a case of him saying something like 'Minty knows, and she's thrown me out; can I crash for a couple of nights until I get sorted?'

No; it was more like; 'Guess what? The cat's out of the bag, I've left home, and I'm yours forever so clear out some drawers for me, darling.'

Since the second he'd arrived, Fiona's head hadn't stopped spinning, and her feet had hardly touched the ground. She lay motionless in bed now (and for the very first time with the *luxury* of time), and thought about the chain of events.

What bugged her the most, she realised now, was that there had never been any discussion about what the landscape might look like, if her and Leo's affair ever came to light. She'd always figured that if he was ever going to leave Minty, it would be a carefully executed exercise in logistics, with nothing happening at all before they'd properly planned what they would do after he closed the marital front door behind him for good. It hadn't occurred to her, that she'd simply end up 'acquiring' a live-in lover with no notice!

The arrangement they'd had, if you could call it such, was that Leo would drop by whenever he could make time, and then he'd leave again when the obligation of being a husband and a good-example father bit him on the backside. He was like the perennial boomerang; bouncing back and forth as the opportunity arose. That was more or less what they'd both signed up for (but only implicitly, because they'd never actually talked about it in any detail) and, as time went by, they'd settled into a semi-regular timetable.

It was a system that suited Fiona well enough. She loved Leo; of course she did! But she also loved her independence, and loving someone wasn't always the same thing as wanting to live with them full-time, was it? Particularly without being asked? After enjoying decades of personal privacy and freedom, being expected to simply budge up without warning and start sharing space with someone 24/7; well, that would be quite an adjustment for *anyone*, wouldn't it?

She'd always hoped that one day they would make it to that, but with *time*; to adjust to both the idea and the reality, of co-habiting. But, as the saying went, the best laid (or imagined) plans of mice and men often went awry, and when the shit had hit the fan at 'Casa McLeod,' Leo had somehow just assumed – on his own, with no consultation whatsoever with Fiona – that he could drop a critical stitch in the tapestry of his life and simply pick up a different one without leaving an adultery-sized hole in the fabric big enough for them *all* to fall through.

She hadn't been prepared for having her space so suddenly and permanently invaded, on the assumption that she wouldn't mind. She'd never seen Leo look sheepish before, either, so she hadn't been prepared for how irritating *that* was.

Her initial attempt at 'discussion' (also known as trying to offer her perspective, and slight objection, to Leo simply assuming she'd be overjoyed to have him suddenly in permanent residence) had ended in a very heated row. It was their first-ever fight, and it didn't bode well for smooth sailing. Leo had been incredulous that she was *audacious* enough, to mildly object to being landed on with no notice, in what he'd assumed was a 'done deal.' The spectre of his accusation hadn't quite gone away yet, and Fiona was starting to wonder if and when it actually would.

I love him, so of course it's right that's he's here! As he pointed out himself, where else was he supposed to go?

She would have been upset if Leo *had* gone somewhere else that first night. It was logical that he came to her. She was his lover, after all. But that wasn't the same thing as wanting him to suddenly hang his hat in the hallway, so to speak, and put his feet so firmly under her kitchen table! It was arrogant of him, and it hadn't even occurred to him that she might be feeling vaguely taken-for-granted, in the process of him having been kicked out of one bed and assuming he could seamlessly and permanently install himself in hers!

But, it was what it was, and they were where they were, and it seemed that this was their life now. They were in love, and they were together. Leo was in her bed *every* night now, and for the *whole* night! She got to see (and appreciate?) the rumpled, sleepy, morning version of the man she loved so much. There'd been many, many times when she'd wished with all her heart that he *could* stay all night; that he *didn't* have to get up and go home to the unsuspecting Minty.

Be careful what you wish for, a little voice whispered, deep in the shadows of her mind. It sounded vaguely vicious, which was anything but reassuring.

It's what I always wanted, isn't it – for us to be together like a 'normal couple'? We were always going to get to here eventually, weren't we? Does it really matter so very much, if it's all happened faster than we expected?

The fact that she hadn't been ready was an uncomfortable truth (and she suspected that Leo was just as unprepared), but it was one that they both had to live with. There were two clear choices, and as Leo had said; what was the point of him leaving his wife, if he and Fiona weren't going to be together at the end of it?

There was just one minor detail in that happy-house-playing scenario that he'd conveniently swept aside, as if it hadn't mattered. He hadn't left his wife, had he? She'd thrown him out. And as much as Fiona hated to admit it, that mattered quite a lot.

Only time would tell if their love was strong enough to adjust to the unexpected change but, given the way she was feeling, Fiona was unable to say with any certainty that it was. And that did not feel good.

Minty's reaction had surprised her. Throughout the decades, she'd never know a single streak of vindictiveness within her pragmatic friend. Minty had always been the sensible one, the even-tempered one, and the practical one. Where there was a problem, Minty found the solution. Where there was hysteria, Minty calmed things down. Where seriousness threatened to submerge someone, Minty was always ready with the perfect joke. She didn't always connect fully with a lot of what was going on around her, but she was kind, generous, tolerant and trusting.

She let herself down, with all that trust! Minty always assumed that everything was fine, in her little bubble-world. It never occurred to her, to raise her head, and be at least a little observant of what was going on around her – right under her stupid nose!

But, as Fiona was finding, it wasn't a comfortable thing for her to admit to how shameless she'd been in exploiting her best friend's trust. It was far *more* comfortable and convenient to blame Minty for her own short-sightedness, and for how easy she had been to take advantage of. Anything was better than having to admit to being a ruthlessly selfish predator. One did have to *try* at least, didn't one, to live with oneself? Any excuse was better than none, that could cover the yawning cavern in her conscience.

So why wasn't that working as well as it should?

Fiona thought back now, to the early days of their lives together. When Minty and Leo had announced that they were getting married, something within her had quietly crashed and died. She was the only person in the entire world who knew how quickly and how hard she had fallen for Leo McLeod, back in the day. It had been an instant fusion, for her at least; that age-old cliché of eyes meeting across a crowded bar. But clichés always stemmed from something, and they always held an element of truth.

That night in the pub, at the end of the Engineering faculty students' final-ever exams, when the lid had come off the pressure cooker and everyone was letting their hair down, she'd taken one look at Leo and she'd adored him in an instant. She'd known, in that *same* love-at-first-sight instant, that nobody else would ever come close. She'd marvelled too, at the time, that she'd never noticed him around campus before. But, she reasoned, maybe she just hadn't been *supposed* to notice him, until that night. As fanciful a notion as it had been, she wondered if maybe fate had been holding them both back from meeting, until the stress of finals was over...

She'd had to work hard, on catching his eye; not because she wasn't beautiful with her gorgeous sheaf of long blonde hair, velvet-brown eyes and willowy figure, but because the pub was so crowded that night, the punters were seven deep at the bar. As they'd clamoured for drinks, the noise had become almost unbearable. Everyone was drunk on relief and real ale, and most were intent on getting even drunker.

She'd eventually managed to catch Leo's attention, through the throng, and he'd grinned as she motioned him over. He came with two friends, and he'd quickly slung an arm around her shoulder, and kissed her on the cheek. It was the happiest moment of her life, but then it had quickly become clear that he was more captivated by Minty. A *lot* more captivated, in fact; to the point where once the introductions had been made, he hadn't so much as glanced at Fiona again; not in the way she'd wanted him to. His eyes never left Minty Cartwright, not that night, and not for twenty years since.

It was a bitter pill to swallow, but Fiona had done it – or at least she *thought* she had. She'd started seeing other guys, including a graduate geologist called George, who she taken as her plus-one to Minty and Leo's wedding. She did her stint as Maid of Honour, smiled as the show went on, and the smile had stayed plastered to her face in one way or another for twenty soul-stripping years.

Marrying George 'the woodpecker' had been the biggest mistake of her life – at least until now. The divorce had been a hard admittance of failure, but she couldn't realistically have expected anything else, firmly on the rebound, and marrying in haste just to prove that someone wanted her, even if the man *she* really wanted didn't.

Minty had helped her to pick up the pieces of that tattered sham marriage, all the while being blissfully unaware of the fact that Fiona had never felt a scrap of love for George, and being even less aware of where her affections *really* lay.

For God's sake! I wasn't that good an actress, was I?

Truly, Minty was the most unobservant person on the planet. That complacent, smug, self-absorbed idiot had never once noticed, in the last two decades and more, that Fiona had loved Leo from the get-go, or how much, *or* that she'd held her torch aloft for all that time.

Well, she knows it now. Maybe a few things are falling into place for her now, like how much she ignored Leo, and for how long, while she was doing her medical degree, and how much that cost her in the long run.

She frowned to herself now. As justifications went, she was struggling to make this one fit. It only made partial sense, because Leo had actually been very happy to be the one at home, raising the babies for the first few years of their lives, while Minty finished her medical degree and got her career established. He'd graduated earlier with Fiona, with a degree in engineering, which took less time to achieve. Minty still had a ways to go, back then, but Leo had wanted them to get married anyway and start their lives together. He didn't want to wait, so he'd made all the compromises, including working fewer hours and organising childcare when he did have to show up for work, and he'd been more than happy to do it.

Fiona sighed heavily now, and turned over in bed. She was in a constant battle, lately, with her self-justifications. She had been for some time now, thanks to keeping the secret of her and Leo's long-term affair, and even more so since it had come to light. It frustrated her a lot that no matter what she tried to tell herself, she just didn't feel comfortable with herself anymore. She knew she only had herself to blame, for her constant state of guilt and turmoil, but that didn't make it any easier to live with.

It had been two full years and a half, since the moment she'd first fallen into bed with Leo, right here in this room. They'd found themselves getting drunk in a bar together after Minty's plan to meet them after work went haywire. It hadn't been the first time she'd stood them up; far from it, and Fiona had spent a lot of time trying to tell herself that in all the ways that mattered, having her affair with Leo was what both women deserved. Minty deserved to lose the husband she couldn't make enough time for, and Fiona deserved the chance to finally have what she thought she'd *always* deserved, and been so cruelly denied.

But none of the reasoning she tried to apply helped her to feel any better.

How ridiculous, to have a moral conscience! I've never been plagued by guilt before, so why now? Why can't I just do this, and get on with it, like I've always done and got on with everything else in my life?

The bare fact of it all was that sneaking around with Leo, and being the mistress of subterfuge, as well as the mistress of her best friend's husband, was a different thing entirely from having everything out in the open. Being exposed as a 'home-wrecking whore' (to quote Belle's eloquent turn of phrase) was a lot harder than she thought it would be. She was grateful that Margie Bluett had at least given her the heads up, in a half-hysterical phone call, about bursting Minty's bubble.

'I've really screwed up, Fi! I just spilled the beans to Minty about you and Leo. I didn't mean to; please believe me. I thought, after what you'd said last week, that he had already left her!'

As furious as Fiona had been with Margie, she couldn't really blame her for letting the cat out of the bag; for wanting to commiserate with another woman whose husband had run off with her friend. Fiona had been so *smug*; so *certain*, that

Leo was going to leave Minty. Something he'd said, during one of their more passionate trysts, had made her believe that his desertion of his family was imminent and she'd mentioned it to Margie as if it already *was* a done deal! It was her own stupid fault for being so loose-lipped and over-confident, after a handful of happy-hour cocktails.

But, honestly! What were the chances of Margie bloody Bluett, who Minty didn't even *like*, running into her at the local supermarket and actually having a *conversation?* Those two had hated one another at school! Never in a million years did Fiona ever imagine there would even be the barest acknowledgement between them, let alone a bloody chin-wag at the check-out, about the state of Minty's marriage and Fiona's claim on her husband!

And now of course, Minty would also know about Fiona's meetings with Margie, that she'd kept from her for years. There were reasons for that, that went back a very long time, but never in a million years would Minty ever understand, or forgive her for it, even if she tried to explain,.

Sometimes fate was just brutal. It came along and put the boot straight into you, without caring how much it hurt.

Oh, stop complaining, you pathetic cow! You got what you wanted, didn't you? Stop trying to blame the person you shit on for the fact that you did it. She trusted you, and she didn't know what you were doing, but in whose fucked-up world does that make <u>her</u> the villain of the piece?

'Oh shut up!' Fiona muttered to herself. Voices in her head like that one, that forced her to hear her own conscience, only made everything harder.

Her attention wandered now, to the slightly sorry state of her finances. Bankrolling Leo's new wardrobe had cost her a pretty penny. She'd had to leave the office at no notice, and rush downtown to John Lewis, after his beseeching (and once again sheepish) phone call to rescue him by footing the bill for his purchases, after all his cards had been declined. It hadn't occurred to him, to muster enough dignity to graciously smile, apologise to the shop assistant and thank her for her time, and leave the store empty-handed. That's what most people would have done, but Leo was not 'most people.'

She understood his pride, and she felt just as outraged as he felt himself, over the fact that Minty had destroyed every last stitch of his clothing, sent his shoes up in smoke, and cut off his access to their money. But having to pay over three thousand pounds for replacement suits, shirts, jeans, t-shirts, underwear and shoes, had been annoying in the extreme. Leo had promised to pay her back, and she had no doubt that he would. He was nothing if not generous with his money, when he had it. But there it was again; that little flash-feeling of being taken for granted; Leo's arrogant assumption that she had the time, the money and the *willingness,* to go and clean up his mess.

The gaping hole in her bank balance had prompted her to tear a strip off Minty, or try to, at least. The woman's behaviour had been outrageous! Fiona had been so incensed by it, and by the fact that she'd felt forced to pay for the result of it, she'd rung Minty and ranted at her for a full five blistering minutes.

She'd been decidedly wrongfooted when Minty had simply let her do it, and hadn't offered a word in response. Fiona had got to the end of her tirade and, faced with silence from Minty's end, had felt strangely humiliated; enough to actually ask her; 'Minty, are you there? Are you listening to me?' Minty had let the silence lengthen and had then clicked off the phone. It had left Fiona thoroughly confused. *Why did she listen to the entire rant? And why didn't she have a single word to say to me, in response?*

It wasn't the action of a friend (or ex-friend?) she though she knew so well. Minty's response to her call had been decidedly unnerving, and verging on spooky. Fiona had been spoiling for a fight, and had imagined she'd get one. After all, Minty had to have been pretty hot under the collar, to have done what she did to Leo's stuff. She had to have been madder than *hell*, to do all that. It was so out of character for her! She'd even poured treacle into the tank of his Goldwing, for Christ's sake! That was pretty extreme.

So Fiona had anticipated a hot exchange on the phone, where both women could unload their feelings, at least in part. Her overriding need to let out some of her own pent-up emotion, even if it was by slating and berating the woman she'd wronged, was something she'd felt driven to do. She hadn't expected to be confronted with silence. The opportunity to go nuts herself, without a response, had left her feeling worse than ever, and she couldn't decide whether that was what Minty had intended, or not.

On the one hand, she doubted whether Minty was even that clever, to be able to turn the tables so effectively, and leave the 'wronger' feeling wronged. On the other hand, she resented her erstwhile friend's capability for leaving her reeling from being hung up on and feeling like the biggest piece of pond scum on the planet, without having said a single word.

She didn't know why it had happened, and the most infuriating thing of all was that the outcome was nearly always the same, now. Every time Leo complained about what Minty had or hadn't done, since he'd left the marital home, Fiona had contacted her to pick a fight about it. She'd ranted her piece, and run to the end of it, only to have the occasional verbal response. Most times now, all she ever got was a quiet click, as Minty hung up the phone.

Fiona had tried to have it out with Leo. 'Leo, why don't you tell Minty how upsetting it is, the way she's treating you? You've got so much to replace and repair because of the way she's handling the split. You do have every right to defend yourself against wilful damage and destruction, you know, which is what this is! I'd be calling the bloody police, if it was me. Don't you even *want* to fight back?'

Why is it me, who defends you? Why am I the one who takes Minty to task about every mean thing she's doing? Don't you have the balls to do it yourself?

Leo had shrugged off the suggestion that he should be calling Minty out on her behaviour. Fiona understood that his failure to respond to his wife was probably down to whatever scrap of guilty conscience he might actually have, at what he'd done to his family. Minty was a woman scorned, after all. If he launched an attack on her, everything would almost certainly become a lot more hostile, but did that give her the right to destroy his property and leave him financially destitute? And did he really have to roll over *quite* so willingly?

'I just want things to settle down, Fi, and they won't, will they, if I start making a shitload of noise as the 'wounded party'? I just need to let Minty be the pissed-off hurricane she needs to be, until she blows herself out. For God's sake, darling, it's just stuff! Material things that can all be replaced!'

Yeah, with my money, so far at least, you pathetic wimp! Fiona had bitten back the retort, because it wouldn't have helped to let it out, but inwardly she'd been raging.

Nobody was listening, or taking her seriously. Minty was treating her as either entertaining or irrelevant; she couldn't decide which. Leo wouldn't take charge and try to convince Minty to stop doing spiteful things like changing the locks on what was still the marital home, selling it for an absolute pittance, or refusing to let him have access to his mail.

To top it all off, Belle had been around to Fiona's 'whorehouse,' as she'd sneeringly called it, and told her in no uncertain terms what a dirty slag she was. She'd thrown her 'piece of trash' locket at Fiona's feet. She had then gone back a *second* time, to throw the keys to the car Leo had bought her directly into Fiona's *face,* and tell her to shove them straight up his arse.

Leo hadn't even gone so far as to try and leave a message for Belle, to say that hurling her keys at Fiona's face and drawing blood was unacceptable, even if it *had* been an accident. Did his desperation not to rock the boat any harder *really* have to include being so dismissive of Fiona's bleeding cheek?

Belle and Ethan were both refusing to speak to their father, and Minty was ignoring the texts he was sending her, all of which were far too polite for Fiona's liking. She hated the fact that Leo had turned her into such a cliché; the sad, suspicious woman who checked her partner's phone while he was asleep or in the shower.

It seemed that nothing could elicit a rage-response from him. Even his own family crucifying him didn't make him angry. It was as if he had simply rolled over and given up on trying to defend his own actions. The only time he got upset was when Fiona herself tried to get him to react appropriately. She was the one person he was willing to fight with, and that wasn't the way the script was meant to run, was it?

So, here she was, lying in bed with the man she'd coveted for pretty much half her life, and trying to convince herself that *this* was the way the script was meant to run. To the victor go the spoils. The problem was, she didn't feel victorious at all. She felt wretched, and while she knew it was because she'd betrayed the people in her life who'd loved her the best and the longest, a small part of her was starting to wonder if the *other* person she hoped would love her just as much, actually really did. The traitorous little voice in the shadows of her mind – the most vicious one of all – whispered to her now, in a way she couldn't ignore or readily answer;

Is he really worth all this to you? And, more importantly, are <u>you</u> really worth all this to <u>him</u>?

Chapter Three

It was time for another cup of tea. Minty lifted one of the chrome hotplate lids on the Aga, and set the kettle on it to boil. The little red oven commanded full attention in Teapot Cottage's cosy kitchen and she was surprised now, to be thinking about her grandmother Clara, who had owned a coal range; a huge black solid-fuel hulk that would be classed as charming and gorgeous (albeit hopelessly impractical) in today's retro-obsessed world. When Minty was small, she used to love it when 'Gamma' would pick her up and sit her on the beat-up old oak sideboard next to it, to watch her make mini pancakes by pouring the batter directly onto one of the old black beast's scrubbed and oiled metal hotplates and flipping them with an ancient spatula.

That old range had been, from what Minty could remember, the sole source of heating and cooking for the tiny, two-up-three-down terrace house that her grandparents had lived in all their married life. It was the original appliance that had come with the house and Gamma had kept it scrubbed clean, like everything else in her much-loved little home. It was beautifully stove-blacked and regularly polished to within an inch of its busy life. It also had a wooden drying rack above it, on a pulley system, identical to the one here in Teapot Cottage.

Gamma's range had always been running, and the kettle had never been more than a few seconds away from whistling its head off, so visitors who came never had to wait long for their cup of tea. As heavily as she'd used her range, Gamma had still always managed to keep it in tip-top condition, and looking like it had arrived from the shop floor just the day before.

Minty smiled fondly, with a lump in her throat, as she remembered Gamma saying many times that the only way she would ever leave that funny little house would be in a wooden box. Her wish came true, as everyone knew it would. It had been a long time now, but Minty still missed her.

She found it comforting to think of her much-loved, rock-solid grandmother at a time when her own life was so turbulent.

I wonder what she'd think of how things have turned out. Would she chide me, for not having seen what was right before my eyes? Or would she decide that Leo and Fiona were such effective masters of subterfuge that nobody could have seen what was coming?

She wondered, for the first time, what had become of Gamma's old coal range. Hopefully, it hadn't been wrecked. She hoped it had been rescued, and perhaps converted to run on a more efficient source of power. If she'd had the presence of mind at the time, she mused, she could have claimed it herself. Maybe in her new home, wherever she chose to make it, she could have another Aga installed, red and glorious like this one, but definitely newer, and maybe a bit bigger too.

A light knock at the back door surprised her, and she opened it to find a tall, slim, smiley woman standing on the doorstep. She introduced herself as Adrienne Raven, the owner of the cottage.

'Hi, Dr Cartwright! I won't take up your time, but I just wanted to see how you were settling in, and check that you have everything you need? There's a storm coming through, quite soon now I think, and I wanted to tell you that there are candles in the kitchen drawer in case the power goes out. It does, occasionally, although never usually for very long.

'This old place doesn't like the lightning much, and occasionally shuts down in protest. The local council usually fixes a power outage pretty quickly though, so please don't be too worried.'

She explained that the Aga was gas-fired; the house would stay warm, and she'd still be able to cook, if the power did go off. She declined Minty's offer of tea, but smiled warmly.

'The hot tub out the back is ready to use, so please do take advantage, although it might be best to wait until the storm passes!' Her eyes danced. She seemed like a very happy sort. Minty decided that she liked her.

'Thank you for the wine, Mrs Raven, and for the other little goodies I found when I arrived. So thoughtful. I wasn't expecting that at all. I hope you won't mind me returning the bacon, but I'm a 'veggie,' and I wouldn't want it to go to waste.'

Adie nodded and smiled gently, as Minty handed her the packet.

'And the cottage is beautiful! So peaceful, and homely. It's made my long journey completely worthwhile.'

'It's a fair old hike up here from Bristol, especially on the train! But you have a good amount of time here, so I hope you'll enjoy it. There are some lovely walks and I think there's an Ordnance Survey map or two, in one of the drawers in the sideboard, that will show you where they are. I recommend the walk that winds around the back of our barn, further up the drive. It leads up to one of the area's little tors that are dotted around the region, that gave Torley town its name. The view from up there is one of the best in the district.'

'Yes, I'll look forward to that. I've quite a lot of head-clearing to do, and I do think hiking will help.'

Mrs Raven laughed. 'It usually does. It helped me a lot, initially, when I first came up here. I wasn't much of a walker when I first arrived, but I quickly became one! My life was a pretty big mess, at the time, but I managed to put it back together quite well, after a stay in here.'

'Well it couldn't have been in much more of a mess than mine is, right now,' Minty confessed wryly. 'Usual cringeworthy cliché of husband running off with best friend, I'm afraid. House being sold, life being turned on its head, friends scattering in different directions to try and escape the fallout, kids wanting to set their father on fire, menopause breathing down my neck, all that bloody nonsense.'

'Oh, God. I'm so sorry! I really don't mean to pry…'

'Ah, don't worry, you're not. It's all fact, so I have to come to terms with it all, which means 'putting it out there,' to quote a phrase. It's the biggest part of what my life is, at the moment, so I can't pretend it's not happening. But it's okay; I'm not one for crying on other people's shoulders. I'm more pissed off that I didn't see any of it coming, really, if I'm honest. He reckoned we hadn't been happy for years. I thought we were. Blah-blah, you know?'

'As a matter of fact, I do! My first husband had an affair. I didn't see it, either, but that was only part of the problem for me. I'd screwed up royally myself, and I was virtually deranged with the menopause too, at the time, which didn't help. I was a blithering hormonal mess! I really did think I was going mad, for a while, there.'

'I'm in peri. It hasn't driven me *completely* crazy, but I'm certainly having my moments, and I think I'm heading into the full swing of things. Sadly, I have the distinct impression that I could perhaps lose my sanity at the flick of a switch, since it's already teetering on a knife-edge! And you're right. It *doesn't* help to be dealing with haywire hormones, when you're already being tested to the limit with other drama.'

'I hear you, totally, but I'm sure you'll work everything out. Try not to beat yourself up about what you didn't see. Just because you didn't see it, that doesn't mean you deserved for it to happen. Betrayal on that scale is a horrible thing. Being kind to yourself is easier to say than it is to do, but you'll get to a good place a lot faster if you can put those two out of your head for a while and focus more on meeting your own needs.'

With that, she reached out and gently squeezed Minty's shoulder, and left through the back door.

Twenty minutes later, the predicted thunderstorm unleashed itself across Torley valley. A match-ready fire had been laid in the grate, so Minty lit it and watched as it took hold, then located the candles in the kitchen, and set them on the bench, 'just in case.'

The stormy weather had turned everything a bit dim and dreary, but as soon as the fire had blazed into life, it transformed the room. It quickly became cosy, and with the two table lamps providing a soft warm glow, the space suddenly felt quite womb-like. Even though it made sense to draw the curtains and keep the heat in, Minty didn't have the heart to close off the dramatic view of Torley Valley that could still be seen through the pretty multi-paned windows, even in the pouring rain. She tipped Peg Tripper's vegetable soup into a pan and set it on the Aga to heat, and slid the quiche into the oven to warm through, before returning to sit in the window, in quiet contemplation.

Here in this lovely space, it somehow felt *safe to* think about everything. Being in the home she'd so recently shared with her despicable 'man of three lions' hadn't done a single thing to steady her state of mind. She'd been desperate to put some space between herself and the house that still held the essence of Leo so firmly within its walls. The home that had borne testament to the highs and the lows of their decades together wasn't a home anymore. The heart had been ripped out of it; so much so that it felt like a hostile place to her now, as if the walls that had seen more happy times than sad ones had turned on her, scorning her for her own inattention. She felt *judged* by the house now, for her failure to see what had been right there in front of her, between the two people who'd spent so much time there with her. It hadn't helped much, when Leo insisted he had never bedded Fiona in their home. She believed him but her desire to stay there had melted like ice-cream in the sun and, just like melted ice-cream, it couldn't be reconstructed.

Mrs Raven had been right, when she'd said that just because Minty hadn't seen her husband's affair with her best friend, that didn't mean she should accept it. The bald truth was that Leo and Fiona had hidden the truth very well. They had both made the conscious, active choice to knowingly and deliberately lie, very convincingly indeed, to her face. So she *shouldn't* judge herself, or let anyone else judge her, let alone a stupid house! It was just plain bonkers, to feel intimidated by her own home, just because Leo had left it. She didn't want to keep living within its walls, but selling up had to be about needing a fresh start, not because of some misguided notion of being driven out by 'hostile' beams and rafters, for heaven's sake!

She had three weeks here at Teapot Cottage. By the time she was ready to head back to Bristol, it would only be a few weeks until Christmas and hopefully, by then, at least some of the thornier issues between her and Leo might be resolved. But, even if the dust *hadn't* started to settle by the time she went back, a few weeks away to gather her thoughts, sleep properly, eat well, walk in the fresh air and consider what she wanted for her future, would all help her to go back stronger and more ready to deal with whatever might come next.

Certainly, selling the house so quickly was a major step forward, and she could look forward to house-hunting, and packing. Belle, bless her, had already pledged her and Tim's help with that, and with the move to wherever Minty was destined to end up. Her strapping son Ethan and his equally able-bodied Canadian boyfriend Kal had also promised to help.

She was determined to keep focussing on the positives. A new start had been thrust upon her, and she had no choice but to run with it. Leo had proved that he wasn't worth fighting for, and what would be the point, anyway? Her life with him was over. An abrupt ending, yes, but given who he'd chosen to betray her with, well… that really didn't leave any way for the door to stay open, did it? There was no coming back from a trust so badly blown. And as for Fiona? Minty hoped she would never have to lay eyes on *that* dirty trollop, ever again in her life.

*   *   *   *   *

In the days that followed, she was surprised, and comforted beyond measure, by the fact that Teapot Cottage seemed to have wrapped her in a warm cocoon. She was alone here, but she didn't feel lonely; not like she had while she'd been rattling around in the marital home after Leo had left. The vulnerability that had cloaked her since Leo's admission had torn their lives apart, had receded. She realised that she didn't feel quite as precariously balanced anymore, between rage and despair. Incredibly, even in the space of just a few days, a fair measure of clarity had dawned, and some of her resolve was returning. As she poured herself a glass of wine, she also realised that her decision to come here had been absolutely bang on the money. It was hard to see how being anywhere else but here, in this gorgeous nurturing environment, would have helped her half as much.

Outside in the back garden, a few chickens were running around, clucking and pecking at the ground. Minty found them hilarious. When she'd first arrived, Mrs Raven had urged her to help herself to whatever eggs she needed, that might be in the laying boxes.

As a lifelong city-girl, Minty had never encountered a live chicken in her life before. When she'd first gone out to the henhouse, in slight trepidation, she'd found four of the hens sitting in laying boxes, their bright red combs flopping lightly across the front of their darting little brown and white speckled heads. They'd clucked gently at Minty, who simply clucked gently back, being at a loss for what else to do or say.

'Book-book ark!' she'd said gravely, to them all. They'd looked at her for a moment, with their heads cocked on one side, then promptly all got up to wander off to the garden. Clearly, they were not impressed with her attempt at chicken-speak! But their eggs had been gorgeous; brown and lightly speckled, and she'd been thrilled to feel the warmth of them in her hands. She hadn't been able to resist scrambling them with a little salted butter on the Aga more or less straight away, and pouring them out onto a piece of hot, home-loaf toast. A deep, rich yellow, they were the best eggs she'd ever eaten. They were certainly the freshest! She truly thought she'd died and gone to heaven.

That's it. I'm never going back to those insipid, pale offerings from the supermarket that they always label as free range when they're not. From now on its proper free-range eggs from an organic farm shop, every time!

So now, every morning, Minty wandered out and had her morning cluck with the comical chooks. It surprised her, how delightful it was to be around them. They were particularly fond of her food scraps and would run along behind her, clucking and shaking their heads, until she placed her offerings in the designated feed area for them. Watching them pecking away with relish at the food she gave them, she actually had something to laugh at, for the first time in weeks.

Sitting now with her tea, again in one of the window seats, she found herself wondering for the first time how Leo might be doing. She suddenly realised that in the midst of all the angst and all her vengeful reactions to his infidelity, her husband hadn't fought back once.

Yes, he'd been apoplectic about her intention to sell the house so cheaply, and virtually boiling with rage over the fate of his golf clubs, but even then he'd backed off more quickly than she'd expected. He hadn't retaliated over the loss of his clothes, his blocked access to their finances, or his destroyed fishing rods.

He hadn't been far off crying, over the golf clubs, and she'd seen the cold fury in his eyes when he'd realised what she'd done to his beautiful Honda Goldwing (the two empty treacle tins sitting on the petrol tank with its cap sitting next to them kind of gave it away), but even then he hadn't come after her with any retaliation. He'd simply had the bike picked up and taken to the local Honda dealership for overhaul and repair. It would have cost a fair bit to have sorted it out, but he hadn't complained, at least not to Minty. Bloody Fiona would probably have had to foot the bill for that too. Leo's 73p had no doubt morphed into more, since his salary would have come in since, presumably to a new bank account Minty couldn't gain access to, but she was sure Fiona had plans for every penny of it, to counterbalance what she'd presumably had to bankroll in the interim.

Leo had clearly been less restrained in complaining to his mistress however, since Fiona had more than made up for his reticence, with her relentless combative calls that berated Minty hard, for her 'unwarranted actions' towards 'poor Leo,' who was 'suffering greatly' as a result.

He did have every right to be upset about the wilful destruction of his property, no matter how much he might have deserved it, but it was Fiona who had assumed the role of mouthpiece, probably by self-appointed proxy. Leo wasn't the type to sit back and allow anyone else to fight his battles for him and he certainly wouldn't have put his mistress into the role of hostile advocate, which gave Minty cause to wonder if he even knew Fiona was calling her. She wanted to believe he wouldn't approve and would in fact put a stop to such nonsense, but she had to concede that he wasn't the man she'd always assumed him to be. Who knew what was going through either of their silly, self-serving heads?

Was Leo's 'sufferance in silence' a ploy to look more wounded than she, when the time came for the divorce to be settled? Or did he genuinely believe that Minty's wrath was fully justified? She didn't know, because while she'd chosen to take the verbal punches from Fiona, she had so far refused to pick up the phone whenever Leo called her, and she was adamantly ignoring his texts. She knew the day was coming when they'd have to have a conversation but that would happen when Minty was bloody-well good and ready, thank you very much, and not when Leo thought she should be.

His texts were always unfailingly polite. There were plenty of 'pleases' and 'thank-you's' peppered in with his pleas for her to talk to him. But she didn't trust his motives. She would never trust him again, with anything. She certainly wasn't in the mood to deal with demands or listen to more excuses.

Had they been unhappy for a long time? Had Leo truly been discontented, or was it simply a perverse form of wishful thinking in the hope that he could hang the blame on Minty for his moral aberration? Twenty-two years of marriage. It counted for *something*, didn't it?

There were a lot of years to look back on, a lot of jointly-faced adversity, a lot of happy memories, two fantastic kids, and a shedload of history. Nobody who was truly invested in a relationship just threw all that away without a second glance, did they? If their marriage hadn't all been a sham (and Minty couldn't bring herself to believe that it had been), then she was forced to conclude that this was not a simple burn-that-bridge scenario for Leo. He might be a lying, cheating, two-faced adulterer, but he wasn't stupid or impulsive, or ignorant of the value of love, time and history; of everything they had built in a time that had spanned half their lives. He also wasn't typically driven by a need to shake things up, simply out of a misplaced sense of boredom. Minty believed they *had* been happy, until Leo had been presented with an apparently irresistible temptation that had devoured the foundations of a previously stable marriage.

This turn of events wasn't just a flash-in-the-pan gone wrong. It wasn't just an idle whim. It wasn't a simple case of a man in the midst of a midlife crisis, deciding he was bored with the status quo and seeking a bit of fun elsewhere, or needing reassurance that he was still attractive to other members of the opposite sex. Minty was forced to conclude that Leo had to really love Fiona, to have taken such a huge gamble with everything else. He would never have done that for anything less than what he thought was a better long-term option. It did, she conceded sadly, amount to real love. Leo had simply switched his love from wife to mistress, and that was that.

Maybe they really couldn't help it, like he'd said. As her mother had once told her, when she first met Leo; 'you can't help who you fall in love with.' As big a stretch as it was, to imagine her husband and her best friend being 'powerless' to resist the 'tidal wave of love that engulfed them,' she had to concede that nobody ever knew for certain what made any person fall for another one.

Christine Cartwright, Minty's mother, hadn't liked Leo much. She never said why, but Minty could always feel a slight tension whenever the two were in the same room together. They were polite, and respectful, but Minty never detected any warmth between them. They were like two circling cats; both well aware of an expectation of appropriate behaviour, but being a little less than comfortable about maintaining the charade.

On the few occasions when she'd questioned Christine, to try to get to the bottom of the reasons why she could never be at ease with her son-in-law, her mother would simply shrug and say that very thing: 'you can't help who you fall in love with.'

It was obvious to Minty that Christine was never going to tell her what the problem was. Minty knew her mother's decision had been made out of kindness and respect, but it still frustrated her. If Christine had sensed something 'off' about Leo, didn't she have a moral responsibility to inform her daughter? Evidently, Christine hadn't thought so.

Minty wished with all her heart that her mother was still alive, *and* that she'd said something, all those years ago. Maybe Minty wouldn't have married Leo. But then, they wouldn't have had their two gorgeous children, would they? Young, newly engaged to who she truly believed was the most incredible man on the planet, and massively excited about the future; would she have listened to Christine anyway?

What a mess, Mum. Did you predict this? Is that why you never warmed to Leo? Did you believe he would one day hurt me like this?

Minty knew that even if Christine *had* said something, she would have told her to butt out and mind her own bloody business, and her mother would have anticipated that. After all, who on earth knew Minty better? Christine had held her tongue and taken her concerns quietly with her to her grave. Hot tears sprang to Minty's eyes, and she let them fall.

Christine had only been gone four years, but it still felt like yesterday to her daughters, Minty and Fliss.

Oh my God! Fliss! I need to call her. She still has no idea about any of this!

Minty's sister, who was four years older, had moved away from Bristol to France not long after their mother had died. She'd married Filipe; a very lovely, lively, exuberant Frenchman, just before Christine had got sick. As a maturing couple who had found love later than planned, they hadn't wanted to have children. Filipe's French family hadn't held back their dismay, but Christine had kept her thoughts to herself about it. There was so much that she never said, *about* so much, Minty reflected now. Her lovely mother had gone to her grave with everything, with no judgement on her daughters.

There were times when Minty envied Fliss and Filipe. She loved the absolute bones of Belle and Ethan, and she couldn't imagine life without them. But she'd occasionally wondered how much more freedom she and Leo might have had if they hadn't unexpectedly become parents.

There had never been an actual *plan* to have children or, for that matter, to avoid having them. They just surmised that it would happen if and when it was supposed to, and they'd deal with whatever life chose to bestow upon them. They had both been bemused at finding out they were pregnant, just a year into their marriage; not exactly ecstatic, but not unduly dismayed. Just bemused. They quickly got used to the idea though, and a year after Belle was born, Ethan had arrived.

There had been a bit of talk, of adding a third child to the family, but Minty's difficult pregnancy and her protracted, complicated labour with Ethan had left her deeply unwilling to have another baby. In any case, after slogging away to get her medical degree, she wanted to have at least *something* of a career. Two kids still made that possible, but three would have made it a lot harder, especially with Leo wanting and deserving his career too. They didn't want their kids raised by nannies, so they'd settled happily into the foursome they became, and it seemed to Minty that they were happy enough.

Nobody expected to still be head-over-heels in lust after twenty-two years, did they? Some loved-up couples were lucky, when the sparks still flew after decades, and Minty and Leo had still had their moments, until very recently. But most people simply settled into their comfortable routines, after becoming accustomed to one another's faults and foibles, and the fireworks of passion evolved (or devolved?) into something more companionable.

That was normal, wasn't it? Putting up with the farting and the snoring, the nagging, and the occasional burnt pan of potatoes? Wasn't that how most marriages survived, with the unspoken agreement for compromise and tolerance, underpinned by a love that grew and matured into something more enduring than the need for passion and jumping into bed with someone else? You certainly weren't supposed to go and fall in *love* with someone else! Not after twenty-two years! That wasn't part of the story you thought you'd written together.

Minty had no idea what Fliss might say about her current situation, but there was only one way to find out. She picked up her mobile phone and scrolled through it until she found her sister's number. Fliss answered within a couple of rings, in her usual upbeat and happy tone.

'Hi, sweetie! Long time no speak. How are you?'

'Hey, Fliss. You got time to talk?'

'Yeah, sure. What's up?'

As Minty filled her in on the events of the past few weeks, Fliss became more and more indignant and outraged, although she did laugh a lot when Minty told her what she'd done to Leo's stuff.

'Fair play to you for being so restrained. I think I'd have done worse than that. I'd have taken to *him* with Gamma's scissors! The boxers, Minty! What a hoot! But at least if the stupid bastard's going to swing his dick around he may as well go the whole hog! What a wanker, though! And as for Fiona?

Well, some friend she turned out to be! And I can tell you *now* that I never liked her. Nor did Mum, much, in the latter years. The skinny bitch was always looking at her watch, like she couldn't wait to be somewhere else. She had a habit of looking slyly to the side too, through half-shut eyes, like she was trying to keep an eye on something but didn't want anyone to know what it was.'

It was Minty's turn to laugh. 'Really? In all the years I've known her, I'd never noticed that.'

'Of course you didn't.'

Minty was taken aback by her sister's comment. 'Fliss? What's that supposed to mean?'

'Oh, nothing, really. It was a silly little comment. Forget I said it.'

'No, come on. That was a pretty *loaded* little comment actually, and maybe it deserves an explanation?'

Fliss sighed, deeply. 'Ah, Minty; there's a lot of stuff you've never noticed going on right under your nose, all your life, sweetie.'

'What? What do you mean by that?'

Fliss blew into the phone. She chose her words carefully.

'Nothing mean, and I probably shouldn't have said that, either. But, now that I have, let's just say that observance isn't one of your strong points.'

Fliss' voice was kind, but the comment made Minty cringe. She felt immediately defensive. 'What, are you saying I should have seen this coming, with Leo and Fiona?'

'God, no! Of course not! I don't think *anyone* could have seen this coming! They've been at it for what, more than two years? Filipe and I were over for your wedding anniversary party, two years ago, and let me tell you, there was absolutely *no* clue – *none* – that they were shagging. And believe me, Minty, everyone was getting pretty pissed at that party, and I have a finely-tuned radar for these things. They had to be very bloody clever indeed, to have hidden that from me. I never saw it, as a hyper-vigilant observer of all things relevant and not, so how could *you*?'

Minty knew that her sister was right. Fliss certainly was hyper-observant, and astute to the point of being downright embarrassing at times when she decided to give voice to something she'd seen.

Fliss spoke again. 'I just meant that there have been things in the past, quite important things actually, that have simply sailed right over your head, sweetie. And to be honest I always envied you for having such a filter. I was never so lucky. I always saw everything, felt *everything*, and sometimes it wasn't great.'

'What kinds of things?' Minty demanded.

Fliss was quiet for a moment. When she spoke again, her voice was hesitant.

'Are you sure you want to have this conversation, Minty? Right now, with everything that's already hurting you so much?'

'Yes, of course I do! If I've been an ignorant fool I would like to know!'

And also why nobody bothered to tell me before!

'What kinds of things?' she pushed Fliss to answer. Fliss sighed gently.

'Well, like Dad having a gambling problem, as well as being an alcoholic. It's why he and Mum eventually split up. She could just about handle the drinking, but the debt he racked up was too much for her. And the fact that she worked herself into the ground on three jobs for six straight years while you were at medical school. The fact that she carried on repaying the loan for your studies, even after you got married, so you'd never have to go into debt. And the fact that she was willing to do the same for me. She offered to fund me through uni too, but I said no, because she was already knackered and I didn't want her to work that hard anymore. And Aunty Angie's cancer; how big a toll that took on Mum.'

Hot tears of shame sprang to Minty's eyes and rolled down her face. She was struggling to breathe properly. She couldn't speak, but her ragged breathing would surely tell the observant Fliss that she was weeping. It did.

'Oh, Minty! Please don't feel bad. That's the last thing I want, especially right now! But you did ask, so I'm just being honest about what you missed, that the rest of us fought pretty hard to deal with.'

'My God, Fliss, how *could* I have missed all that?' Minty's voice cracked.

'You were in your own world, sweetie! You were still recovering from the trauma of being badly bullied at school. You missed Dad. You missed Poodle-Sally, because Dad took her with him when he left. You had glandular fever and hardly got out of bed for almost a year, then Poodle-Sally died, then Dad up and died too, halfway through your med school years. And then you got married, and that was expensive too.'

Fliss' voice became gentle now. 'Even before the wedding, you never got home much. Whenever you did you still always had your head into your books, studying like mad. I get it, Minty. Mum got it too. You were already finding things such a challenge, and your life was changing, and your confidence was low. We just thought it better not to drag you into anything else that might make you feel even worse, like distractions that would take away from the medical degree we all wanted so much for you to have. It would have killed us all, if you'd damaged or even *failed* your degree, through being distracted or upset. You needed to be focussed, so we made sure you were.'

'You should have told me, Fliss. I'd have coped.' Even to her own ears. Minty's voice sounded wooden and flat.

Her sister sighed again, and was quiet for a moment.

'Maybe you're right, Minty. I'm sorry. Maybe you *would* have coped, especially with Leo to help you bear the load. But if you hadn't, we'd never have forgiven ourselves! Besides, with Mum working her arse off to get you through med school, all that would have been wasted if you'd failed to finish. We were trying to be practical and supportive, to get you to your goal. I guess it backfired a bit, but we kept you out of the loop with the best intentions, Minty. Please believe that.

‘To be honest, if you had noticed what was going on around you, like Dad’s car being repossessed, like my dance lessons being cancelled because there was no money to cover them, well, we would have told you everything. *I* would have told you. I *wanted* to, sometimes. I *did* have times when I resented the fact that you were so oblivious to the reality of our struggles, while I had to try and deal with it all, but there weren’t many of those. Most times, I just wanted you to keep your head above water and triumph over your own set-backs.’

Minty suddenly felt cold. ‘Fliss, Mum told me she’d paid for my medical degree with inheritance money. Tell me the truth about that too, please. Did she ever really inherit anything?’

Fliss snorted. ‘Only a mess of debt from Dad. Then he went and died on us, before he could even start to make good on his promise of helping to reduce it. He left her a hundred and forty-eight thousand pounds in debt, Minty! She officially went bankrupt to clear it all, a few months before she died, so we wouldn’t be left with it. She’d worked all her life, and even after she got the cancer she still tried to clear as much of it as she could. When it became obvious that she was going to die before she could even make a decent dent in it, that was the route she took.’

‘Oh Jesus, Fliss! Why the fuck didn’t I know that? I’d have willingly given her my money from Gamma, if I’d known.’

‘Don’t worry. I didn’t know either. I found the notice among her things when I was clearing them out, after she’d died. As soon as she got confirmation that the cancer was terminal, she filed for bankruptcy. It was all done and dusted before she even told anyone how ill she was.’ Fliss sounded sad.

‘Your inheritance money; we both know she’d never have accepted that from you. She’d have thought it would have been a waste of it, and I think she’d have been right.’

‘So she carried that burden, Fliss; hiding it from both of us, then *you* took it on and carried on hiding it from *me*.’

'I only carried the *knowledge* of it, Minty, not the debt itself. If Mum had wanted either of us to know, she'd have told us. By filing for bankruptcy she shielded us from having to take responsibility for that crippling debt.'

'She should have gone bankrupt years before! It was probably the stress of the debt that caused the cancer.'

'Yeah, maybe. It couldn't have helped, put it that way. But who really knows? She was very proud, Minty. You *know* what she was like.'

Minty did. She knew that her mother wouldn't have shunned her responsibility, never in a million years, even for a debt she'd acquired through someone else's folly, but she wouldn't have saddled anyone else with it either. It must've been incredibly hard and humiliating for her, to file for bankruptcy, but she'd done it for her daughters. What a truly extraordinary woman Christine Cartwright had been.

'I miss her so much.' Minty was crying openly now, fat salty tears sliding down her cheeks.

'I do too.' Fliss' voice broke. Then she cleared her throat and continued;

'Minty, I'm sorry I had to give you the home truths like this. I know it's the last thing you need, to feel worse about things than you already do. I didn't mean for that. But as far as Leo and Fiona are concerned, you *will* get through this. Come out here, and stay with us for a few weeks, if you like? Maybe even for Christmas? Filipe would love to see you too. He would urge you to come.'

Minty smiled at her sister's generosity, so predictable and so sincere. She thanked Fliss, promised to go to France and spend time with her and Filipe very soon, and she went on to describe the gentle, joyous little space of Teapot Cottage. When Fliss was completely satisfied that Minty was in a safe, supportive, quiet place and getting her head back together, she ordered her to keep her in the loop, told her she loved her, and rang off.

Oh Fliss! My poor darling sister. Did you want to go to university too? Why did you never tell me any of it? That money I had, that I used for the house? Gamma's money? You could have had it all, every last penny, if only I'd known.

It was hard, to discover how much her mother and sister had kept from her, growing up. Minty understood why they'd done it, but that didn't help her to feel any less uncomfortable. It seemed that failing to see what was going on around her had been a problem for a very long time.

Have I really been that oblivious to such big stuff raging around me? What else have I failed to see, over the years, and how has that ignorance shaped my life?

She didn't know how much different her life could have been, if she'd known what her mother was dealing with. She would certainly have made different decisions about buying the house that she and Leo had decided on, all those years ago. It wouldn't even have been an option, if she'd known that poor Fliss had missed out on going to university because of lack of funds! Her sister had always been massively resistant to going into debt, so that would have precluded student loans, and Minty now understood exactly *why* Fliss was so loan-averse! It was a terrible thing, that she missed out on higher education because Minty hadn't known what Christine was up against. Ironically, her inheritance actually *could* have cleared her mother's debt *and* sent Fliss to university, albeit as a 'mature' student by then. She still could have gone, and got a degree!

Gamma's inheritance had been Minty's alone. Her grandmother hadn't split it, and nobody ever understood why, but Fliss had never been bitter about it, and neither had Christine. Nobody ever asked about it, and nobody ever made Minty feel guilty. That had always mystified her and it still did; now more than ever, as she realised what her mum and her sister had been up against. Having had all that money to herself, she was now more uncomfortable about it than she'd ever been.

Poor, poor Fliss! I'm so lucky she's like she is. If she was resentful in any way, or angry at me for having my head so far up my own arse that all it did was make me selfish, I couldn't count on her for support, could I?

But Minty wished now that her mother and her sister *had* been honest, back when it was still possible to change the course of their lives. Until the gargoyle of infidelity had rocked up and smashed her world to pieces, she'd more or less had a charmed life. The rude awakening, of her world now being in tatters, burned like fire. But maybe it was nothing more than she deserved, since that charmed life had come at such a huge cost to Christine and Fliss.

A knock at the back door distracted Minty from reflecting any more on the revelations that had come out in her conversation with Fliss. She wiped her weeping eyes with the back of her hand, straightened her hair a little with her fingers, took a deep but wobbly breath, and opened the door.

Mrs Raven stood on the doorstep, holding a bunch of long-stemmed pink protea flowers. She treated Minty to a beaming smile.

'Hi. I thought you might like a few of these for the coffee table? I grow them in a greenhouse up at the farm and for some strange reason I've had a really bumper crop this year. I normally sell them at the Saturday Farmers' Market, but here, please have a few. There's a good vase for them under the kitchen sink.'

'Oh, look at these, they're *gorgeous!* How lovely, and how kind of you! I've just made a pot of coffee, so please stay and have a cup.' Minty opened the door wider to allow her 'landlady' to come in. Mrs Raven grinned at her, apologetically.

'Coffee sounds great, thanks. It's a shame about the weather, isn't it? I hope you're not too disappointed. We do get it, up here, I'm afraid. Being so high up the side of Torley valley means we often get stuck with cloud-cover drifting in, that can't seem to find its way over the tops of the fells. It can get stuck in the valley and hang around for days. The winters can be damp and soggy, if they're not snowy. November is always a lottery. We can have four seasons in one day here, especially in the run-up to Christmas. They're saying we might even get a bit of snow this week!'

‘I don’t mind. As you know, I’m what you might call ‘in transition,’ and I’m just here for a bit of peace and quiet, while I figure a few things out. The weather is the last thing on my mind, to be honest. So is bloody Christmas.’

Mrs Raven looked at her kindly. ‘Yeah, it can certainly be a tricky time when you’re on your own, especially if you don’t want to be. But maybe you don’t have to think about it quite yet, with everything else that’s hit you. A lot of people are in transition and thinking about a change of direction, when they come here. It’s a nice, gentle place to regroup. There’s good energy here. You might feel a bit differently about things, by the time you’re ready to leave.’

She shared a little of her own story, and parts of it really resonated with Minty. It was as if the same history was repeating itself, with a different character in the foreground. She said so, and Mrs Raven cocked her head on one side and looked at her with a slight smile playing around her lips.

‘I was thinking that. It’s kind of weird, but then a lot of what happens around here *is* pretty weird! Believe me, I’ve long since given up on marvelling at coincidence. I no longer believe it exists. Sometimes it takes a while to figure out why certain synergies occur, but I think we all cross paths for a reason in this life, for however long or short a time it may be.’

Minty suddenly found herself opening up a little more about her own marriage, and how it had ended.

‘What baffles me the most, is that I didn’t even realise we weren’t in a good place – or that *he* wasn’t, at least! I’d taken my eye off the ball completely, and I don’t even know how that happened.’

Mrs Raven nodded. ‘Well, you mentioned that you’re peri-menopausal, and I think it’s only fair to attribute some of your inattention to *that*. The ‘change’ really messes with the mind, and it’s quite common to miss a lot of what’s going on around you.’

‘For me it’s mostly forgetfulness,’ Minty admitted. ‘I can run hell-for-leather up the stairs on an urgent errand and by the time I’ve got to the top I’ve completely forgotten what it was. And the sweaty palms, and the aches and pains in my joints; it's all driving me crazy. I'm a doctor, as you know, so I understand what's happening biologically, but I don't think that *I* can be fully prepared for the maelstrom that's about to hit me!'

Mrs Raven rolled her eyes. 'My menopause was a pretty bumpy ride, and still is, to some extent. I'm a long way from being out of the woods, with mine, and I didn't really have a peri, to prepare, like you. At least you have some warning. I saw friends dealing with it, and I had a few things going on, like the occasional night sweat, memory loss and confusion, but the full Monty came without much warning at all, and it was like smacking into a brick wall!' She shook her head in frustration,

'I still have sleep disruption, hot flushes, and occasional bouts of feeling like I could cry until my head falls off. I've finally stopped keeping the tampon industry alive single-handedly, thank goodness, but I now feel like I'm keeping the vaginal lube industry afloat instead, since my nether regions sometimes feel like they've stumbled into the Sahara desert!' She grinned and blushed a little, self-consciously, at her own confession.

'Sorry! That probably wasn't very appropriate, but I'm used to talking openly about it all, because I have good friends going through the same thing, and I do think it helps to be frank about it. We talk about it a lot, so we share some great support that way. But all kinds of things happen at this time of life that you're never quite prepared for. So I sympathise. It's no fun, especially when other elements of your life are so up in the air.

'As I told you last time I popped in here, my ex-husband Bryan was having an affair too. His went on for six years and I never had the slightest inkling, in all that time, of what he was up to. I can see *now* that things weren't right. Hindsight is always the clearest, isn't it? I had some dark secrets of my own that didn't help us but, in retrospect, even if I'd told him what they were I don't think it would have changed the choice he made in taking a long-term mistress. She was in his life long before I spilled the beans about my own stuff. But I was like you; I thought we were okay. I thought I was enough, that our marriage was worth more than the gamble of having an affair. But he loved her. How could I challenge that?'

'And Leo loves Fiona. Ah, Mrs Raven, I feel like such a fool,' Minty confessed. 'I know you said I should be less hard on myself, but it's easier said than done. It's *incredible* to me, that I was so unsuspecting. I trusted him, and I trusted *her*, my oldest dearest friend! I had no idea that either of them would or even *could* betray me so badly!'

'I can't even imagine how hard it must be, to come to terms with all that. I didn't know my husband's mistress at all, and I think that may have helped me in some way, to accept things. It would've been a lot harder, I'm sure, if she'd been a friend. Is your name Araminta? May I call you that?'

Minty vehemently shook her head. 'God no! Please don't! Only my solicitor calls me that! Call me Minty, please. Everyone does, although they're all probably calling me Mrs Pathetically Oblivious, behind my back.' She felt the tears spring to her eyes again. She wiped them away, but Mrs Raven reached over and touched her hand. Her voice was gentle.

'Don't deny the grief, Minty. It's important that you acknowledge how you feel. It's all part of the process. Everything is still very new, and raw. Let it come out, as it needs to. And my name's Adrienne, but you can call me Adie, if you like.'

Minty nodded through her tears. 'I'm sorry. I didn't mean to fall apart on you. It's just that I haven't really told anyone about it since it all blew up last month. I've told my son and daughter, obviously, and my sister, but she lives in France, and I had a really difficult conversation with her about that and other things, just before you arrived actually, so that's why I'm a bit wobbly.

'I'm not very well supported, to be dealing with this. There's nobody else around me that I feel I can really talk to who won't judge my situation – and judge *me* – in a way I don't want. Feeling like a fool is bad enough. I don't want to be *seen* as one, too. A fair few of my friends don't know about this yet, and I'm not sure how they'll react when they do. That kind of scares me a bit too, if I'm honest; you know, who'll be in my camp, and who won't be? Leo and I have friends going back to when we first got married. It would hurt to lose any of them.'

Adie nodded too, but pensively. 'I totally understand where you're coming from on *that* score! It's always the big question, isn't it, after a marriage split; who keeps 'custody' of the friends? People can be very unpredictable. The ones you expect to support you often don't, and the people you think don't give a damn are sometimes the first to rally around you.'

Minty described how she'd come to hear about Leo and Fiona. 'I didn't expect the woman who told me to be so nice to me, after she realised what she'd said. She thought it had already happened and she was beside herself, that she'd put her foot in it. I actually felt a bit sorry for her, she was so distraught! It's ironic that she was, to be honest, because when we were at school she used to hate me. She made my life hell.'

Adie nodded slowly. 'Well it sounds like she grew up, which is good. It's nice that she tried to be kind, in the aftermath. That might count for more than you realise.' She frowned and pulled her bottom lip with her thumb and forefinger.

'For my part, I felt *incredibly* foolish, when everything came out into the open, because so many people I thought were my friends knew all along what my husband was doing and they never told me. Others just dumped me when I was at my lowest ebb. There were two, in particular, that treated me so badly, I actually felt violated by them. That was indescribably painful.' She grinned now, and rolled her eyes.

'It's actually not painful at all now, with the benefit of that all-important hindsight! They were truly awful women! My best friend Miranda calls them 'Nincompoop and Pickitt,' and I'd love to cheer you up sometime, over a glass of wine or three, by telling you what they were like! I can laugh about them now, on the rare occasions when they do come up in conversation, because they really were the kind of terrible you could write a decent book about. But, at the time, I felt devastated by how horribly they were treating me. Not just by being absent when I needed support, but one of them *actively chose* to be vindictive. That's the one we call Pickitt. She was a complete narcissist, and absolutely vicious with it, and it was pretty hard to deal with that, especially with everything else going wrong too. I was all at sea, for ages, with no idea how to get out of my own head.'

Adie let her smile fade, and she frowned to herself again. 'But, you know, I came to realise that even as the people who treated me badly were hurting me, they were teaching me valuable things. Everyone teaches us something, Minty; if not about us, then about themselves. The woman who gave you the news, and then tried to help you; that's a form of gold, just in itself. We like to think that most people don't want to hurt us, and feel bad when they do, but it's hard to know who to trust after something like this. It's good that that lady was honest. In my situation, I felt completely *brutalised* by so much dishonesty, meanness and betrayal. I kind of went into myself for a while. I withdrew from everything and everyone. It was the only thing I felt I could do.'

'How did you learn to trust again? You've remarried, haven't you?'

Adie smiled gently. 'Yes, as a matter of fact I have, just a few years ago. I spent a few months here in this cottage, house and pet sitting over Christmas, for the people who owned it at the time. I eventually got together with my husband Mark, after he invited me to the farm's annual Christmas party. I'm sure you'll meet Mark at some stage, by the way. If you're out walking and he's out and about, he'll make a point of coming over and introducing himself to you. He has a gruff manner, but he's really very sweet.

'But to answer your question Minty, I trusted him completely, right from the get-go, because he's very down to earth. He calls a spade a spade, and people always know where they are with him. He doesn't have a dishonest bone in his body. What you see is what you get, and that made it easy for me to trust him.'

Adie drained her cup. 'That was nice cup of coffee. Thank you, Minty. Do check out the Farmers' Market on Saturday, won't you? You'll find most of what you need there, and it supports the local growers and producers. It's an easy walk down to the town, and if you like you can leave your purchases there with me to bring back for you after the market closes, at around one o'clock.

'And please, you really must stop beating yourself up about not noticing what your husband and best friend were up to. The fault lies with them, not with you. People can be remarkably clever and convincing when they have something to conceal. A guilty conscience can often result in extraordinary levels of subterfuge. Believe me, I know all about that – from *both* sides of the fence! And the hormonal ping-pong is part of it too. Don't forget that. Just because the peri hasn't been dramatic, that doesn't mean it *hasn't* been affecting you mentally, in ways you might not have noticed.'

She stepped forward and gave Minty a quick hug.

'You'll get through all this, darling girl, and you'll be stronger for it. It might not feel like that just now but it will, in time. Don't let your husband's and your friend's actions define who you become, or rob you of your confidence. Their choices probably had less to do with the state of your marriage than the fact that they just had itches they selfishly chose *one another* to scratch, instead of doing the slightly less indecent thing and looking elsewhere.

'But, if you can spend more time looking for the silver lining than dwelling on the bad stuff, you'll notice there are more positives in all this than you might think. You'll start to see them once the dust begins to settle.'

'I hope so. Thanks so much, Adie. And not just for the flowers.'

With a brief nod and another gentle smile, Adie left, quietly closing the back door behind her.

Chapter Four

These windows needed washing on the outside, Adie noted as she walked back towards Ravensdown House. She tried to remember the last time they'd been done, and couldn't. *I must phone the window cleaner. He can come early next week, and clean out the guttering too, I think.*

She stopped and listened. Sounds were coming from the barn, so she knew Mark was in there working. She always liked to know exactly where he was, on the farm. He was pretty good at telling her, but then he'd go off and do something different somewhere else and there were often times when she didn't have a clue where he might have gone. His accident just a few years ago, when he fell through the barn's rotten mezzanine floor, was never far from her mind. Knowing where he was, and roughly how long he might be, was her way of making sure he was safe in what he was doing. If she lived to be two hundred, she would never forget the sight of him lying stock-still on the stone floor of the barn with blood seeping from his head. Her own blood had run cold. He'd suffered a torn liver and a nasty neck fracture. He'd been lucky to survive.

They hadn't been married, at that point. They'd both known they were in love, but neither was at the point where they'd known how the other one felt. Mark's life hanging in the balance had been enough for Adie to acknowledge how *she* felt, and Mark realising how lucky he was to be alive had been enough for him to do the same. They'd both poked their heads out of their protective hard shells, and the rest, as they say, was history.

Mark had been widowed, years before, and Adie had been going through a painful marriage break-up. Neither imagined they would find love again, and Adie never let a day go by when she didn't thank her lucky stars for Teapot Cottage and the man it had brought into her life. Mark Raven was a no-frills, salt-of-the-earth farmer. He was as rugged as the day was long; a true diamond in the rough, but he had a solid gold heart and he'd given it to her.

Inheriting a beautiful, unusual step-daughter had also been a blessing. Feen Raven was a true fairy-child, being totally at one with the natural world, and possessing the rare gift of foresight and a kind of 'knowing' that very few other people had. Feen possessed portals to other worlds that she could see directly into, and it gave her a unique ability to understand and guide people in crisis. She was a modern-day 'white witch,' gifted with the wisdom of aeons past to heal the sick, injured and grieving, in ways that most people couldn't fathom. Her craft came directly down the familial maternal line, passed from her grandmother to her mother, and then to her.

Many people called her an oddity, because in her own sweet way she was quite eccentric, as well as being ridiculously tiny in stature; almost childlike, and a lot of people found it hard to comprehend how small she was, as a 'grown-up.' Those who couldn't or wouldn't try to understand her, who chose instead to distrust or fear her capabilities, generally gave her a wide berth. Feen would just smirk and let it roll off her back. The young woman had a unique understanding of such people and never let their opinions bother her.

She and her husband Gavin were regular and frequent visitors back at Ravensdown. Although they spent most of their time in London because of Gavin's work as a songwriter and composer, Ravensdown would always be Feen's primary home, no matter where she went. She and Gavin had the twins, Alder and Willow, and Adie saw quite a lot of them.

She adored Feen, and was continually fascinated by her. It was nice, to have her step-family around so much, because she didn't see any of her own kids as often as she would have liked. They were scattered across the south of England, in jobs and relationships, and all pretty busy with different things.

Her first-born daughter Ruth was a university lecturer, and she lived in Guildford with her wife, the acclaimed Italian dress designer Gina Giordano. The couple had a young daughter, Chiara, who was a complete delight to Adie. The little family spent a lot of time in Italy, near Gina's family in Calabria.

Her son, Matty, never liked to venture too far from his home in Epsom. He'd settled down quickly, after a big family-blow-up, a slightly shady past, and a pretty rough ride from the police over a crime had hadn't committed. He was a quiet family man now, working as a computer engineer, and living contentedly with his wife Marie. They had two small daughters, Amelia (Milly) and Sophie.

Adie's other daughter Teresa was yet to settle down. She'd done a few years of travelling but was now working and enjoying life in London. She still kept heading off somewhere in Europe for city breaks, whenever she could. The girl had itchy feet, and was trying to find a compromise between earning a living and seeing what the world had to offer. So far, her wanderlust wasn't showing any real signs of being resolved, but there was plenty of time to settle down. If she could find a balance between working and travelling, it would keep her happy for a while.

Adie relocating to the Lake District certainly hadn't made it easy for any of her kids, but they came to Torley occasionally, sometimes for Christmas (and her birthday, which fell on Christmas Eve), and Adie and Mark went to London a couple of times a year, so they would all make the effort to meet up for lunch or dinner whenever they could fit it in.

She'd come to expect little effort from them all. It had only been a few years since the family had suffered some devastating blows. Adie had brought Ruth back into her life again as the grown-up baby she'd had and adopted out when she'd been just fifteen, and Bryan, Teresa and Matty hadn't known a thing about it. Adie had kept dark secrets for her entire marriage, and probably would have continued to keep them, if a catastrophic series of events hadn't brought everything out into the open in a way that nobody could ever have predicted. As the saying went, 'the truth will out,' and it certainly did, leaving everyone reeling from the shock. When the storm finally passed, it had left the acrid taste of betrayal on the lips of everyone involved. Coming back from all that had taken a lot of time and tolerance. The biggest casualty had been Adie and Bryan's marriage but, as she later came to realise, that was already fatally compromised by Bryan's long-term affair – *his* secret that *she* hadn't known about.

They still weren't completely out of the woods, as a family, and Adie doubted if she and her children would ever go back to the easy-going relationships they'd enjoyed before all of that. But, at least everyone was civil now, and making a decent effort, and some semblance of trust and kinship was gradually returning. It was a good start.

As she'd confided to Minty Cartwright, she no longer missed the 'friends' that had fallen by the wayside, largely because of how badly they'd treated her when she'd needed their support. They'd turned out to be such two-faced, fair-weather friends – the kind that no one needed. A few of them had tried to get back in touch a couple of years after the dust had settled on her dead marriage and family fall-out, but probably only to try and make themselves feel better about what they'd done to her. She never answered their emails, or picked up the phone to them, and she never returned their calls.

Some scars ran very deep, didn't they? Sometimes you didn't ever fully come to terms with emotional devastation and the best you could hope for, after being mortally wounded on multiple levels, was that you'd be able to find a way to live with the pain of it all. It wasn't the same thing as being 'at peace,' but finding an acceptable level of adjustment provided the kind of comfort that helped you to have something resembling a normal life.

Minty certainly seemed to have a lot of emotional pain to work through. Adie felt keenly for her, knowing exactly what it was like to find out in circumstances you could never have foretold in a million years, that your husband had been consistently cheating on you with someone he'd actually fallen in love with. For poor Minty, the fact that the woman in question had been her closest friend for her entire life was an unimaginable betrayal.

It had been mortifying in the extreme for Adie to learn, when Mark Raven was still just a friend, that he'd inadvertently overheard her husband Bryan in conversation with a woman who had clearly already been his mistress for six years, at the time. It was one of those astonishingly random coincidences that sometimes happen in life that force you to believe in fate; where you pretty much have to accept that no matter how much it hurts, the universe is actually working in your favour to help move you forward from where you were emotionally stuck; from where your wheels were spinning, even if you didn't know they were, and even if it hurt you to be moved.

Poor Mark had simply been in the wrong place at the right time to have discovered what was going on. He hadn't told Adie about Bryan's affair, but he had forced her cheating rat of a husband to do it himself.

The end of a close relationship you've given your all to is always devastating, no matter what the circumstances. No matter who was at fault, who had been blind, or who had more pieces to pick up, it's like any other death. Poor Minty. What must it feel like, to be so badly betrayed like that, with two of the founding pillars of your life giving way at the same time?

Destabilising wasn't the word! Adie hoped with all her heart that Minty would recover and go on to make a good and happy life for herself. Despite the fact that she was on good terms with her kids and would probably have them around for at least some of the festive season, it was likely to be a pretty tough Christmas for her, and Adie knew all about that too!

The front door slammed shut, making her jump. Mark came through to the kitchen, dripping wet. 'A'reet lass? It's pissin' down again. We'll know in't mornin,' if that repair we did to't barn roof'll 'old.'

Adie threw him a towel and he wiped his wet face. 'I could murder a brew, if kettle's on?'

'It is now,' she said with a grin, and lifted one of the giant Aga's hotplate covers and stuck the kettle on it. The gorgeous, dark blue beast was three times the size of the one at Teapot Cottage. It dominated the big farmhouse kitchen and Adie adored it. She wouldn't cook with anything else, now.

'I've just been down to see the tenant at Teapot. Took a few proteas for her. I'm glad I did that, because I think she's in need of a bit of cheering up, bless her.' Adie briefly explained to him about Minty's circumstances. Mark harrumphed a little.

'Well, she's in't right place to find a different way o' lookin' at things, any road.' He peered keenly at his wife.

'I know 'er story sounds a bit familiar t'yer own, but yer do know it's not yer job to fix all these bloody lame ducks that keep showin' up 'ere, don't yer, lass?'

She laughed. His broad 'Lanky' twang always cheered her up. His accent was like someone from generations past, and nobody could really explain why his pronunciation of the old Lancashire dialect was still so strong. It made him unique within the family, because his sister Sheila's accent was a lot less dramatic. She dropped her 'aitches' whenever she spoke, but she'd been married for a very long time to her husband Bob Shalloe, whose accent was more like a 'rounded BBC,' so while everyone could tell where she came from, she did sound a little more refined. Mark sounded like exactly what he was; an occasionally-smelly sheep farmer with no airs and graces but he was, in fact, utterly and completely gorgeous and adorable to all who knew and loved him.

But he was also cringingly pragmatic, and sometimes that did annoy Adie. She held up her hands in mock surrender. 'I know, I know, Mr Sage, and I won't interfere down there, I *promise*. I just hope she'll be okay.'

Mark nodded and sat down at the table. Evidently, he'd decided to finish work for the day, and Adie didn't blame him. The farm could be hard work, at different times of the year. Sometimes she had to gently nag him to slow down a little but, for once, he seemed content to call it quits a few hours earlier than normal. It was a rare occasion when he did, and she sent a silent message of thanks to the God of Weather, who was responsible for it today.

'Are you okay yourself, darling? It's not like you to lay down the tools so early. You look knackered. Is your back playing up?'

Mark nodded. 'Aye, a bit. Not so bad, but it's 'avin' a bit of a sing-song twang, an' I don't want it gettin' any worse.'

Adie agreed that it was wise to stop. To be fair, he'd been better than she'd expected him to be, in the wake of his accident, in listening to his body and taking things a little easier when it told him to. They'd had a big talk about that, after he'd come home from the hospital. Adie had let him know in no uncertain terms that she wasn't about to condone him going at the farm like a bull at a gate anymore. He was a solid barrel of a man, with more than enough enthusiasm to do what needed to be done, but his body wasn't as strong as it had been. Making an 'honest woman' of her would be fine, she'd told him, but making a widow of her wasn't. He needed to button off a bit, and take things easier.

There was more than enough money to employ a farmhand, so that was what they'd done. They now had a young, fit chap called Mike Evans coming in part time, just for the weekday mornings, and it had taken a lot of the physical strain off Mark.

''Alf an 'our upstairs wi' you might fix't twangin,' though,' he said thoughtfully, half to himself. She ignored the gleam in his eye, and turned her face away so he wouldn't see her smirking at his predictable attempts to drag her into bed for a bit of slap and tickle. He was always trying his luck but, bless him, he never took offence if she batted him away like an annoying fly, which she sometimes had to do.

‘It might make it worse, have you thought of that? In any case, I’ve got a big pot of chilli con carne to make this afternoon for the pot-luck dinner on Saturday night,’ she reminded him. ‘You hadn’t forgotten about it, had you?’

Mark shook his head. ‘No, I ‘adn’t. ‘Oo’s comin’? The usual suspects I tek it?’

‘Yep, Bob and Sheila, Carla and Dave, Egg and Peric, the Murphys, the Davies,’ and Trudie and Kevin. Stuart Thomson’s coming, if only because Meghan’s babysitting for Debby and Darren, and he has to drop her off and pick her up. You know how he hates to leave the stables for long. Hopefully we’ll see Han and Stazel Walton, too.’

She shook her head, laughing at herself now. The family had adopted some of Feen’s Spoonerisms in describing certain members by name with their consonants switched. It was quite hilarious. Egg and Peric, and Han and Stazel were just two. Darla and Cave was still being established, as the ‘Spoony’ term of endearment for Gavin’s mother and her new husband, but it wouldn’t be long before that was how they’d be referred to forevermore, within the family.

Mark thought for a moment. ‘I don’t suppose we can get ‘em all to bugger off ‘ome early, so can get yer into bed before midnight for a bit of ‘ow’s yer father?’ His eyes danced at Adie, and she grinned. This time she let him see it, but she also rolled her eyes, and she let him see that too.

Oh, this man; he was *full* of mischief, always trying to wind her up. She pulled a face at him and giggled.

‘Don’t bank on it, but you never know your luck, you old letch! You never give up, do you? I think you need a cold shower!’ But she couldn’t stop herself from laughing, and he grinned back at her, like a cheeky schoolboy.

Adie thought back to the time when she was staying at Teapot Cottage herself. She’d just arrived there, with her life in tatters, feeling much the same way as Minty Cartwright was probably feeling right now. Mark had very kindly invited her to the Ravensdown Christmas party. Her first impulse had been to reject the invitation, imagining she’d be no sort of company, but then she'd been persuaded by her new friend Peg Tripper, who ran one of the local cafés down in the town, to go along to keep her company. Adie had agreed, and the party had been the beginning of a whole new life. She often wondered how differently things might have turned out, had she not gone along, that Christmas night. A smile played around her lips, and Mark chuckled at her.

'I dunno what yer thinkin,' lass, but it's givin' me twinges in places I shouldn't be 'avin' any, considerin' yer keep turnin' me down!' There was that mischievous twinkle again. He sat at the table, shaking quietly with laughter at Adie's reddening face. He still had the ability to catch her off guard with the innuendo, and he loved how it made her blush. She shook her head at him.

'Well, it's the middle of the afternoon and I've loads to do! Rain-check at bedtime though?'

'Aye, go on, then, if yer up fer it by then. Yer normally snorin' yer little 'ead off as soon as yer 'ead 'its pilla.'

Adie did really fancy him, and their relationship was as passionate as any could be, for couples their age. Having found one another late in life, they'd started off just as friends, but the friendship had very quickly deepened. By the time they'd got around to getting physical it was more about a deep desire to truly fulfil one another than it was about fireworks for themselves, although there were still a few of those occasionally! They were lucky to have found one another, and they both knew it.

Adie pulled her attention back to her tenant. She decided she would go back down to the cottage straight away, and invite Minty to the pot-luck dinner party. It was something she and Mark did once a season; invite friends over, with each guest to bring a shared food contribution. It was called a 'pot-luck' because that's exactly what it was. Nobody knew what anyone else would be bringing, and what ended up on the table was always a random and fascinating assortment of dishes.

From chilled orange and almond soup to chicken stew and dumplings, from Hungarian goulash to ham and asparagus pie, from rum-laden trifles to cappuccino profiteroles with whipped cream, the selection was always interesting. And of course, most times, everyone knew one another. Adie knew from her own experience that any party at Ravensdown could be quite an intimidating prospect to a new guest, but she resolved to try and persuade Minty to come along anyway.

As she pulled on her wellies and dragged her raincoat down from the coat stand inside the front door, she almost called back to remind Mark to get a couple of two-kilo packs of minced beef from out of the big chest freezer in the barn, then thought better of it. *He's already dried himself off. Since I'm going to get wet anyway, I may as well get it myself, before I come back in.*

Minty was surprised to see her at the back door of the cottage again, and opened it to let her in. Adie shook her head. 'I swear to God I'm not a stalker! Really, I'm not. I'm wet through, so I'll stay in the porch, but I just wanted to invite you to a pot-luck dinner up at the house on Saturday night, and meet a few of the locals.'

Minty looked slightly baffled. 'Pot-luck dinner? That's a term I'm not familiar with.'

'Ah, yes, sorry! My daughter Teresa picked up the term 'pot-luck' in Australia, when she was travelling around out there. It's a kiwi term, apparently, for inviting a bunch of people to dinner, letting them bring whatever contribution they want, for the table, and seeing what you end up with! It's always interesting, and lots of fun.'

She could see by Minty's reluctant expression that she didn't find the idea tempting, so she tried another tack. 'There will only be about fourteen of us. When I was here, when I thought my whole life had ended, I was invited to a Christmas party. It was the last thing I wanted to do, so I get your reluctance. But honestly, I made myself go, and it changed my whole life. Besides,' she added, 'I could use a hand in the kitchen, even just for an hour or so, from someone else who understands how an Aga works. You wouldn't have to stay if you weren't comfortable.'

Adie elected not to say that her sister-in-law Sheila Shalloe, the all-time-master of the Aga from whom Adie had herself learned everything she knew, would also be at the party. She wanted to appeal to Minty's potential for being of help.

Anything to get her there, and out of her funk for a while.

Minty thought for a moment. 'Well. . . you're right in saying I don't feel very sociable but I could come for a bit to help in the kitchen, I suppose, if that's what you really need?'

Adie nodded briskly, keen to leave again before Minty changed her mind. 'Great. If you could come about seven, that would be brilliant. And of course you won't be expected to stay if you don't want to. They're a pretty relaxed, easy-going crew, so nobody will mind at all if you decide it's not your scene. Thank you, so much, Minty! I really appreciate it.' She gave Minty a beaming smile and a wink, and stepped back out into the rain.

As she headed past the farmhouse and over towards the barn to get the frozen beef out of the freezer for the chilli con carne, she heard the landline phone ringing inside, and wondered who was calling. Most people called her or Mark on their mobile phones, these days. Usually, apart from cold-callers and canvassers, the only person who usually called them on their landline was Feen. Adie smirked at the thought of Mark answering the phone to someone who was hoping to scam him or sell him something. They'd definitely get a lot more than they bargained for, in being told 'no.'

The barn roof did – so far – appear to be holding. Mark and Mike had done a very neat repair. It looked great and seemed to be doing its job, so far at least, in fending off the sheeting rain. Adie shuddered when she looked at the floor. It was always bittersweet, coming in here. The first time she'd ever come into this barn was to rescue Mark, who was unconscious and bleeding on the stone floor, after his terrible, life-threatening fall through the mezzanine floor, with Feen in hysterics beside him. While he was in hospital, Adie had gone on to spend a lot of time in here, locating what was needed and keeping everything straight, as part of taking over the interim running of the farm with Feen. She now knew the barn like the back of her hand, but she still had very mixed feelings about it. Thankfully, now that the mezzanine floor had been repaired, it didn't feel like an unsafe place.

Back in the house, she took off her dripping wet coat and boots, and made her way back into the kitchen. Mark was still on the phone and he waved to her to take it. 'Feen,' he muttered, as he handed her the headset. 'I'm off for a shower.'

'Hi Feen, everything okay? Are you guys still coming up on Sunday?'

To Adie's delight, Feen was ringing to say that a day of music recording that Gavin had scheduled on Saturday had been brought forward, after someone else had cancelled their Friday booking. It meant they could come up on Saturday morning instead. 'That's *great* news! Be warned that we're having the pot-luck dinner on Saturday night, though! The house will be full.'

Feen laughed and told her that was exactly why they were keen to come up ahead of schedule – to be there in time to join in. Adie rang off, after telling Feen to do a sun dance, or at least have a stern word with her 'spirit guides.' The weather needed to improve a *lot* by Saturday.

The ongoing downpour wouldn't be much fun for the twins, when they came. It wouldn't be so great for her poor tenant, either. Although Minty Cartwright had clearly come here for reasons that had little to do with the weather, it always made life a lot less difficult when it wasn't pouring with rain. Few people appreciated getting soaked to the skin every time they set foot outside their front door. A break in the rain was sorely needed.

Chapter Five

Hmmm. A party invitation, Minty mused. She felt mildly irritated that Adie Raven had presented it in a way that made her feel vaguely manipulated into being a kitchenhand, of all things, but she deliberately set that thought aside. It had been an incredibly kind gesture, to be offered an opportunity to get out of her own head for an hour or so and help someone else.

Minty suspected that Adie didn't really need much help in her kitchen. She seemed like the most capable person on the planet, and if it was a shared dinner, with people bringing contributions that were presumably already prepared, what would need to be done in the kitchen involving the Aga that she couldn't manage by herself?

It had been a thinly veiled attempt to get Minty to focus on something else for a brief time and meet some new people. But, as with most things, she had two choices about how to take it. She made the choice to be gracious, and grateful, that someone who hardly knew her cared enough to invite her to a party where she knew precisely no one. 'Only about fourteen people,' Adie had said. That seemed like a lot, to Minty. Maybe she really did need help in the kitchen!

Minty hadn't even met Mark Raven yet, Adie's husband. Walking into a house full of strangers was certainly the most nerve-wracking prospect she had faced for weeks, and she may yet bottle out of it. However, having given Adie her promise to help, it would seem a bit mean and wimpy to change her mind, wouldn't it?

So it seemed that she was stuck with going, and although Adie had said it was an informal affair, Minty wondered if she even had a scrap of clothing with her that would look halfway respectable at a 'pot-luck' dinner, however relaxed it might be.

Everything she'd bought with her had pretty much consisted of casual gear; comfy jeans, jumpers and trainers. She hadn't imagined running into anyone she'd have to make the slightest effort for. Feeling fairly frumpy and ugly in any case, as a newly-rejected wife and best friend, she hadn't given any thought to packing anything even mildly flattering or pretty when she'd decided to 'get out of dodge' for a while.

She pulled down the well-thumbed little Torley Directory from the shelf next to the fireplace, and flicked through it. There was a boutique in the town, a place called GladRagz, where she might just be able to get a decent top to go with her one respectable pair of jeans. She quickly called the boutique to check its opening times. The voice that answered sounded friendly; a woman announcing herself as 'Trudie speaking.' Minty confirmed the opening times and said she would pop down in the morning to take a look at what was on offer.

She hoped she would find what she needed. The prospect of taking the bus from town all the way to Carlisle, to find something to wear for an event she wasn't even sure she wanted to go to, was just a little too much.

The following morning, after a lazy late breakfast, she took the walking trail down across the fields into Torley town and quickly located the boutique. It was tucked into the corner of a cluster of shops behind the town's little 'supermarket,' and just along from the back entrance to the Bull and Royal pub.

She was warmly greeted by an attractive, smiley woman, who Minty estimated to be somewhere in her early fifties. 'Hi. I'm Trudie, welcome to GladRagz. Are you looking for something special?'

Minty confirmed that she wanted something to wear for an informal dinner. Trudie invited her to take a look around. She wasn't at all 'hard-sell,' which was something Minty had always hated. Being pounced on the minute she walked through a shop door, and being harangued to try something on, or followed around like she was under suspicion of being a rampant shoplifter was a cast-iron guarantee to make her turn around and walk straight out again.

Mercifully, Trudie left her to it, and she soon found a rack towards the back of the shop that held a lovely variety of autumn jumpers and tunics. Everything was of excellent quality, and not too exorbitantly priced, for wool and cashmere. A forest green-coloured cowl-neck tunic caught Minty's eye. It wasn't a colour she normally wore, but somehow it seemed to beckon her. It looked a little on the large size, but she decided to try it on anyway. Slipping it over her head, she felt the indisputable, warm caress of cashmere.

The tunic was lightweight but lovely. On her body, it didn't look too big, just slightly oversized, which was the fashion of the moment anyway, if the different magazines she had flicked through (Fiona's magazines, as a matter of fact) were anything to judge by.

'What do you think?' She asked Trudie, stepping out of the fitting room. Trudie narrowed her eyes, chewed the inside of her lip, and thought for a moment.

Well, that makes a nice change! Here's a woman who isn't going to tell me I look lovely in a burlap sack just so she can make a profit on it.

'The colour is gorgeous on you, with your dark hair and eyes, and your beautiful, honeyed skin. I had this in a few good colours actually, but most of them got snapped up quickly. I think there's another one left on the rack, in blue. Not sure if you saw it, but it's a pretty one too.'

'No, I didn't, but could you get it for me, if it's the same size?'

'Of course, and I do think it is! But just hold on a sec.' She disappeared into the recess in the back of her shop, and quickly came back holding up a pretty, delicate gold chain belt. Its open, looped links were in the shape of elegant little sixties-style daisies. It was quite retro, but since that was apparently all the rage at the moment too, it didn't look out of place.

‘These belts just arrived yesterday, and I haven’t got around to properly unpacking them yet. You have a pretty waist, so let’s try this.’ She stepped forward and draped the gold belt around Minty’s waist in a way that left a few of its petal links dangling slightly, at the side of her body. The belt instantly transformed the tunic from simple to stunning.

‘Oh my goodness! What a difference! I can’t believe that!’ Minty was thrilled. The gold chain subtly accentuated her waist. ‘Wow! You know, I’ve never worn belts? I never even think about them, as accessories. But this is beautiful, and what a lift it gives to the top! It’s a lovely top anyway, but this makes it look so much more elegant!’

‘But still quite casual,’ Trudie offered.

‘Yes! It’s perfect for what I need, I think. Thank you so much!’

The belt didn’t have a price tag on it, but Minty didn’t care. It was gorgeous. She had to have it. Trudie also rolled up the sleeves on the tunic a little to add a chunky cuff effect to it, and wound a light bronze chiffon scarf around Minty’s neck. The little touches made the whole thing look fantastic.

‘You have a really good eye! But I suppose a lot of people have told you that.’

Trudie grinned as she came back and handed Minty the same tunic as the one she was already wearing, but in a gorgeous ‘Airforce’ grey-blue.

‘Yeah, one or two have mentioned it, but I’ve been in this game a long time. What I know is that very few women really appreciate their own assets. They tend to just focus on the faults, as they see them. I try to help them understand exactly how sensational they can look with just a teeny tweak of help.’

And it *had* been a teeny tweak of help. The simple acts of turning up the cuffs and adding an elegant belt and scarf to a very plain top had Minty feeling like a million dollars. She held the blue tunic against herself, and decided she liked that too.

‘Well, I think I’ll have both tunics *and* the belt and scarf. I’m so thrilled!’

‘Did you say you were going to wear jeans with the tunics?’

Minty nodded. ‘Yeah. I hope they’ll go okay together, but it’s all I brought with me. I’m here on a last-minute break, and I didn’t imagine, when I packed my bag, that I’d be going to a dinner!’

Trudie held up a finger. ‘Well hang on a minute then. D’you like leggings? I’ve got some really nice ones. They’re a bit pricey but they’re very well made. Unlike the cheapie ones you get every winter in the chain stores, which fall apart after a dozen washes, these ones will last three times as long, probably more if you look after them.’

Minty was amused. ‘Leggings? No, I’ve never owned a pair. I’ve seen enough women who certainly *shouldn’t* be wearing them. That’s put me off for life!’

Trudie nodded and laughed. ‘I know. A lot of ladies don’t bother to check in a mirror before they leave home, do they? Especially the ones who really should! But you’ve a lovely figure. Leggings would look great on you.’ She shrugged. ‘It’s just a thought.’

Minty suddenly felt mean for so readily dismissing the other woman’s suggestion. Trudie didn’t seem like the sort who would try to flog anything to someone who didn’t want or suit it, but she was rather good at ‘up-selling.’

‘Go on, then,’ she giggled, in spite of herself. ‘Just for a laugh, I’ll swallow down my horror and try a pair on.’

Suddenly she was in the mood for a bit of adventure, and it wasn’t as if she had to be anywhere else in a hurry. Trudie reached for a pair of black leggings off a nearby rack.

‘You look like a size twelve? Try these, with the top and the belt.’

Minty did as she was told, and when she looked at her reflection, she was astounded at how chic she suddenly looked. ‘Oh, my God! I look amazing! Even if I say so, myself! I have legs!’ She sounded incredulous to herself. Trudie threw back her head and laughed.

'That you do, and rather shapely ones, if you don't mind my saying so. These leggings have a good amount of Lycra in them, which makes them hug the legs, and it means they don't go baggy around the bum and the knees like the more mass-produced cheaper ones do. They also won't fade to grey with washing, like a lot of others. They'll stay black. See how these have a slight sheen to them? Very flattering.'

She stood back and scrutinized Minty. 'The tunic properly covers your bum, so the look isn't vulgar at all. It all looks very casual-chic, in my humble opinion, and very age-appropriate. If you were worrying about that, you shouldn't.'

Trudie then backed off completely and left Minty alone in the fitting room, tactfully giving her the space she needed to make her decision without pressure. But Minty had to agree with her. She did look pretty good, and she suddenly looked and felt like a different person. A much more modern one. It occurred to her that without her even registered the fact, her dress sense had somehow become quite 'dowdy,' in recent years

When the hell did that happen? When did I become a mumsy frump with no fashion sense?

Minty thought back to her wardrobe at home, jam-packed with 'sensible' things to wear under her white med coat at work, and couple of ancient 'safe' dresses that would have done (at a push) for an evening out but would probably never draw any compliments. Her mind drifted to the drawers of jeans, with holes that *weren't* part of their design, and track-suit bottoms whose colours had terminally faded, sitting alongside serviceable but boring jumpers, and a handful of t-shirts with fraying necks and holes under the arms.

No wonder Leo looked elsewhere. You really let yourself go, a vicious little voice whispered in the back of her head. She tried to ignore it, but it wouldn't quite fade away when she asked it to.

And what about Bloody Fiona, her so-called 'best friend?' Wasn't it her job to draw Minty's attention to the fact that she was starting to dress more like a homeless woman than a professional one who hadn't even turned fifty? Surely, it's what any good friend would do? But Fiona hadn't been a good friend in the end, had she? And maybe it suited her quite well, to look a lot more glamorous than poor old moth-eaten Minty.

Yes, it seemed that Fiona Winterson had let Minty down in more ways than one, and for a very long time, without her even having noticed. Minty couldn't remember the last time she'd been prompted to go shopping for something nice to wear, unless you counted the cocktail dress Fiona helped her choose for her 20th wedding anniversary party, and that was one item that could *definitely* go in the bin. She doubted if she could ever bring herself to look at it again, let alone wear it. Shame, given how beautiful it was, and the fortune it had cost. Maybe she could get a few quid for it on eBay or Vinted. That would be another adventure she hadn't experienced before – the prospect of online selling!

Yes, maybe it was time for a make-over in general. Maybe Mrs Minty McLeod – or Ms Minty Cartwright (as she was going back to being in *all* aspects of her life from now on) needed to reinvent herself, quick-smart, in preparation for the different direction her life was going to take.

Consultants generally reverted to Mr, Ms, Miss or Mrs for their titles, but Minty had never got hung up on the intellectual snobbery of medical formality, so she never minded much when people called her 'Doctor.' She *was* one, after all, and she'd slaved for nearly a decade to become one! 'Doctor' was absolutely fine but, for the purposes of officialdom, she decided now to ditch her 'Mrs' and officially become a 'Ms.'

'Oh! Is everything ok?' Trudie gave Minty a worried glance. Minty realised her sadness must have shown on her face, and she made a conscious effort to push it aside and concentrate on the moment. She mustered a smile that she hoped would make her look a little more confident.

'Yes, absolutely. I was just thinking about things I probably shouldn't be thinking about! I will take the leggings, in fact if you have any more in my size I'll take two pair. I think I could get used to the new look.'

She looked down at her feet, suddenly not wanting to put her battered, scruffy old trainers on again. 'I don't suppose you have any nice shoes or boots that could pull all this together, do you?'

Trudie winked at her. 'Of course I do. I have some great slouch boots. I just didn't want to push too much at you, since you really only came in for a top.' She pointed towards another small annex at the side of the shop that Minty had walked right past as she'd come in, and hadn't even seen.

'Gosh, this place is full of surprises!' Minty found to her delight that the annex was full of individual little shelves, each displaying a different kind of boot or shoe. Trudie must have all the boxes and sizes out the back or upstairs, because there was very little room for anything other than the display and a seat to sit on while you tried something on for size. But Minty's eye was immediately drawn to the slouch boots Trudie had mentioned. They were black suede with gently tapered toes, a two-inch heel, and gold-clamped tassels at the back. She knew they would go perfectly with the leggings. Trudie offered a pair in her size, so she tried them on, loved the look of them too, and decided to buy them as well.

She burst out laughing. 'I can't believe I'm actually buying pixie boots and leggings!'

'Well you do look fabulous in them,' Trudie smirked. 'Just make sure that you *always* wear the leggings with a top that fully covers your rear end, to keep them looking respectable and trendy. It's important, as we get older. Oh, and in case you were looking for anything else, there's a sale rack at the back. It's mostly stuff left over from summer, fairly lightweight and well picked-over now I'm afraid, but you might find a bargain or two, if you have time to look.'

She smiled at Minty and went back to writing in a notebook on the counter. Clearly she wasn't a woman to pressure her customers into anything. Minty did take a quick look, but she didn't find anything suitable for the colder climate that now prevailed. Summer was long gone, winter was almost up on them all, and the sale stock really had been well and truly pawed and picked over. Some of it was badly shop-soiled. There wasn't much of anything left that anyone would want.

She came back to the counter and handed over her credit card. Trudie placed a pair of gold-tone, delicate drop earrings in the shape of flowers not dissimilar to the belt, on top of the items Minty was buying. 'These are old stock, and they go with the belt. Please take them as my gift.'

'Oh, no! I couldn't. They're lovely, but please let me pay you for them.' Minty felt confused, but compelled to do the right thing, as she nearly always did. It hadn't occurred to her to buy earrings, but it seemed a little mean-spirited to say she didn't want them. She swept aside the quick stab of resentment at feeling more or less *obliged* to buy them. She needn't have felt alarmed however, because Trudie flatly refused to add them to the bill.

'They're old stock. Nobody's bought them in a year, and I hate having old stuff hanging around that my regulars constantly see and ask themselves why it hasn't sold. It's not good for business. I'd generally send them to the charity shop with the summer sale stuff that doesn't sell, but I'd rather gift them to you.'

'Well in that case, I'll gladly accept them with grace and gratitude. They are lovely, and you're right. They do go with the belt, and the gold on the boot tassels.'

Minty gave Trudie a heartfelt smile, and thanked her again for her help. As she opened the door to leave the store she was surprised by the fact that it was, once again, bucketing with rain. She chided herself for having forgotten to check whether there was an umbrella at Teapot Cottage.

Trudie looked up, grimaced at the weather, reached over to the side of the counter, and pulled out an umbrella from a holder containing about half a dozen. 'Here, take this. Drop it back next time you're passing.'

Minty thanked her profusely again. Trudie waved her thanks aside. 'All part of the service.'

It was a small, simple thing, to be offered an umbrella in the pouring rain, but it touched Minty in more ways than

Trudie could ever imagine. It was both a metaphor and an irony, that a stranger would seek to shield you from the rain, while the people you trusted the most would gladly throw you out and leave you standing it.

So Minty waltzed out of GladRagz with two entire outfits. She laughed to herself at the small thrill her little shopping spree had given her.

See? Life goes on. You will be happy again. One day at a time, and count the blessings as you go.

She decided to call into Peg's café for a hot cuppa and a snack lunch, and was surprised and humbled when Peg remembered her, and asked her how she was settling in at Teapot Cottage.

'It's a gorgeous little place, Peg! You were absolutely right! I'm really happy in there. Can I please get a cup of hot chocolate with all the trimmings, and one of your veggie sausage rolls?'

The vege-based sausage rolls in the cabinet by the counter looked fat and succulent, and made her mouth water.

'Of course, love. Get yourself settled and I'll bring it over.'

'I've just noticed those big pies you've got in the cabinet too. Are they home-made as well?'

'They are, but I've only got two creamy veg and one chicken and mushroom left.'

'Okay, wrap me up a creamy veg. I can heat it up in the Aga, and that's tonight's dinner sorted, and probably tomorrow's lunch as well! Perfect. Thanks, Peg.'

'No problem. Will you be wanting another taxi called, love? It's a bit of a hike up to Ravensdown at the best of times, and a proper bloody trudge in the rain.' She looked out through the window and grimaced. 'This doesn't look like passing off anytime soon. In fact, if I'm honest, it looks like it's getting worse. Perhaps I should call Adam, to come and get you.'

Minty nodded. How kind of Peg, to realise how much of a help that would be! She remarked that it looked like being the perfect afternoon to get the fire going, and fall asleep in front of it, and Peg agreed.

Adam Driver arrived soon after, in his taxi, and she was grateful when he greeted her like an old friend. He was around forty, she supposed, and he had twinkly blue eyes and a cheeky grin. She was quietly delighted to see again the photograph of his wife and children that he'd mounted into a little frame and fastened to the dashboard of his taxi. A family man then, and a happy one, by all appearances.

'I do have to stop meeting a pretty woman like this, you know, Ms Cartwright,' he grinned at her. 'People will start to talk!'

They made a few minutes of friendly small-talk, and Adam dropped her off back at Teapot Cottage just as the first clap of thunder came. Hot on its heels was a bolt of forked lightning that literally tore the sky apart. The rain was falling so hard she could barely see through it. Scrambling from the taxi to the front door, she managed to get it open and hurl herself through it just as a gust of wind threatened to whip her shopping bags clean away, and off to God-knows-where.

Bloody hell! This is one angry storm!

Another clap of thunder shook the cottage, followed by another massive bolt of lightning that lit up the sky like a strobe light. Minty was grateful that she'd had the foresight to lay the fire ready, before going out, so all she had to do was set a match to it and it let it take hold. She switched on the living room lamps and, mindful of Adie's previous warning about the possible loss of power, she quickly jammed a couple of the tall, tapered candles into the holders that sat atop the sideboard in the living room, and made sure the matches were alongside. The last thing she needed was to have to scrabble around in the dark to get them lit.

She filled the kettle and set it on the Aga. Snuggling into a window seat with a good book seemed like the most realistic plan for the afternoon, but once she was settled with the fire roaring and another steaming mug of chocolate, she was content to just watch the storm, as it played out dramatically across the hills that flanked the Torley valley, against the darkened sky.

She was still amazed at how much she'd told Adie Raven, the day before, about her situation. That wasn't like her at all. She normally kept her business to herself, especially when it was unpleasant, and she certainly didn't make a habit of confiding in complete strangers! But something about Adie had invited confidence and trust. The woman was a born listener. Not only had she shared some of her more intimate menopausal struggles, but she had also made a couple of very astute observations. Minty already knew that Leo and Fiona's betrayals had been their choice, and not her fault, but having someone else say it, who'd been through something similar and survived it, counted for something.

It somehow *validated* everything she was feeling. It also proved that she wasn't going mad in wondering, in her highly emotional and hormonal state, how much of their creeping around behind her back had been her own fault. None of it was, and Adie had been right, in saying how clever duplicitous people could be, especially when they had something to lose. Leo and Fiona really *had* been surprisingly adept at keeping their affair from her for two and a half years. With everything to lose, Leo had turned into a master of deception. That wasn't Minty's fault, nor was her best friend's decision to shaft her in the worst way, by being exactly the same.

On reflection, Minty conceded that Fliss had been right in saying how little she had noticed of what was going on around her at different times. But that didn't make it okay for anyone, least of all the people who were supposed to love her, to use her lack of attention to nuances, as an excuse to betray her. The fact that Fiona had decided she loved Leo more than Minty, and the fact that Leo didn't love Minty anymore at all, really smarted and stung. But the subterfuge and lies hurt more.

Another question came to her as she sat there, staring at the vase of Adie's pretty pink proteas reflected in the window. She'd punished Leo in every way she could, but why had she not struck back at Bloody Fiona? If anything, her anger towards Fiona should be greater, shouldn't it? If Minty's husband was to have an affair, wouldn't it be a bit less devastating if it was with someone she didn't know, instead of her very best friend?

Maybe an excuse could be found by some stranger Minty had never met, for feeling entitled to bed her husband, but Bloody Fiona made the choice to do that in full knowledge of the potential devastation. She knew Minty better than anyone did. The horrible, two-faced bitch would have been in no doubt at all, at least initially, about the amount of pain she'd be causing to someone she was supposed to love. She'd made her selfish decisions anyway, and then she'd gone on to be even *more* of a bitch, about *everything*, in being unable to leave Minty in peace, to try and pull her life back together.

The fact that Fiona had fallen in love was irrelevant. Even if she hadn't actively led Leo on initially, she certainly hadn't repelled his advances out of loyalty to her best friend, had she? No. While Minty wasn't fully conversant with how the scenario had played out, one thing was crystal clear; Bloody Fiona had helped herself to what she wanted, without enough conscience to stop herself, knowingly stomping a lifelong friendship into the dirt and enabling her so-called best friend's husband to be a cheat, in the process.

Nice woman. I wonder how she sleeps at night.

Having an irresistible weakness for someone else's husband was one thing, but being elaborately dishonest about it was quite another. So why *had* Minty been so reluctant to defend herself against Fiona's rantings? Why *had* she consistently accepted the other woman's whining, bitching and moaning, and volleyed so few objections in return? Why *had* she foregone every opportunity to tell her to 'fuck off and die'? The most vindictive thing she'd done was cancel Fiona's stupid magazine subscriptions, which hardly amounted to a vicious comeback. Why was she so willing to accept Fiona's abuse?

She supposed it was shock that had made her so compliant at first. Reeling from events, she hadn't given herself the chance to examine how she really felt about Fiona's betrayal. The truth was, and she now felt compelled to acknowledge it, that the initial shock of her husband's infidelity had literally eclipsed the other half of the equation. Now, she had to confront the fact that Fiona's treachery had hurt even more than Leo's.

He was a man, and men often thought with their dicks and little else. While that was a pretty big generalisation, and never enough to excuse infidelity or pretend it didn't matter, it tended to be true and most people understood that. A home truth far less often acknowledged, was that women often placed *their* own sexual needs above other important things too. Fulfilling their own lustful urges meant more to some of them than the fact that doing so involved someone else's husband and risked someone else's marriage. It wasn't always just men, to whom sex became more important than friendship or conscience.

Minty knew she wasn't the first woman to be betrayed by the people she loved, and she wouldn't be the last. But one thing was for certain. Bloody Fiona actually *did* deserve every last shred of her anger, and from now on she would not be tolerating the deranged idiot's vitriolic calls, or feeling like the bad guy for wanting to defend herself but forcing herself not to add any fuel to the fire by fighting back.

It was time for Minty to come out swinging; to be true to herself in dealing efficiently with a problem that clearly wasn't going to solve itself. She needed to put a stop to Fiona's self-serving nonsense, for once and for all.

Fiona had already tried to phone twice this morning but, strangely, there hadn't been any reception in the GladRagz boutique while Minty had been having a little fun for the first time since the shit had hit the fan. Her phone had shown two missed calls after she left. Next time Fiona called (and Minty knew there would be a next time, and probably sooner rather than later), she vowed that the reception she'd get would be rather different from the one she'd be expecting. Minty would draw her line in the sand, and leave her ex-friend in no doubt about where it was.

Next time you call, I'll be ready for you; you dirty slag.

And Minty didn't have long to wait. She washed her mug and put it away, and settled down with her book, and she'd only got about three chapters into it when the shrill sound of the ringtone she'd dedicated to Fiona started up on her mobile phone; Lady Gaga's 'Poker Face.' She'd set up that ringtone for Fiona's calls after a raucous 'hen do' for a mutual friend, where they'd all got royally pissed and started singing. It had been one of the best nights out that Minty had ever had, and every time Fiona called, it reminded her and made her smile.

Well, not anymore. *No more smiles for you, Miss Winterson. And I really must change that ringtone,* she thought, as she braced herself. *Maybe I could download the theme tune from Jaws for her calls, given that she's such a fucking predator, sinking her teeth with such relish into my husband? That's if I decide to keep her in my contact list at all, and why should I?*

She clicked onto the call. 'Hello Fiona,' she said, managing to keep her voice even. 'What do you want this time?' Her heart suddenly ached, but she did notice that for the first time since the world had shattered, she wasn't wary or sick to her stomach, and bracing herself to deal with a barrage of abuse. She was just sad. The grief process had already started – the process of detaching and letting go of what she had to acknowledge was lost.

'Um... well, hello. I hear you've had an offer on the house, that you've accepted, which is even lower than your pathetic asking price. The agent's just been on the phone to Leo confirming it. He is furious! Minty, why are you doing this? It's so unfair! Leo poured his heart and soul into that house, and if this is to punish him, it's a bit pathetic, don't you think? Maybe you'll be less smug about everything when he drags you through the court.'

Minty quietly counted to ten. *Don't let her rile you. Don't let this get the better of you. Stay calm.*

'Are you there?' Fiona snapped. 'What is it, with all this silence shit?'

'Mm-hm. Yes, Fiona. I'm here.'

'Well? What have you got to say for yourself?'

'What have I got to say for myself? Hmm. Let's see. Well not much, as it happens, at least not to you, since the sale of the matrimonial property I have the larger share in, and which I also poured my *own* heart and soul into, is none of your fucking business.'

Minty took a quiet, deep breath and continued. 'And, by the way, speaking of all things pathetic, I'm done listening to your outrageous attempts to mitigate your own guilt over trashing my life, by ringing up and ranting at me.'

'What? Oh, don't flatter yourself! I don't give a flying fuck what you think.'

'Well, clearly!' Minty said evenly. 'But I'm going to tell you anyway, what I think. You're the most selfish bitch I've ever met. You're even more self-serving and lacking in conscience than my scumbag, shit-for-brains husband, and that is saying something! You fully deserve one another, and I hope you'll be very happy, lying in the stinking little bed you've made for yourselves. If anything about this whole situation is 'pathetic,' Fiona, it's you. You are dead to me. You will never again have anything to say that I will want to hear, so I will never answer the phone to you again. Stop calling me. If you don't, I will file for a restraining order, and then we'll see who ends up in court, if you're stupid enough to ignore it.

'And in all the pathetic mistakes you've ever made in your sad little life, believing that I wouldn't drag *you* through the court you seem to be so fond of referring to, for stalking and harassment; well, that would be the worst. I'd have you locked up, if I could.'

Minty didn't wait to hear Fiona's response, before she clicked off the call. She was breathing hard, and her hands were clammy and shaking, but *boy,* had that felt good! She half-expected Fiona to ring straight back, but she didn't. Her phone stayed mercifully silent.

Oh God! I feel like I've finally woken up from a horrible nightmare.

She looked out over Torley Valley, through the window, and she felt a gentle new peace settle over her. She noticed that the fire was failing, and she sprang to get it going again. She was getting pretty adept with it now, after a few days' practice. She just had to make sure she had enough newspaper or cardboard underneath it, and lay her kindling over the top properly, before resting a couple of dry, smallish pieces of wood across the top. Once they caught alight, the fire would then be established. Keeping it going was merely a matter of making sure she didn't forget to put more wood on it before it got too low. It wasn't rocket science, but she'd only just caught it in time today, as distracted as she'd been with other things.

With the fire roaring again, and the sublime smell of her creamy vegetable pie emanating from the Aga, Minty felt as if Teapot Cottage was almost hugging her, as the thunder rolled and rumbled all around her, and the lightning flashed and tore the sky apart. This was a beautiful little place. Not for the first time, she congratulated herself on having chosen such an excellent bolthole. Nobody knew where she was, not even Belle and Ethan, and that was exactly the way she wanted it, for now.

She made sure to keep reassuring Belle by text though, that she was safe and doing ok. Her daughter could be a real worry-wart and, of course, she was having to deal with all this trauma too! Minty thanked the lucky stars for Tim, Belle's boyfriend, who had his feet firmly on the ground and would support her as she came to terms with the shock of her family falling apart, and worked her way through the grief, towards some form of acceptance.

She didn't have to worry so much about Ethan. He was doing just fine. As the more pragmatic of her two children, he was less likely to lose his temper or panic when things got difficult. His boyfriend Kal was similar in nature. He was a stabilizing influence too. They were a sweet young couple, and Minty was profoundly glad that Ethan had such a lovely, stable relationship. She knew that young gay men often struggled to achieve that; even the ones who desperately wanted it, at his age.

The boys had invited her to go over to Kal's place in Swindon for dinner, after she got back to Bristol. It was less than an hour's drive, and she was looking forward to having a nice, normal evening where the topics of conversation would quickly extend beyond discussing the 'gorillas in the mist' who had betrayed them all. Ethan would pay lip service to his father's conduct, but he wouldn't say a thing about Fiona, and they would very quickly be talking about things that were infinitely more interesting and positive.

He and Kal were flying to Toronto for Christmas, to spend it with Kal's family, and they were going to a very big 'Pride' party on Boxing Day with a handful of Kal's Canadian friends. Minty was looking forward to hearing about that. The trip had been booked for many months, yet the boys had generously offered to cancel so they could stick around and see her through her first Christmas without Leo.

As touched as she'd been by the gesture, she wouldn't hear of it. Belle and Tim were going to be around, she'd reminded them, and if she wanted she could probably 'do the Christmas thing' with them. But she really wondered if it might be nice just to let the event go by without much fanfare, this year. She was a lot more relaxed about Christmas being a family washout than everyone else seemed to be. Even if their lives hadn't been blown apart by Leo's infidelity, it would have been a slightly weird family Christmas anyway, with Ethan away for the first time.

She did need to do some shopping for presents, but she could do it all from up here in Torley. Her kids didn't have massive expectations in life, and she was grateful for that. Ethan and Kal were getting backpacks and hiking boots this year, so she could buy those online. Belle and Tim just wanted vouchers for a big DIY superstore, and since there was a branch in Carlisle she could probably pop over there by taxi and buy those, before she got the train home.

Fliss and Filipe would get their usual gift of a bouquet of seasonal flowers through Interflora, and Minty could do her food shopping online too, and just get Waitrose to deliver everything. That way, she'd be fully sorted in plenty of time, with no need to do a last-minute panic shop, and end up buying all kinds of expensive and inappropriate things. Leo, of course, would get nothing and, as for Fiona, well; it was a little hard to resist the temptation to get a t-shirt printed with a picture of a vagina on the front of it and the words 'I'm a dirty Doxie' written underneath it, and have *that* delivered. But Minty quickly decided that Fiona wasn't worth the effort or the money it would cost.

All of a sudden, Christmas was starting to look a lot more manageable and simple. Everyone would understand if she didn't do the usual tradition of 'stockings' or Christmas cards this year. She would simply post something on her Facebook page to apologise and say she was making a donation to charity instead. Everyone was doing that, these days. Some were just lazy misers, who didn't want to make much of an effort, and wouldn't give to a charity at all. Others would though, and Minty was one of those.

She wished she could stay longer than three weeks in this lovely cottage, but work would soon beckon her to return. A leave of absence could only stretch so far, and while she wondered if she could feasibly push it out to another fortnight, or even until after Christmas, she wasn't sure if the cottage would even be available to keep renting. Someone else may have booked it. Staying longer was only an idle thought, but Minty made a mental note to speak to Adie Raven about it anyway, next time she saw her, which would no doubt be at the 'pot-luck' dinner on Saturday night.

Being in a different place, particularly one as restful and gentle as this one, allowed a certain perspective that Minty knew she wouldn't have found so readily at home. Moping around in the space she'd shared with Leo, it was impossible to separate the past from the present, and the present from the future. It hadn't felt possible to try and accept all that had gone wrong, or focus on whatever might have to happen next, while she was still there; in a place with so many cherished memories, hopes and dreams still held within the walls.

The love she'd always felt for the house was gone; hopelessly overshadowed by betrayal. Minty knew she could never again be happy in a place that reminded her, in so many miserable ways, that one of the biggest commitments she'd ever made in her life had failed. Selling the house was the right thing to do.

When she and Leo had got married, Minty had been a struggling medical student, and Leo hadn't long started his first 'proper' job as the smallest minnow in the pond of a firm of architects that was set to expand but only a little. It hadn't been – and still wasn't – the sort of company that would ever set the world on fire. Leo's prospects for promotion or partnership there were never going to amount to anything enormous, but the job offered stability, and that had meant everything to them, in the beginning.

He'd been at pains to point out how much more valuable stability was over everything else, when you were newly married. The big bucks could and probably would come later, but stability had to be your starting point, if you wanted to buy a home and raise a family. Minty had readily agreed.

Over the years, the firm Leo worked for had won a couple of prestigious awards, and had secured a handful of lucrative, high-profile contracts, so the family fortunes *had* significantly increased. From starting out as a minnow, Leo was now earning a very respectable salary but, as an eminently respected A & E Consultant (a position she'd worked her socks off to achieve), Minty was still the higher earner.

It was Gamma's inheritance that had enabled them to buy the house in the first place, with a deposit big enough to make the mortgage manageable on Leo's starting salary. A solicitor friend of her mother's had ensured, after much arguing and opposition from Minty herself, that since she had bankrolled the acquisition with her own money, she would always have the casting decision on what was done with it in the event that the marriage ever foundered.

At the time, she'd been insulted at the idea of anyone insinuating that her marriage might not last, but she had grudgingly agreed, trying to ignore the idea that the relationship might then be jinxed as a result. Christine, her ever-patient and long-suffering mother, had gone to great lengths to explain that all the legal contract was trying to do was protect her interests in the event that she ended up without her husband, for *any* reason.

As resistant as Minty had been at the time, to that thinly-veiled pre-nuptial agreement, there were no words to describe how grateful she was for it now.

The documentation as to who owned the lion's share of the property was clear for anyone to see. Leo wouldn't have a leg to stand on if he tried to take Minty to court over the undervalued house, especially since however low the sale price might be, he would still get his promised half. Any divorce lawyers worth their salt could find an appropriate loophole to construct a successful, watertight case for her to give him a hell of a lot *less*. He was an adulterer! Had he not been, they would likely have remained a married couple with a substantial and incredibly valuable matrimonial property to enjoy until death did them part, or at least until their dribbling dotage forced either one of them into a care home that needed to be funded. Leo didn't have much ammunition to fight the reality of that.

Was that the underlying issue in the foundering of the marriage; that she earned more than he did? Did he feel inferior because of that? It was something Minty had frequently invited him to talk about, over the years, but he always said he wasn't bothered by the fact that her salary was higher than his. They'd had that conversation enough times for Minty to have been convinced, so she really didn't think the reason he'd strayed had been about a need to prove his capabilities in other areas simply because his wife hauled home the bigger piece of the pie each month.

And it wasn't as if Leo hadn't had opportunities to advance his own career. He was just comfortable where he was. Over the years, he had grown from that miniscule minnow just starting out, into a fairly important fish in the firm's pond. He was now an important asset to the company he'd stayed loyal to from the beginning. While his financial package was never going to put them into the financial stratosphere, like working for a bigger go-getting firm might, Leo had always been happy where he was. Like he'd said from the start, stability was the key to the success of everything else, and he wasn't an overly ambitious man. Like most people, he simply wanted to use his talent and be recognised for it. He had all that now, and a salary that really *wasn't* to be sneezed at, without the cut-and-thrust pressure of continually having to try and prove himself.

It was what he'd always *said*, but Minty had no idea these days what was true and what had always been a bare-faced lie.

Not that it mattered anymore. What was the point in raking over cold coals? Wherever the bulk of the blame lay, there was little to be gained by undertaking a big postmortem, other than to understand the lessons that came out of it all and move on. And that was precisely what Minty was determined to do; move on.

It was interesting, she reflected, how far she'd come in the last few days, on that score. Paralyzed by shock, anger and sadness in Bristol, she had undergone a radical transition since arriving here in Torley. She was still feeling hollow, and kind of 'scraped-out' after the terrible revelations. It hurt like hell that her marriage was over, and probably would for a very long time, but anyone who said a change of scenery couldn't result in a change of perspective didn't know what they were talking about.

It was all a matter of what you wanted. If you wanted to wallow, you could take forever to bounce back. If you were determined enough not to let other people's actions knock you down and keep you there, you could do the spade-work and get yourself back on your feet, dust yourself off, and keep walking forward with your head held high. Minty Cartwright might well have a cheating rat for a husband, but that didn't mean her life was over, or even compromised.

Lady Gaga started up again, and this time, she ignored it, and let it ring out. She waited calmly for it to stop. As soon as it did, she promptly blocked Fiona's number.

Suddenly, irrationally, she was glad she'd had the locks changed on the house, and had reset the alarm system before leaving, complete with new 'arm and disarm' key codes. She wasn't going to take any chances. If anyone had asked her, just a few weeks ago, if she thought that either her husband or her best friend would ever dream of robbing her or vandalising her home, she'd have laughed in their face. But not now.

She wondered, now, if she should block Leo's communications too, but maybe she shouldn't, quite yet. A conversation would need to happen at some stage, she knew that well enough, but it could wait until she was good and ready to have it.

Chapter Six

'Eh, up! They're 'ere already,' Mark chuckled, as Feen and Gavin's car drew up outside the front door. Adie breathed a sigh of relief.

'That's good! I've been worried about them driving so far in this weather. It's like this all over the country at the moment, from what I understand. It was bad enough just coming home from the Farmer's Market in town! What a washout *that* was, today! I think the rain kept most people away.'

She'd just got back from the market and had started preparing a quick lunch, in time for her step-family's arrival. She opened the door to Feen and Gavin, who each held a sleeping twin in their arms.

'We made it,' Feen said quietly. 'We left at six this morning but my God, this rain is a killer, isn't it? Typical for November, I suppose, but still…' She trailed off, but Adie understood her frustration.

'Yes. It's been horrible all week. Storm after storm. It's actually supposed to snow next week. too. I've almost forgotten what the sunshine looks and feels like. November is so often really settled and nice, but not this year.'

She knew that as frustrating as the weather was, it never mattered too much to Feen. She was always just glad to be back in her childhood home.

Adie fully understood why Feen adored Ravensdown. It was incredibly special. The farm, and in particular the old house, had been a real discovery, and a big labour of love for Feen's parents. Before Beth Raven had fallen ill with bowel cancer, she and Mark had lovingly restored the old, abandoned stone wreck to its former gorgeous glory. It had taken years. Feen often said that she could still remember her mother wandering around with plaster dust in her hair while her father hammered away in the hallway, relaying newly stripped oak floorboards and fixing the wonky lintels at the tops of all the doors.

Ravensdown House was well over two hundred years old. Built of solid stone, it had a handsome wide front, flanked by two symmetrical gables with gorgeous, mullioned windows complete with leadlight panes. Ivy grew all around the west gable, giving the place a distinctly romantic air.

But it wasn't just the cosmetics and the meticulous attention devoted to the quality of the finishing, that gave it that. Mark and Beth Raven had adored their home, and one another. The spirit of that love still lived within the walls, the floorboards and the rooftops. Long after Beth had died, Mark had found love again with Adie, and she also truly loved the house. It deepened the air of warmth and welcome that spilled forth to all who came to its heavy old oak front door, furnished with its forged knocker, hobnail studs, and ancient iron hinges.

After Feen and Gavin's marriage, and the birth of their twins, Mark had blocked off half of the upper floor of Ravensdown House for them, so they could have their own space and plenty of privacy during their time here. It was a temporary measure, since Feen would one day inherit the house and would no doubt want to restore it to a single dwelling without incurring too much work. For now though, it served the family very well as two semi separate homes. They usually all had dinner together anyway, down in the big kitchen, but the little 'kitchenette' Mark had installed just inside the new door on the landing at the top of the stairs leading to the East gable was enough for Feen and Gavin's needs if they wanted to cook for themselves.

Feen smiled down at her daughter Willow, asleep in her arms, and glanced over at Gavin. She spoke softly.

'It seems a shame to wake them, so I think we should take them straight upstairs and let them carry on sleeping.'

Gavin nodded. 'Yep, that makes sense. They'll only be grizzly if we wake them now.' He grinned at Adie. 'The joys of being on the on the tail end of the 'terrible two's.' She grinned back at him and nodded.

Mark sauntered into the hallway, yawning, and gave his daughter a hug. 'Welcome 'ome, team! These little 'uns aren't afeared o' storms are they? We've 'ad a couple o' right bloody bangers already this week, an' another 'un comin' tonight, just in time fer't potluck.'

Adie wiped her hands on a tea towel. 'You've made good time. Lunch is almost ready, I'm just making chicken, cheese and pesto paninis to have with some home-made butternut soup. We'll all be able to pig out properly later when everyone arrives with their bucketloads of food.'

She looked down at twins, still sound asleep. 'Why don't you just take those two into the living room, and leave the door open? The fire's going in there. We'll be able to see and hear them from the kitchen when they wake up.'

Feen nodded. 'Yes, that's a much better idea. I've got a big bag of abric foff-cuts for you, by the way, that Gina said she'd promised you? She came to our place to pick up my design prototypes, on her way home from work, and she gave me the hag to band over. It's in the car. I'll get it once the rain stops, if it ever does!'

The rain hammered hard against the kitchen window. 'It's brutal weather for a party. D'you think everyone will still come?'

Adie nodded. 'I've rung the ones I didn't see at the market, which finished really early, as there was hardly anyone about. They're all still coming.'

She ladled out soup into bowls and took the paninis out of the Aga's warming oven. Feen spied the huge pot of chilli con carne set at the side of the oven. 'Ooh! Is that what I think it is? And is it for tonight?'

Adie laughed. 'Yes! And yes! I had to make it a few days ago and freeze it, otherwise I'd never have had time to get it done. I've been flat out with all the stuff I've had to do for the Farmer's Market. It was busy earlier in the morning before the rain got so heavy, and I sold out of most of what I'd taken down there, so it's back to the grind for me from Monday, sadly.'

Feen looked at her and rolled her eyes. 'Oh, don't give me that! I know how much you love making your aprons and pot-holders from different abric foff-cuts, for the market, and your baking and preserves.'

Feen was right. Adie did enjoy her commitment to the market. She sold quite a lot there each week, mostly to fill regular orders. Her 'kitchen linens;' pretty potholders, oven gloves, aprons and trimmed tea towels were a new thing, and were what she called a 'slow-burn,' sales-wise, but her eggs and jars of jam nearly always sold out and her lavender shortbread had been a subscribed product for a long time now. She never seemed to be able to make enough of it. She'd had to plant a lot more lavender to get enough of the corollas she needed for it. It was a well-loved delicacy in the Torley area now, and people were always disappointed if they hadn't ordered in advance and couldn't get any on the day. Rarely did Adie ever have to bring any home from the market.

Things were getting busier in the town, and next week was the official start of the pre-Christmas trading. Many of the market traders would start taking orders for things like turkeys and hams, Christmas puddings and gourmet mince pies, special 'festive-flavoured' chutneys and sauces, and a host of other things. Adie had already ordered a roll of cellophane and a few packs of purple ribbons, so she could start gift-wrapping some of her fabric items and her jars of jam and ginger marmalade, for people to buy ready-wrapped to give as gifts. She'd already swapped the regular labels on the jam jars for some Christmassy ones that she'd found in the local craft shop, Patchwork 'n' Pen, and she'd wound a bit of thin tinsel around the lids.

The Christmas tree also had to go up, but that was all in hand. The Youth Club, who used the hall on Friday nights and always set it up for the Saturday market, would be erecting and decorating the tree *and* the hall as their evening event next Friday. Under their leader Ian Handlett's watchful eye, the kids always did a nice job of making everything look welcoming and festive.

The hall had also started hosting a flea market, one Sunday a month, from 10am until 3pm. That was a new initiative that Adie had set up, in response to a number of enquiries from people wanting to sell second-hand goods. They'd wanted to do that at the Saturday market, but although there was one small bric-a-brac stand there every Saturday, that had been there since the market had first begun, decades before, Adie was reluctant to change the lovely vibe of the traditional Farmer's Market by introducing stands that catered for a very different group of shoppers. In any case, there simply wasn't room, and after at least half a dozen people had asked about selling used goods, her hunch was that perhaps there was scope for a stand-alone flea market. It had first been offered as a one-off experiment, but it had proved so popular that the townspeople had clamoured for it to be a regular event.

Mike Hawkins, the local vicar, had graciously given permission for the hall to be used one Sunday a month for the purpose. So far, the flea market was a rip-roaring success, and Adie didn't mind giving up a dozen Sundays in the year, to oversee things. It meant she got to know a few more of the townsfolk, and she'd had a few bargains herself, not least of which was a large box of traditional preserving jars, complete with lids and seals. Feen, of course, had been over the moon at the idea of a flea market, and was always frustrated when the event fell on a Sunday when she wasn't up from London. She'd been very lucky there once, with a trader who was clearing out her grandmother's wardrobes. Feen had managed to score a few beautiful vintage and retro dresses, skirts and jackets, and had floated around on cloud nine for at least two days after.

'So who's coming tonight, then?' Feen enquired now, drawing Adie's attention back. Mark pulled a wry face, and she laughed. 'Daddy! Don't pretend it's a chore. You know you'll enjoy yourself, so drop the humpy Humbug act!'

Her father made a mock scowl. 'I'll be 'appy to see 'em come, an' I'll be just as 'appy to see 'em go again.'

Feen looked at Adie, rolled her eyes, and raised her eyebrows.

'It's just the usual crowd,' Adie responded. 'Oh, but there's a guest coming; someone you won't have met! The lady staying at Teapot Cottage. Her name's Minty Cartwright. She's mid-forties, I think, and she's on her own, so I invited her up. There's nothing worse than a party happening right next to you and not being invited to it. She's had a bit of marital trouble, and she's a bit wobbly, so even if she does come she might not stay very long.'

'Don't worry, we'll all make her weel felcome, won't we Daddy?' Feen looked enquiringly at Mark, who pulled another face and said nothing.

Adie laughed at her husband. Mark was as sociable as anyone else, even though he tried to make people think otherwise. He liked his home and hearth, and he never minded too much sharing it with others, because he genuinely loved his family and friends. But he was always glad when everyone left again and he could have his house back to himself.

Adie went along with his grumpiness, knowing it was a bit of a front, knowing that he was infinitely kind, and as soft as butter beneath his gruff exterior. Everybody knew it, and Mark knew that they did, but it never stopped him from rolling his eyes, shaking his head and heaving dramatic sighs, at the idea that anyone was coming to call.

'Aye, lass,' he muttered now. 'O' course we bloody will.'

'Well, I'm had to glear it,' Feen grinned. 'What a gunny old foat you are!'

Mark then got into conversation with Gavin, about the younger man's songwriting work with a new up-and-coming band. Mark didn't know a lot about such things, but he always made an effort to ask, and Adie knew how much Feen and Gavin appreciated it.

She laid out the lunch and let everyone help themselves. After they'd all eaten and cleared up the kitchen, Feen and

Gavin went to get the still-sleeping twins, take them upstairs, and generally get settled in. Mark went back to the barn to carry on fixing his old rotary hoe, and it was really too late for Adie to do much else except put her feet up and enjoy a quiet couple of hours with a book, before she had to start preparing everything for the evening's pot-luck dinner.

She knew Feen had been hoping to catch up for coffee with her best friend Josie Valley for an hour that afternoon, but the time had somehow evaporated, and neither woman had wanted to head out in torrential rain. It was only mid-afternoon and already it was almost dark, with the storm rumbling around the ranges and threatening to roll right in.

Regrettably, coffee with Josie would have to wait, but Feen and Gavin were up here for a whole week, so Adie was sure there would be time, perhaps on Josie's half-day off work on Wednesday. She was always busy, with her job as the local postmistress and her toddler Matilda (Tilly), who was just a few months older than the twins. The times when she and Feen usually set aside to face-time in the evenings when Feen was back in London invariably got put off for one reason or another. Feen was often out at night, at gigs and after-gig events that Gavin often felt obliged to show up for, as part of his work. He hated going alone, so Feen usually went with him. Any spare time she could get, to catch up with friends, was precious. Weeks would go by when the best she and Josie could manage was a conversation by text.

Adie made a mental note to ask Feen to invite Josie for lunch on Wednesday. She could bring little Tilly, and the kids could all have a run around under Adie's watchful eye while the two women had a decent catch-up. Josie was pregnant again, and due not far into the New Year, so there was lots for the women to talk about.

Gavin would probably spend the week working. These trips to Ravensdown weren't really breaks for him, but he was pretty happy to be here anyway, and it was always nice for him to see his mother Carla, and the friends he'd made up here during their visits over the last couple of years. Adie figured she could also babysit all three toddlers if the Valleys and the Raven-Blacks wanted to go to the pub for a few hours, one night, or out somewhere nice for dinner. Gavin got on very well with Josie's husband Tony.

Feen would probably want to go ferreting around in the hedgerows for herbs and autumn flowers too, while she was here. She'd mentioned that London's parks and gardens had incredibly slim pickings for natural remedies. She pretty much had to buy what she needed from a dried herb seller. Feen much preferred to make her potions and lotions from scratch with fresh and self-sourced ingredients wherever possible. She had a few things growing in pots, since they didn't have much of a garden at the back of their flat in Mayfair. It was a shared space so it didn't feel fair, to hog what bit of grass there was and turn it into a herb farm. She had also planted a few herbs in the borders around the lovely fenced-off garden square in front of all the houses. Most people wouldn't know what they were, so she had a few things growing that she thought would be safe enough in there, but it was all a long way from what she had growing up here at Ravensdown. Adie figured that Feen would be very keen to go out for her herbs here, even in the foulest weather.

Adie plumped a couple of cushions behind her and settled down to read, and she was a surprised to find herself struggling not to nod off.

Hmmm.. perhaps a short power nap might be a good idea, before everyone starts arriving, with enough food and drink to sink a battleship.

The Ravensdown pot-luck dinners were always boisterous and slightly noisy affairs, especially when everyone had had a bit to drink, and they could be quite exhausting. But they always resulted in plenty of leftovers that nobody ever wanted to take home, so the fridge and freezer would typically be bulging with enough weird and wonderful food to ensure that she didn't have to cook for about a week. As trade-offs went, that wasn't a bad one.

Feen woke her, an hour and a half later, by poking her head around the door. 'Do you need any help, Adie? I'm going to take a quick shower, while Gavin keeds the fids, and I'll come back down and give you a hand, if you want?'

' Yes, that'd be great, thanks darling.' There isn't much to do, but I do need to shower and get changed myself, and I'd love some company while I'm pottering about in the kitchen after that. Minty Cartwright, from Teapot Cottage, is coming at seven, I think. It will be nice for you to meet her.'

Feen asked her if Gavin's mother Carla Walton was coming tonight, and Adie nodded. Feen gave her a wink and a nod, and disappeared.

Carla and Gavin had a lot of history and a lot of it was difficult. But, after being estranged for many years, they had managed to resolve a lot of their issues. There was a tricky bit of history between Carla, Mark and Adie too, but Feen and Gavin's wedding had been a turning point for everyone, and all of the affected relationships had been a lot easier since. Adie genuinely liked Carla now, for all her prickliness, but she doubted if the two 'blended' families would ever be as close as others she knew. To be fair, everyone had moved, first from hostile to civil, and then to cordial, so they weren't so uncomfortable around one another anymore. The current level of comfort might be the best they'd ever get to but, if that proved to be the case, she supposed it was good enough. After all, they had to be realistic, didn't they? They were never going to be The Brady Bunch.

She loved Gavin's grandparents though, Stan and Hazel Walton. Everyone did; they were the quintessential grandparents you couldn't improve on if you sat down and tried to design the perfect pair. 'Han and Stazel,' as everyone now called them, were kind, loving and generous to a fault. Adie would never forget how they'd opened their home and garden to everyone who'd been invited to Feen and Gavin's wedding there, and they'd welcomed every last guest with open arms.

It had been the most wonderful summer's night, under the stars, in a garden that had once graced the cover of a magazine. Adie would never forget the sight of Feen and Gavin having their first dance as a married couple, in Han and Stazel's beautiful white wrought iron bandstand that could rival any in the best public parks in England. Gavin had given it a fresh coat of paint the week before, and strung fairy lights all across the pillars and the roof. It had looked magical and almost ethereal.

Gavin adored Feen. Adie and Mark had initially been more than just a bit worried at how quickly he had stormed into her life and turned it upside down, but now they were profoundly grateful for it. Feen and Gavin had found themselves in a love-at-first-sight, whirlwind romance, but they *were* true soulmates. Anyone with half an eye could see that, and the fact that the enigmatic and unusual little 'white witch' had found her one true love; well, everyone was thankful for that. Gavin was a keeper. He was the one in a million he needed to be, to understand, love and cherish the one-of-a-kind Feen.

The doorbell rang just as Adie was setting her pot of chilli con carne on one of the Aga's hotplates. She checked her watch. If it was Minty Carwright, she was right on time.

Feen got to the door first. 'Hi! You must be the lady from Ceapot Tottage? Welcome! Come on in. I'm Feen Raven-Black, daughter of the house, and this is my husband Gavin.'

Gavin heard his name and looked up from his conversation with Mark, smiled, and nodded briefly. Adie stepped forward. 'Hi, Minty! I'm so glad you're here. You've met Feen and Gavin, and this is my husband Mark.

'Ow do?' Mark's voice was as gruff as usual, but he tempered it with a warm grin.

Minty looked nervous. 'Where do you want this?' She handed Adie a delicious-looking brown rice, sultana and orange-segment salad, showered with sliced spring onions. Adie took it from her with a smile and ushered her through to the kitchen. Feen followed. Minty was clearly well outside of her comfort zone, and Feen evidently decided to put her at her ease at the same time as Adie was enlisting her help in the kitchen, to put cutlery, plates and dishes on the table.

'How are you finding the cottage? The weather's awful isn't it? I dunno about you but I love a good storm, as long as I don't have to be out in it! But it's horrible when I do.' She smiled generously at Minty, who smiled gently back.

'The cottage is wonderful and cosy, thanks. Perfect for this time of year, I think, with the open fire and everything, but I do hope the rain clears soon. I wanted to try some walking, but I don't fancy going out when it's bucketing down like this.'

'Are you from the city, then?' Feen enquired. Minty nodded.

'I currently live in Bristol, but I was born and bred in Cheltenham, originally. I've never spent much time in the countryside, even though the Cotswolds were more or less on the doorstep when I was growing up. I never took advantage, but I think I could enjoy doing some country walks up here, if the weather ever lets up.'

Adie chimed in. 'It's supposed to clear by Tuesday afternoon, but be warned. It mightn't last long. There's meant to be a bit of snow coming in on Thursday or Friday. They're never clear about snow. It's pretty hard to predict, but I'd be ready for that, if I were you. I'll make sure Mark drops some more firewood by the back door for you.'

The doorbell rang again, and this time it was Bob and Sheila Shalloe, with Darren and Debby Davies right behind them. Adie ushered them all in quickly, out of the rain. Feen was thrilled to see them, and embraced them warmly.

'Hi guys! It's great to see you both. It's been ages, hasn't it? How are your little ones; Ruby and Thomas?

Debby grinned at her. 'They're fab, thanks. Ruby's at home with her devoted babysitter Meghan, and Thomas is asleep in his bassinette, in the car. I'm not ready to leave him with anyone yet. He's still too tiny, at barely a month old, and I'm breastfeeding him, in any case. I wanted to ask where we could put him? He's sleeping like a rock.'

Gavin piped up; 'Bring him in, and I'll take him up to Alder and Willow's room. The cots are still in there, and the baby monitor's on, so it'll be easy to keep an ear on them all.'

Feen nodded enthusiastically. 'Yes, let's do that. And I'm so glad you've got Meghan. She's fabulous, isn't she!'

Gavin cocked his head to one side and looked at Debby.

'Meghan. She's the girl with the horse, isn't she? Astro, the one that Darren found? Didn't her father buy Beaconsfield Stables?'

Debby nodded. 'Yeah, last year, and he's really started to turn things around up there. I think he's going make a real success of that place, especially since Meghan's totally into the horse thing, too. They're a perfect pair for that business, those two. Meghan's only sixteen but she's already clear about her future, which is amazing. Coming up here was a real catalyst for them, just like it was for us. Stuart's right behind us, actually, should be pulling up outside any minute,' she added.

Gavin nodded slowly. 'Yeah, I remember them both. He was a convicted drunk driver, wasn't he, her father? And they had all that trouble, with his carpenter's ex trying to kill him, not long after moving in there. Nice to hear that they're on their feet now.'

Debby pulled a face. 'Well, they're getting there, but it was touch and go for a while. It was a really tough time, especially for poor Meghan. I wouldn't have been at all surprised if they hadn't stayed, after their carpenter's murderous ex showed up, and with Meghan's horrible abduction, and everything. Even Darren had nightmares about it all for a while, since he was the one who unwittingly stopped that psycho Keith Brockett for good. But Stuart and Meghan are both made of strong stuff. I talk to Meghan a lot, and I know you do too, Feen.'

Feen nodded. 'Yep, and it's so nice that things are turning out well for them. God knows they've had to overcome enough to get to here. I like Meghan. I have all the time in the world for her. I must pop over and see her before we head back to London next weekend. Maybe us girls could all go for dinner one night, down at the Bull, and leave all the kids with the boys!'

The doorbell rang again, and everyone in the hallway took that as their cue to go and put their dinner contributions in the kitchen, and move into the living room. Adie was happy to see Stuart Thomson, and Trudie and Kevin Sangster, all stepping over the threshold. Trudie grimaced as she shook out her umbrella. She was carrying what looked like a heavy pot wrapped in a padded bag with a sturdy handle, and she gave Feen an air kiss and went straight into the kitchen. Stuart handed Adie a spectacular tray of sushi, and wandered over to talk to Mark, Gavin and Darren, who were heading into the living room.

She heard exclamations coming from the kitchen, as Trudie and Minty greeted one another. It seemed that they'd already met, when Minty had gone into Trudie's store, GladRagz.

I'm going to leave this door slightly ajar, rain or not. I'm not here to be the bloody butler, and everyone seems to have conveniently disappeared!

She hurried back through to the kitchen, keen to make sure poor Minty wasn't either alone or overwhelmed. As she passed by the living room door, she heard Darren talking about Silverquick, the new band Gavin was writing music for. Darren had heard them recently and wanted to know more about them.

'D'you think they'll do a tour soon?' he was asking Gavin.

'I dunno if they've enough material yet, to be honest. They've given me a lot of lyrics, and I've written the music for some of it, but we're only talking about eight songs in total. If they did a tour now they'd have to use a lot of cover stuff, and I don't think that's what they want to do. They plan to be completely original.'

'Did you write the music for 'Take You Back'? That's a great song.'

'Yeah, thanks. That one's doing okay. It came off the back of listening to them as they played together, to establish what kind of sound they have. I spent a day with them, watching them jam, listening to their stories, their philosophies, that sort of thing. Knowing all that stuff really helps me to write what they'd really want to play and be *good* at playing. You have to work with their strengths, to help them be successful, but a lot of the time they don't even know what their own strengths are! Sometimes you have to lead them by the nose until they get it, but Silverquick are starting to. They'll do really well, I think.'

'They're a good band.' Darren acknowledged.

'Yes they are. They'll go places, if they stick to the knitting and don't stray too far from what they're really good at. Time will tell.'

Darren wandered into the kitchen now, and stood with one shoulder propped against the door. Adie introduced him to Minty. Then Trudie wandered back in and beckoned Minty to go with her.

'Let me introduce you to a couple of other people. Can you spare her, Adie?'

Addie laughed. 'Of course! Go! Get a drink and meet some of our favourite weirdos!'

At that moment, Peg and Eric ('Egg and Peric') also turned up, and Adie was pleased to see that Minty had also already met Peg. Andy and Madeleine Murphy arrived next, and everyone was duly introduced to the new guest. Adie watched as Minty engaged gently with different people as the introductions continued. When Stan and Hazel Walton arrived, with Carla and Dave, she was surprised that they had brought a guest with them too. It was their son Tristan, Gavin's uncle.

He must be visiting the family! How lovely it was, to see him again! Adie really liked him. She hadn't seen him since Carla and Dave's wedding. He was a doctor who lived and practised on the outskirts of the Berkshire market town of Newbury. Adie had asked him, at the wedding, if he knew a woman called Penni Pickitt, who lived in a nearby town. Penni had once been a friend of Adie's, many moons ago, before the friendship had turned spectacularly sour. With a couple of drinks under his belt, Tristan had laughed and said that while he 'couldn't possibly comment' on a 'familiarity he might have,' with anyone who 'might be a patient of any of the local practices,' he was fully aware of how horribly hypochondriac and self-absorbed some people could be.

It had been the most hilarious, thinly-veiled admission (with full disclaimer) that Adie could ever have hoped to get. Tristan was far too professional and far too much of a gentleman to actually say; 'yes I do know that woman and she *is* an absolute cow,' what he *had* said (with a very big twinkle in his eye) was close enough. Adie had decided she'd take that, and she'd laughed until her sides were aching. When she'd told Miranda, she had laughed hard, too. 'It's a small world darling,' she had said, 'and it's good to know that we're not the only intelligent people who have the full measure of that odious, spiteful creature!'

Tristan Walton *was* an incredibly funny man. He was charming, well-read and attentive. He genuinely listened when other people spoke, which was a valuable virtue, and he shared his sister Carla's dry wit and razor-sharp observations of the worst in other people. Both siblings would also show no mercy to themselves either, with their self-deprecating quips, which made them even funnier. Being in their company was always entertaining, often hilarious, and people sometimes did end up literally crying with laughter.

Tonight, Tristan enveloped Adie in a warm hug. 'Hello, you gorgeous lady! Do tell, has there been any word from 'Pee-Pee?' he'd asked with a smirk. Adie had smirked back and said, 'Mercifully, no! She's off destroying someone *else's* misguided faith in her, I expect.' Tristan gave her a wink, and another gentle squeeze.

As the evening got underway, Adie found herself keeping a close eye on Minty, who started off looking a bit like a frightened deer, about to bolt at any moment. But, part-way through the night, she kind of 'found her groove' and was more than holding her own as she moved between the living room and the kitchen, helping out, and talking to different guests. She seemed to be getting on quite well with Tristan. They were both doctors, so they probably had a lot in common. Typically, Tristan was telling some story to Minty now that was making her laugh.

I hope she has a nice time, tonight. She has a lot to process, but I hope that for a few hours at least she can take her mind off some of it and enjoy a chat with a few bods here.

Adie and Mark's friends and family were a nice bunch. They were all making Minty feel welcome, so Adie decided that she didn't have to worry about her at all, and she actually *didn't* need any help in the kitchen. That had been a ruse to get Minty here tonight, and it seemed to be working well. She hadn't made a run for the door, at least not yet, which was a good sign.

As time passed, and everyone became more replete with good food and drink, Adie stacked the dishwasher and decided to be a bit more sociable herself. For the first hour or so, it was always pretty hard to get out of the kitchen. She was usually too busy to talk much while food was being dished up. People were constantly moving about while they were eating and drinking, too, and they had a habit of putting their empty plates and glasses down wherever they happened to be, so there was always plenty of ongoing clearing to do. Most people didn't think about helping with that.

She wandered through to the living room, and wasn't at all surprised to find that Feen had swooped on Minty, and the two women were deep in conversation. Adie was sure that Feen would have picked up on the fact that Minty's world was ever-so-slightly in tatters.

The hurt was huge, bubbling away beneath her tenant's calm facade. Nobody could see it, but Adie knew it was there, and she was certain that Feen would have felt it. It was nice, that the two women had connected. Adie hoped that Feen could offer some wisdom and encouragement to poor Minty, who had the weight of the world on her shoulders, and was struggling with the load.

She tuned in now on Sheila and Peg, who were chattering away about the fact that Christmas was nearly upon them. There would be another party here at Ravensdown – on Christmas night – as per the tradition that had been started by Beth Raven too many moons ago to count. Sheila and Peg always did the bulk of the catering, and they were discussing it now, with their heads together.

Mark wandered over, kissed Adie on the cheek, and handed her a fresh glass of vodka tonic, with a lovely lime twist.

''Ere yer go, lass. Looks like yer in need o' some sustenance. Get this down yer neck.'

Adie gave him a grin and a wink of thanks, and settled herself on the sofa next to two of her dearest friends. She finally allowed herself to unwind, and help them with the Christmas party planning.

Chapter Seven

The 'pot-luck' dinner party was in full swing now, and it was a lot more fun than Minty had expected. She'd dragged herself here unwillingly, hoping she could 'hole up' safely in the kitchen so she wouldn't have to talk to anyone or feel like she had to explain herself to a dozen or more complete strangers. The last thing she'd been prepared for was to be in no hurry to leave!

It was a very informal event, as Adie had promised, and although all these 'strangers' had been a bit intimidating at first, Minty had soon got into stride and was grateful for their openness and willingness to engage with her, without asking too much of her.

She found herself working hard to remember the names of the people she was being introduced to. Names were something she'd always struggled with; it was worryingly common for her to be introduced to someone, only to have forgotten their name in the next second. Everyone did seem nice, but it had been a big relief when Trudie, the owner of GladRagz, had walked into Adie's kitchen! She'd greeted Minty like an old friend.

'I know you!' she'd exclaimed with a laugh, treating Minty to a warm and unexpected hug before turning to Adie and explaining that she'd sold Minty the lovely leggings and tunic she was wearing, just a few days earlier. She'd beamed back at Minty. 'When you said you were going to a party, I didn't realise it was this one! How lovely that you're here, and I really like what you've done with your hair!'

'So do I,' Adie had affirmed. 'Wearing it loose, with those gorgeous gypsy curls; it really suits you. And I recognize those earrings, don't I, Trudie?' She'd grinned at Minty. 'Let me guess, a gift of old stock?' She lifted her fingers to put quotation marks around her words.

Trudie and Minty had looked at one another and laughed. 'Damn,' Adie had stage-whispered, grinning widely. 'I wanted those!'

Trudie had laughed again. 'Well Lord knows you had enough bloody time to make up your mind about them!'

All three women had chuckled as another woman appeared carrying a tray of elegant glasses filled to their brims with bubbly. Adie had introduced her to Minty as Sheila, her sister-in-law. Sheila had beamed at her. 'Ello, love! I'm 'appy to meet you. I'll introduce you to me 'usband Bob, when I get a spare minute.'

As introductions had gone, it couldn't have been any better. Everyone was super-friendly and warm.

'You do look gorgeous,' Trudie reaffirmed to Minty now, causing her to go pink with pleasure. She was secretly thrilled to be complimented so sincerely, after the battering she'd taken lately. She doubted if Bloody Fiona would have been so spontaneously generous with praise for her appearance.

The only thing Fiona Winterson has ever been generous with was the body she threw at my husband.

She tried to quash her random, unwanted thoughts by knocking back her bubbly in one quick gulp.

The kitchen table was filling up with delicious-looking food as people kept arriving. Minty was introduced to Maddie Murphy, the owner of Torley Tresses hairdressing salon in the town, and to her husband Andy, who ran his own plumbing and gas-fitting business. Maddie explained that she knew Teapot Cottage very well, because it used to belong to friends of theirs, Sue and Glenn Robinson, who had decided to move back to Australia after Glenn's father had died unexpectedly. They'd sold the place to Adie, who'd been looking after it for them.

A lot of the conversations around the room were about the general area; what was happening on the farms, in the business sector, etc. There was a lot of social and environmental history around Torley and Minty was content to simply listen to the conversations. Everyone seemed very happy to be living in this part of the world.

One guy she met was interesting to chat to. His name was Tristan Walton. He looked to be in his mid-fifties, and he was a GP based in Berkshire. He was up here visiting his family and had been hauled along to dinner, more or less under protest. He didn't appear to mind too much though, and he seemed like a nice guy. It was fun to 'talk shop' for a while with a fellow doctor, especially after they realised they knew one or two of the same people, and had both been at a couple of the same medical conferences in the recent past. It really was a small world, when you thought about it. Tristan had a cheeky smile an upbeat style of conversation, and self-deprecating sense of humour. He was openly gay, with a long-term partner who was currently away visiting his own family in The Netherlands. Minty felt very comfortable, chatting to him.

Everyone was as welcoming and friendly as Adie Raven had promised her they'd be. Only one woman she was introduced to (she thought her name was Carla Holloway) had seemed a bit frosty, almost as if she wasn't particularly comfortable with the crowd. She was Tristan's sister. Minty had a brief chat with her, and she was pleasant enough, but it hadn't felt like a conversation that would go anywhere. And she had the impression that Carla could wipe the floor with someone she didn't like, if she wanted to. Her husband (Dave?) was a lot more affable and open.

Carla and Tristan's parents seemed lovely though, and Adie's husband Mark was *very* easy to be around. He made Minty laugh. He was a delightful man, with a broad, old-fashioned Lancashire dialect she found incredibly funny. It was all she could do not to burst out laughing at his indignant retort, after someone had left the front door wide open and the rain came sweeping in, was 'Fer swine's sake, can some bugger not've 'ad bloody gumption to jam't wood in't piggin' 'ole?' She loved his earthiness. He was probably the most 'real' person she'd met in a long time.

Part-way through the evening, the tiny woman who had opened the door to Minty when she'd first arrived came over to her. At first glance, Minty had thought she was a child but she'd then seen, on looking more closely, that the diminutive woman was probably in her mid to late twenties. She had to be a size six, or eight at best, and about four feet eight inches in height. She was absolutely tiny, but perfectly proportioned. There was something quite ethereal about her too, almost fairy-like. She was dressed in a pair of drainpipe jeans, an outrageously beautiful, snowy-white vintage lace top with a high neckline, and strung with a dozen different silver necklaces that cascaded down the front of it. Edwardian-style black ankle boots with tiny buttons up the sides completed her stunning outfit. She'd threaded a bright red silk scarf through the belt loops on her jeans, and tied it on one hip, in an elaborate bow, and the overall effect was absolutely gorgeous. Feen Raven had a unique but beautiful sense of style, and a timeless, almost unworldly beauty. Perfection in miniature and, seemingly, very lovely with it. She'd refilled Minty's glass to an over-generous level, and given her a kind, knowing smile as she did so.

'Hi Minty! Not feeling too overwhelmed, I hope? This lot are a bun funch, and they'll always budge up and make someone feel welcome, but they can get a rit baucous, especially after a few drinks. Have you forgotten everyone's name yet?'

Minty grinned, and decided that she quite liked this tiny woman, who seemed to hold untold mysteries behind her gentle smile and wise eyes, framed by the longest lashes imaginable.

'Surprisingly for me, I think I've managed to remember most of them. Your Dad is lovely. He's hilarious, actually.'

Feen's blue eyes had danced. 'That he is. What you see is what you get. He's a darling; probably best described as a 'rough diamond.' As duff as the gray is long, with a marshmallow heart underneath. Carla, my mother-in-law is very similar, actually. She's a proper porcupine, when it suits her, but she's soft as butter beneath. I never tell that I'm onto her, but I expect she probably knows.'

Minty decided she'd just have to take Feen's word for that. She was surprised, when the little woman suddenly looked right into her eyes, almost like she could see what was behind them. It gave Minty a vaguely uncomfortable feeling, that her mind was being gently but thoroughly examined and rummaged through, in a way she couldn't quite describe. It was a little unsettling and unexpected, but not acutely unpleasant.

Feen moistened her lips with the tip of her tongue. When she spoke again her voice was very quiet. Minty had to strain to hear it.

'Forgive me if I'm talking out of school, but I feel a great need to tell you something. There are two very hot-headed demons in your head, who have already puck their stitchforks into you. They are causing you much anguish, but you will overcome it, Minty. Keep the faith on that. They will only continue to have power over you if you continue to let them. For your own meace of pind, try to put them out of your thoughts and focus on other things.'

Minty stared at her, dumbfounded. Oh no! Had Adie Raven betrayed her too, by talking to her step-daughter about Minty's problems? She didn't want to believe that. Feen just slowly shook her head.

'Minty, I swear, this is coming solely from me. I see stuff, and I feel stuff. You're in pain, and I feel it. I also know that you need to mix what's fessing with your head, and quickly, because some really big changes are coming, and sooner than you think. You need to be ready for them.' She bit her lower lip and continued, just as quietly.

'You have yet to be tested, I'm afraid, far more than you already have, and it'll be hard. But if you can acknowledge the injury, the pain of what's happened in your life, and know that there is no going back, you'll be deady to real with what comes. Just do it on your own terms. That's really important.' She'd shaken her head, with a tiny frown, as if she was trying to clear it of something that was buzzing in it.

'There's a storm coming, Minty. The lessons within it are painful, but they will take you to a much better place. Let go of wondering what you could have or should have done differently in the past, because there wasn't anything, and you must believe that. It's *critical* that you do. Concentrate on what you can do going forward, and be ready for what comes. And don't worry. Everything will turn out okay for you.'

The front door had opened again, and Feen had looked up, smiled broadly, and gently excused herself. A small smile played around her mouth as she took Minty's hand and gave it a surprisingly strong squeeze, before melting almost mercurially away, into the throng of people all standing to greet the latest arrival. Minty struggled to work out the meaning behind what Feen had said to her.

Two demons. They'll feed off my thoughts, but only if I let them. I'll prolong my own misery, in other words, by continuing to give Leo and Fiona any headroom.

That made perfect sense, but what didn't so much was Feen's predictions of big change coming. Not big change already *here*, as was the case, but big change *coming*.

More upheaval? Seriously? Feen did say 'change,' not 'upheaval,' and she also said that she thought that everything would work out. Oddly, although Minty felt she had every right to feel offended by a bunch of uninvited observations about the state of her emotional health, from someone she'd never even met before, she somehow felt a little lighter instead; a little *relieved*. It was hard to describe, but it felt as if something had kind of loosened its grip in her head, like a fist letting go of what it was holding.

Many people would dismiss what Feen Raven had said as outrageous, perhaps even disrespectful, but Minty instinctively knew that there was something very special about her. She couldn't put her finger on what it was, and while it wasn't exactly 'spooky,' it was enough to make her sit up straight and take notice.

Feen had meant well. There was no denying that, and Minty found her fascinating. Her Spoonerism, where she swapped the consonants on a pair of words, seemed to be quite unconscious, and it was all the more interesting for that. Minty thought it was as charming as Feen was, herself. All in all, it really wasn't possible to be offended by the little woman taking the very great and uninvited liberty of saying what she had. She'd simply been trying to help.

Minty drained her drink and went in search of another. The flurry around the front door had settled, and people were now wandering about again, with piled-high plates of food, and she suddenly remembered that she was supposedly here to help her hostess! As she headed back towards the kitchen, she collided with a tall, light-haired man coming through it from the opposite side. He reached out to steady her as she almost took a tumble.

'Whoa, there! I'm so sorry, I nearly sent you flying didn't I? Wasn't watching where I was going. Please, forgive me.'

He grinned at her. Slightly embarrassed, she steadied herself and smiled tentatively back at him. 'No problem,' she mumbled as she pushed past him and almost ran through to the kitchen.

Adie was ladling what looked like chilli con carne into a serving dish from a huge pan. She looked up at Minty. 'Ah! Hello, lovely! Could you please rescue the rice from the hotplate for me? There's a strainer at the side, hot water in the kettle to rinse it with, and a big serving dish at the other side of the sink for you to tip it into. That would be fabulous.'

Minty was grateful to have something to do. As she sorted out the rice, different people kept coming into the kitchen to help themselves to food. They really were a friendly, jolly bunch. She was glad she'd come, even though she wasn't as comfortable as she would be at a social gathering where she maybe knew more of the people, and maybe hadn't had her life completely blown apart just a few weeks before!

Don't give the demons headroom.

This was a party full of strangers but, curiously, she didn't feel *completely* like a fish out of water. Tristan Walton was a GP, and one of the other women, the vet's wife as she recalled (Debbie, was that her name?) was a theatre nurse, so the medical fraternity was quite well represented, which made some conversations easy, and Minty was grateful for that. With farmers, business owners, musicians and vets adding to the demographic, nobody could argue about the diversity of the little group.

A lull in the surge towards the table gave Minty the chance she needed, to ask Adie about staying on at Teapot Cottage. Unfortunately, it was booked for the full week after her tenancy ended.

'I'm so sorry,' Adie wailed apologetically. 'It's free again after that, for the fortnight right up until Christmas, but I guess that doesn't help you much, does it?'

The man Minty had bumped into earlier had returned to the kitchen, waving his empty plate at Adie. 'Someone told me the best chilli in town was lurking in here?'

Adie held out her hand for the plate and duly piled it high with rice and chilli.

'Thanks Adie,' he said with a smile and turned to leave the kitchen. But he suddenly stopped and turned back towards the women, looking a bit sheepish. 'Um... I wasn't ear-wigging, before, but I did hear Adie saying Teapot Cottage wasn't available for longer than you've booked. I dunno if it's of any interest, but I have a converted barn on my property that I rent out to people who come to do horse trekking or rider training at the stables. It's currently vacant, because it's a bit out of season. We're usually only busy in the spring, summer, and very early autumn. It's very nice, actually. Newly finished in fact.'

He looked a little self-conscious. Promoting himself was clearly outside of his comfort zone. 'It's also quite big, so you might rattle around in it a bit, but you'd have a choice of bedrooms and bathrooms! If you did want to continue your stay around here for a bit longer, it might be an option?' He smiled, almost shyly.

Adie's eyes flew wide open. 'Stuart yes, that would be a *great* option! Minty, I can absolutely vouch for Stuart's barn at Beaconsfield! It really is gorgeous, brand spanking new, and presumably Stuart, you could do a good out-of-season rate on it?' She turned to her friend with her eyebrows raised.

The man – Stuart – shrugged lightly. 'Yeah, I'm sure we could come to some arrangement.' He leaned forward and put out his hand.

'I'm Stuart Thomson.' Adie was immediately apologetic that nobody had introduced him and Minty already. She swiftly stepped in as Minty shook Stuart's hand. 'This is Dr Cartwright, current Teapot tenant. Her friends call her Minty.'

'Pleased to meet you, Minty Teapot, if you don't mind my informality? I run the Beaconsfield riding and trekking stables a few miles from here. It's on the other side of Torley Valley, on the Carlisle edge. You can Google us if you like, take a look at the photos of the barn, on the website, and let me know if you're interested. No problem if not.'

With a quick nod, he left the room, presumably to demolish his chilli con carne before it went stone cold.

'Stuart's barn really is beautiful. It has a hot tub too,' Adie advised her with a grin. 'He bought the place as a failing business, but he and his daughter Meghan are really turning things around. It's lovely and peaceful up there, especially if you like horses.'

Minty had to admit that she didn't know the first thing about them; 'Only that they're huge and totally intimidating.' She confessed that the nearest she'd ever come to a horse was talking to a mounted policeman at a summer steam fair, years ago, to ask for directions to the porta-loos!

‘Ah well, I don’t think horsemanship is a prerequisite for staying there. It’s often booked by families, and I’m sure not everyone rides. I know you don’t have a car, but the stables is on Redemption Road, and there’s a good round-robin bus service between Carlisle and Lancaster that stops along there.’ She frowned, and shook her head. She was genuinely contrite. ‘I’m so sorry I can’t offer you the cottage for longer, Minty. The people who have booked it are hikers who come twice every year, in late spring and early winter, and I think they’re pretty unlikely to cancel.’

Minty shook her head. ‘It’s no problem. I should get back anyway. I’ve taken a leave of absence from work, and there’s still a lot to sort out with the house sale and everything, before I go back in. I probably shouldn’t stay away any longer. It just seemed like a nice option if I could have stayed on. The cottage is so beautiful.’

‘Well, don’t make a decision about going home until after you’ve taken a look at Stuart’s barn. You’ll probably get an even better rate than mine, if you take it. You can negotiate something, I’m sure, and it really is such a fabulous treat, to stay there. Out-and-out luxury. I’d stay there myself if I could justify it!’ Adie winked at her and grinned.

Minty had to concede; it was a pretty good endorsement, and Stuart Thomson seemed okay. He was polite, and not in the least hard-sell; in fact, he seemed not to care one way or the other if she wanted to stay there, but he had cared enough to offer. It was just a little more of the kindness Minty really needed in her life right now. Maybe she would take a look at the barn. If she found it irresistible, she might book it for another week or so, and see how she felt after that.

‘Your step-daughter Feen is an interesting character,’ she remarked, as she rinsed a few plates under the tap. Adie rolled her eyes and grinned good-naturedly.

‘Oh dear. Go on then, what’s she been saying?’

‘Nothing alarming, but let me ask you something. Does she have some kind of seeing gift or something, or was she just pulling my leg?’

Adie's face became serious. She moved across and pulled the door to the kitchen so it was partially closed. She regarded Minty for a few seconds, as if weighing up what to say, and took a deep breath.

'Feen does have unique abilities that most people would struggle to understand. Mark and I call them 'portals,' like windows to different spheres of life that she can see into, but others can't. Her mother and grandmother had similar abilities, and I think her little daughter Willow does too, but it's still a bit too early to tell for sure. When I first met Feen, she really unsettled me, but as I got to know and love her, I realised how rare and gifted she is, and how genuinely driven she is to help people.' Adie stared out into the middle distance, clearly thinking about what to say next.

'One thing you have to appreciate is that Feen doesn't have the same kind of social filters that most of us have. She will sense something, but she isn't always the best judge of when to pick her moment to come out and say what's on her mind. She'll very often just say it, at the time she feels it. Her timing isn't always appropriate, and there have been times when it's caused more offence than gratitude, but you can rest assured that it is absolutely *always* well-meant, and absolutely *always* intended to be of help. It simply wouldn't occur to her, to string someone along, or mess with their head.'

Minty considered this for a moment. 'She told me big change was coming. Not here already, but *coming,* and that she thought it would all work out alright. She somehow picked up that I've fallen into the role of victim; that the way I'm thinking is dragging me down. She said I had to change my perspective. I'm usually not too bad at doing that, by the way, but I somehow seem to have lost the art of objectivity, in the middle of *this* particular shit-storm.'

Adie nodded. 'Well, if you ask me, she probably sensed that, and it sounds like good advice. I'm sure she'd have told you more if she actually knew more, but she has obviously sensed something big happening for you; something life-changing.'

'She said I had to clear what was in my head so I'd be ready for it. I'm just not sure if I can deal with any more big upheaval though, Adie. I'm battered beyond belief here, already.'

'I know you are, Minty. But I do think you can deal with whatever else comes, *if* you're in the right frame of mind. It sounds as if that's what Feen was trying to tell you, from what she could sense about you; that you needed to reclaim your emotional strength, to be free to confront or embrace what happens next. I guess with menopause breathing down your neck, that might seem more daunting than usual. But you're a strong woman. You *can* get through *all* of this, if you're in the right headspace.'

Minty shrugged, as her mind kept racing. Adie expressed concern that Feen had upset her, but Minty assured her that wasn't the case. 'No, she didn't upset me at all. She mystified me a bit, but she kind of took a weight off me, I think. The reassurance that all would be well is actually helpful, now that I understand that she wasn't just being silly, because right now I still can't see the wood for the trees about the future, and I'm grateful for every positive I can find, even if it's tiny, or even if it's only a maybe!'

'You know, I think we all create our own positives, Minty. We just have to want to. And sometimes we need to have a little faith, especially when the days are dark. Feen probably picked up on the fact that you needed exactly that right now – a little bit of faith – and she handed it to you in her own way.'

It sounded profound, yet simple. Maybe that was the secret. Rather than over-thinking the situation, maybe Minty should pull right back from it and start taking each day just as it came; more simply, and with a little bit of faith. She'd already put paid to Fiona's spiteful calls. There wouldn't be any more of those to drag her down and, even if there were, she wouldn't answer them. She'd delivered the message to the mistress; no more shit from that quarter would be tolerated. That was a pretty good start.

Feen had said there would be no going back. That meant Minty needed to stop thinking about the past. It was easy to say, and a hell of a lot more difficult to do, to draw a definite line under her old life, especially since everything was still so fresh, certain things still had to be resolved, and Minty was still feeling so raw. How do you write off and square away a twenty-two year marriage, a lifelong friendship, and the excruciating pain of betrayal, all in such short time? She wasn't at all sure, but she knew she had to try and do it, one way or another.

Someone once said that a grief process lasted roughly half the length of time the relationship being mourned had lasted, but that couldn't be right, could it? If it was, Minty would be condemned to spending a huge chunk of the rest of her life mourning the loss of her husband and best friend. What kind of emotional prison was that, to find oneself in?

Researchers had produced a good deal of empirical evidence suggesting something quite different; that most people remarry within two years of a failed relationship. A lot of those new relationships didn't last, presumably because of the impact of the unresolved baggage that invariably came from the split that had preceded it, but a lot *did* last. That meant people did move on, readjust, claim a new future, and sometimes rather more quickly than they first anticipated. Adie Raven was a classic example of that! She hadn't been expecting to find new love, but she did have the courage to embrace it when it came.

Right now, Minty couldn't imagine feeling better or looking at a different future, especially since the last thing she wanted to do was get involved with another man. But maybe in two years' time, when she looked back, maybe she'd be in a place where the anguish of this time would have faded, and would simply have settled into place as a part of her life journey, rather than the abrupt ending to it that it felt like, right now.

We all have a choice, don't we? I wouldn't go back, even if Leo woke up tomorrow and realised he'd made the biggest mistake of his life and begged me to take him back. I wouldn't. I couldn't! I could never trust him again. And the friendship with Fiona, how could I resurrect that? No. Those relationship are over. Feen Raven was right. There is no going back, so do I wallow or do I work through it and figure out how to get my balance back?

She looked at Adie, who was smiling gently at her. 'D'you think I should start thinking seriously about the future yet, or just take things day by day?'

Adie shook her head, and shrugged. 'I can't answer that for you, Minty. It's your life, your emotions, and your choices. All I can tell you is that when I first arrived here I was an emotional wreck with no idea what my future was going to look like. I was in a slightly different position though, because I needed to repair a lot of relationships that I had damaged *myself*. A clean break for me, from my family, was never what I wanted or needed. From my husband yes, in the end, but not from my kids.'

She came over to Minty and gently placed a hand on her shoulder. 'It's different for you; I realise that. A clean break is what you really need, because as much as you loved your husband *and* your friend, those relationship are no longer possible. The kind of trust that was broken really isn't the kind that can be rebuilt, at least not to the extent where you could have those relationships back the way they were. If you did have them back, they would have to be very different. And somehow I don't think you'd want to settle for anything else than what you really wanted or deserved from either of them.'

Adie looked sad for a moment. 'But, for what it's worth, until I got to the place in my head where I knew what to do next I just took each day as it came. I stayed quiet, I licked my wounds, I was kind to myself, and I focussed on nothing except each day as it came. I got through each one, just focussing on my needs and not my wants, which was easier than I thought, because at the time I didn't know what I really *wanted*, but my needs were crystal clear. I concentrated on fulfilling those, and gradually I regained the strength to lift my head, to consider what could come next, and I mended.'

'You have a great life now, by the looks of it,' Minty remarked with a small smile.

Adie nodded. 'The future revealed itself to me; I didn't go in search of it, and you know what? I think that's the key. I do believe there is a grand plan for all of us, and if we can find enough patience to let the process unfold as it's meant to, where we're meant to go and what we're meant to do in this life does somehow become clear. I'm happier now than I ever dreamed possible, especially after being such an emotional wreck when I first came here. My old life was okay, but I had secrets that dragged me down. I never knew how much, until later. I was happy enough, to be sure, but I wasn't *free*. My secrets were shackles that prevented me from having the kind of life I really wanted and could truly have, with everything out in the open.'

'D'you think you were *supposed* to go through the fire, Adie, in order to get here?'

The other woman considered Minty's question, and then shook her head. 'Honestly? I really don't know. But I did go through the fire, and I dragged my family through it too. I don't know if that was part of the grand Universal plan, or whether life just put an unhappy fork in my road because of other people's mistakes and bad behaviour. I don't even know if that kind of thing can influence the grand design. All I know is that when a storm passes, there's usually more settled weather at the other side. I think we just have to trust the process.'

Adie went onto explain that her faith in Universal Law came about from different conversations she had, over time, with Feen.

'I was never much for religion, Minty, and I still don't hold much truck with the Christian faith. I've seen and felt for myself how brutal the church and its dogma can be. I guess I lean more towards the Buddhist teachings these days, but only indirectly. There is a lot of sense in them, in terms of how humanity can be kinder, and what is gained from that. Personally, I think that mainstream religion, in the ways that we are all expected to understand it, has too much to answer for that it really can't; at least not for me. There are too many so-called explanations that I just can't bring myself to accept.'

Adie pulled her bottom lip with her thumb and forefinger. She seemed to be weighing up whether to say something further, but then she decided she would.

'Certain terrible things happened to one of my children, in her adoptive family. It's a very long story for another day, but let's just say that what happened to her, with mainstream religion at its heart, has made it impossible for me to accept those things as being part of some divine plan to help her, or anybody else who was involved in that terrible situation. I can't believe religion is supposed to work in ways that hurt people so badly.

'I have my own belief system, Minty, and it's not what most people would even want to know about, let alone understand, but that's the point, isn't it? What we believe in is personal to ourselves. But I believe the Universe is fundamentally in our favour. It wants us to be happy and, to that end, it somehow just sorts everything out if we let it! Happiness is actually ours for the taking. It's only our thought processes that stand in the way of it.'

'In other words, we're only ever as happy or as miserable as our thoughts allow?' Minty mused. 'I guess I've always understood that, on some level, but I've never really felt the resonance of it. I never realised exactly how responsible I was for my own misery or joy.'

Adie cocked her head on one side. 'D'you realise it now?'

Minty chewed her bottom lip thoughtfully. 'Well, not exactly, because I still feel that I was betrayed by people I trusted, and I'm struggling to see how that was my fault!'

'Yeah, That's a tough one. But we are impacted by other people's choices, aren't we? And we don't have any control over those. Your husband and your friend had your trust, and they made the choice to break it. That wasn't within your control. It *wasn't* your fault. The key here isn't what happened; it's how you interpret and go forward from it. Dealing with what you *can* control. Your own choices *now*. D'you see?'

Minty nodded, as something slid gently and quietly into place, in her head. 'Yes, I do. You know, maybe I have a portal of my own, opening up. I am starting to feel that I can choose which side of the coin to look at, sort of like that glass-half-full or half-empty thing. I don't have to keep gnashing my teeth and wailing. And I do believe in karma, as it happens. I guess a good example would be for Fiona and Leo to get married and then for Leo to lose his job and for them both to end up homeless, penniless beggars, living in a cardboard box.'

Minty smiled in spite of herself. Adie did too.

'Yeah, that would be one form of Universal payback, wouldn't it? Let me just say though, that we can bring bad karma upon ourselves if we try to direct it elsewhere. That's the Universe's job, not ours.'

Adie was thoughtful again. 'I think it's important to grieve for what you've lost, Minty. It's a necessary part of being able to eventually come to terms with everything. But I also think it's a good idea to keep some focus on your capability to rebuild. You don't need to have big plans – that's just pressure. Finding the balance between being sad and being hopeful is enough right now. If you can take it day by day, until you feel more confident in considering a bigger picture, you'll be able to nurture yourself through the grief process without falling into a bloody big hole you can't haul yourself back out of.'

It was the most constructive advice Minty felt she had ever been given, but was she really capable of simply sitting back and letting the future unfold in its own way, in its own time? That kind of faith felt alien to her. She'd always felt she needed to steer the ship; to be in full control of whatever happened in her life going forward.

The biggest problem right now was that feeling of utter and complete failure that she'd lost control of the life she had before. Grieving for her marriage to Leo, and for her relationship with Fiona, well that was one thing. But simply trusting that things would work out?

That was a whole different kettle of fish, but maybe Adie Raven was right. Maybe the way your life turned out really was all part of some grand plan you couldn't fight or control, so maybe trying to steer the ship was all a waste of effort. Maybe you *were* supposed to hit an iceberg, from time to time, to learn a lesson from not paying enough attention to something that could sink you. Maybe you *were* at the mercy of a spring tide that had a plan for sending you somewhere other than where you wanted to go. Maybe those things were actually 'protective measures,' thrown down by the universe, in its grand plan to keep you from some kind of terrible harm if you did keep going in the same direction.

And maybe she and Leo were never supposed to last, and this horrible experience was the biggest lesson she had to learn in life; to relinquish the need to control everything. To let it take her where she was really meant to go.

The sceptic in Minty railed against the idea. But it occurred to her now that her refusal to surrender to the inevitable might be the biggest stumbling block to getting through it all. It was the kind of philosophical debate you could have with yourself that would only make your head hurt more, the longer you wrestled with it.

The meaning of life. That was always the big question wasn't it? Everyone had their own theory, but Adie's seemed to make more sense than most. Minty hadn't been brought up with a religious faith. The only objection she had to Adie's was the idea of giving up the need be in charge. It felt like a stretch too far, right now at least, to imagine that the best plan for her life would be the one she didn't have much of a hand in designing.

The door swung open and Feen's husband Gavin came through it. 'Oops! Sorry, I hope it's not a private conversation

I've barged into?' He looked confused, as well he might, at the idea of two people trying to have a private conversation in a busy kitchen in the middle of a party.

Minty shook her head. 'Not at all. Just girl talk.'

He grinned broadly at her. He was incredibly good looking, with long flowing black hair and startling green eyes. He had perfect teeth, and he wore black jeans and a tight t-shirt that hugged his body like a second skin. He was in *very* good shape! Minty wondered how many women would fall for those sexy charms if he was on the market. Had he been, and had she been, and fifteen or twenty years younger to boot, she'd be trying pretty hard to get him to notice her.

She had the idea that she'd seen him before, somewhere. His face looked familiar, but she couldn't put her finger on why.

'So are you staying at Teapot Cottage, then?' he asked, and smiled again when she nodded. 'I spent some time there when I first met Feen. It's quite a special little place, isn't it?'

His Home Counties accent seemed a little at odds with his rock-God appearance. Minty decided he wouldn't look out of place on a stage somewhere, wielding some screaming electric guitar.

Then it hit her. She knew where she'd seen him. It was in one of the magazines she'd reclaimed from Fiona. He'd been photographed at a high society soiree thrown by the dress designer Gina Giordano, to launch the newest collection from her GinGio brand. Now that Minty thought about it, she also recognised Feen, as the woman who was photographed with him. She'd been wearing a very posh frock and a lot of make-up, and her hair had looked completely different, so it hadn't been easy to make the connection. But Gavin was in the music industry, she recalled now. He was something of a celebrity, and evidently so was Feen. It didn't surprise her at all, now that she recalled it. As 'beautiful couples' went, they had to be pretty high on anyone's guest list.

Gavin turned his attention to Adie, and they started to have a conversation about the twins. Minty excused herself, and threw Adie a small, grateful smile as she left the room. Adie winked at her, in response.

The decibel level in the living room was steadily rising. More and more laughter bubbled up within the conversations, thanks largely to the free-flowing alcohol and the fact that most of the guests knew one another well. Minty had a quick word with Maddie Murphy to ask if she could fit her in for a trim and blow-dry. Maddie nodded enthusiastically. 'Of course! Ring on Monday morning and we'll sort out a time.'

The vet's wife (Debbie?) was a chatty sort, telling Minty about her work as a theatre nurse in Carlisle hospital, and asking her about her own work as an A & E Consultant. She did seem genuinely interested in Minty's work. The very delightful Tristan Walton asked her if she'd like to go for a drink the following night, and she smiled and accepted with a nod. He was 'safe territory' for her, as a gay guy in a committed relationship, who wouldn't hit on her if his life depended on it. The chance to chew the fat with someone who didn't have a hidden agenda would be very welcome. He offered to pick her up and drop her back at the cottage, after she'd mentioned that she was here without a car.

She tried to catch Stuart Thomson's eye, to thank him for his kind offer off ongoing holiday accommodation, but he was deep in conversation with a solidly built guy with dark hair and an alarming number of tattoos (she thought it might be the vet?), and she didn't want to interrupt them. She thought she could take a look at the Beaconsfield website and email Stuart, to thank him, even if she decided not to take him up on his offer.

The party was a lot of fun, but she was starting to feel like it was time to bow out and head 'home' to Teapot Cottage. She located Adie, who had finally made it out of the kitchen proper, and was standing next to her husband Mark. They were talking to Mr and Mrs Walton, and as Minty looked around, everyone appeared to be deep in conversation. They probably wouldn't notice her leaving. She found her coat in the hallway and was just about to open the big front door, when Feen came down the stairs.

'Oh! Are you going?' Feen seemed disappointed.

'Yeah, I'm off, but it's not because I haven't had fun. I truly have, and I *really* like your friends! I'm just feeling a bit wiped out, and I promised my sister I'd call her tonight. If I leave it much later she'll be in bed, since they're an hour ahead. She lives in France,' Minty added, by way of explanation.

Feen nodded. 'I've just been checking on the twins. They've had a big day, with the journey up here, and then with different people going up to see them, waking them up every five minutes.'

She gestured up the stairs, and shook her head little. 'They're asleep now, thank goodness. Hopefully, I'll see you again while we're here, Minty. If I don't, I wish you all the best.' She stepped forward and gave Minty a quick hug. As she did so, she whispered, lightly; 'just keep your mind open.'

'Thank you for your insights, Feen,' Minty said to the tiny woman. 'I appreciate them very much. You take care, too.'

It was still pouring with rain. The rumbling thunder was faint, in the distance. The storm wasn't as big as the one they'd had earlier in the week, but the rain was just as heavy. Back at the cottage, Minty made a quick reassuring call to Fliss, and another to Belle, then had a look at Stuart Thomson's Beaconsfield Stables website.

He'd described his barn as 'very nice.' That had been an *epic* understatement. It looked *gorgeous* – the epitome of luxury! As she got herself ready for bed, Minty decided that she'd 'sleep on it,' and maybe give him a call in the morning to see if he would accept her offer to rent it for a week.

She told herself that she did deserve that kind of treat. She'd more than earned the right to indulge herself in a little shameless luxury, just for a change.

Chapter Eight

It was totally terrifying. Being this high off the ground, on an animal with a clear mind of its own, that could do whatever it pleased at the drop of a hat, was *not* Minty's idea of a good time. At least, not yet. Stuart and his daughter were both very confident around the horses, which was reassuring, but Minty still felt incredibly vulnerable. Her horse was called Finnegan, and he was apparently the most docile horse in the Thomson's business. They always put rookie riders on 'Finny.' He was guaranteed not to bolt, buck them off or disobey an instruction. Or so they said. As the horse shook his head and sidestepped, clearly fidgety and keen to get going, Minty decided that she wasn't about to blindly trust those endorsements.

Two other people were also here for a horse trek today. Stuart had approached Minty yesterday to ask if she would be keen to come along, and she said she wouldn't. She meant it too, until he cocked his head on one side, smiled a little self-consciously at her, and asked again very politely if she would – perhaps to help them out? At this time of year, he'd explained, business was traditionally slow and the horses still needed exercise. The fact that she didn't have a scrap of experience on a horse hadn't mattered, he'd said. He'd told her about Finnegan, the bomb-proof stalwart of the stable.

Since Stuart had given Minty a laughably low rate on the hire of the barn for a week, she felt it would be churlish to refuse. Being offered a horsey day out 'for a bit of fun' was something she could politely turn down but, if the Thomsons needed an important favour that was within her capabilities (even as a greenhorn), she felt it would be throwing the man's kindness back in his face if she said no.

So here she was, having been gently 'manipulated' once again, by someone *else* she hardly knew, into something she really didn't want to do. This time, she was astride a horse that was even taller than the corral fence over which different saddles had been slung, waiting for everyone else to get saddled up. She felt impossibly high up, off the ground.

It's a long way to fall, she muttered to herself, anxiously.

She had quickly arranged to move to Beaconsfield Barn after her tenancy at Teapot Cottage had ended, after seeing it on the website, talking to Stuart Thomson, and being offered a rate that was simply too good to turn down. The call to the hospital where she worked, to advise them that she'd be away another week, was met with the expected frustration, but her boss had understood. As he'd acknowledged, Minty would be more of a liability than a help if she went back to work with her mind still in a scrambled mess. A semi-retired consultant was filling in for her, and he didn't mind hanging around for a bit longer, if more time was what she really needed. That was a comfort. It took a lot of the stress away from feeling like she had to return to the full-on coalface before she was really ready.

Her mind was no longer a tumultuous mess, though. In fact, she thought a lot of people might have been as surprised as she was herself, at how far she had come in wrapping her head around her husband's infidelity with her very best friend. Consciously refusing to ruminate on the actions of her 'two demons,' as Feen Raven had described them, had helped a lot, as did Adie's wise advice about allowing herself to grieve for what had been lost without falling into the snake-pit of guilt, self-recrimination or energy-sapping hostility.

She had taken an opportunity to go shopping over in Carlisle with Adie Raven, where she'd picked up a decent pair of hiking boots and a few more suitable items of clothing. After that, suitably attired, she had immersed herself in nature during long days walking the fells, even when it was raining.

That, and a good healthy diet and better sleep than she'd had in years had done wonders for her state of mind.

Teapot Cottage had continued to provide Minty with an almost womb-like shelter from the tornado that had torn her life apart. Leaving the little house after her three-week stay had been a poignant moment, but as she said her heartfelt goodbyes, expressed her gratitude for the peace and strength it had given her, and closed the front door, she hadn't felt like she was leaving a part of herself behind. It felt more like she was *ready*, for a new adventure; another supportive step on her journey towards a life that was now forever changed.

Beaconsfield Barn was actually called Ford's Haven. It was, apparently, named after the people who had owned the property before Stuart. He had renovated the derelict structure and turned it into a generous, luxuriously appointed holiday home. The barn boasted four bedrooms, two with their own en-suite bathrooms, a staggeringly well-appointed kitchen, and a generous living space with a free-standing log burner and separate conservatory, where the sun could flood in and offer warmth, even in the wintertime. The quality of the appliances, fixtures, fittings and decor was first rate. When Stuart had confessed to having sourced a lot of stuff online and from reclamation yards, Minty honestly couldn't believe what he'd managed to achieve.

'I've turned into a bit of a scavenger! I'm a salvage yard rat now, and a car boot convert,' he'd confessed, laughing, when Minty admired various different, unusual or extraordinary things within the house. While the place was a testament to style and quality, it was living proof that even if something looked ridiculously expensive, that didn't mean it really was. Without bragging, Stuart had quietly told her the difference between what he'd paid for things, and what they would have cost if he'd bought them new. She'd looked at him, incredulous.

'Are you kidding me? That's a *massive* amount of money!'

‘I kid you not. Virtually everything you see here is salvaged, reclaimed, recycled or second hand. Even the kitchen.’

Stuart had gone on to say that he’d learned to appreciate second hand quality over shoddy new materials. That included the appliances. The huge American double-door fridge freezer in one corner of the kitchen, with an ice-maker and cold-water dispenser in the doors, had been given to him for free. He’d bought a stainless steel dishwasher and clothes washer-dryer machine from a family who was emigrating to Australia. The double-sized stainless steel gas cooker and range hood that sat opposite had come out of a cafe that was being refurbished. The central island housed a pristine white double Belfast sink and a top-quality shower-head tap. The kitchen surfaces were cream granite, and the drawers and doors had a rich wood finish.

‘I can’t believe all this stuff was second hand! Either you got seriously lucky, or you have a real eye for a bargain.’

Minty couldn’t hide how impressed she was. Stuart looked almost embarrassed.

‘I’ve *developed* an eye. I had to, Minty. Buying this place tapped me out, and I wasn’t in a position to go into debt. Everything had to be done on half a shoestring, so it was, but it meant it took longer than I hoped to get the place finished to the standard I wanted, because I had to wait for what I needed, to appear at the right price. It was finally finished a few months behind schedule, but I think it was worth the wait.’

Stuart Thomson certainly had an eye for quality, there was no disputing that. But he was also a man who knew what things were worth and he wouldn’t waste money by paying more than he needed to. It was an admirable quality, all tied in with another one; of having the patience to wait. But, from what he’d said, he’d had to *learn* to be thrifty and creative. He hadn’t started out that way. His vision forced him to adjust his approach to achieving it, because he wanted it badly enough.

It's interesting, isn't it, how effectively we can adjust our sails when the winds change? We just have to want something badly enough. Do I want to move on badly enough, to put Leo and Fiona behind me? Can I commit to moving on from the past, adjusting my sails and going in a new direction?

A shout brought her back to the present. Stuart was rounding up the other two riders, and they were all preparing to leave, with him as their leader. His young daughter Meghan was to ride at the rear. Abruptly, Finnegan lurched forward, and Minty had to grab hold of his neck to steady herself, as unaccustomed as she was, to the movements of a horse. Meghan briefly came up alongside her on her own mount, a beautiful part Palomino horse called Astro, to check that Minty felt she was under control with Finnegan.

She didn't feel in control at all, in fact she couldn't remember *ever* having been this far out of her comfort zone! But she nodded and smiled bravely, not wishing to seem too inept to even remain upright on the horse!

As they set off in single file from the property, and rounded the first hill, she was astounded at how beautiful the view was, across the valley. It felt like she'd inadvertently wandered into some kind of Nirvana.

She'd been warned, prior to the trek, that Finnegan might stop in his tracks in the centre of the stream. Apparently it was one of his funny little habits that his rider would need to be prepared for, but he came to a halt so abruptly that Minty had to struggle to stay in the saddle. As instructed, she gave the horse a few beats to enjoy the water as it rushed around his knees, then she clicked her tongue and put her heels gently into his sides. As Meghan had promised, he promptly moved forward again, but her heart was pounding in her chest. Just as she was trying to concentrate in getting safely out of the stream, her mobile phone vibrated in her front pocket, and she heard the faint ringtone – The Lion Sleeps Tonight – that signalled a call from Leo. Irritably, she sighed.

For God's sake, when will you get the bloody message that I'm not ready to talk to you yet? Leave me alone!

Leo just needed to shut up, go away, and get on with the very thing he'd been so preoccupied with before; shagging his bloody mistress.

Without warning, Finnegan stumbled slightly on getting up the bank at the other side and, to Minty's sudden terror, she felt herself sliding slowly but inexorably off him, as he tried to regain his own balance. Caught completely off guard, she screamed involuntarily, just as she hit the water, right before her left shoulder struck a gigantic, jagged rock. The last thought that went through her head was the desperate hope that she wasn't about to die.

* * * * *

The vibration and noise of the air ambulance rotors thudded through her brain as the helicopter gently left the ground. They were headed for Carlisle, the paramedic told her. She appeared to have fractured her shoulder and was being taken to A & E.

Great. This is all I fucking need. You try to do someone a favour and this is where it gets you.

Stuart Thomson was in the chopper with her, his face a mask of horror and contrition. 'Minty, I'm so sorry! I can't believe what happened! One minute you were absolutely fine on your horse, the next you were in the bloody water, screaming in pain. I didn't even see you fall!'

Minty tried to move herself slightly on the stretcher, but only increased her own discomfort. They'd given her some pain relief that had made her drowsy. She could still speak, although her voice sounded small, and slurred, to her own ears.

'It wasn't your fault. It was me. He moved awkwardly, and then he stumbled. My mind was elsewhere, and it caught me off-guard. I just wasn't focussed or prepared, and I lost my balance.'

‘Well, I feel responsible. I knew you were a brand new rider! I should have been keeping a better eye on you. I let you down and now you’re injured. I’m so sorry.’

Stuart sounded utterly wretched, and he looked like he was about to cry. Minty tried to shake her head at him but a wave of nausea hit her and she turned her head away from him and managed to vomit neatly into the bowl the attending paramedic had been holding. ‘Concussion,’ she heard him mutter to the pilot.

The helicopter landed within what only felt like seconds from when she’d been lifted into it. The hospital was no real distance, as the crow flies, so the air ambulance had been dispatched and they’d managed to land it in the field on the other side of the treeline from the stream. They hadn’t had to carry Minty far. It was a lot easier than it would have been trying to get her back across the fields and over to the hospital by road. That would have taken an hour at best, and it would have been tortuous, even with pain relief.

Minty could hear Stuart on the phone now, presumably to Meghan. He was instructing her to tell the riders that Minty was going to be okay, and to call him back as soon as they’d all returned to Beaconsfield and handed back their horses.

Stuart never left Minty’s side, insisting that he wanted to be there when they x-rayed her. Minty herself was hopeful that it would be a clean fracture that wouldn’t require surgery, but the pain was excruciating, despite the pain relief and she knew instinctively that it was more serious. Sure enough, her luck didn’t hold. The x-ray showed a break of her left proximal humerus with displaced fragments of bone. ‘A proper job of it, then,’ she muttered, when they showed her the slides.

It was clear to her own trained eye that she’d be needing surgery to screw the bones back together, and then she’d have six to eight weeks in a shoulder sling. So much for only another few days left of absence! She definitely wouldn’t be back at work this side of Christmas. She was looking at the end of January, now, at best. *At least it was my left arm, and not my bloody right.*

As soon as the emergency team were informed that Minty was an A & E Consultant, they started talking to her in more medical terms. She understood everything she needed to know, just from looking at her own x-rays, but she appreciated the respect and support they gave her. As they prepped her for surgery, Stuart reappeared from the corridor after talking again to Meghan. He still looked anxious and shame-faced, and she tried to reassure him yet again, as insistently as she could, that she'd been the one responsible for falling, not him.

'Stuart, I've had a lot of things rolling around in my head lately, and my mind was wandering, like it seems to be doing a lot, lately. I wasn't concentrating as much as I should have been. This was nobody's fault but mine. Please don't feel bad.'

He seemed inordinately distressed, but there wasn't much else she could say to him to try and ease his unnecessary guilt. He'd just have to work through it in his own way. She appreciated how much of a fright she'd given everyone though, and she was relieved to be reassured that everyone else on the trek was absolutely fine, including young Meghan. It sounded as if she had stepped up well, and taken the other riders for the adventure they'd paid and come for, after making sure they were both happy to continue.

'She's a great kid,' Minty observed.

'Yeah, she is. We've had our moments, over the past few years, but she's as solid as a rock.' Stuart stepped back as two orderlies came in to wheel her through to theatre. 'I'm going to stay right here in this room. I'll be here when you come back. Is there anyone you want me to call?'

Minty thought that maybe she should call Belle, or Fliss, but quickly decided against it. What was the point in worrying them? What could they do? It wasn't as if Fliss could drop everything and come over from France, and Belle was busy enough without having to feel she needed to come haring all the way up to the Lake District. No; it would be far better to ring them after her surgery, so she could at least reassure them that she was on the road to recovery. She shook her head at Stuart.

'Thanks, but I'll wait, and make a few calls once I'm back on the ward, assuming my bloody phone still works after I ended up in the stream. You really don't have to stay if you'd rather not,' she added. Stuart looked aghast.

'Are you kidding me? I'm not going *anywhere!*'

After the operation, Minty felt incredibly groggy, and her head felt like a lump of lead. Her mouth was dry, and she slowly started to remember what had happened. From the corner of her eye, she could see Stuart heading for the door. 'Someone come, please? She's waking up!'

A duty doctor quickly came in, and told her that the operation had been successful. After eight weeks or so in a sling, and taking things easy, she should be back to full strength.

Eight frickin weeks! Bloody fantastic!

As she came around a little more, she could see other people in the room; another doctor, a nurse, the surgeon who'd operated on her, and Stuart. True to his word, bless him, he'd stayed until she returned and woke up. Her surgeon was telling them both that Minty had to stay in overnight, but would probably be discharged some time tomorrow, after she'd been checked over. The nurse gave her two powerful tablets to help keep the pain at bay.

Once they were all satisfied that she was in the best possible shape, all things considered, everyone left and Minty found herself left alone with Stuart. She hastened to let him know that she didn't mind one bit, if he wanted to go. She wondered vaguely how he might get home, but she didn't ask. No doubt one of his friends would be able to give him a lift, or he could get a taxi. Beaconsfield wasn't far from the city.

Stuart cleared his throat. 'Umm... I'm not sure if I did the right thing, but while you were in surgery your mobile phone rang, in your jeans pocket, and I answered it. I thought it might be important, so I was just going to take a message for you. It was a guy called Leo? He wasn't very friendly, I have to say.

He was a bit demanding, wanting to know who I was, and why I was answering your phone. He said he was your husband.'

Minty closed her eyes. *Great. This is all I bloody need.* She sighed heavily and looked squarely at Stuart. '*Ex*-husband. It's complicated. I'm sorry. I hope he wasn't rude to you.'

'Well he was pretty obnoxious, as a matter of fact, but I don't take it personally, although it did make me stop short of telling him what's happened, or where you are. I just said you were busy and you'd get back to him. I don't think that suited him very well, but it wasn't my place to tell him anything, and I only had his word for it that he really is your husband. *Ex*-husband, should I say.

'And I'm sorry,' he added quickly. 'I really probably shouldn't have answered it. I just wanted to help. I hope I haven't dumped you in it, instead.' He pulled an apologetic face. He handed her the phone.

'Don't worry about it, Stuart. Thank you, and also for being circumspect about me. It's a long story, but I really *don't* want Leo to know where I am right now.'

Minty wasn't ready to give anything more away, although she supposed there would be a time when an explanation might be appropriate, considering this nice, hospitable man was doing all he could to help her. 'But hey, you should get home to Meghan. She'll have had quite a day of it. She'll be keen to see you home, I'm sure.'

Stuart nodded. 'Yeah, she's put away all the tack and dealt with all the horses. She's a real trooper, and she's been worried about you, so at least now I can reassure her that you're going to be fine.'

'Do that, and tell her 'thank you.' She's sweet, to care. And maybe, if it's not too much trouble, could you pick me up tomorrow and bring me back to the barn? I need to figure out what to do next about all this.'

Minty gestured ruefully with her right hand, at her slinged-up left shoulder.

'Of course I will! That goes without saying! And please don't make any plans until we get you safely back there, okay? Promise me?'

Minty nodded. She was too tired to think about much. She was literally wiped out. The painkillers were kicking in, and she was craving sleep, now. Maybe things would feel a little more positive tomorrow. At least her phone was working and hadn't been flooded after her fall into the stream. That was a stroke of good luck.

Stuart waved as he left the room. She waved back, then checked her phone. There was a long list of missed calls from Leo. Stuart, clearly, had elected not to pick them up. That was probably wise. Minty would figure out tomorrow, what she needed to tell Leo. She wriggled back and settled into her pillows as comfortably as she could, and promptly drifted off to sleep.

A few hours later, The Lion Sleeps Tonight ringtone permeated her sleep and woke her up. It took her a few minutes to bring everything into focus, but as she shifted slightly and a bolt of pain shot through her shoulder, she quickly remembered where she was, and what had happened.

Shit!

Minty checked her watch. It was ten to seven in the morning and she'd slept right though breakfast, if the cup of cold tea and the congealing plate of scrambled eggs and toast on the table in front of her was anything to judge by.

Getting home to Bristol on the train was going to be tricky. Hiring a car was out of the question too, as she knew she'd be unable to drive for the better part of two months. There were calls she needed to make. It was time to come clean and let everyone who mattered, namely her boss and her daughter, know where she was. Leo could wander off and hang himself for all Minty cared. She ignored his call, and saw, on scrolling through her phone, that he had called a total of nineteen times since she last checked.

What? *Nineteen calls*? That was bordering on obsession – unless there was an emergency he urgently needed to communicate to her. Belle? Ethan? What if something had happened to one of the kids? There were also a couple of missed calls from Ethan, several from Belle, and a couple of texts from her too, begging Minty to call her.

Minty's heart leapt into her throat. She steeled herself to listen to her voicemail messages. There were seven from Leo. She clicked onto the oldest one first.

'Right, so who the fuck's the rude bastard who's answering your phone, even though you seem to have stopped doing so yourself? And where are you? We need to talk. Call me please.'

No mention of Belle, Ethan, or any other emergency. Minty sighed, shook her head, and deleted that one.

'Minty, I don't know what you're up to, and I really don't care, but I need to speak to you about the house. Some of my stuff is still in there and I want it back, so if you can tear yourself away from your fancy man, please call me so we can sort out a time for me to come and pick it up. That's if any of it is still in one fucking piece, that is.'

Again, no mention of anything other than what Leo wanted for himself. Delete, again.

'Minty wherever you are, presumably in some love shack somewhere with a guy who's keeping you busy, I'm running out of patience. Call me.'

Delete.

Look, Minty, you've made your point. If you want to fuck someone else, fine. Knock yourself out. Like I give a shit. But at least have the courtesy to answer my calls.'

Delete.

'You're pathetic, you know that? What is this, tit for tat? Didn't take you long to replace me, did it? Playing the wronged wife, maybe you already had this guy up your sleeve. Maybe he's been in the picture all along. I will find out, and when I do, we'll see how the divorce settlement shakes down in court.'

Delete.

'This isn't funny, Minty. If you've already replaced me with some guy you're holed up God-knows-where with, which it very much seems you have, then fine. But we do need to talk about the house. So please just do as I ask, get off your arse and call me, as soon as you've finished shagging whoever it is that answered the phone on your behalf. Interesting, how you never used to let <u>*me*</u> *answer your phone.'*

Delete.

Minty, I'm starting to wonder if something's wrong. Who was that guy? Are you safe? I'm thinking of calling the police. Belle says you went away to get your head together but she doesn't know where. Does anyone know where you are? I know you're with some guy, but please just let me know you're safe, otherwise I'm going to the police. I mean it, Minty.'

Minty stared at the phone, incredulous. Now, more than ever, she wished Stuart hadn't tried to be so helpful in answering her phone while she was in surgery. Leo clearly had the wrong end of the stick, and Minty would have found his indignation pretty funny, if he hadn't then got worried and started talking about going to the authorities. She imagined he'd probably told Ethan and Belle, and they would be besides themselves. Minty called Belle straight away.

'Mum! Bloody hell! Where are you? I've been worried *sick!* I must have called you twenty times! Dad thinks you've been kidnapped!'

Minty reassured her daughter that all was well and explained about her accident, but she didn't bother to mention much about who Stuart was, other than to say he was a friend who'd taken her to hospital.

'The *Lake District*?' Belle's voice was incredulous. 'What on earth are you doing all the way up there? And *horse riding*? Oh, never mind, Mum, it doesn't matter right now, does it? As long as you're ok. Look, we need to get you home, don't we? Tim and I will have to come and collect you, and I can drive your car home.'

'I didn't come by car. I got the train, and I can sort myself out for getting back, darling. Please; stop worrying! I'm fine, and I'll be back in Bristol when I'm ready, but not before, okay? There's no pressing need for me to come back, as it turns out, and right now I really don't want to. It's just a broken shoulder. I can still do everything I need to do, as long as I take it carefully, and I'm very happy up here, just relaxing. Please don't tell your father anything about where I am or who I'm with,' she added. 'Just tell him I'm safe and I will call him soon.'

Belle reluctantly agreed, and Minty clicked off her phone. A small smile played around her lips, at the fact that she'd told Belle she would be staying up here in the Lake District. It was clearly a subconscious decision, and she'd more or less made it without checking with Stuart Thomson about whether he'd let her stay on. Ah well, if not, she would simply go back to Teapot Cottage. And if the worst were to happen and it turned out she couldn't stay there either, then she *would* go back to Bristol. If the universe decided (as Adie Raven would probably have observed) that Minty should go home, it would be because she was meant to.

And there it was. The abandonment of control.

Chapter Nine

Damn! Stuart was starting to wonder whether, if it wasn't for bad luck, Beaconsfield would have any luck at all. By her own admission, Minty Cartwright had been thinking about other things, instead of concentrating on her horse and what he was doing, when she slid into the stream on the trek she hadn't really wanted to go on in the first place. But it wasn't good enough, to allow the poor woman to take full responsibility for the accident which had busted her shoulder good and proper and rendered her unable to go back to work this side of next February!

It was the first accident they'd had with a rider, and of course it was inevitable that someone would fall off their horse at some stage. The fact that a trek was always a fairly slow walk meant that the capacity for serious injury would typically be small. The stables did of course have an appropriate disclaimer for people to sign. While all care would be taken, with all realistic eventualities covered, riders were ultimately responsible themselves for their own safety, provided they did what they were told.

If they paid attention, instead of letting their minds wander to God knows where, and if they were fully engaged with the process of riding in a group and had been honest from the get-go about their level of experience, accidents could be kept to a minimum. Only very experienced riders were allowed to go any faster than a walk. They could let rip with a canter, or even a full-on gallop, in the five-acre field at the midway point on one of the trails, but only when Stuart was already satisfied that they were competent enough to do it safely.

His lawyers, good friends since the days when he was still practising contract law himself, had made absolutely sure that Beaconsfield's disclaimer and declaration forms were a hundred percent watertight, to protect the business. He'd drawn them up himself, knowing contract law like the back of his hand. His legal buddies merely ratified them, leaving no wiggle room for Clients to complain once they'd signed them. It wasn't possible for them to then try and hold the business accountable for the results of any failure of responsibilities they'd accepted in writing as their own.

Minty was insisting that it was all her own 'silly' fault. Had Stuart still been the type to shirk his responsibilities, and do something like drink too much and get behind the wheel of his car with no thought to the potential consequences, he'd have been content to let Minty take the blame. But he wasn't that person anymore. The arrogant, over-confident man who had driven drunk, who had killed a woman and her unborn child as a result, was long gone. He'd kissed his career as a solicitor goodbye and said hello to six years in a prison cell. By the time he came back out of it he was very much a man changed for the better.

Poor Minty. The break in her shoulder was incredibly painful, and had needed an operation. It had all been straightforward and successful, but that wasn't the point, was it? He should have been watching her more closely. He knew that Minty was an inexperienced rider and more than slightly nervous to boot. She hadn't wanted to be there; that much had been obvious, and he felt now as if he'd railroaded her into going on the trek. If he hadn't, she'd still be in one piece.

Meghan had been pulling up the rear, and she should have been paying more attention too, to the novice rider directly in front of her. It hadn't been that long since Meghan herself had been at the mercy of Finnegan's baulking midstream, for God's sake! Surely she should have remembered how disconcerting that had been? Surely she ought to have been ready to coax the horse forward herself, to safety on the other bank?

Stuart shook himself and checked his thoughts. *Stop it! That's not fair.* Nobody could have foreseen Finnegan slipping. It was simply a random, unfortunate event, so there was no point in trying to blame Meghan for it. The poor girl was probably already beating herself up. She didn't need Stuart banging on, making her feel even worse.

Throwing blame around wouldn't help anyone, but maybe they needed to take a closer look at Finnegan. Maybe the horse was getting a bit past it. Stuart didn't want to think so, because the thoroughly bomb-proof, perfectly pedestrian Finny was such a huge asset to the Stables as the ideal horse for first-time riders. But Stuart had to be sure. They couldn't risk another incident like this one. If the old beast was no longer up to the job, they needed to stop using him straight away. Stuart figured if that was the case they could certainly put him out to pasture. He was a good horse. If it really did prove to be time to retire him, so be it, but Stuart wouldn't even consider getting rid of him. He'd ensure instead that Finny had a good retirement in the home he'd known all his life, and with his friends around him, which was important for horses, as thoroughly social beings.

Glancing at his watch, he decided to try his luck and call his friend and stables vet, Darren Davies, who luckily answered on the first ring. Stuart usually made a point of not ring him during working hours, unless it was for something important. So, if Darren saw a call from him, he invariably did try to answer it. Stuart was a client as well as a friend.

Happily, Darren wasn't far away, on a routine early-morning call to a neighbouring farm, and he promised to swing in on his way back to the surgery within the hour.

As usual, he was as good as his word, arriving at Beaconsfield before nine-thirty. After giving Finnegan a thorough going-over, Darren deemed him healthy and strong enough to continue.

'He's fine, Stu; he just had a stumble, I think. Shame it had to be right there and right then, with someone on his back, but it's just like you, me, or anybody else. We sometimes slip or trip, without warning, and that's all it is. Maybe Finny himself had his mind on other stuff.'

Darren shrugged. 'It's just one of those things, mate. He's as fit as a fiddle, as far as I can tell. His feet are fine, and there's no hoof imbalance. His hearing and eyesight are ok, there's no pain responses anywhere to indicate muscle or joint pain. His knees are fine and I can't see any problems with his reflexes. He's as strong as an ox.'

Reassured, Stuart invited his friend to stay for a quick cup of coffee. The two men sat on the terrace outside the kitchen. It wouldn't be long before a big new conservatory would be built here, which would make it possible to sit more or less in the garden even on the coldest winter days. Stuart planned to have it as the new dining room, with a couple of armchairs beyond, at the far end, by the door to the outside. The current dining room would become part of an extended living room, once they'd knocked the wall through.

It was just over a year since Stuart had bought Beaconsfield, and although he and Meghan had lots of plans, including the conservatory, the renovation of the old barn on the property, ultimately for guest accommodation, had been the biggest priority. That had taken longer than anticipated, and had turned out to be a bit of a money pit for Stuart after a series of unfortunate events that had occurred there. The upheaval had resulted in delays they hadn't foreseen or budgeted for, but he'd always known the importance to the business, of getting the barn completed.

So the work on the house itself had taken a back seat for longer than he'd wanted, but they were now ready to go ahead with the conservatory at least, and he wasn't too bad with a sledgehammer, so he figured on knocking the internal wall down himself to extend the living room. The bigger room would need a more powerful log burner, but he'd managed to get one for a song, on a local for-sale site. It was currently sitting in the shed next to the stables, ready to replace the little one that was coming out, hopefully in the next couple of months, before the winter really set in. Darren had agreed to come and help get the wall down, and Meghan promised to make herself scarce by going down to visit her grandmother in Taunton with Darren's wife Debby, who was also taking their toddler Ruby and new baby Thomas to visit family, on the weekend Stuart had scheduled for the work. They'd kept the bookings diary clear for that whole weekend.

Stuart felt the need to confide in his friend. 'Minty, the woman who's had the accident, has issues with an ex.' He cringed as Darren's eyes predictably rolled.

'Oh, shit! Shall I just ignore the sirens going off in my head, or should I be asking; what kind of issues?'

'I'm not sure exactly, but while she was having her op yesterday, I was waiting in her room, and her mobile went. I thought I was doing her a favour by answering it, but the guy on the phone didn't seem impressed that I had. He was really rude, bordering on nasty, in fact. When I told Minty, she said it was her ex-husband. She said it was complicated, and she didn't seem too pleased that I'd tried to help by answering the phone to him.'

'Christ, Stu! It was none of your bloody business. I know you were trying to help her, but really? After what happened with that mad carpenter and her ex-husband last year? You know, the one they all thought I'd bumped off?'

Darren seemed suddenly angry, but Stuart couldn't really blame him. He refrained from stating the obvious, that he carpenter he'd hired last year, Caroline Swift, wasn't mad at all. Her ex-husband had turned out to be, but it had only been the most freakish of coincidences that had led him here to Beaconsfield. Caro had kept her head down, and would never knowingly have put Stuart, his daughter or his business at risk. He reminded Darren of that at least, and Darren was slightly mollified, but the vet wasn't about to let it go without saying his piece.

'Stu, I know you've said your new friend can stay here for as long as she needs to while she recovers, but do you really want to run the risk of another hot-tempered bastard turning up here looking for his missing ex-wife?'

He had a point, and Stuart acknowledged that the same thought had occurred to him, but he'd made the offer before he realised the implications, and it felt a bit mean to withdraw it. He sighed, heavily, wondering if there was any way he could get out of it. Darren, as usual, was reading his mind.

'She's not your responsibility, mate. She's admitted the accident was largely her own fault. You offered her the barn at a knockdown rental, you've seen to her care at the hospital, and you're picking her up today and bringing her back here. I think you've done enough to exonerate yourself from whatever it is you think you have to make up for.

'I know that you and I are almost permanently in 'pay-it-forward mode,' but there has to be a limit, Stu. You have to get her out of here. You have Meghan to protect. She doesn't need any more trauma, especially now, while she's preparing for her A-levels. It wouldn't be fair to her, to run that kind of risk. And *you* don't need it either.'

'I know, and you're absolutely right. Minty's not my responsibility. Meghan is. I just feel bad, that's all. The poor woman can't go back to work for weeks, and she has a real mission ahead of her, to get home.'

'She must have family or friends who can help her, Stuart. You have to think about yourself, and what's best for you and Meghan. And another thing, mate; I'm sure you're tempted to let her have the barn for nothing now, for as long as she needs it, but having it occupied for low or zero rent isn't helping the business, especially if it means you'd have to turn away full-paying bookings! You need to be sensible about this. Acting out of some kind of misplaced conscience means you can't be realistic about what's best for Beaconsfield or for you and Meghan. However altruistic you might feel driven to be, the bills won't pay themselves.'

His friend was making as much good sense as he always did, and as always Stuart was grateful for the reality check. He didn't bother to say that the barn wasn't likely to be booked until well into next spring. There *was* always an outside chance that someone would want to come and stay before

Christmas, or be here over the festive season, and it wouldn't make sense to turn that down. Christmas and New Year were premium dates for charging more, if the opportunity came.

He checked his watch. 'Speaking of picking Minty up, I need to get a move on, or I'll be late.' Darren also checked his watch and jumped, exclaiming that he'd be late too, if he wasn't careful, for a scheduled surgery back at the practice. As they made their way out to their cars, Darren turned to him.

'It's been a year or so now, since you took this place on. D'you feel the time's flown or dragged?'

Stuart pulled a face. 'Mostly flown, especially since what happened last year.'

The 'Brockett incident' was still very fresh in everyone's minds. Stuart had employed a carpenter to renovate the old barn, who had escaped an abusive relationship, only to be tracked down by her ex-husband to Beaconsfield after he'd recognised her in a coffee-shop photo a friend of his on holiday had taken, with Stuart and his daughter in it.

Keith Brockett had been a deranged head-case, who had gone to great lengths to identify and abduct poor Meghan. He'd threatened her unspeakably, to find out where his wife Caroline was. Brockett had then dumped the poor traumatized teenager in the middle of nowhere, and it was only because Meghan had had the foresight to call Darren after failing to reach her father, and they'd got to the Stables in time to stop Brockett from killing Caroline *and* Stuart, that they were all alive to tell the tale. Darren had tried to disarm the wood-wielding Brockett, who had stumbled and fallen, cracking his head on a pallet of concrete blocks. The fall had killed him instantly.

And that hadn't been all. A few months prior to the Brockett affair, Warwick Ford (the guy who Stuart had bought the business from) had unexpectedly died, just as he was about to start helping Stuart renovate the barn. The shock had been immense, mostly because the barn was being done principally for Warwick to live in while he helped show Stuart the ropes in running a stables and horse trekking business he had, at that point, known nothing about. Stuart had found himself suddenly cast adrift, without enough specialist knowledge to complete the building work *or* efficiently run the stables.

They'd felt like dark days indeed, until the boat righted itself. Good friends, including Darren and Debby Davies, the Raven family and some of his buddies from the legal fraternity, rallied round and helped Stuart and Meghan make sense of everything. After wondering for many months if the place might just be a little bit jinxed, Stuart now felt that they'd overcome the setbacks. They were finally on track with getting Beaconsfield running and heading towards making a profit. He certainly didn't need any more horrible complications to result from being kind to an injured stranger!

Darren was grinning at him. 'Yeah, that one's going to hang around in people's memories for a long time to come, isn't it? It took me months to stop having nightmares about that day. But Meghan seems to be coping well, after the counselling.'

Stuart nodded. 'Yeah, she's in a much better place, and of course Debby has been a big help with that too, and Feen Raven. Those two are worth their weight in gold, rallying around her the way they have. It saved her. I think it saved us both, to be honest. I thought I'd go mad, after I found out what had happened in the back of that van. You lot kept us *both* from going crazy.'

He looked at his friend kindly. Darren Davies was one in a million. He had a shady past of his own that he'd managed to overcome, and had transformed his life after a series of scarcely believable events had made it possible for him to reinvent himself from a petty criminal to an extraordinarily gifted veterinary surgeon. Darren knew a lot about overcoming adversity, and also about self-forgiveness. Stuart had learned so much from his new friend. Sometimes the gratitude he felt for his new life, and the people in it, left him struggling to breathe.

Darren looked at him sagely. 'Just don't make any decisions that could leave you wide open to dealing with any more of someone else's shit.' Stuart saluted him, and Darren grinned, got into his Land Rover and backed away.

Stuart started his own car and made his way towards Carlisle hospital. He sent Minty a quick text to say he be running about ten minutes late, and she pinged one back straight away; 'no problem.'

Stuart knew that having Minty staying at the Stables would depend on him being honest about his misgivings, and her being honest about her circumstances. He got the feeling she was an honest and straight-up person though, so he hoped that would be enough for her to appreciate his position and act accordingly. He knew she probably wouldn't want to stay if doing so was likely to make him or Meghan feel nervous.

Once she was in the car, after a bit of a process getting her settled with the pain and awkwardness of her injury, he lost no time in taking the bull by the horns.

'Minty, as I said before, I'm very happy for you to stay on at the barn until your shoulder heals, if that's what you would want, however I do need to tell you a few things.'

He went on to explain everything that had happened since he'd taken on the stables the previous year. He first told her about the background of his own life, and his fall from grace as a solicitor after being convicted of drink driving causing death, and spending time in prison, and he told her about the impact of that on his second marriage, and on his daughter. He then told her about the shocking, unexpected death of his brand-new mentor, and he told her about taking a chance on a female carpenter with an unhappy history, who'd brought terrible trouble to their door.

Throughout the horrible description of exactly what that trouble had been, he was very glad that he was driving, because he didn't have to look at Minty to gauge the impact of everything he said. It was a lot to tell a stranger. He finished the entire sorry story with one final, simple sentence.

'So, forgive me for asking, but I'm aware that you're in a complex situation with your ex-husband, so I need to know that if you do stay here, my daughter and I will be safe from being involved in that.'

Minty didn't answer straight away. After a couple of minutes, he risked a glance at her, and he could see that she was struggling not to cry. That wasn't what he wanted at all.

'Minty, please, don't be upset. I didn't tell you all that to make you feel uncomfortable, or try and lever you out of here. When I said you're welcome to stay, I meant it. But I do have to protect my daughter. She's been through enough. We need real stability here. The truth is, I just don't know how we'd cope with any more unnecessary upheaval, so I hope you understand why I'm asking, about Leo.'

Minty's mouth was set in a straight line. Either she was furious at him, or she was trying to keep her feelings in check. He didn't know which it was. Eventually she broke the awkward silence.

'Of course I understand, Stuart. Under the circumstances, it's absolutely the right question to be asking. I have a daughter myself, slightly older than Meghan, but I feel the same. I'd protect her until my dying breath, and I'd *never* put her in harm's way.' She directed her gaze out of the window at the road ahead. They were nearly back at the stables.

'Leo and I were married for twenty-two years, and I found out a month or so ago that he'd been having a long-time affair with my best friend. He's in love with her, and wants to be with her. He's already moved in with her, actually, so there's no danger of him declaring his love for me again, let alone coming all this way to do it. He's annoyed at the thought that I might be moving on too though, I think, and to be honest you answering my phone didn't help matters, even though you were trying to be helpful.'

'So he thinks I'm a rival?' *Deja vu – Keith Brockett thought his wife was shacked up with me and it nearly cost me my life.*

'He doesn't know what to think, but I've told my daughter how things really are, and I think she'll put him straight, if she hasn't already. But I've decided not to stay here anyway, Stuart. It's nothing to do with what you've just told me,' she added hurriedly. 'I'd made up my mind before that, to be honest. Now that I can't go back to work, I don't really need to go back to Bristol just yet, so I'd like to see if Teapot Cottage is available again for a few more weeks after this weekend. Please, *please* don't be offended.'

Minty went on to tell him that she thought the barn was 'absolutely beautiful,' but simply too big for one person. It was cavernous, particularly in the kitchen and living areas, and it made her feel a little lonely, rattling around in there on her own. Families would love such a big, open-plan environment, but for one person looking for cosiness and time away from everything, it didn't feel like quite the right place. She finished her explanation by saying; 'if I still had a husband and a couple of dependent kids, I'd love to spend a holiday here, truly! But for me, Teapot Cottage just somehow fits more with what I need right now.'

'What if it's not available?'

Minty shrugged. 'Then I guess that'll be the message that I probably should go home, and my daughter and her partner can come and get me, and take me back. That would be ok too.'

'It might be more sensible to be at home anyway, mightn't it, so you're nearer to the people who can help take care of you, instead of miles away, and all by yourself?'

Minty laughed. 'Being by myself is exactly what I came up here for, and it's still what I want. I can get groceries delivered, and I can still walk, and read, and cook well enough one-handed. I don't need taking care of. I'll be just fine.'

Stuart had no doubt that she would be. Minty had a lot to process, and time alone was important, to get the necessary perspective on how to pick up the pieces of her shattered life and put them back together again on her own terms. He'd had six years in a prison cell to do that. Minty needed time too. He understood completely, and he told her so. She smiled at him gratefully.

'So you're not offended, then? At me not wanting to stay?'

'God no! I totally get it, and I get how special Teapot Cottage is too. Meghan and I stayed there when we came up here after I got out of jail. We were living with my mother and it was all fine and everything, but I wanted to have some time just with my daughter, to give us a real chance to get to know one another again. She met her horse over there, Astro, and that's what started off a whole chain of events that ultimately led us to here.'

They'd pulled up at the stables, and Stuart gestured through the window at his little empire.

'We needed a new start, and I definitely needed a job, and this turned out to be it. Things kind of fell into our laps a bit, and although it hasn't been an easy first year, I do think we can make it work. It's a future for Meghan, anyway, after she leaves school.'

He told Minty about Meghan's desire, that had developed from her own experience, to become an Equine Therapist, to help people heal from trauma. He could hear the pride in his own voice. Meghan had come on in leaps and bounds since moving up here, morphing from a snotty, belligerent teenager with too much bad attitude and a crippling inability to see anything positive, to a delightful, insightful young woman dedicated to horses, and to using their awesome power to help people in emotional crisis.

'Wow! That's amazing, Stuart. Good for her! I can fully understand how difficult your lives have been, and what a real milestone it is, that you've reached this point together. Life can teach us so much can't it, if we let it?'

He nodded, smiling. 'Yes it can. Why don't you give Adie a call over at Ravensdown, to check on the dates for Teapot Cottage? Stay here until you can move back, and we can take you over there and get you settled.'

'Thanks, Stuart. You're a good friend. And really, you don't need to worry about Leo. He's not *really* interested in me or anything I do anymore. He doesn't know where I am, and even if he knew, he's not the sort of person who'd turn up and try to throw his weight around. He might be a bit resentful that I'm managing just fine without him, but that's about as far as his chagrin goes.'

She told Stuart some of what she'd done to Leo's belongings, and added the fact that he'd taken it all on the chin without much reaction at all. Stuart didn't know whether to laugh or cry. In the end, he laughed, and so did Minty, and before long the two of them were literally shaking with laughter, with tears rolling down their cheeks.

Stuart finally got control of himself. 'As a man, I should be horrified and really indignant that you did all that! Really, I should, Minty! But to be fair, I think he probably deserved that and I guess her realised it.' Still chuckling, he climbed out of the car and helped Minty do the same.

'I need a hot bath!' she proclaimed, and when he'd walked with her to the barn, unlocked the door and shepherded her inside, she turned to him. 'Stuart, thank you so much, for being so kind and understanding, *and* tolerant! I doubt if I'll ever get back on a horse again, even though I know the 'done thing' would be to do exactly that, but I appreciate everything you're doing for me. I'll see you later.'

'If you need anything, just send me a text. I'll be around the property somewhere but I'll have my phone with me.'

She winked at him, and closed the door. Feeling vaguely dismissed, he headed for the house, to get changed into work clothes. There were stalls to muck out, and water troughs to replenish, and spending time with the horses always made him happy. He felt a big sense of relief that Minty would be going soon. It wasn't that he didn't like her; he did. She was a nice woman, but he didn't need the complication of having someone around who had big issues to deal with. She wasn't here through a love of horses, in fact she would probably never go near another one again in her life, so even if the barn had been small and cosy, there was little point in her being here among creatures that held no interest for her. Teapot Cottage would suit her much better.

It was, on reflection, the best solution all round.

Chapter Ten

It was official. Anger had now skyrocketed straight past incandescent, and was headed directly for the stratosphere. Minty fought really hard now, with the impulse to fling her phone through the nearest window. Bloody *fucking* Fiona, the one person in the world whose head she could cheerfully rip off and walk away from with absolutely nothing on her conscience, had texted her *again*. She must have figured that Minty had blocked her because she was now using Leo's phone, to make contact.

Honestly, if we were allowed to murder just one person each, in this life, and be allowed to get away with it, I would not be wasting time on my mongrel, turd-faced ex-husband. I'd be going after Fiona Winterson, with a double-barrelled sawn-off shotgun. What is it, with this head-case bitch? Why can't she leave me the fuck alone?

It was time for a change of number. As monumentally inconvenient as that would be, it seemed like the only realistic alternative to being continually harangued by someone so demented that they couldn't leave you alone if their very existence depended on it. Forget stalking! This was the kind of off-your-head obsession that landed people in straightjackets and thrown into padded cells.

Minty knew, though, that even if she did change her number it would only be a matter of time before Leo managed to convince someone who had it, to give it to him. When it suited him, Leo Carleon McLeod could charm the hind legs off a donkey. He'd certainly managed to charm the pants off Fiona, hadn't he?

She also knew that this kind of anger and upset, so out of character for her, was unsustainable. She couldn't have anyone in her life, no matter who they were, who could make her feel like this. Clearly, she hadn't dealt with Fiona's obsessive vitriol as well as she thought she had. She looked down at the latest missive.

Aren't you being a bit of a coward, Minty? Why don't you just come home from wherever you are and face this situation, instead of hiding away God knows where?

Screenshot. Delete.

There are still things in the house that belong to Leo that he needs. If you have destroyed it all, at least have the courtesy to tell him. If you haven't, at least have the courtesy to let him have what's his. Stop being such a bitch.

Screenshot. Delete.

Enough was enough. Fiona using Leo's phone to continue trying to be as obnoxious as possible was a pretty low blow. Minty wouldn't mind betting that Fiona would be deleting her texts from Leo's 'sent' folder, and would certainly delete any response Minty might make. She'd bet the bloody house and contents on the fact that Leo wouldn't know what Fiona was doing. Despite what had happened, and his damnable falling for another woman, Minty knew for a fact that Leo wouldn't stand for *anyone* haranguing her, and using his phone to do it. Whatever principles he was lacking, standing by and allowing someone to be bullied wasn't one of them. He hated bullies with a vengeance.

It was time for Minty to have a conversation with her husband.

Leo played squash with Henry on Thursday nights. She knew they unfailingly booked the court for forty-five minutes from 7pm, and Leo would arrive about ten minutes beforehand. He would sit in his car checking his emails before going into the gym. Unless his routine had drastically altered, Minty figured it was a pretty safe bet that she could call him at exactly nine minutes to seven, and he would answer his phone. If his routine had changed, she would simply leave a message for him to call her from a place where he was alone, without Bloody Fiona's flapping ears within hearing distance.

She waited, and made the call. Her heart was in her mouth. If he answered, it would be the first time they'd have spoken since the minute he'd walked out of the garage at home, after safely seeing his Honda Gold Wing loaded onto the back of the bike repair shop's trailer.

Leo answered on the third ring. His voice was wary. 'Hello? Minty, is that you? Is everything alright?'

'Yes, it's me, Leo, and everything is fine. I will make this a short call, but you need to listen hard, and please don't interrupt me.'

'Umm, right. Okay.'

His voice sounded even more wary now, and Minty lost no time in filling him in.

'I don't know if you're aware, but Fiona has been harassing me a lot, first with horrible, nasty phone calls, then with texts from *your* phone after I blocked hers. I'm sure you're *not* aware of the fact, and I wasn't going to speak to you about it, but enough is enough. I want it to stop, Leo. If it doesn't, I will be taking out a restraining order, and since your phone has been used for part of this campaign of outright bullying, you will be implicated. I thought you should know.'

There was silence at the other end of the phone for a second or two. For a moment, Minty wondered if Leo was even still there, or whether he'd clicked off without her noticing. Then he spoke.

'Are you sure? It's a big accusation, Minty, that Fi is bullying you.'

Minty was prepared in advance. 'I will send you a screen shot of every text she has sent me, including the two I got today from your phone. You can then decide for yourself. But let me tell you, Leo, there is only one way for anyone, including the police, to view these texts. It is bullying and harassment. The police *will* be told, and action *will* be taken, if it doesn't stop.'

A long, frustrated sigh came down the line. 'Minty, I do know that Fiona has been calling you, but she told me they were amicable conversations. She has said more than once that she has sorted a lot of things out with you, and that you were in a much better place about us, me and her, I mean.'

'Did she? Well she is lying to you Leo. The texts will prove it. There's at least a dozen of them, some from your phone, and all telling me I'm a pathetic, mean, vindictive, cowardly bitch. I will send the screenshots to you as soon as we're off this call, so you can read them for yourself, and you will see that they have come from your phone.'

Minty took a deep breath and carried on. 'For your information, Leo, I am *nowhere*, about you and her. I'm not in a good place, I'm not in a bad place, I'm just nowhere. But, for a woman who's claimed the big victory and made off with the 'spoils,' for want of a more appropriate way to describe you, I think it's high time she stopped crowing, and stopped trying to make herself feel better about her betrayal of me by claiming that everything that's happened since I fairly threw you out is my fault.'

She took another deep breath, and ploughed on. 'I am not the bad guy Leo, at least not to her. If you want to berate me, punish me more than your actions already have, for not being the perfect wife, or indeed the perfect *ex*-wife, go ahead. But clearly, unbeknown to you, she is fighting your battles for you, some of which may not even be battles in your own eyes, and quite frankly it is making you look like a monumental fool.'

'I'll talk to her.'

'See that you do. Because I've had enough, and I will be doing something about it if it doesn't stop. Don't think I'm kidding.'

'I wouldn't be silly enough to think you're not capable of *anything* anymore. Not that I'm picking a fight, Minty. I do realise how much I've hurt you. I wish with all my heart that I could have done all this without causing so much pain to you, Ethan and Belle, because you don't deserve it, and I *have* deserved everything you've done to my stuff. It was all small, considering what Fi and I have put you through. But Minty, if I could have avoided falling in love with her, don't you think I would have?'

Minty didn't answer. She heard him sigh again, and she could imagine him raking his fingers through his hair, which he always did when he was frustrated or trying to think of what else to say.

'Minty, I hope that one day you'll forgive me. I've come to terms with taking the loss on the house. I do have to point out that we could have done so much better for ourselves, and for Belle and Ethan, without that kind of stunt, but I do understand why you did it. It's okay. I'll survive.'

'I don't care whether you survive or not, Leo. And don't bring our kids into this. They are the innocent party here. They'll be just fine, financially. I will see to that.'

'Oh, come on, Minty! They're my kids too! I'll see to it as well, of course! You must know that!'

'Right. Well, I've said my piece. I don't want to talk about anything else right now. Just get that bitch off my back please, Leo, and make sure she stays away from now on. No calls, no emails, no texts, nothing. Okay? Can you at least do that for me, please?'

Yes. I absolutely *can* do that, and I *will* do that. Let me know if you need anything else.'

Minty didn't bother to say goodbye. She didn't bother to say that it would be a cold day in hell before she'd ever ask him for anything else. He would know that already. She clicked off the call, and immediately sent the screenshots of her call log and all Fiona's texts. She allowed herself a small frisson of glee, that there would probably be quite a row in the 'whorehouse' tonight, when Leo got home from squash.

Oh, to be a fly on the wall!

Chapter Eleven

White noise was a funny thing. People heard it sometimes, when their radio inexplicably lost reception for a few seconds, or when a T.V. signal crashed. The horrible hissing sound had always set Fiona's teeth on edge, ever since her childhood. It made her cringe; like nails being dragged across a blackboard.

She'd had white noise in her head for a few days now, but it wasn't the typical, tooth-jangling external sort, and that somehow made it easier to bear. She couldn't have explained that, if anyone had asked her to try, not in a million years. She couldn't explain why this white noise didn't set her teeth on edge at all, but felt almost like a *comfort*; a protective shield *inside* her head, against thoughts that would otherwise set her screaming, with no idea how to stop.

Breast cancer. Two tiny words. Three small syllables. Twelve little letters that never failed to strike the deepest fear imaginable, into the heart of every woman on the face of the earth.

It was, apparently, 'IBC.' Such a small set of letters. Just three; but the viciousness that underpinned such innocuous-sounding jargon justified a hell of a lot more words, didn't it?

One of those might be 'hospice.' Another two might be 'death sentence.' Three more might be 'manageable but incurable,' with another six saying 'it's only a matter of time.' What the hell, why not throw in the twenty most important ones of all; 'the justice you fully deserve, as a lying, cheating husband-thief who dragged your best friend's life through the dirt.'

Thirty-two words that summed up the rest of her life, if 'husband-thief' was in fact two words. If it wasn't; if a hyphenated word only counted as one, it was even worse. It would mean only thirty-one meagre words, after all the many millions of words she'd spoken, read and heard throughout her life, to sum that life up now.

When she'd rung the surgery, and described her symptoms, she'd expected to be offered an excuse for why she 'couldn't' be prioritised. Everyone knew that the NHS was in tatters. People wanting a consultation often had to wait more than a month to be seen, for anything that was classed as 'non-urgent,' usually by receptionists who were no more qualified to make those decisions than Fiona's neighbour's cat. Everyone had started learning to swallow their fear and outrage at no longer being 'important' enough to be seen quickly, no matter how sick they were. The system simply couldn't cope. The poor staff in some of those overloaded clinics and hospitals struggled to even provide a decent standard of emergency care. Non-critical patients didn't have a hope.

Nobody could even say, anymore, what constituted an emergency. A seventy-two year-old man with two hip replacements, one knee replacement, high blood pressure and a history of heart attacks still had to lie in the middle of the road for four hours after being knocked off his motorcycle by an inattentive bastard in a beat-up old banger of a car, who said he 'hadn't seen him,' before an ambulance could be dispatched to collect him. Fiona knew that because she'd seen the accident happen and she'd sat in the road, holding the old man's hand, and talked to him for all that time.

With ambulance bays chock-full of people waiting hours for admittance to unilaterally overstretched A & E's, and the chronic shortage of beds that had people lying on gurneys in hallways in hospitals that couldn't offer anything better, Fiona hadn't even expected to be treated as human, let alone as a priority.

She hadn't been prepared for being given a telephone consultation within the hour, and asked to present herself at the GP's surgery within the next one.

She'd said nothing to Leo, or to anyone else, about that initial appointment. She'd almost convinced herself that she probably had some kind of infection, and she'd expected to be offered a prescription for a week of antibiotics. She hadn't been expecting to be shunted off to the local hospital that very same day for a biopsy, of all things.

The news that followed; that she had a rare form of cancer with a five-year survival rate of only fifty percent, had hurled her against a brick wall.

Her oncologist had explained everything, and had outlined the course of treatment. Fiona knew she'd need to have another conversation with him, to go over things again, because only half of what he'd said had sunk in. Before she could latch on fully to his explanation of what the grand plan of treatment or management might be, the white noise had descended. The next thing she knew, she was lurching and stumbling with disbelief, along the High Street, like a half-deranged, blind-drunk vagrant.

Her first thought had been to call Minty. Her second was to tell herself how stupid she was, for thinking that after shitting where she slept, she could expect her oldest, dearest and most loved friend to even pick up her call, let alone respond to it in a way that might help.

While she'd been at the hospital, Leo had called and left a message. He wanted to talk to her 'quick-smart,' about something to do with Minty, and he'd sounded quite annoyed, but she'd told herself that whatever it was, it would have to wait, because her news was more important.

Somehow, that day, she managed to make it home – but she couldn't have said how she did it.

Leo had been horrified, of course, when she told him. He'd held her, they'd both cried, and he'd promised to bankroll the very best of care, to make sure that everything that could be done would be, to pull her through to the other side of the nightmare. Neither of them was prepared to acknowledge the spectre that hovered around the edges of the room; the spectre of five years at best, no matter what interventions were currently on offer.

She'd phoned the hospital a couple of days later, for clarification on what was to happen next, and was put through directly to her oncologist. He'd explained everything again, with a patience and kindness she really didn't feel she deserved.

I have an oncologist. I know there are a hell of a lot of people in the world who can say that, but I never expected to be one of them.

Now, she was a little clearer, in her head. Apparently, chemo was the first form of attack; what they called 'neo adjuvant treatment,' to help shrink the cancer. Then there would be a mastectomy; probably a double. And then, if required, hormone therapy and radiation.

'We'll get you through this, Fi,' Leo had promised. 'Don't worry about a thing. We've got this. It's a terrible thing, but we're onto it. I suppose your hair will probably fall out, won't it? But we can get you a couple of nice wigs. And of course we'll find the best cosmetic surgeons. Once your boobs have been reconstructed, you'll be back to your old self in no time. Mark my words, darling; at the end of all this, you will be just fine.'

His continued breeziness was starting to grate on her, a little. After his initial shock, and tears, he had bounced back to being positive, and she figured he was trying to convince *himself*, as much as her, that she was going to be 'just fine.'

She appreciated his attempts to see things in the best possible light, but he also made quite a big deal about her impending hair loss, how long it might take to grow back, and the fact that she would be breastless for a while. He'd even gone as far as voicing his concerns about what degree of nipple sensitivity she might be left with, if she even had nipples at all, and it hadn't impressed him, that she couldn't easily answer his questions.

He'd been expecting her to have the reconstructive surgery more or less immediately after the mastectomy, and he'd been nothing short of petulant about it when she'd quietly informed him that it was likely to be at least six months before a reconstruction could even be considered.

His concern that she might not actually survive the cancer seemed to be pretty well eclipsed by his ongoing preoccupation with what the treatment was going to do to her appearance! That was kind of hard to swallow but, as Fiona tried to reassure herself, he was still in shock, and people in shock sometimes focussed on the oddest things. She remembered Minty telling her once about a woman who'd been admitted to A & E after a head-on car crash, and she was screaming through a broken jaw, a half-severed tongue, and a mouthful of shattered teeth, that her newly-done fingernails were broken!

Leo just needed more time, that was all, to absorb the reality of her situation. He needed to understand the process and timetable of treatment and, once he had got it all clear in his own mind, he'd know what his own role would be, and he'd be able to support her a lot more effectively.

She was sure of it.

Until she got home from work a few days later, to find that he had moved, lock stock and barrel, out of her house. The bedroom had felt hideous; like all the breathable air had been sucked out of it. Empty coat hangers mocked her, from Leo's side of the wardrobe.

His note was brutally short, and to the point.

Fi,

I'm sorry, but I can't go on this journey with you. I thought I could face what's coming but I can't. The thought of you being ill and disfigured is too much for me. I'm a shallow coward, a terrible person, and you are better off without me. Good luck and I'm sorry.

Leo

And there it was again; the white noise, except this time it was internal *and* external, and it obliterated everything, except for the sound of her own hysterical, high-pitched keening as she sank to the bedroom floor, in fear and disbelief.

* * * * *

In the days that followed, Fiona couldn't have said what she did. She went to work, which was pretty much all she could remember. What she did there, she couldn't say. What she ate, who she spoke to, even where she parked her car; all of those, and a million other minor details of her day to day life, stopped being of any consequence. They slid from her consciousness like a handful of sand through her fingers. She spent a couple of days trying to contact Leo; that, she did remember; but he wouldn't return her calls or texts. It had quickly become clear, in the cruellest way imaginable, that he wasn't up to the job of seeing her through her treatment for Inflammatory Breast Cancer. He wasn't even prepared to discuss it.

To call him shocked, or even scared, and acting out of character, would have been generous, kind and understanding. But, once Fiona had emerged from the initial, stupefying shock of everything herself, she decided that for the sake of her own sanity and her vital need to focus, she really couldn't be generous, kind or understanding towards him. She had to call him what he really was; a self-centred, gutless fucking coward.

So much for love! So much for 'bankrolling the best possible care!'

Fiona could do that herself; she didn't need or want anyone else to meet her financial obligations, but it staggered her how easily Leo had lied about something so important. It threw up the question, didn't it… what else did he lie about? Did he lie about being in love? Did he lie about no longer having enough feelings for his wife to want to stay with her?

Would he really ever have left her, if she hadn't found out about us?

Fiona understood now that whatever might happen next, no matter what Leo might ever come back or pick up a phone and say, there would never be a way of knowing for sure how truthful he'd been about *anything*. Not anymore.

At the same time as she was finally beginning to understand how devastated Minty must have been, at her husband's betrayal, the true reality of her own predicament started sinking in too. The desolate life she was now left with, through her own selfish choices, was suddenly clear and keenly felt.

Not only was she facing a gruelling regime to battle one of the deadliest and least forgiving forms of cancer in existence; she was doing it without her best friend in the entire world, who had unfailingly been there for her through the best and worst of times, for more than forty years. She was doing it without the man she had loved for more than twenty, by her side. She was doing it without her inspiring and sunny-natured goddaughter, whose love for life would have shone at least a little critical light into the darkest of tunnels that Fiona was about to start stumbling through.

She was facing the biggest and most brutal battle of her life, with no certainty of winning it, and she was doing it alone.

There was no one else to rely on. Her parents had been dead for nearly thirty years, and as for other friends? Well, there were a handful, and they were nice enough to spend time and have a laugh with. But nobody knew her like Minty did. The only person she really wanted anywhere near her right now was Minty – the woman whose life she had irretrievably trashed beyond belief. That relationship was done, dusted, and ground so deep into the dirt, there wasn't a spade big enough to dig it back up again.

Minty's pain was extreme, and Fiona knew it. She had *always* known what her affair with Leo would do to her dearest friend, but only now was that knowledge sinking in, and making its presence felt. Only now, when she could see and imagine the end of her own life, so much closer and more painful than she imagined it could be, was it clear how important it was to live the best life you ever could, and let others do the same.

Minty had had a good life. She'd worked her arse off to rise above her own childhood adversity. A drunk, gambling, abusive, waste-of-space father who had a chip on his shoulder as big as Barbados, about being a black man in white society, who ended up deserting his family. Being virtually bed-ridden for an entire year with glandular fever. Being horribly bullied at school to the level where she once even admitted to wanting to kill herself.

Fiona remembered how horrified and panicked she'd felt, after Minty had confessed that she'd actually sat on the side of her bed, with a overfilled glass of wine in one hand and a handful of her mother's sleeping tablets in the other, and seriously considered suicide. She'd wanted to end the torment of being bullied by a handful of girls at her school who hated her for her intellect, and her reticence.

Minty hadn't made many friends. She'd been too shy, and 'brainy' for most other kids to relate to. Margie Bluett and her bitchy friends had picked on her relentlessly, for more than two years, until they'd managed to grow up enough to understand that there were other things they could do in life that could make them feel *positively* competent and powerful – in ways that actually mattered.

Fiona hadn't been overly popular herself, at school, but that had always been by choice. She was beautiful and smart, and everyone wanted her in their 'cliques,' but she'd always kept more to herself.

Maybe even back then, I had demons I didn't know about, that made it too hard to get close to people.

However, she had never been shy about using her 'mystique,' as some would have called it, to get what she wanted from someone. She'd been so distraught at Minty's confession about wanting to end her own life, she'd determinedly stepped out of her self-contained bubble and spoken to Margie Bluett herself.

She'd done it in the most diplomatic and engaging way she could manage, and her conversation with Margie had been brief, but she'd admitted to her that she was a little confused. She wanted to know why a girl who was so smart herself would waste her time with such trivial nonsense as picking on someone else, especially when she actually had nothing to be envious, angry or defensive *about*. She'd asked Margie to explain it, and Margie couldn't. Fiona had asked, then, if it was possible for Margie and her friends to do something better with their 'obvious intelligence' than waste it being bullies.

She'd expected a backlash from the 'Bluett clan,' as she'd called them, but none had been forthcoming. Instead of being tormented herself, after such an audacious overture (which she'd been fully prepared for), she found that Margie had considered her options and decided instead to treat her more like a friend; someone who had recognised her intelligence!

Over the following couple of years, when they'd all still been at the same school, Margie had consulted Fiona about all kinds of things, from skincare to career choices. Fiona had had to hide the alliance from Minty, who would have been heartbroken at what she'd inevitably have seen as the worst kind of traitorship, but Fiona's plan had been to keep her safe, and it had worked. Margie and her friends had backed off.

Surprisingly, Margie Bluett had turned out pretty good. At Fiona's suggestion she'd joined the school debating team, and had proved to be a persuasive and articulate debater. She'd secured the team's captainship after her first year, and it had ultimately set her up in the career she had now; as a highly skilled business negotiator. She'd followed Fiona and a bunch of others to Bristol university, and she was now pretty high up the food chain at a big firm in the city. Fiona always had to laugh whenever Margie credited her with providing 'the shove that had got her started.'

Minty Cartwright's achievements were no small thing, either. She had clawed her way through her early adversity and had gone on to have a beautiful family, create a warm and welcoming home, and carve a career that made her happy too. There was nothing Minty had, that she hadn't fully deserved. Everything in her world had been more or less as it should have been, before Fiona had waded in with her size six boots and stamped it all into the dirt.

The irony struck her now, that she'd hurt Minty herself more than the people she'd so carefully constructed an alliance to protect her from had *ever* done. The mean-spirited actions of Margie Bluett and her sorry bunch of mates were a drop in the bucket compared to what Fiona had unleashed upon her unsuspecting, gentle and sunny-natured friend.

On reflection, coveting Leo and taking the chance to have him for herself had all been a monumental waste of time, hope and heart. He simply wasn't worth it. She'd sought to trade a pretty decent (if a little lonely) life for a very different one; a riskier one; the one she thought she'd always been destined for. But it never had a hope of working out, did it? For God's sake; Leo had *never* been her destiny! That was crystal clear right now, even if nothing else was.

Funny how you think you know someone, after more than twenty years, but they still have the power to surprise you in the worst possible ways.

When a horse balks at a gate it could easily jump over, it usually just needs another run. But that wasn't Leo McLeod. Supporting Fiona through her cancer wasn't just something he was away trying to figure out how to do, and would come back to with some resolve. Unlike the horse that would eventually make the jump, he was never going to help her over that IBC hurdle. He simply didn't have the moral fortitude. The clarity was decimating, of just how pathetic and weak he had turned out to be. His shallowness, his cowardice; those things were deeply ingrained, life-long traits. She wasn't sure which hurt the most; the fact that he had them, or the fact that she'd never seen them.

The dream she'd had for more than twenty years had disintegrated in not much more than twenty days. To want to have the old life back, before the affair, before the cancer, before the series of earthquakes and aftershocks that had left her under a pile of rubble, was a waste of time and effort. To want to turn back the clock, and do things differently before the tide had so spectacularly turned, was as futile as trying to keep water in her hands.

If I needed love that badly, why couldn't I have looked somewhere else? Why didn't I try harder, to get over Leo? Why did I stay so fixated on him for so very, very long, to the exclusion of anyone else who could have made me happy, if I'd given them the chance? Leo is weak, and I'm condemning him for that, but I was weak and selfish too, wasn't I? Why couldn't I have been a better person, and left well enough alone?

One thing she couldn't get out of her head now was the old adage; 'you reap what you sow.' And there was another one too, wasn't there; 'what comes around goes around'? It was impossible not to see this latest cancer-filled curveball, so impossible to confidently catch and volley back, as punishment for what she had done.

For the first time, she started to think about karma; that Eastern notion, born of Hinduism, that proposed a tenet of cause and effect. What we do in our life comes back to us, in this life or the next. So maybe the cancer was payback. Fiona's oncologist had said that it had been in her body for a very long time, maybe even decades, so it wasn't a direct manifestation of the bad karma she'd put out into the world in recent times.

But that wasn't very reassuring, was it, when she knew she'd been a selfish cow for all of her adult life?

She knew it was being selfish yet *again*, to try and contact Minty, but she didn't know what else to do. Teetering on the edge of the abyss, she would make one last attempt to try and prevent herself from falling into it by reaching out to the only person who mattered in her world anymore. Maybe Minty would grab her hand, and save her from oblivion. But maybe not.

If that didn't happen, so be it. If that was what karma really wanted; if she was really meant to, she *would* fall into the abyss, and so be it. There was nothing left to lose. As the tears fell, and she tried to smother her terror, she picked up the burner phone she'd used for calls from Leo, and texted her old best friend.

Chapter Twelve

A few days after her operation, Minty was back in the blissful cocoon of Teapot Cottage. She sat in the window, staring down into the valley, as the wind whipped the leaves from the trees and whirled them about in the wintry air. Autumn was officially over and the cold, stealthy fingers of winter were sliding slowly across the valley. It had only been six degrees this morning. There had been a little random snow, but it hadn't settled anywhere, except on the roof of the cottage and in random drifts across the farm, in places where a half-hearted sun hadn't managed to melt it.

There was condensation on the windows every morning now too, as a telltale sign that the cold weather was about to start biting. She had lit the fire early and decided that a walk could wait. It simply wasn't warm enough to go out and potentially catch her death, just to prove to her waistline that she was indeed keeping an eye on it. She could probably do some one-armed chair yoga later, if she could force herself to 'show up' for the online class.

Minty's peri symptoms were still driving her mad at times, but they had settled quite a lot, compared to how they'd been when she'd first arrived here. She wasn't as weepy now, and her desire to run a sharp knife through her husband (or any other man who dared to look even remotely smug and self-assured) had more or less dissolved. She had also taken some active steps to stay ahead of at least a few of the 'potholes,' in the inevitable journey towards menopause.

Her hair, which had gone dry and brittle virtually overnight, had been nicely styled into a new and healthy cut by Maddie Murphy at Torley Tresses, and Minty was using a hair mask now, to help keep it in good condition. She had allowed Maddie's beautician to tidy up her eyebrows, wax her fuzzy top lip, and file down the ridges on her nails. She changed to a more organic diet with less sugar, salt and processed foods. She also changed her skincare regime, away from a highly-scented and stupendously expensive moisturiser, to one that Feen had offered her. She had made it herself, and it was paraben-free, unscented, and pH balanced. It felt like a 'hug' to her skin, when she applied it, in a way that the more expensive one hadn't done. It was significantly cheaper too, as an added bonus.

Her last period had been unusually heavy again, but she knew that this aspect of being in her pre-menopausal phase was probably just par for the course. Two months before, she hadn't had a period at all. The one before that had been spotty. It was all unpredictable now but, unless any of her symptoms got dramatically worse, she figured she simply had to accept it, and run with the changes as best she could.

It all made for a more settled mindset; so much so, that she'd even begun to think about where she might want to live after the house was sold. She'd more or less decided that she wanted to move away from England. Italy was very appealing, but so was southern France. Minty felt, on some deep level, that moving to a kinder climate would be a wise choice. She wasn't getting any younger, and the English weather was starting to get her down. Vague twinges of the arthritis that plagued the older women in her family were starting. The Heberden's nodes that her mother had suffered from had already started appearing, disfiguring two of her fingers and one of her toes. A knee injury she'd sustained as a teenager, while skiing, had started to ache a little too. The writing was on the wall, that osteoarthritis was quietly stealing upon her. A warmer climate might be gentler to her slowly ageing bones.

Fliss loved living in southern France, and Minty grinned to herself, imagining how excited her sister would be if Minty suddenly announced she was moving to be closer. Fliss would be off house-hunting like a whirling dervish, as soon as she heard the news, and Minty would probably have very little say in the process. Fliss was the human equivalent of a border collie, organising and shepherding people in classic, effortless but meaningful style. It wasn't uncommon for some of the people she somehow managed to take charge of, to suddenly find themselves at the happy end of a process they'd been dreading, simply because Fliss had stepped in and organised everything so beautifully on their behalf, whether they wanted her to or not.

It actually might not be a bad thing, if she were to phone Fliss and say; 'Hey, sis, find me a house' and leave her sister to it. There might be some merit in simply sitting back and allowing herself to be organised by one of the few people left who loved her the most in all the world. It would be fun to go house hunting again, this time as an independent woman. She could certainly get Fliss to organised the viewings on a handful of properties she'd know Minty would approve of. All Minty needed to do was give her sister a list of what she wanted in a home and – just as importantly– what she *didn't* want, and Fliss would happily start looking around.

It all came down to two things. Minty had to decide if France really was where she wanted to be, and make the slightly more disconcerting commitment to giving up full control and letting things unfold, by way of her highly-organised and massively determined sister. Things would pan out in the way the Universe intended. How impressed would Adie Raven be about *that*?

Minty thought back to what Adie had said at her pot-luck dinner, about relinquishing the stranglehold you thought you had to have over the direction of your own life, and letting things develop the way they are supposed to. It was perfectly reasonable to help the process of course, because tied in with it all was the inherent freedom of choice. To find out where a ball goes, you first have to set it moving.

But was Minty ready for that? Was she ready to throw the ball to Fliss and let her run to home base with it? She wondered at how much of herself she had yet to discover in the process of finding and reinventing herself.

And, as it turned out, it was just as well she hadn't gone out for her walk as planned. If she had, the dodgy phone reception around these parts meant she might have missed the text that came in, on a number she didn't recognise. When she opened it she was stunned, to see that it was – once again – from Bloody Fiona.

A deep wave of wretchedness washed over her, and she swallowed down the urge to cry. For the better part of a week there had been nothing. Not a peep, and Minty had begun to relax, thinking that after she'd sent screenshots of all the texts, Leo had been as good as his word, and had demanded Fiona back off and leave her alone. She had enjoyed a peaceful time at Teapot Cottage, and had gone some way towards a final acceptance of everything, until Fiona's text, via an unknown number, turned her inside out again.

It's Fi. I know you don't want to hear from me and I don't blame you, but I am alone and truly terrified and I need to talk to you right away. Can I call you, Minty? Please? It's not a ruse, I promise.

Minty's heart lurched in her chest. This text was out of character for the hostile, whiny woman she'd been fending off for weeks now. Its tone was entirely different, and while Minty didn't have an atom of trust remaining for her former friend, this message tugged at something deep within her.

It *didn't* feel like a ruse. It felt like a genuine cry for help. Fiona appeared to be in trouble. She was confessing to being afraid, which she had never done in forty-one years. Minty didn't owe her a damn thing but, as much as she hated to admit it, the love that still lingered, deeply buried beneath the thick, dark layers of hurt, wouldn't allow her to ignore what seemed to be a genuine cry for help. She texted back.

Ok. But if you start on me, I'm hanging up and calling the police. I mean it.

Her phone had rung, seconds later.

'Minty.' Fiona's voice was shaky, and clogged with tears. Minty was immediately alarmed.

'What's happened?' *Was it Leo? Has something happened to Leo?*

'Minty, I've got breast cancer. I've had a biopsy, and the results have just come in. It's stage three IBC.'

And suddenly, with no further warning, the world was in free-fall. Struggling to breathe, Minty tried and failed to find words. She stayed silent, as she tried to wrap her head around what she'd just heard.

'Minty, it's aggressive. It's in the surrounding lymph nodes. I need a lot of treatment, and it's not curable.' Fiona was crying openly now. 'I'm probably going to die. I've got around five years, they said, at best. I'm so scared.'

Suddenly, again without warning, an image, a memory long-forgotten, flooded Minty's mind; of two little girls, aged about eight, one dark-haired, the other blonde. They each had a doll, sat on a swing at the playground. They were pushing the dolls and laughing loudly with pure delight. Young mothers-in-waiting, except Minty was the only one who got there. Fiona didn't get to have a child. Minty forced herself to focus.

'Where's Leo? Is he with you?' There was a short silence at the other end and, as the hairs gently prickled at the nape of her neck, Minty recognised it as an acutely embarrassed silence. Finally Fiona spoke again.

'Leo's gone, Minty. He left.' Her voice was dull and flat.

'What? What do you mean, he *left*?'

'He left, Minty. He left *me*. Said he was sorry but he couldn't deal with the cancer. With me. I think he went to a hotel. I don't know which one.'

Minty's brows fused into a frown of confusion. 'But he's coming back, isn't he?'

'I don't think so. He left me a note, and he took all his stuff with him.' Fiona sounded utterly defeated. She was still crying, but softly now. Minty hadn't a clue what to say. The silence lengthened until, finally, Fiona filled it.

'I know it's my punishment, this, for what I did to you. It's God's way of making me pay for destroying your marriage and our friendship. I understand that, and I'm working on accepting it. But I don't understand why Leo left. He said he loved me, but how can someone who really loves you walk away from you when you're at your lowest ebb, Minty? How does that work?'

You're asking me that?

Minty tried and failed again, to find the words to answer. What the hell had happened? Leo did a runner because Fiona was *sick*? Even by the poor standard of behaviour he'd displayed over the past two and a half years, that was pretty low. As much as Minty had tried, in her own way, to retain some vestige of respect for her now ex-husband, she now felt the last of it flying away from her, as the reality of her own and Fiona's situations hit home.

What an utter coward Leo was! He was the worst kind of human being. Not only had he trashed his marriage to move in with his mistress, but he also then left *her* high and dry when she needed him the most; when the love he'd professed to have for her mattered the most. He was breathtakingly selfish, to the bitter end. It just wasn't possible to find a decent excuse for the way he had behaved. In spite of herself, Minty felt torn apart for Fiona.

'Minty, Leo said he can't deal with the cancer. He can't cope with me being sick, and disfigured, having to care for me, all that stuff. He said he wasn't capable of it. He said he was sorry, and I think he meant it, but I just never imagined I'd ever have to face something like this, the end of my own life, without either of you holding my hand. The two people I've loved most in the world are gone from my life, and I know it's my own stupid fault, but I've never felt so alone, and I've never been so scared.'

Fiona was crying again. 'They gave me some leaflets, at the hospital, for agencies to contact for support, all that kind of thing, but what I really want is to be with people who love me.'

Minty was crying now too, quietly, and she was still at a lost for what to say to her former friend, which somehow made everything seem so much more wretched and sad.

It couldn't be a simple case of abandoning her own pain to minister to Fiona's. There had been too much damage done for that. Minty realised she had some self-protective barriers to demolish before she could be of any help to *anyone*, let alone Fiona.

Did she even want to demolish those barriers? Yes, of course she did! But just because someone you love is in pain, that doesn't automatically cancel out the pain *they* inflicted on *you*, and how much it hurt. The human psyche wasn't that malleable. Everything was a process and it took the time it took, to change in any direction. There really was no blueprint for how quickly or successfully you got over being decimated, no matter what the circumstances, or no matter who left you in pieces, or why. As much as she would like to think herself capable, Minty couldn't just pretend that what had happened hadn't. Going back to the way things were, and being of the kind of support she would have been without hesitation before she'd found out about Fiona's and Leo's betrayals, was out of the question.

But, as a medical professional, Minty knew that if the IBC followed its typical path, Fiona was very probably going to die within the next five years.

What must it be like, to be told that your life is going to end? How does it make you feel? What does it make you say, or do, or want?

With her heart in turmoil, Minty suddenly felt compelled to offer something.

'Why don't you come up here?'

Fiona was quiet for a moment, then she sniffed noisily. 'Where is 'here'?'

'I'm up in the Lake District. In a cottage, in a small town you've probably never heard of. I hadn't heard of it myself, until I found it on the internet while I was looking for a bolt-hole. It's a nice cottage, and there's a spare bedroom. Why don't you come up for a couple of days or so, and we can talk?'

No promises, she thought herself, but she didn't say it. Fiona would have understood that anyway; there was no need to say the words.

No promises. Maybe I actually can't be of any help to you. But for the sake of all that went before, all that we've always been to one another before all this horror happened, I'm willing to try. I couldn't live with myself if I didn't.

Fiona was silent. Minty tried again. 'If you come up, I can talk you through the treatment options. I know they've already done that with you, but maybe I can answer some of your questions, and help you focus on what you can do, you know? What's achievable? If it would help,' she added, wanting to give Fiona the choice.

'Well that's incredibly kind of you, especially under the circumstances, Minty.' Fiona's voice was stilted. 'I know I don't deserve your support. The truth is, I didn't know who else to call. There wasn't a single other person I wanted to talk to, about any of this. None of my other friends. Only you.'

What about your bosom buddy, Margie Bluett? Why don't you call her?

Minty closed her eyes and made sure the heavy sigh, that rose unbidden from within her, was quiet enough for Fiona not to hear it.

'Well, I mean my invitation. I don't think we can ever be friends again, after everything that's happened, but there's a lot of history between us, and for most of our lives it was good. No matter what's happened, I don't want you to have to face this alone. So please come up to Torley. You can drive, or you can get a train from Temple Meads to Carlisle and get a taxi. I can't come and pick you up because I can't drive. I have a broken shoulder.'

'A broken *shoulder?* What the fuck have you been doing, Minty? Jesus!'

'It's a long story. I can explain when you get here. But the train might be easier for you, although you might have to change at New Street and again at Preston. It's quite a long journey, but at least you could relax.'

So it was settled. Fiona would arrive tomorrow afternoon, by train, and would stay for two nights. Taking the train would definitely be a lot safer, Minty reasoned, since Fiona's head was bound to be all over the place. Torley was a bit of a trick to get to. Driving wouldn't be the wisest way for her to get here, considering how deeply distracted and traumatized she was.

Full of trepidation about exactly what having her primary antagonist under the same roof might mean, Minty also felt she should tell Adie Raven there would be another person at the cottage for a couple of nights.

The following morning, after a restless night of fitful sleep, and all sorts of terrible images flashing through her mind, she put on her coat and headed up the drive to Ravensdown House.

It really was a gorgeous old place. Nobody could help but be impressed by its imposing stone frontage as they approached it. Someone, presumably Adie, had turned on the lamp in the living room window, a beautiful old pale pink art deco one in the shape of the planet Venus, with a ring around it. It threw a warm, soft, peachy glow across the leadlight windows. Even in the pouring rain, the house was beautiful, like something you'd see on the lid of a chocolate box.

Adie answered the door with a tea towel in her hands. As usual, she was working in her kitchen. She smiled expansively at Minty and opened the door wider for her to step in. 'Oh, hi Minty! Do come in, out of the chill! Is everything alright?'

She went back to the kitchen, leaving Minty with no choice but to follow her. Adie lifted the kettle off the edge of the Aga hotplate and waved it at her. 'Tea?'

Minty nodded. 'Yes, a quick one would be lovely, thanks. What are you making?' Her eyes strayed to one of the granite work benches where pastry had been rolled out, in preparation for being made into something that would no doubt be delicious.

‘Steak and kidney pie.’ Adie pulled a face. ‘I hate the whole offal thing, but it’s Mark’s favourite, so I make one occasionally, to keep him happy. It’s for his lunch today, and I’m counting on him either demolishing the whole disgusting thing, or giving what he doesn’t eat to the dogs. What’s happening with you? How’s that shoulder healing?’

‘It’s doing well, thanks. I’ve an assessment appointment at the local medical centre in a few days, and I imagine they’ll be happy enough with how it’s healing, and report it to Cumberland hospital as requested. I’ve been doing my exercises, and keeping it mobile, within a fair pain threshold. I’ve come to check if it’s ok for me to have someone stay at the cottage with me for a couple of nights; tonight and tomorrow night?’

Adie nodded, distractedly, as she took a bowl of cooked steak and kidney out of the fridge and set it on the bench beside the rolled-out pastry. ‘Yes of course it’s ok. You’ve paid for the entire cottage, not just one room! It’s no problem at all, to have a guest to stay.’

Minty was grateful that Adie hadn’t pushed her to find out who would be coming. She wasn’t going to say, but somehow she found herself blurting it out anyway. ‘Fiona’s coming.’

Adie’s eyes widened. ‘Fiona! Isn’t she the woman who stole your husband?’

Minty nodded, smiling ruefully. ‘Yes. There’s been a few developments.’ She watched as Adie poured the hot water into a spectacularly battered old enamel teapot, on top of the two teabags she’d thrown into it, and set it on the table. She took a couple of mugs down and set them out also, along with a jug of milk from the fridge, and gestured at Minty to sit. She sat down herself, and looked squarely at her. ‘D’you want to talk about it?’

Minty nodded. ‘Yes, as a matter of fact I do.’

And then, the whole story came out. At the end of it, Minty wrapped up by simply saying; 'and I haven't a bloody clue if I've done the right thing, or how I really feel about any of it.'

Adie let her breath out through her teeth, as she poured the tea and handed a mug to Minty. 'Wow! How would *anyone* know how to feel about all this?'

She was thoughtful for a moment. 'It says a lot about you, though, that you could invite her up here under the circumstances. You know, I mean with what she's done to you and everything.'

The heavy sigh that escaped Minty felt like it had come from the bottom of her boots. 'Well, there's a high chance that she's going to die from this, Adie. The cancer she has is particularly aggressive, and can only be managed for a while; around five years as an optimum. There currently isn't a cure. She will probably run out of time, unless she can go into remission, or unless a cure or at least a better management protocol is found, before her D-day. If she feels she has peace to make with me, I guess I have to let her do it.'

And if I can help to ease her suffering, I want to do that too.

Adie reached across and gently squeezed Minty's hand. 'Well, you're a better woman than me, for granting her that. I don't know if I could be that magnanimous to someone who'd betrayed me like that, even if she had been my best friend. Probably *because* of that, actually.'

'No, Adie.' Minty shook her head emphatically. 'I truly think you would do the same thing. It's a question of doing what's right, even if it doesn't feel fair. We have to live with ourselves, don't we, after the fact? You, know, the definition of integrity; doing the right thing for the right reasons?'

Adie nodded slowly. 'Yeah, you're right, of course. I probably would do the same as you. I'd hate it, but I guess I'd hate myself more if I *didn't* do it.'

'Exactly. And I think I have to let *her* think I've forgiven her, even if it's not true. And who knows? By the time she leaves the world, maybe I *will* have forgiven her. That would be the best thing for me too, right?'

Adie nodded gently. 'Absolutely. And what do you feel about your husband, now that he's done this?'

'Honestly? I think I was living with blinkers on for a long time, and I just didn't see how deep his selfishness and cowardice really ran. I'm still trying to get my head around how he could have done this. He's thrown away *everything*, and I just keep coming back to how much of a waste it all is, because if he had loved her enough, he'd have wanted to stay with her, to the end, wouldn't he?'

Adie was pensive. 'Maybe he had love confused with lust. It's a common enough thing, and it can go on for years. Maybe he only thought he was in love with her because of how exciting the affair was. Perhaps it took this horrible reality, this very real situation, to show him what real love means, how you step up to the plate without question for someone you love, no matter how hard or cruel it gets. Maybe he realised he couldn't get there; that what he felt for her wasn't true love at all.'

Minty closed her eyes. 'Yeah, and it begs the question, doesn't it? If he'd still been with me, still loved me, would he have run out on me too, if it had been me that got sick? Or would that love have been real enough for him to want to stay and be what I needed, until the end?'

Adie looked at her sadly and shrugged. "Who knows? Who ever really knows how others will treat them, when the chips are down? You could drive yourself completely mad, trying to work it out. It doesn't do to dwell on these things, sometimes.'

Minty swallowed the last of her tea and stood up to go. 'You're right about that. Thanks for the tea and chat, Adie. I bet you're glad most of your other tenants aren't such headcases.'

Adie grinned and shook her head. 'It's no trouble. Truly. Any time you want a chat, I'm happy to lend an ear. Good luck tonight, Minty, and for the time that Fiona's here. I hope she appreciates you, and I hope you can mend some fences.'

'I'm not sure we can, but that doesn't matter. I'm doing what's right, Adie. I'm doing what's kind, and *that's* what matters.'

Adie gave her a quick hug, and let her out, back into the mid-morning chill. As she made her way back down to Teapot Cottage and let herself in through the back door, Minty felt the warmth of the kitchen enveloping her like an embrace. She had never been more grateful for anything than she was right now, for this incredibly lovely, quiet little sanctuary. She could only hope that by coming here, Fiona Winterson with her cancer and her appetite for other women's husbands wouldn't end up tainting this lovely sacred space.

Chapter Thirteen

Adie clicked off her phone, made Mark a hot cup of coffee, and went to find him. Predictably he was in the barn, working on flattening some gate hinges that had buckled badly in the last storm. High winds had torn the gates to the top field clean off their posts, and if it hadn't been for someone delivering dog food up the driveway alerting Mark and Adie to the fact that the sheep were all out and making their way down towards the main road, they could well have lost some.

Mark had decided he could salvage the gate hinges, saying there was no point in paying for new ones when the existing ones were still strong and could be fixed without too much trouble. He was the typical resourceful farmer. He wasn't a stingy man, by any means. He never minded spending money where it was justified. He just didn't spend it when he didn't want or need to.

He looked up as Adie came into the barn. She smiled and loosened her coat. He'd lit the wood stove to take the chill off the working area and this part of the building felt warm and cosy. In spite of its cavernous size, Mark had arranged the space into sections, for different types of work. His wood lathe was set up in one corner, behind some tall metal shelves that helped to shield it from the rest of the space, and a similar arrangement had been made nearby to create partitioning around his welding equipment. Various work benches had been set up to ensure that for day-to-day work, nothing was ever more than a few steps away, and this had created a cosy quadrangle of industry that was more or less just inside the barn doors. A walkway on the other side led to the rest of the building, where the heavy farm machinery was kept, along with different work benches, winches and all kinds of paraphernalia that all had its own particular place.

Back in the brilliantly arranged workshop area, Mark's old woodstove had provided winter warmth for decades, and on a day like this, when it was damp and soggy outside, and the freezing fog couldn't seem to find its way out of the valley for days on end, the stove staved off the chill and made everything toasty-warm.

''Ello, lass! Yer a sight fer sore eyes! An' is that coffee in yer 'and, b'chance?'

'Yes, and I've a blueberry muffin in my pocket, but you'll have to chase me for it!' Mark chuckled and grabbed her by the arm.

'Gotcha!' He pulled her into his arms and gave her a good, sound kiss. 'D'yer fancy a quick roll around in't hayloft?'

She grinned, kissed him lightly back, then pulled away from him.

'No thanks. Been there, done that, still picking the hay out of my bum, thank you very much. As experiments went, that wasn't one of our better ones, as I recall. Minty Cartwright just popped in – did I tell you she's back for another fortnight?' Adie explained to him about Minty's accident, and how she wasn't going to be able to work for at least the next six weeks. Mark shook his head.

'Bloody 'ell! Poor woman in't 'avin' much luck, is she? Would she not be better off at 'ome, wi' 'er daughter lookin' after 'er?'

'Yeah, probably, but she doesn't want to go home just yet. Personally, I think she probably should, not that I'm ungrateful for another fortnight's booking that takes me right up until a couple of days before Christmas.'

Mark shrugged. 'Ah well, she knows 'erself best, I suppose. If she thinks she can cope a'right, she may as well be linin' yer pocket as not.'

Adie nodded, chewing her bottom lip. 'I guess so. I'm glad the cottage is available for that long for her. It means there's no real down time at all in there now though, before early January, since Miranda and her new man-friend Max are coming for Christmas and New Year.'

She was still surprised at how popular Teapot Cottage had proved to be, since she'd renovated it and turned it into a holiday let. Torley was a lovely little Lake District town, with a population of less than two thousand but, even with its quaint little shops, and romantic rolling fields peppered with dry-stone walls and charming old cottages with pretty lead-light windows, it wasn't on the tourist trail. Funnily enough though, that seemed to be precisely what a lot of people liked about it. Not everyone wanted to be slap-bang in the middle of a throng of tourists, queuing for tables in crowded cafes, and struggling to find a parking space in an over-burdened High Street.

Teapot Cottage suited those who wanted to be a bit off the beaten track and have a peaceful retreat to return to after their time out walking or visiting the various sightseeing spots on offer across the beautiful county of Cumbria. They were exactly the type of tenant Adie wanted. She couldn't be bothered with the party types who needed little excuse to get drunk and leery. They invariably left a mess behind them, and Adie was lucky that she hadn't had to deal with many. The website listing made it clear that it was not a place for hen or stag parties. It was simply a retreat for walkers and others who wanted peace and quiet. 'Party Central' it definitely was not.

She was constantly amazed at how many people ended up here to work through big life changes and other events that pushed them into different modes of retreat while they figured things out. Some of the tenants had turned into life-long friends, and the cottage was also a nice retreat for her own family members when they needed a little time out from their busy lives. She was always happy to let any of the kids have it if they wanted it, because it wasn't really about the money.

The rental did provide a nice little income, but she and Mark didn't need it. He already had substantial wealth and Adie didn't need much of anything beyond what they wanted or did together. The cottage, and what was re-invested from the sale of the home she'd shared with her ex-husband, would provide her with a decent retirement fund when the time came.

In the meantime, the income from the cottage and the Farmers' Market meant she never had to ask Mark for money or use the joint account for anything she wanted just for herself.

A lot of Adie's bookings now came in through word of mouth. She couldn't recall a single tenant who'd ever been anything less than thrilled with their stay at Teapot Cottage, and some came back at least once every year. Many regarded the cottage as 'theirs,' in their own way, but most who'd stayed had been respectful and considerate. It was almost as if the little place *demanded* respect for itself. Most people who stayed there automatically took great care of it, and the most damage Adie had ever had to deal with was a couple of broken plates, a cracked cup, and replacing a spark-scorched woollen rug with a new one after someone had forgotten to place the fire guard in front of dying embers when they'd gone to bed. Adie's Visitors' Book was packed with praise and gratitude from departing tenants, and she consistently had five-star feedback on the ratings sites.

'I do have to get the chimney swept before the winter sets in. I keep forgetting to do it. My menopausal 'sponge-brain' is still playing havoc with my short-term memory. I should make a call today, and get it booked in, as I'm now running out of spare days where they can come. I think it will have to be done while Minty is still there.'

Mark put his arms around her again and pinched her backside. 'Well, she'll just 'afta make 'erself scarce fer a bit, won't she? And, Missus, if I can't get yer up inta th'ayloft fer a roll around, yer'll 'afta bugger off. I've 'inges to fix!'

Adie giggled, winked at him, and left him to it. Gorgeous man. Maybe they could have an early night. Just not in the bloody hayloft, thank you very much!

Minty booking in for longer meant that Adie would probably now have to spend the morning of Christmas Eve cleaning, in time for Miranda and Max arriving mid-afternoon. That was fine, she supposed, although she had been hopeful that she would have everything done and prepared by then, and could just relax and enjoy her birthday.

Being born on Christmas Eve wasn't as 'magical and charming' as most people thought it was. In truth, it was bloody inconvenient, and although she never minded much not going out on the night (she always used to have a Christmas Eve cocktail party, in her past life), she did try to make sure the day was one where she could indulge herself a little. She could spend the day just relaxing, having a bubble-bath or going out for a facial or a massage, reading a good book, and just enjoying herself in whatever way she felt like. She so seldom ever had a day like that, and her birthday was the one day of the year that was *hers*, so she was never very keen to give it up. It did mean being properly organised well ahead of time, and she usually was. Unwelcome spanners in the works, like having to do a full house clean all morning, were things she could do without.

Maybe she could get Peg, her friend who ran Ye Old Torley Tea Shoppe, to come and clean the cottage instead, which she did occasionally when Adie was snowed under with other things and tenancies were turning over. Even if Peg had to do it the evening before, maybe she could fit it in. Adie and Mark already had plans to have dinner that night at The Beeches, the big hotel on the main road to Carlisle. That was a new tradition they'd already established; having a nice dinner somewhere, the night *before* her birthday. This time, they'd planned to go ahead of time, and pop into Carlisle, to pick out a new bathroom suite and tiles for one of Ravensdown's bathrooms that was in desperate need of an upgrade. Mark had already arranged his day to take the afternoon off so they could do that, which meant they'd be away from the farm from after lunch until fairly late that night.

Adie dialled Peg's number, praying that she could help. Her friend answered just as she feared the phone was about to go to voicemail, and she sounded a bit flustered.

'Hiya, Adie! Sorry, I could hear this damn thing ringing away, from the front of the shop, but I just couldn't remember where I'd put it! Found it behind a pile of bloody tea towels, would you believe!'

Adie grinned to herself. Peg was one of the most organised people on the planet, and she hated it when anything was amiss. Not being able to locate her ringing phone would have driven her nuts. Peg agreed to come and clean the cottage on the evening before Christmas Eve, for the usual fee, and Adie promised her they would catch up before then for a glass of wine. She made a mental note to make sure she had a nice bunch of flowers, a good bottle of wine, and an extra little bonus in Peg's payment envelope, when they did that.

Peg Tripper was a very dear friend. Adie loved spending time with her. She thought back to the time when, in the wake of Mark's terrible accident in the barn, Peg would always turn up at Ravensdown on Friday nights with a takeaway and a bottle of wine after Adie and Feen had finished on the farm.

The women would sit around, relaxing, and 'chewing the fat.' They'd done it for weeks; first while Mark was still in hospital, and then while he was recovering at home, from the fall that had nearly killed him. During those weeks, it hadn't taken long for Eric Tripper, the temporary Farm Manager they'd employed to run the farm, to take a shine to Peg. He would come in, every Friday evening, and offer Adie and Feen a round-up report of what he'd managed to achieve that week.

At the time, Peg Wilde was a confirmed widow. She'd said, many times, that her tolerance for the general grumpiness of most men of her own age was at rock bottom since she'd gone through the 'change of life.' Fancying one was probably never going to be on the cards because when her menopause had finally waltzed off into the sunset, after years of playing cat and mouse with her body and brain, it had dragged her libido away with it. In her own words; 'my sex drive is long-dead and buried, apart from the occasional date with a toy of a certain shape, and I'm happy enough with my cats, thanks.'

She hadn't been looking for romance, in any shape or form. But it found her anyway, in the shape and form of Eric, and they'd been married a short time later, at the Carlisle Registry office. Thanks to Feen and Gavin's shared and hilarious penchant for Spoonerism, the newlyweds had quickly become 'Egg and Peric,' and were as close to the Ravens as anyone who wasn't family could be.

Peg knew where the spare key was kept for Teapot Cottage, and Adie knew she would do the job to a top standard, with fresh linen, re-stocked shelves and fridge, and everything spick, span and spotless.

It was a wonderful thing, to have people you could rely on. Peg would know that Adie would never ask her to help unless she was stuck. Everyone understood how important it was to her, to take care of her beautiful cottage herself. But, as everyone *also* knew, being married to a farmer and staring down the barrel of Christmas, with friends descending on her for the holidays, meant that her time was in pretty short supply!

She mentioned to Peg that she had ordered a bunch of Christmas lilies for the cottage from Heavenly Blooms, the local florist, that may or may not be on the doorstep when Peg got there. In the run-up to Christmas, Fiona Frost and her busy little team of deliverers were snowed under, so she hadn't been able to guarantee exactly when they could be dropped off.

'Oh, don't worry about those, love! I'll pop along to the shop and pick them up, and I'll bring them with me when I come. Fiona can strike it off her to-do list.'

'Thanks, Peg! That would be wonderful. I'm sure she'll appreciate it as much as I do! Have I told you lately that you're gold, to me?'

Peg laughed into the phone, and sang a cheerful goodbye.

Chapter Fourteen

After she'd made her bed, and tied up the cottage a little, Minty searched around for the earrings Belle had given her last Christmas. She was surprised that they were nowhere to be found. Normally she was conscientious about her jewellery – especially the stuff she really liked. She loved the little silver crystal studs. They were elegant, with the fine gold chain hanging off them, with a tiny diamante-studded gold crown dangling at the end. She sat on the edge of her bed and wracked her brains now, to try and remember when she'd last worn them, and remembered that it had been at Stuart Thomson's barn, when she'd been staying there.

She quickly rang Stuart's number, and was surprised when he answered on the second ring. She'd been prepared to leave a message, thinking he'd probably be busy. She was pleased when he confirmed that he'd found the earrings on the floor next to the bed, when he'd gone in to clean the room.

'I was going to call you, to see how you were, and to arrange to drop these over to you. They clattered up the vacuum cleaner pipe as I moved it under the bed, and I'm glad I was paying attention, because I'm usually distracted with a million thoughts, and cleaning is an autopilot thing for me.'

He went on to explain that after taking the machine apart, to try and work out what the noise had been, he could see the earrings lodged in the filter. 'I remembered seeing you wearing them, just before the accident.'

'I'm so glad they were in the bedroom, and not at the bottom of the stream! They were a gift from my daughter, and I'd hate to have lost them.'

'Yeah, I figured you'd want them back. I know how upset Meghan gets, whenever she loses an earring. It's always the end of the world as we know it, even though they're usually just cheapies that she gets from her friend Jayde at the Farmer's Market over in Torley. I figured you'd be upset at the thought that you'd lost these. They look expensive.'

Minty laughed. 'I'm not sure they are, but I'm glad to be getting them back! I don't know how I was ever going to tell my daughter that I'd lost them!'

'Well, I thought I'd pop over and see you anyway, to make sure you're okay. It's been a few days now since you went back to Teapot Cottage, and I know you're fine, but I still want to lay eyes on you if you'll let me, to reassure myself that you really are? I still feel bad about what happened.'

When Stuart had dropped Minty back at the cottage she'd casually invited him to pop back over for coffee as and when it might suit him to come.

'Okay then; why not come for that coffee we talked about. Are you free today, by any chance? Around mid-morning?'

'Yeah, today would be good, but would later in the afternoon, be alright, after I collect Meghan from school? She could come with me, about four o'clock.'

Minty thought for a moment, then said regretfully, 'I'm sorry Stuart, but that won't work. I have a visitor coming to stay for a couple of days, and that's around the time she's due to arrive. It's another part of my complicated situation, I'm afraid, and it's not going to be an easy visit. I think it would be best if you *could* come over earlier in the day, to save any awkwardness, or you could leave it until the weekend, when she'll have left again. I'm not in a rush for the earrings, now I know they're safe.'

'I can come mid-to-late morning. I can tie the visit in with getting some supplies I need from Darren, at the vet surgery, for the horses. Why don't I bring a couple of brunch paninis and an evil chocolate éclair each, from the bakery in town?'

Minty smiled. 'That sounds perfect. Thank you so much! A veggie panini for me please. The horses are all okay, aren't they?

'They're fine. A couple are on a course of supplements, that's all, and I'm running low. I don't want to leave it until I actually run out, and there's never any guarantee that Darren will be in my area before then, to drop any off. I have to be proactive about it, as Meghan would say!'

He chuckled, and Minty chuckled back. She was looking forward to seeing him. With everything going on in her life, she could certainly do with an hour of light relief, and brunch with a nice new friend.

The day turned a little brighter, although not much warmer, and Minty lit the fire. She wanted the house to be cosy when Stuart arrived.

She'd just set the kettle on the Aga to make the coffee, when she heard his four wheel drive pull up outside. She opened the door before he had chance to knock.

'Wow, look at you!' He beamed at her, as he came through the door. 'Looks like you're doing pretty well. I like the new haircut, and you have a little sparkle in your eye! I guess the shoulder is healing well?'

He handed her the earrings with a flourish, and she laughed with delight. 'Oh, my God! I'm so glad to see these! It feels like a good-luck omen, and right now I can use as many of those as I can get!'

Stuart pulled out a chair at the kitchen table. 'I love this place,' he declared, looking around. 'When we were here, me and Meghan, it somehow helped us to put everything into perspective. Maybe we were ready for that anyway, and maybe just being in a different environment was all we needed for everything to start falling into place. But, as mad as it sounds, I've always felt that being *here specifically* helped us in a way that I don't think we'd have experienced anywhere else.'

Minty smiled at him gently. 'You know what? That doesn't sound mad at all. Different people have said that there's a little bit of magic in here, and for what it's worth I believe it. I've felt it myself.'

She didn't feel compelled to share any details. If Stuart hadn't answered her mobile phone that day at the hospital, he would probably never have known she had a complicated marriage, since her wedding finger was conspicuously bare of rings, but it wasn't an easy thing, to lay yourself open to someone who hardly knew you, about the crap that was going on in your life. Stuart was a new friend, and she hoped he would continue to be one, but that was all.

As they sat there, eating their brunch and chatting about the weather and the fact that Minty's shoulder was quietly progressing, they heard a car pull up outside the cottage. Minty vaguely wondered who it was, and went to the window. Craning her neck she looked out, and felt her stomach lurch.

'Are you ok, Minty? You've gone as white as a sheet!'

She looked over at Stuart, took a deep breath, and gave him a wobbly smile. 'Yes, I'm fine. It's just my visitor, but for some reason she is about five hours early.'

She opened the front door and there stood Fiona Winterson, larger than life; the woman she'd thought was her soul sister for more than forty years. Seeing her was painful in the extreme. This was going to be a difficult visit. Minty wasn't prepared for how upsetting it was, standing here looking at her lost best friend.

Stuart mumbled something about needing to leave. He'd probably sensed Minty and Fiona's awkwardness, and she felt a bit sorry for him. She was about to introduce them, when Fiona got in first.

'I hope you don't mind, Minty, but I got on a train last night instead of this morning. I just couldn't sit around in the house anymore, I had to get out. I arrived at Carlisle last night and I stayed at a hotel near the railway station. I didn't think you'd mind too much if I came early.'

'Well, what would you have done if I hadn't been here?' Minty enquired.

Fiona shrugged, and looked a little confused. 'Well, I'd have sat on the doorstep, I guess.'

'Lucky it's not raining then.'

'Yes, I suppose so. Oh!' Fiona suddenly realised that Stuart was standing in the entrance to the kitchen. She seemed startled. 'You have company, Minty! Sorry if I've barged in on anything.' She looked and sounded acutely embarrassed.

Minty shook her head. 'It's no problem. Fiona Winterson, meet Stuart Thomson, local businessman and friend. Stuart came by to see how I was after I fell off a horse at his stables last week. He was just returning something I'd left behind.'

Stuart seemed relieved to have a chance to speak.

'Hi, pleased to meet you. I was just leaving, actually. I've a lot to do, so I won't intrude.'

Minty felt even more uncomfortable as Fiona openly appraised him. He met her gaze and whimsical smile, and she held *his* gaze and blinked a few times, clearly at a loss for what to say to him. He didn't seem to know what else to say either, so he shook himself a little and headed for the door. As he drew level with her, he heard her murmur, 'No, please don't leave on my account. I'm the one who's not supposed to be here. Not yet, anyway.'

Minty knew the atmosphere had turned frigid, and she wasn't at all surprised that Stuart could sense it. It was also clear that he knew the situation wouldn't be made any easier if he stayed. He was uncomfortable. It was exactly the scenario she'd been trying to avoid, in asking him to come earlier.

At least we managed to finish our brunch and coffee!

Stuart turned to her. 'Hey, will you walk me to my car? I have a favour to ask you, concerning my daughter.' He nodded to Fiona. 'It was nice to meet you. Enjoy your stay.'

As he and Minty left the cottage and walked to Stuart's car, he turned to her. 'Look, I know that what's going on in your life is none of my business, and I don't feel the need to know what any of it's about, but I can sense that this visit is really uncomfortable for you. You're clearly on the back foot, here, and the logical, sensible and considerate thing to do is leave you to it. I'm just following my instinct in saying that I can stay if it would help.'

Minty regarded him for a long moment. 'Stuart you're a good friend. I appreciate you, and since you've told me your story I do feel I can at least tell you that all of this is horribly complicated. I can't go into the details right now, but you're right. It *is* uncomfortable, and difficult, and sad, and a whole lot of other things. Maybe we can get together for a drink in a couple of days, after she's gone back, and I can explain things? I'd like to, actually. A man's perspective might be useful, with what's been happening lately. Can we do that?'

She was relieved when he nodded. 'Sure. Maybe we could meet at the Bull and Royal for a pint and a bite to eat on Friday night? I'll be bringing Meghan over to the Youth Club. It would save me going home and coming back again, and from cooking, of course.'

Minty nodded. 'Ooh, yes. That sounds perfect, actually. Let's aim for that. Thanks. Can you pick me up?'

He winked at her. 'Of course I can! Good luck for now, Minty, and remember I'm only a phone call away. If you need anything sooner, you know where to find me.'

She moved forward and gave him a quick, one-armed hug. He got into his Range Rover and drove off, and she waved as she watched him go.

All of a sudden, she felt weary to her bones. The last thing she wanted was to go back into Teapot Cottage right now, to deal with Bloody Fiona. But the situation couldn't be avoided, could it? She'd invited her up here, after all. What was she going to do, pretend that she hadn't?

Back in the house, the two women stood staring mutely at one another. Neither knew quite how to start the conversation, and it was clear to Minty that Fiona was waiting for her to take the lead.

So she did. 'How are you feeling? Do you want to have a lie down, or would you like some coffee?'

I can't say the word 'welcome.'

‘Coffee would be great. I haven’t started my chemo yet. I’m already prepared for feeling wiped out more or less permanently, once it starts next week, but for now I have a bit of energy, so it’s probably the best time to come. I’m sorry I’m early.’

Fiona’s voice was the quietest Minty had ever heard it. It was almost as if she didn’t want to use it, to create any vibration at all.

Minty moved past her and headed towards the kitchen. As she was making the coffee, black with one and a half sugars, she felt a sudden, sharp spike of resentment. She tried to stifle it but decided that no, actually, she wasn’t about to let Fiona completely off the hook. Stage-three invasive breast cancer or not, there were ground rules that needed to be laid here, expectations that needed to be managed, and limits set, and she knew she had to do it straight away.

‘I’m truly sorry you’re ill, Fiona. Believe me, if I could wave a magic wand and make it all go away, I would do exactly that. Nobody should have to face what you are facing. But I have to be honest. I don’t know how to feel about you being here, even though I’ve invited you. I asked you here because it felt like the right thing to do, but if you’re expecting the open arms of forgiveness absolute, for what you’ve put me through, I can’t give you that.’

Fiona pressed her lips together in a fine line, which Minty knew she always did when she was about to show her own humility. *God, I can read you like a book! Shame I somehow failed to do it while you were shagging my husband behind my back.*

‘I know, Minty, and I’m not expecting that, believe me. Being invited here at all is more than I deserve. It’s messing with *my* head too. But there’s nowhere else that feels right for me to be. There’s no-one else I’d rather be with right now than with you.’

‘What, not even Leo?’ Minty hated herself for her waspishness, but she simply couldn’t help it. Then, digging monumentally deep, she checked herself.

I have to make a real effort here, to be kind, or at least inoffensive if I can't manage kind. I didn't haul her up here just to torment her, did I? Did I?

Fiona shook her head resolutely. 'No. Not even Leo. I can't pretend I'm not devastated about how he's dumped me, at the worst time of my life, but right now he is the last person I want around me while I come to terms with this. His note said he can't stand the thought of being with me disfigured! He can't go there, apparently; can't get into bed with someone who only has half a rack at best, and a bloody big scar where the other half should be, and that's the *best* case scenario. God, it was such a cruel way for him to end it.'

Tears welled in Fiona's eyes, but she blinked them away. 'How did I not know how cruel he could be? It's so horrible I can hardly breathe.'

Minty felt a quick stab of sympathy. Yes, Leo's words and actions had been cruel beyond belief. She tried to tell herself that he must have been terrified, and reacted badly as a result. As excuses went, it was pretty poor, but what else could explain such a brutal reaction? Was Leo Carleon McLeod utterly devoid of empathy as *well* as moral scruples?

Minty had always vaguely wondered, but never too deeply, about his capacity to shoulder certain responsibilities, such as caring for someone who was sick. She had occasionally wondered what would happen if she herself had fallen seriously ill while they were together. Leo wasn't the kind of man who would cheerfully hold the bucket while you puked into it, and whenever Belle or Ethan had been sick as children, he'd always bolted, leaving it to Minty to clean up the shit or the sick and administer the medicine. Even when they'd been helpless babies, Leo would rarely change a nappy and whenever he did, it was always with the worst kind of grace. He didn't 'do' vomit and poo, but Minty always figured he'd surely step up in that regard if he really had to, for someone he loved. It was all part of the package you took on, wasn't it?

I'd have done it for him in a heartbeat of course, but we judge by our own standards, don't we?

She was dumbfounded beyond description that her erstwhile scumbag husband couldn't find enough compassion to support the dying woman he'd professed his undying love to, and left his wife for. Did it all have to hinge around the sexual? Could he not just be with her, and love her the way he was supposed to, until she died? What a terrible coward he was, not just a *fallen* idol to the women he'd wronged, but a totally *shattered* one, with feet of crumbled clay.

Minty had no idea what to say. Wordlessly, she handed Fiona the mug of coffee, and gestured for her to sit at the kitchen table.

'Have you eaten?'

'Yes, thanks. I had breakfast at the hotel. The coffee is welcome though, and it's good. Theirs was pretty shyte.'

Minty couldn't bring herself to smile. *You're here, and yes, you may be dying, but I'm still not quite ready to be nice to you yet.*

Fiona looked at her sideways, through half-closed eyes, and Minty realised with a jolt that her sister Fliss had remarked on this very habit, saying she thought it was furtive, like Fiona didn't want someone to know she was looking at them. Minty marvelled at how, in more than forty years, she'd never noticed her friend do that – until just now! Fliss had been right. It *was* furtive, and it *did* make her feel uncomfortable!

'There's food in the fridge, pots, pans and plates in the cupboards, and cutlery where you'd expect to find it. You can help yourself to whatever you want, whenever you want it, as long as you clean up after yourself.'

With the underlying message: *I'm not waiting on you.*

Fiona nodded, took a gulp of coffee, and set her mug down. 'Right. Thanks. I haven't been eating much. Overdosing on coffee, as usual, but my appetite is zero, and no doubt set to slide into the subterranean once the treatment starts.'

'You mean your appetite for *food* is zero. Your appetite for other people's husbands seems absolutely fine.'

Minty's own jaw dropped in disbelief. She was utterly horrified with herself. *Oh my God! Did I just actually say that out loud?*

Fiona blinked and pressed her lips together again. 'Maybe coming here was a mistake.'

Her voice was very quiet again, and she couldn't look at Minty. She really did look as if she were about to cry. In decades, Minty could only recall Fiona ever being in tears a handful of times, and then only for a very brief spell. She normally got control of herself fairly quickly, whatever the circumstances. Her father had been a staunch army man. The stiff upper lip had always prevailed in the Winterson household. Fiona was simply a chip off the old block. Usually.

'No, it wasn't. I'm sorry I said that. Truly! It was below the belt. I didn't mean it.'

'Yes you did,' Fiona returned softly, with a light shrug. 'Whatever we say, we have to think it, first. Nothing comes from nowhere. All speech comes from thought. But it's okay, Minty. I deserved that. I deserve a lot worse than the hospitality you've extended to me. You're right. I did steal your husband from under your nose. You have the right to throw whatever punches you like. You have every right to be as angry and mean as you want.'

'I don't *want* to be angry and mean,' Minty retorted hotly. 'I want to be better than that, and better than *you*, and better than my scum-cake husband, but I'm struggling to get my head around it all. You and me, me and Leo, you and Leo, selling my home, the cancer, you being here, and let's not forget this broken bloody shoulder and being unable to work. I fell off a fucking *horse*, for God's sake! It's a lot to deal with, all at once. You'll have to bear with me if I'm not my usual calm and level-headed self, Fiona.'

To her chagrin, Minty felt herself on the verge of a full-on rant. Mightily, she pulled herself back from it. Fiona had barely been here for five minutes.

Fiona nodded. 'I know, Minty. I get it. I know what it's like to have your head so full of the kind of shit you can hardly believe is real, you almost forget to *breathe* properly.'

Yes, that was exactly it. Breathing properly was something Minty had struggled to re-master too, before she'd arrived here at Teapot Cottage, but she made no comment about it.

'Let me show you where you'll be sleeping. It's the bedroom along the hall from mine. The bathroom's in the middle. There's only one.'

She led Fiona up the stairs and showed her into the spare bedroom. It looked pretty, with its multi-coloured crochet throw, and navy and white gingham curtains at the window. The view down into Torley valley was one of the best features of the cottage, and the bedrooms made the most of it too, with west-facing windows. A watery shaft of sunlight did its best to offer a mild degree of warmth to the room.

'It's lovely! The whole place is lovely.' Fiona seemed genuinely impressed by the cottage. She only had a small bag with her, more of a large handbag than a holdall, and Minty guessed it would contain a small bag of makeup and travel toiletries, a change of knickers and bra, a nightshirt, spare pair of jeans and a couple of tops. Over the years, Fiona had developed the best knack Minty had ever seen, for travelling light. She could look a million dollars, every day and night for a week, out of what she could fit into a miniscule holdall.

It was a talent Minty had always envied, especially on those bargain-basement, hot-week holidays they always used to go on, with Fiona breezing her way through from breakfast to bedtime, via at least one beachside nightclub, with little more than three mix-n-match bikinis, four complementary sarongs, and a tiny bag of 'bling' – transformational accessories – in her hand luggage.

Minty, by comparison, would be labouring under the load of a fully laden suitcase, packed to account for every possible eventuality, and dangerously approaching the weight limit on the *outward* journey. By the time she'd bought souvenirs and the odd bit of clothing, and her duty-free Pimms and perfume, she'd be relying on Fiona's luggage allowance as well as her own, with a cheap and cheerful bag she'd invariably have bought from a local bazaar or market, whose buckles would be busted well before the flight home even landed.

'I might just have a bit of a rest if you don't mind, Minty? I didn't sleep at all well last night.'

You and me both, honey.

'Of course. Take all the time you need. I've had some food already, with my friend who was just here, but you can fix yourself a sandwich if you want one.'

I'm not waiting on you.

Fiona nodded absently, and Minty left her to it. As she made her way downstairs she heard the curtains being pulled in the spare bedroom.

She tried to settle her thoughts. She was low on provisions. She'd intended to make a dash to the little supermarket in Torley town to stock up before Fiona was supposed to have arrived this evening. She'd planned to ask Stuart if he'd run her down to the supermarket and back. That opportunity had gone, but she could probably put on a raincoat and go now, since Fiona was probably going to be asleep for a while. Even if she wasn't, even if she did wake up and come down, she'd soon see that Minty wasn't around, and figure she'd popped out on an errand.

If I'm not here, you'll work it out.

She threw on her coat and grabbed her handbag. There was nothing in the cottage for Fiona to snoop at, so she felt okay about leaving. Before she did, she tossed another log onto the fire and put the fire guard in front of it. At least, for whichever one of them would be first back into the living room, it should still be warm and cosy.

Just over an hour later, Minty was back at the cottage, to find that Fiona still hadn't surfaced. She quietly unpacked the groceries; a foil tray of Mediterranean vegetables for roasting, a pack of fresh pasta, a cob loaf of bread, a bag of grated mature cheddar, a head of garlic, some tomato paste and a jar of passata. She'd also bought a cauliflower to prepare with cheese sauce, some fruit, a big wedge of brie and some crackers, a large carton of orange juice, and a couple of bottles of wine.

They certainly wouldn't starve, and if Fiona didn't want to eat much or any of it, that suited Minty just fine. While she'd been mindful to shop for things she knew Fiona would eat, she didn't buy anything she didn't like herself. Whatever her semi-wanted guest didn't eat in the short time she'd be staying, Minty would polish off herself.

Fiona surfaced about half past two, looking pale and drawn. Her pillow had left a pleated imprint on the left side of her face. Looking at her properly for the first time, Minty could see she'd lost weight, and her hair needed a jolly good cut and colour. She looked somehow diminished, and the presence she normally had, that aura of command that made everyone look at her whenever she walked into a room, was gone. She was a far less shiny, less bold version of the woman Minty had always known. It couldn't have just been the cancer that had caused that – she'd only just found out about it. It had to be something more, that was making her so much less 'present' than the way she used to be. Guilty conscience, maybe?

Minty didn't comment. It wouldn't help to say anything. While it was a struggle to be kind, there was nothing to be gained by being critical, insulting or downright mean. She wasn't about to debase herself with that.

She'd made and eaten a toasted cheese sandwich and a bowl of tomato soup while Fiona had been sleeping, and she had left an identical snack on the bench, so all her 'guest' had to do was put the sandwich in the grill machine, and reheat the soup on the Aga. Fiona did it without complaint, and Minty was glad, in part, to see her eat something, even though she stayed in the kitchen to eat her food, and only when she had finished, and washed and put away the dishes she'd used, did she venture into the living room. She volunteered to make a cup of tea, and Minty graciously accepted.

They were clearly walking on eggshells around one another, which was to be expected, she supposed. She wondered if perhaps an all-out row might make it easier to break down the barriers that were so painfully evident in their overt and extreme politeness, and the way they consistently avoided direct eye contact.

She decided it probably wouldn't, but thought she should take the bull by the horns anyway, and when Fiona came back in with the mugs of tea, she gestured for her to sit in the armchair that faced the windows. She sat sideways in the window seat of one of them herself, with her socked feet on the cushions and her knees bent. It would be of great help to them both, to not be facing one another (as if in confrontation), but able to fix their gaze instead on the stunning panorama in front of them, if talking to and looking at one another proved to be too much.

She laid her head against the windowpane, and took a deep breath. 'So, the cancer. Tell me about the timeline.'

Fiona gently cleared her throat and, when she spoke, her voice was so quiet that Minty had to strain to hear it.

'One night, around ten days or so after Leo moved in, my left breast became really red and swollen. It had been a bit tender for a few days, and I thought it was just some peri-menopausal thing; you know, breast tenderness? It's something I've always had, around the onset of my periods, as you'll probably remember. But it's one of the symptoms of peri too, and that's where I'm at, so I had half a mind it was just something else on that list.'

Minty did remember. Her own menstrual cycle had always been straightforward, with only an occasional cramp or bout of irritability, until peri had started turning it into a monthly lottery of severity, on the months when it turned up at all. But she knew that Fiona had often had a difficult time with hers.

'So I hadn't thought too much about it, but I didn't sleep well that night, and when I showed Leo in the morning he made me phone the GP surgery straight away. They made me an appointment for later the same day.' She blew a breath out, before continuing.

'The doctor I saw examined me, and arranged for a biopsy at the Nuffield Hospital. I have private health insurance, so that got me fast-tracked to consultancy. Leo took the afternoon off, and came with me. After the biopsy we went home and had a very quiet day. I think we were both in shock, to be honest, and neither of us really knew what to say. I didn't want to tell anyone else what was happening, because I still didn't really know what was wrong. I wanted to wait until we knew what we were dealing with. The doctor hadn't made any suggestions about what it could be, so I still thought it was something pretty minor, like an infection or something hormonal, and I'd just be given some pills to clear it up.

'Anyway, the doctor called asking me to meet him, to discuss the results of the biopsy. I went alone, and as soon as I looked at him, and he asked me if I wanted to have someone else with me, I was scared. I knew he was going to say it was cancer, Minty, and it is. Its IBC.'

Minty nodded, grimly. 'Inflammatory Breast Cancer. That's a tough one, Fi, and you're quite young to have that. You said it was Stage three?'

'Yes. Stage three. It hasn't spread beyond the surrounding lymph nodes. My Oncologist recommends aggressive chemo, then mastectomy, and whatever ongoing treatment might be necessary after, so that's the route I'm taking. I'm already scheduled for chemo. It starts next week, and if that's successful they'll give me a mastectomy, sometime after Christmas I think, and then I can have radiation, and they'll put me on medication. I think it's called Herceptin?'

'Yes, that's right. But, from what I understand of IBC, the five-year survival rates are as high as seventy percent. And with different clinical trials, and new ground being broken with treatments, and everything… well, I think it's way too soon to start planning your funeral, Fi. Remission is a definite possibility.'

Fiona nodded, slowly. 'Yes, hopefully. But everything's happened very quickly, and I'm struggling to get my head around it. I had to go into work and tell my boss and my colleagues. That was hard, but they were all really encouraging, and I felt better about it all when I left. Until I got home, of course, and found the note from Leo, telling me he couldn't cope with me being sick and maimed for life.'

Fiona blew her nose, and wiped her eyes with the back of her hand as her tears fell.

'All his stuff was gone. He'd just vanished. He didn't even wait, to tell me to my face. He won't even answer my calls. I feel so scared and alone, Minty, and so completely and utterly stupid. I'm everything you said I was, and more.'

Minty chose not to buy into that conversation. It was one they would probably have eventually, but she wasn't going to get into it yet.

'What have they told you, so far? Do you know everything, you need to know, d'you think, or do you have more questions?'

Fiona closed her eyes for a moment. When she opened them again, they were swimming with tears. Minty reached over to the coffee table and picked up the box of tissues that were sitting on it. Fiona took the box and sat it in her lap, but she didn't pull any out. She sniffed, hard.

'No. I think they've covered all the bases. They gave me a heap of information, leaflets, printouts, website addresses, that sort of thing. They've rated my chances of survival for three to five years as about fifty percent, but they said with good care, diet, and so on, I could live longer. They also said though, that its possible I could deteriorate a lot faster. Some people do. There's no real way of determining who's likely to do better or more poorly. It's all a bit of a lottery, from what I understand.'

Minty looked up to the ceiling and blinked hard, as the tears pricked her own eyes. Fiona continued.

'I need to get my affairs in order, and I think I probably *do* need to organise my funeral, despite what you've said. I need to at least pay for it, before the prices go even further through the roof. It costs a lot to shuffle off the mortal coil, these days! I also have to make a will, organise a Power of Attorney, decide whether to have a DNR in place, figure out whether I want hospice or home-based palliative care, all that stuff.'

She sighed deeply. 'I never imagined I'd be doing anything like this before I'm fifty. I certainly never thought I'd be doing it alone.'

Clearly, Fiona was angling to talk about Leo, but Minty wasn't ready to talk about him yet on *any* level; certainly not about him leaving Fiona alone, and running for the hills at a speed that beggared belief. She wasn't ready for a conversation about Fiona and Leo as a couple, but she was able to talk about *herself* and Fiona; as far as the cancer went, at least.

'You won't be doing it alone. In spite of the fact that you've betrayed me in the worst way possible, in a way I'm still not ready to talk about, and in a way I'm not sure I'll ever fully recover from, I won't leave you to face this alone. We go back too far for that.' She looked at her friend, her *erstwhile* friend, the woman who had meant the absolute world to her for more than forty years.

'You and I have the kind of history that most people don't get to have. Few people can say they've been one another's staunchest ally for more than four decades. Even fewer can say they have more than one person like that in their lives. I can't, and I know *you* can't. I have other friends – good ones, in fact – but they've never been in the same league as you were, until everything changed.

'So I will support you, Fi, because underneath the agony you've caused me, and even though you've been anything *but* my staunchest ally in recent years, I still love you. Not enough to be able to forgive you, and go back to the way things were before. The damage is too great for that.'

Tears swan in Minty's own eyes again now, but she ignored them and continued. 'The love I had for you? You tore it from me with such force, when you helped yourself to Leo.

What's left is all there is, and I'll give it to you gladly, but it's nothing like it was. I don't trust you anymore, and I doubt I ever will, but I won't abandon you and leave you to face dying alone, without the kind of support any dying woman deserves.'

'You're a better bet than Leo, then' Fiona observed wryly. 'And before you ask, no. Even if he came crawling back on his hands and knees, begging me to forgive him for what he's done and said, I wouldn't have him back.' She sounded resolute, but she was crying again. It was obvious to Minty that she desperately wanted to talk about Leo, but Minty had already said that she wasn't ready to go there, and she figured it wouldn't hurt to make the point again, one more time.

'I *wasn't* going to ask, actually. I'm not interested in your relationship with my ex-husband, or even whether there is one anymore. You and Leo have nothing to do with me. Our marriage was over the minute he started fucking you. I just didn't know it, at the time, did I? But the fact that he left you? I can't help you with that, Fi, and as I've said, I'm not ready to talk about it.'

Minty made sure her tone was final. There was no way she was going to be pulled into a painful discussion about what her ex-husband had done. It was all still far too raw. In any case, even if Minty did want to talk to anyone about it, Fiona would be the last person she would choose, and of course she didn't have to say that. Fiona already knew she'd blown all rights to hearing the finer points of Minty's anguish.

No way are you getting a front-row seat at the suffering you've caused in my life.

'Fair enough,' Fiona conceded with a slight nod. 'But just let me say one thing, for what it's worth. I didn't *want* to be in love with him, but I was, and when he walked out I guess I got a glimpse of how you would have felt when he left you to come to me.'

No you fucking didn't! Your 'glimpse' was a drop in the ocean compared to the reality of my husband of twenty-two years walking out on me with no warning, and realising you'd been the cause. It was a drop in the fucking ocean, compared to witnessing the agony and confusion on my daughter's face when I had to tell her what the two of you had done. Don't you bloody dare compare your pain to mine!

Minty didn't say the words, although her face must have shown her fury, because Fiona slumped down in her chair, in what looked like an effort to make herself as small as possible, and focussed on the view beyond the window. Minty leaned forward and cleared her throat, determined to retain the dignity she was in real danger of losing.

'As I said, I will support you through the cancer, and I will do so out of the love I still have for you. But it's a different kind of love to what I used to have. I now love what you – what *we* – used to be. All those years, when it was just the two of us, and then even when there were three of us, before whatever point it was when you started coveting my husband, we shared everything of ourselves with each other, you and me.

'The you I used to love; that's who I will do this for. Not the 'you' who's sitting in front of me now. Because the 'you' who exists now is not the same person to me. I will honour our past. And when you're gone, if this cancer does claim your life, I will continue to cherish what was, before you ruined it. I will remember the 'you' that used to exist, but only because it's too big a part of my life *not* to remember with love.'

Even to Minty's own ears, it hardly made sense. But whether it did or not, it was how she really felt, and there wasn't a better way of saying it. It would simply have to do. Or not.

Fiona was still crying, and looking around the room, at anything and nothing, desperately avoiding eye contact with Minty. 'Well, don't feel you have to help,' she muttered, almost to herself. 'I don't want to be anyone's *obligation*.'

Minty forced herself to shrug. 'Take it or leave it. I'm telling you that part of me still loves part of you. If that's not enough for you, under circumstances where you don't have the right to *any* of my love, since you've butchered me like a pig in a slaughterhouse, that's fine. I can leave you to it, and you can fuck off home whenever you like. It's your choice.'

Fiona flinched, but said nothing. Instead, she started voraciously biting the inside of her bottom lip, pushing the knuckle of her forefinger against it for more leverage. Minty know this was a nervous reaction, and sometimes Fiona would tear at the skin so much with her teeth she would make her own mouth bleed. Minty always told her off for this, but not today. It didn't feel appropriate to show so much caring for anything other than the cancer that was slowly but surely going to ravage her, maybe until there was nowhere left to invade.

That was really cruel. She is dying and she is alone and afraid, and yet I can't bring myself to be any kinder to her than this. Am I that wounded? Yes, if I'm honest, I am. I can only do so much here. Her wounds are heartbreakingly real. I know that. But my heart is broken too. My wounds are real too, and they were inflicted by her. Of course I don't want her to be afraid, to face dying alone, this fully-grown only child of now-dead parents! But I can only do so much. I'm just not a good enough person to be capable of more.

A lengthy pause prevailed. At last, Fiona spoke again, almost in a whisper. 'Look, Minty. I don't expect forgiveness. I shouldn't even be here. But as I've said before, you're the only person I want to be around, right now. I don't want to be anywhere else but here, no matter how hard it is to face you, and it *is* hard, believe me. Nowhere else, no *one* else, makes sense. I can't explain it any better. That's just the way it is.'

'I get it, Fi. I do understand. And, like I said, part of me does want you to be here. But I'm still in the place where you put me, on the other side of a broken bridge I don't know how to cross back over safely, and you're a very long way from where the small part of me that does want to reach you can actually do it. I can't explain *that* any better. *That's* just the way it is.'

‘So where do we go from here?’ Fiona’s voice was still quiet, as if she was afraid it might shatter what looked and felt like the beginnings of a fragile truce.

Minty shrugged. ‘I don’t know, but I guess it’s like I tell people at work who are facing rehabilitation, and what someone wise has said to me recently. One day at a time. We take things one day at a time, or even one moment at a time if we have to, until *some* of this starts to make sense.’

Fiona nodded. ‘Yes. *That* makes sense. We can do that, while I’m here. But there are things I do want to say to you, Minty. Things I *need* to say, and you have to let me say them. I know you don’t want to talk about Leo, and I understand it, but you have to let me say what I need to.’

‘Actually I don’t have to let you, at all,’ Minty responded coolly. ‘I don’t have to listen to a single one of your excuses, your apologies, your self-justifications, or anything else. Maybe the moment will come when I’m ready to listen, but now is not that moment. If you really do have stuff to get off your chest, and I’m genuinely sorry for the ill-judged pun there, you will have to wait until the time feels right for me.’

She turned her face towards the window and looked down over the view. There was such strength here, in this vista. You could drink it in with your eyes until you were full to the brim inside, and it somehow made you feel stronger and more able to face your own reality. Minty knew the time would come when she *would* let Fiona say her piece, but it would only be when she’d gathered enough of the strength that existed within these walls to cope with it. It would be soon, but not right now.

‘I’m going out for a walk,’ she announced. ‘Do you feel up to coming with me? I’m going up to the Tor. It’s a bit of a climb, for about twenty minutes, but the view from the top is worth it.’ She checked her watch, before adding; ‘we should still have time to get up there and back well before it goes dark.’

It may be a good thing for her half-invited guest to get out in the fresh air, but she wasn’t going to push. Fiona agreed to give it a go, and the two women put their coats on and headed up past Ravensdown House to the start of the track to the Tor.

'Wow! What an amazing place!' Fiona gaped at the arresting spectacle of the big old house. Grateful for a neutral subject for discussion, Minty explained about Mark and Adie Raven. She also talked about the remarkable Feen, and her rock musician and songwriter husband, and the fact that they generally lived in London for at least half of the year.

'Sounds like an interesting family,' Fiona remarked. 'And how romantic, how wonderful, that Adie and Mark found one another later in life. I do so love a happy ending.' Her voice was wistful, the unspoken words hanging in the air; '*but I'm not going to have one*.' Minty refused to make any comment.

As they moved towards the gate beside the barn that led to the track, the front door of Ravensdown House opened, and the diminutive Feen came out. She was carrying a traditional old wicker basket. She looked up and saw Minty and Fiona and raised her hand, a bit tentatively, Minty thought. Feen looked unusually hesitant, so she beckoned her over.

'Hi Feen, are you guys here for the weekend? This is Fiona Winterson.'

Feen smiled gently at the women. 'I'm here, but not with Gavin. He's working on a project that's graking him a bit mumpy, so I left him behind in London. I just needed to get out of the city for week with the twins. The pre-Christmas bonkers-ness is everywhere and it was starting to pive me drotty. People seem almost hysterical about it all. I feel like the place has gone mad.'

She rolled her eyes. 'We've been here for a few days, actually, but the weather hasn't been brilliant so this is my first real chance to get out and horage around in the fedgerows for an hour or two!' She held out her hand to Fiona. 'Hello, Fiona, pleased to meet you. I'm Feen Raven-Black. Are you visiting for the weekend?'

'I'm just here for a couple of nights. I go home the day after tomorrow. It's beautiful here,' she added.

‘Yes it is. Are you heading up to the Tor? Be careful, it will be windy up there, and there’s been lots of rain so there’ll be some mippery slud on the track. Take your time and watch your footing, especially you Minty, with that shuff doulder!’

With that, she smiled broadly and turned to go, and within seconds she was halfway down the driveway towards the main road. For one so small, she seemed to move incredibly fast, as she scurried away. Fiona frowned and turned to look at Minty. ‘What in the world was she babbling about? And what, pray tell, is a shuff doulder?’

Minty explained about Feen’s use of Spoonerism; transposing the first consonants on a pair of words. ‘Nobody can say for sure if it’s a speech disorder or a form of dyslexia. There’s research, but none of it’s definitive. Anyway, its unconscious, and quite charming, I think. She does make me laugh at times.’

‘She’s so tiny! I can’t believe she gave birth to a set of twins! She’s beautiful too, with those incredible blue eyes, and lashes to kill for. She seems nice.’

‘She is, and you should see her husband! He is *drop* dead gorgeous! The epitome of tall, dark and handsome, with the most gorgeous green eyes you’ve ever seen, and a body to *die* for. They’re a really nice family, actually, all of them.’

Minty started walking again and opened the gate to the track, holding it open for Fiona. It was a bit of a slog to the Tor, mostly uphill, and Feen had been right – there was a lot of mud on the track, but since it was a well-defined pathway with plenty of rocks dug in underfoot to offer traction in poor weather, they didn’t find it too difficult. They reached the top and went to sit on the ground, on a flat rock, with their backs against the stone Tor. The view from here, all across the Torley valley, was incredible. Adie Raven had told Minty that on a clear day it was possible to see right into Scotland.

‘It’s nice up here,’ Fiona remarked. ‘Kind of makes you glad to be alive, doesn’t it? I could stay here forever.’

‘Maybe you bloody should,’ Minty muttered. Before she could stop herself.

Fiona turned to her. 'You assured me that coming here wasn't a mistake. I don't expect you to be nice to me, Minty, but I would appreciate you lightening up on the snide remarks. All things considered, they really don't make things any easier.'

Minty was incredulous. 'Don't they? Oh, I'm so sorry! My apologies, Fiona, for being less than tolerant of what you've done to my life! I should have more sensitivity, shouldn't I? After all, we wouldn't want *you* to be any more upset with the way things have ended up, would we? God forbid!'

Fiona stared out to the middle distance, and sighed quietly. 'Okay. I'm going to leave, when we get back down to the cottage. I'll call a taxi to take me back to Carlisle for the night, and I'll get the train home again in the morning. It really *was* the wrong thing to do, to come here.'

'Well, if you came here hoping to hide from the truth, or imagining I could somehow ignore it myself, that was pretty naïve, don't you think?'

'Right, so I'm the naïve one? Of all the ways for a pot to call a kettle black, that has to take the biscuit.'

'Naïve is the least horrible thing I'm entitled to call you, I think, under the circumstances; you, with your stupid mixed-up metaphors.'

Well, don't let me stop you from speaking your mind, Minty, since you're clearly not interested in letting me speak mine.'

'Oh, trust me! If I was to *really* unleash everything that was on my mind, by the time I was finished there'd be nothing *left* of you!'

Fiona sighed heavily. She looked away, back out to the middle distance, and her voice was tired and quiet. 'Well, maybe there shouldn't be. Perhaps being left in shreds is no more than I deserve.'

Something inside Minty finally snapped. 'Oh please! Stop with the whining victim deal! '*Poor me! What a mess I've made of everything!*' What the fuck do you want, Fiona? Sympathy?'

'Maybe a little sympathy, for the fact that I'm dying, yeah.'

'We don't know if you're dying. This thing, this cancer? It's beatable, Fiona. Its stage three IBC, but people do achieve remission from it. You can win this fight; you just have to *want* to, but you don't stand a bloody chance if you keep playing your shitty little 'poor-me' card.

'Self-pity won't heal you. It will almost *certainly* kill you, with this disease, and if that really is what you want, then just fuck off somewhere else and do that would you, please? Because I can't help you if you're not prepared to help yourself. I'm not sure I really want to anyway, after what you've done to me and my family, so don't come here moaning about your lot in life if you're not prepared to do any spadework of your own, to change it.'

'That's great. Thanks so much for that, Minty. Fuck off and die? Right. And why would you even care?'

Minty felt white-hot with rage. 'Well why *should* I care? Tell me that! What did you expect, when you came here? I mean, *really?* What did you *really* expect? That I'd be standing here with open arms, saying; 'ah come on, poor baby, all is forgiven'? You tore my life apart and destroyed everything I held dear. You broke my daughter's heart too, and that's even *worse*, as far as I'm concerned. What did that girl ever do to you, to deserve you blowing *her* world apart? Here's a clue; she loved you! D'uh! And so did I, but that didn't count for anything, did it, in your fucked-up world? All you seem to know how to do is serve yourself with whatever you want, no matter who you have to shit all over, to do it. You don't seem to have a scrap of remorse for ruining the lives of the people who care about you.

'Oh, and as if that wasn't enough? You've harangued me with your miserable, whingeing tirades on the phone for *weeks* now, in an effort to try and make yourself feel better about what you did. You're pathetic! What the fuck do you want from me?'

Minty found herself fighting the impulse to start slapping Fiona. She knew that if she started, she probably wouldn't be able to stop. For the first time in her life, she actually felt like beating the crap out of someone.

She's not even a pretty crier! Red-eyed and snot-faced. Look at the bloody state of her! And anyone who makes me feel like this can never be good for me, can they?

Fiona sniffed snottily, wiped her eyes with the back of her hand, and then looked Minty up and down, with a disdain that made her catch her breath.

'What do I want from the woman who has everything and sees nothing? Well that's quite the question, isn't it?'

Minty's mind flooded with confusion. 'Is it? What the hell are you talking about? If it's 'quite the question,' as you put it, then fucking answer it, you stupid cow! You demolished the two critical cornerstones of my life, and you sit there talking in riddles and still trying to insinuate that helping yourself to my husband was *my* fault?'

'Critical cornerstones! Well, you've still got your bloody kids, haven't you, you smug cow? What are they, if not 'critical cornerstones'?'

Minty narrowed her eyes. She was trying, desperately, to understand. 'Is that what this is about; the fact that I had kids and you didn't?'

Fiona's laugh was harsh. 'Don't flatter yourself! I never *wanted* kids! You always knew that! We talked about it often enough, when we were growing up. It was *you* who wanted the good old 'two-point-four.' Me? I just wanted to be free of all the bullshit you thought was so important! I had a miscarriage, actually, but you didn't know about that, did you?'

'What? You had a bloody miscarriage? *When?* Of course I didn't know about it, Fiona, but *why* didn't I? How could I have known about *anything*, if you didn't fucking tell me?'

'It was before George and I broke up. I didn't even know I was pregnant. I had a horrible session on the loo, and I realised I had to call an ambulance, because the bleeding wouldn't stop, and neither would the cramps. Turns out I was two and a half months gone, by calculations, but I'd had a semi-normal period, so I was none the wiser until it happened.'

She made a wipe-away gesture with her hand. 'Oh, don't sweat it, Minty! Best thing that ever bloody happened to me, if you want the truth.'

Minty didn't believe that for a second. 'Why didn't you tell me?' she demanded.

Fiona laughed again, but there was no humour in it. 'What would have been the point? So you could have felt superior about that too, that you had two great kids, while poor Fiona the loser ended up with nothing, *again?*'

Minty was incredulous. '*Superior?* What the fuck? Is *that* how you saw me? I could have supported you! That was a terrible thing to go through alone! We were friends, weren't we? Or had you decided, even back *then*, that I was just a hateful thorn in your side? Actually, I'm curious, now. When *did* you start to hate me, exactly? I'd like to know, so I can trace back to everything you've ever said to me since, about anything. I'd really like to understand how long you've been my enemy, instead of my fucking friend.'

'I was never your enemy, Minty! I was just pissed off that despite the fact that we both worked our asses off to get our degrees, you ended up with everything; even more than you already started with, which was shitloads more than I *ever* had! I ended up with little more than the crumbs from your table. I got to be the friend who came to dinner, who got to be Maid of Honour when you married the man I wanted!

'I was allowed be godmother to one of your kids. Whenever you went on holiday I got to water the plants in your beautiful big house, and feed your adorable cats and dogs. I could stay over, and watch your hundred-and-fifty-inch TV with its Bang and Olufsen speakers at twenty grand a pair, and a thousand movies to choose from. When my car was in the garage being fixed you lent me your 'spare' Mercedes. You let me help you plan your big fancy twentieth wedding anniversary party, where I had to stand alongside, yet again, like I did at your wedding and on so many miserable social events after it, smiling through the agony while the only man I ever loved stood smiling next to *you!*'

'I was trying to be the friend who included you in my world, Fiona! When did you ever tell me, that it felt like I was rubbing your face in anything? How was I supposed to figure that out, with no clues? Never my enemy? Good God. I'd hate to see what you'd do to someone you *didn't* like!'

'Christ, Minty! There were *plenty* of fucking clues! You just never noticed how patronising and smug you always were, and what effect it had on people. It wasn't up to me to tell you!'

'Yes it bloody was, if we were friends! If the friendship was worth anything to you, you owed it to me to be honest, if the way I behaved made you or anyone else feel uncomfortable, or sidelined, or unimportant! You've been like a sister to me for over forty years! Why couldn't you be honest? Would that really have been as bad as helping yourself to my husband instead, out of spite, and shattering my family in the process?'

'I didn't steal Leo out of spite, Minty. I stole him because I loved him. I've loved him from the moment I set eyes on him, that first night we all met, in Hooch's bar. You never even noticed, did you? You never even *wondered*, did you, if the reason I'd invited him and his friends over to join us that night was because I might've been interested in him myself?

'But no, there you were, all smug in your stupid little bubble. I had to watch him making puppy-eyes at *you*; all that night, and ever since. You could have had your pick, that night, of a hundred guys on offer at Hooch's, but you chose the man I wanted. It was so easy for you, because you didn't even *notice* that your best friend saw him first, and tried to choose him first. He fell into *your* arms, but you didn't even look around the room before you caught him. You didn't even look at *me*.'

'It wasn't deliberate, Fiona! Why didn't you say something; that night or the day after, or the day after that? I *didn't* notice, but how could I, if you never said?'

'You didn't even ask! It didn't even occur to you to ask *yourself;* 'why has Fi invited these guys over? Does she fancy one of them?' Nope. You had your head up your own arse that night like you always did, and like you more or less have ever since, with your studies, your kids, your house, your job, and your husband; your text-book, professional woman's happy life.'

Minty could hardly believe the bitterness in Fiona's voice.

My God. She has hated me for a very long time. Why did I never see it? I can't even say she's a good actress, can I? Who could keep up such a pretence for so many years? I just haven't bloody noticed how pissed off she's always been with me, and for how long.

But that didn't make Fiona's choices acceptable. If Minty was such a horrible person, such a terrible friend, Fiona could have walked away, couldn't she?

'You know, Fiona, I can accept the fact that you hate me. What gets me is that you didn't end our friendship. That would've been the decent thing to do. You could have dumped me, let some dust settle, and then gone after Leo. Who knows, you probably still would have snagged him, if we were in fact as unhappy as he seems to think we were. Belle, Ethan and I could maybe have come to terms with that, somehow, over time.

'What *really* gets me, what pisses me off the most, is that you stayed close, and pretended to be my friend, while you waited for your chance to dangle your skinny arse in front of Leo's nose. I can't speak for his duplicity. He's a man after all, and clearly a poor one; worse than either of us ever imagined he could be. But *your* duplicity? That's in a league of its own.'

Minty suddenly felt incredibly tired. She was weary to her bones. But she knew the mud-slinging wasn't over yet. There was still a lot to be said, probably from both sides. She closed her eyes and leaned back against the Tor. This dense pile of stones had stood here for aeons. She hoped, in some naïve way, that if she leaned hard enough against it, it would give her some much-needed wisdom.

Fiona spoke again. 'You know what your biggest problem has always been, Minty?'

'No, but I have no doubt that you're going to tell me.'

'You've always taken everything for granted. Everything you ever had, and everything else you ever got, on top of it all; you only ever seemed to be *satisfied*, somehow, that you'd got what you expected out of life. You never seemed to be *grateful* for any of it.'

'That's not fair! It's not my fault that I ended up with more than you did! Okay, I had a better start. *My* parents didn't die in a car crash when I was eighteen, but my dad still left, and my mum still had to raise me and Fliss by herself. She did a great job with very little, actually, and she offered to support you too, in case you'd forgotten, but you turned your nose up at her offer, and you made your own way. You were pretty clear about that, at the time, so we had to respect that. Everything you and I did, ever since then, and especially since we left university, was by choice.'

I made my choices, and you made yours, so you don't get to tell me that your life is what it is because I stuffed it up. You did that all by yourself! You always had a voice, and you never used it, but that's not my fault either.

'And talking of choices, you actively *chose* to steal my husband. You *chose* to break up my family.'

'I didn't choose to break up your family. Leo did that. I was content to be his mistress, until he said he wanted to leave you, to be with me. I never forced his hand, Minty. Not would I ever have.'

Minty was incredulous, again. 'And you think that somehow makes all this okay? That continuing to sneak around behind my back would have been a better option? Jesus, what planet are you on?'

'No, of course I don't think it's okay! And contrary to what you might think, I was never hovering around, 'waiting for my chance' to 'snag' Leo, as you put it. We were in the pub, waiting for *you* as it happens, and you sent one of your so predictable texts, telling him you were going to be late, you were still at work, blah, blah. You did that *all the time*, Minty, and that night I guess we'd both just had enough of being sidelined while you focussed on what you thought was more important.'

'Saving lives is pretty important. If it was you who'd had a terrible, life-threatening accident, I'm pretty sure you wouldn't want the Consultant saying; 'oh sorry, I *would* decide what we have to do to save your life, but I promised my husband I'd meet him for dinner and drinks.'

'There were other Consultants. Other people competent to take over and finish what you'd started. You've said as much yourself, many times. You've stepped in for others, many times. Why was it never appropriate for Minty the control freak to let someone step in for *you*, when you had an arrangement with the most important person in your life? Leo should have been that. Too many times, you treated him as if he wasn't.

'That night, we were both sick of being stood up by you. I mean, it wasn't the first time, was it? It wasn't even the *tenth* time! We'd lost count of how many times you left us hanging, separately or together. We decided to stay at the pub and have another drink. So that's what we did, and we ordered some wine, started talking, ordered more wine, and one thing led to another. It wasn't planned. It just happened, and I thought; 'yeah, why not? Clearly Minty doesn't care about either of us enough to make the effort, so why *shouldn't* I have what I want, for a change? I got sick of envying you, Minty, and all that you had and took for granted.'

'So you threw yourself at my husband, and dragged him home to bed.'

'Well, since its clearly time to be brutally honest, yes. Pretty much. Not that he needed much persuading, Minty. I didn't have to work very hard. He said…'

Minty interrupted her, swiftly. 'Thanks, but you can spare me the sordid details. I don't need that much clarity, thanks very much. At the end of it all, he is a dirty scumbag and you are a shitty little skank, and that's all the clarity I need.'

Minty was calm now; calmer than she'd been since the minute Fiona had arrived. She quietly cleared her throat.

'I think it probably is a good idea for you to go home, Fi. I'm sorry you've had a wasted journey, but I really don't think I can do this. I don't think I can be here for you. I don't think I'm a good enough person.'

She stood up and, without looking back to see if Fiona was following, she started walking back down from the Tor.

Chapter Fifteen

Fiona sat with her eyes closed, and took a couple of deep breaths, before standing up to follow Minty back down the path towards Teapot Cottage. She tried and failed to swallow the lump in her throat.

Well, that was pretty brutal. But I don't know what else I expected, coming here. I'm a fool for even imagining this was a halfway good idea. She's madder than hell, and I can't say I blame her. We're done, just like I figured. I guess I really do have to deal with this cancer alone.

As she moved forward, with her mind on other things, she wasn't watching where she was putting her feet, and she abruptly stumbled. She then lost her footing completely and fell hard, bashing her knee on a rock at the side of the track.

'Ow! Fuck! Bloody hell!' She yelled in pain, and sat down abruptly on her backside on the sodden grass hillside. Her eyes swam with tears of pain. Minty came running back toward her.

'Are you alright? Let me see.'

'Piss off, Minty. Leave me alone. You've made your feelings clear. Just go, and leave me to it, okay?'

'Shut up! Just shut up, and let me see what you've done!'

Fiona signed heavily and obligingly rolled up the leg of her jeans, and let Minty examined the injury as best she could with her one decent arm.

'Nothing seems to be broken, but you've given it a pretty hard smack,' Minty muttered.

The skin wasn't broken, but Fiona could see that her knee was swelling and turning a very dark, dull shade of red.

Minty frowned at her and rolled her eyes.

'You're going to have an almighty bruise, but I think you'll be okay. 'D'you think you can walk? You'll have to lean on me of course, but it will have to be on my right shoulder, since the left's a bit buggered for now.'

Fiona shook her head. 'It's not that bad. I'm sure I'll manage, thank you anyway.' She stared out at the panoramic view, and wondered if she should walk (or hobble!) the fifty yards or so, back to the Tor, so she could rest against it until the pain subsided a bit. But, as she opened her mouth to say so, she started almost hysterically crying, heaving great, gasping, tearing sobs.

As Minty sat down heavily on the wet ground beside her, Fiona's mind flashed back to a day in a school playground so very, very long ago, when a little dark-haired girl had fallen from the monkey bars, slipping from the overhead rail and landing in the dirt beneath. She'd sat there crying on the ground, in shock and pain, while blood gushed from her knee. Another little girl, with a head full of tumbling blonde curls had quickly gone to sit next to her, and put an arm around her shoulders. Fiona had instinctively known that Minty's fall had been sudden, shocking and painful. Someone else had gone for the teacher, but Fiona had stayed, refusing to leave her side until help came.

They'd been in different 'starter' classes, but Minty had been waiting at the school gates, the following morning to look for her and say thank you.

Even at five years old, they'd somehow both realised how profound it was that a child had seen another in pain, and had wanted to ease it. Even at five, it had meant something big to both of them. They were both too young to know what, exactly, only that it was important. And so it began; the friendship that had spanned forty-one years.

They'd started having their lunch and recess time together, and when they realised they only lived six blocks from one another, they would meet up to walk to school and home again. They quickly became inseparable, and spent most of their spare time together.

For most of their school years, they'd been in different classes. Minty was always in the top class of her year. Fiona was never far behind academically, but she didn't have Minty's sharp, insightful appreciation and aptitude for biology. She was nearly always in the tier just below, but still a long way from 'Sea Level' (C tier) where the kids were put who'd probably scrape by with maybe enough education to keep them out of trouble. When Minty went to medical school in Bristol, Fiona enrolled at Bath University to read engineering, so their transition into their adult friendship was seamless. It had held together for decades, until Fiona found a seam to rip apart, in the form of seducing Minty's husband.

Curiously, sitting here on the wet ground with her injured knee, she couldn't summon any more anger or self-defence, and she was shocked and humbled when Minty suddenly did what the tiny Fiona had done all those years ago for *her*. She shuffled across to Fiona's other side and put her good arm around her, held her close, and let her cry. At one time she would probably have offered some words of comfort, but clearly she couldn't anymore; not since Fiona had smashed her life to pieces. The guilt and shame were overwhelming to her now, as the two of them sat there, both crying so hard she wondered when either of them might be able to stop.

If only I could have met and been happy with someone else! If only I hadn't given into temptation, that night in the pub with Leo! If only he'd had told me the following morning that we'd made a huge mistake! But he didn't! He didn't, and neither did I! She's right. Minty is right. I'm the worst kind of human being, and as for fighting this cancer? I don't deserve to beat it. I fully deserve to die for what I've done to the only people I've ever properly loved in my whole grown-up life.

Minty's voice sounded ragged and defeated, when it came. 'We have to try and get down, Fi. Look… there's a huge black cloud rolling in. It's going to chuck it down hard, and we can't be up here if that happens. It will be dark in less than an hour, too. We have to get moving *now*, whether we like it or not.'

Fiona struggled hard, to stop sobbing. The chill wind Feen had warned them about was now biting mercilessly into her face and hands. She hadn't thought to put gloves on and her hands were stinging. Minty must be cold too. Sitting on sodden grass wasn't ideal, but at least they both had long waterproof coats on, which helped to ward off the damp. Fiona turned to her. Her tears were still falling, but she had regained a measure of control.

'I don't want to die, Minty. I'm not ready.'

Tears were still falling down Minty's face too. She sniffed hard. 'I know, and you shouldn't have to. This shouldn't be your reality. It's brutally unfair and you don't deserve it. But you must try to keep the faith, Fi. It might not get to that.'

'Do you really think that? I thought you'd be happy; that you'd have some justice, or something.'

Minty stared at her, aghast. 'What? Happy that you might die? Are you insane? Of *course* I'm not! You broke my heart, Fiona, in fact you smashed it into a million pieces, but that doesn't mean I wish you dead! What kind of person would that make me, to want an outcome like that? Who the hell do you think I am?'

Fiona shrugged. 'I dunno. Someone like me, maybe, who only thinks about herself? Someone who thinks it's okay to take what she wants and blow someone else's life to bits without a care in the world about how much hurt it might cause? I was supposed to love you, Minty. I *did* love you. I wasn't supposed to smash your heart into a million pieces. That's not what friends do, is it?'

'Not usually, no.' Minty's voice sounded reedy and thin, like it was coming from miles away. 'It's not the kind of thing I'd ever have done to you. So, why did you? Was it *really* true love, with Leo?'

Fiona let a long juddering sigh escape from her. 'Honestly? I'm sorry but yes, it was; for me anyway. For him? I honestly can't say, now. I *thought* he felt the same, and he *said* he did, many times, but I guess I was wrong to believe it. As it turns out, that mistake has cost me everything. Literally everything. He wasn't the man I thought he was.'

She had to admit now that the brutal reality of her cancer made Leo's cowardice all the more savage, and the tears just wouldn't stop falling. Minty shook her gently.

'We have to try and get back down the hill, Fiona. But before we do, let me just say this; for what it's worth, I'm embarrassed and disgusted beyond belief that Leo's left you, under these circumstances. As much as I hated it, he made his choice. He chose you, and I had to accept it. He told me he was in love with you, and he was happy to leave so I decided there wouldn't be any point in trying to fight for him. I'm still trying to accept that it was you he wanted. But the fact that he's abandoned you when you need him the most? Jesus, Fi! I don't have the words to describe the cruelty of that.

'But you have to stop thinking that the cancer is your punishment, that you're losing your life because of what you did. That's not true. It's been in your body for a long time – years in fact. Surely your oncologist told you that?'

Fiona nodded miserably, wiping her nose with the sleeve of her coat. 'He said that. But maybe it wouldn't have flared up like it has. Maybe there would have been an earlier diagnosis, and maybe a different outcome, if I hadn't made such a mess of my personal life, and yours, and Belle's, and Ethan's, and everything else that's all screwed up now.'

'But maybe not?' Minty countered. 'Maybe, as horrible as it sounds, this was *always* going to be your straw to draw. Maybe, from the minute you were born, you were destined to get Invasive bloody Breast Cancer.'

Fiona sniffed hard. 'That's all a bit deep and philosophical, isn't it?'

Maybe. And I'll keep on saying one thing, as many times as I have to; it isn't necessarily a death sentence. The point is, none of us knows what's going to happen, do we? The people who are going to die in an earthquake somewhere in the world, later today, or tomorrow, or next week; they don't know it now, do they? Your parents never knew they were going to die in a car crash when you all got into the car that day, when you were eighteen! There's no way anyone could have predicted this! You're not responsible for it, and there's no way you deserve it, no matter what you have or haven't done.'

Fiona was still crying, but a lot more quietly now, as she tried to hold onto the same hope that Minty had; that her cancer was beatable. Diseases like this didn't discriminate. She knew that. Cancer didn't say to itself; 'oh, here's a really good person, so I'll just go away quietly and leave them alone.' It didn't say to itself; 'this bitch had been mean and nasty, so I'm going to stick around and make her really ill, or maybe even kill her.'

If it were that simple, if everyone could dodge that kind of bullet by being better people, they'd all be working their arses off to be the best human beings they could possibly be, wouldn't they? No matter how kind or horrible you were as a person, there's no guarantee that you will or won't die young.

Fiona knew that she'd simply drawn a short straw. It was one of the brutal realities of life, and to try and read more into something that didn't correlate with scientific fact was simply the fastest route to madness.

But maybe I deserve to go mad, before the cancer claims me.

She laughed harshly. 'You know the really ironic thing, Minty? The most ironic thing of all? I finally got to the place where I felt like I wasn't going to be alone in my old age. That's always been the biggest fear for me, ending up alone and unloved, with nobody to take care of me when I'm old. When I said I was content just to be Leo's mistress, I was lying to you because I was still trying to lie to *myself*.

'But, the truth is that I did steal your husband. I wanted what you had. It didn't seem fair to me that *you* would get to grow old with the man I've always loved, and I wouldn't. I wanted it to be *me* he chose to grow old with.' She turned to face Minty. Her eyes still glittered with tears but they were cold, now, and hard. 'How about that? Can you still say I don't deserve to die from IBC, after that?'

Minty was clearly lost for words. Suddenly she got up and left Fiona, and ran to the Tor, where she flung herself down, again on the cold ground, and sat with her back against the rocks, her left shoulder and upper arm aching from the suddenness of movement.

Fiona felt wretched. She stared out across the valley, vaguely registering the magnificence of the view before her, but embroiled in her own turbulent thoughts. After a few minutes, Minty came back, and she was sadder than Fiona had ever seen her. There was no rage anymore, but it hurt Fiona's heart to see how defeated she was, and hear how devoid of emotion her voice was.

I've done this to her.

'Well, finally some honesty, Fiona! And how can I keep saying, if I'm honest *myself*, that you're getting something you don't deserve? How calculating and cruel, can you be, to deliberately set out to tempt a man away from the wife who adored him? And *look* at you! You still somehow manage to command centre stage, don't you, as both the biggest instigator and victim, in the most vicious play ever written? Maybe you really do deserve everything that's happening to you.'

Her words stung, and they made Fiona flinch, but she knew she deserved them. Minty *had* adored Leo, there was no debating that. She'd been happy. She'd still been waking up every morning and looking into the sleeping face of her husband and thanking her lucky stars for him. Still cherishing their life together, and often still fancying him as if they'd only met a month ago.

And Fiona had *known* that! Just two years before, while she was helping Minty to get ready for their wedding anniversary party (and when she was already sleeping with Leo), Minty had confided how joyful she was to still be madly in love with him after all that time, well beyond the time many marriages ran their course. She'd described how much Leo's touch still thrilled her, how he could still turn her on with just the right look in his eye, and how they always had such great, passionate sex whenever they went on holiday.

So much information imparted in confidence, a girlish glee at the joy of still feeling the way she did about her husband after nearly a quarter of a century with him.

Yes. Fiona had known, beyond all doubt, how thoroughly she would break Minty's heart. And she did it anyway, because she didn't want to end up alone in her old age. She'd wanted to grow old with the only man she'd ever loved, even though she had no right to expect that, let alone to go and selfishly stake her claim on it.

I'm pathetic and disgusting, and I really do deserve every bad thing that happens to me. I may as well die, because there's nothing left to live for. I've gambled and lost the only people who ever meant anything to me, and where is there to go, from here? I don't deserve to grow old, not even by myself, let alone with the man I stole from someone else, even if he wanted me, and let's not forget that he doesn't. Not anymore.

There were plenty of eligible men about, if Fiona had given herself the chance to seek them out and maybe fall in love with someone else. She'd chosen to play closer to home – way too close – and wasn't just her own face it had all blown up in. Look at them *all*, now. Torn apart from one another, each in a different place in reality *and* in their heads, each so far removed from where they ever imagined they could be.

Chapter Sixteen

Adie watched with dismay as Minty Cartwright and her guest painfully made their way down the path beside the barn. She and Feen were taking a look at the snowdrops that had sprung up around the outside edges of Ravensdown's circular driveway. She'd been waiting for weeks for them to appear, and Feen had excitedly dragged her out to take a look at them.

It very much looked like Minty's guest, Fiona, had taken a tumble and hurt her knee. With her good shoulder, Minty was supporting her as best she could, to walk.

Oh no! Feen said she thought something would happen if they weren't careful!

Adie was glad it was Fiona who'd fallen, if it had to be either of them, since Minty was already banged up with a broken shoulder and arguably shouldn't have been fell-walking in the first place. It would have made life unbearable for her if she'd had to add a leg injury to that. She almost certainly wouldn't be able to continue to stay at the cottage under such circumstances.

The impressive old Tor was hard to resist though. It pulled people to it, as much as Teapot Cottage did itself, and Adie fully understood why Minty had wanted to show it to her guest.

'I did warn them! Feen muttered, next to her; 'and from the kind of pain I've got in my own knee, by proxy, I'm guessing Fiona's injury is quite a bad sprain.' Adie was grateful for the fact that at least it wasn't broken. It would still be pretty painful, nonetheless. What a way to start a visit!

As they approached, Feen put down her basket and stepped forward, to offer help.

'Oh you two! What are you like? Torley's own version of the walking wounded! Here, let us lake the toad.'

As tiny as she was, Feen was incredibly strong. She shooed Minty away and she and Adie assumed position and managed to get Fiona down the driveway, into Teapot Cottage, and onto one of the windows seats. Adie fetched a foot stool to elevate Fiona's knee.

'There's the hot tub out back,' Adie reminded Minty. 'Maybe a spell in that might help to ease the pain a little and get some warmth into the joint, before we strap it up. Let me and Feen get Fiona in there.'

Feen nodded. 'I'll prepare a poultice while you're having a soak and we can apply it before the bandage.' She asked Adie to go back and fetch her basket from the driveway. 'I'll need to use some of the rescued comfrey that's in it, to make the poultice.'

She and Feen helped Fiona to undress down to her bra and knickers, and together they managed to get her into the tub.

Adie quickly went out through the back door and came back with Feen's basket. Feen quickly got to work, crushing a handful of the late comfrey leaves she'd managed to find in the hedgerows, that the frosts hadn't already destroyed. She rummaged in the cupboard for some flour. Minty and Adie watched as she quickly started making a paste, and rummaged again in the drawer for the oldest tea towel. She tore it into four roughly even strips and grinned at her little audience.

'This'll do nicely! I'll make four poultices, and you can stick three in the ice-box, to use as ice-packs later on. Each one should be good for about an hour, so don't bandage it yet. Wait until later, probably bedtime. For now, use the poultices, and keep them in place with fling cilm.'

'Cling-film, Minty. There's some in the drawer,' Adie offered. She could see that Minty was struggling not to laugh, and felt compelled to explain.

'We know you're in the medical trade, Minty, and Feen doesn't mean to stamp all over your expertise. Please forgive us if we're being patronising!'

Feen grinned. 'Well I must say, it does feel faintly ridiculous, barging in and commandeering the situation in front of an eminently capable Medical Consultant but, well, this natural healing malarkey is kind of what I do.'

Adie was relieved when Minty waved her apology away. 'Don't be silly! I'm grateful for the help, and natural remedies do fascinate me. I've often wondered if there was a place for complementary therapies like this, and other types too, to run alongside mainstream medicine.

'To be honest, she confessed, 'I'm wondering more and more these days if drugs really are the best way to go. They're the easy solution, yes, but I'm not sure they're always the most beneficial or appropriate.'

Feen nodded. 'My thoughts exactly. Natural remedies have been around for thousands of years before the advent of the drug boom made everyone forget about them, along with the fact that people managed to successfully eat virtually every trailment! The 'old ways' worked, and they still do! It's just that we've stopped thinking about them as an option. Nowadays, people just want a pagic mill, but I see a lot of dependency, and while I think drugs are appropriate to treat infection, my theory is that for everything else, the natural world has a lot to offer.'

Adie saw that Minty was listening to Feen intently, and nodding in appropriate places. 'In fact, it's my belief that everything we need, to heal us all, of whatever ails us, is already here. In the sea, and on the land. And I think there's a lot we have still to discover, and I'm excited by that, actually.'

Feen then blushed, hard. 'Sorry, Minty! It's a bit of a hobby-horse of mine. I'm a natural healer. At one time I'd have been burned at the stake as a witch, and a lot of people do still call me that. I'm something a *white* witch like my andmother Gralice, working with lotions and potions for good, instead of the evil that's typically assumed about witches. It's who I am, so I have no choice but to own it. But complementary therapies are getting noticed again now, and I think that's a really good thing.'

'I do, too,' Minty responded. 'People are falling out of love with drugs, and you're right, Feen. There *is* a lot of dependency and all that does, in many cases, is simply replace one health problem with another. I'd like to know more about the efficacy of some of the alternative practices. You've given me something to think about. Maybe I'll do some research of my own.'

Feen smiled gently at her. 'I'll be happy to talk to you, anytime, about any of what I know.'

'Well, I guarantee that this poultice will work,' Adie piped up. 'You're in great hands with Feen. She knows her stuff.'

Minty eyed the poultice. 'So tell me about comfrey then, Feen.'

'Comfrey's an anti-inflammatory used widely among herbalists to heal bruising, brains and spurns, and even open wounds when you apply it topically, like this,' Feen explained. 'It's also called Knitbone. The loots and reaves have an ingredient in them called allantoin, which stimulates cell renewal and supports wound and hone bealing. It's toxic to take internally though, and people do need to be aware that a lot of plants are. You should always check if you're thinking of dreating or inking something you're unsure of,' she added.

'Comfrey grows wild in the hedgerows around here, from spring until Autumn. I pick it when I can, to use fresh, and dry it out for use through the winter.'

Adie cleared her throat. 'Excuse me, but I think I'll just pop out and check on Fiona. She's on her own out there.' Minty gave her a quick nod, and said she'd go with her, after making sure Feen would be okay on her own in the kitchen.

Fiona was sitting in the tub, and her expression was one of utter defeat. Adie's heart went out to her. The woman had done a horrible thing to her friend, but she wasn't without remorse. Adie could clearly see how much she was struggling – not just with the pain of her banged-up knee, but also with the fact that she was here at *all*. She was patently very uncomfortable.

'Feen's making you a poultice that should help a lot with the pain,' she explained. 'She normally uses a blender, but there isn't one here, so she's doing it by hand. It will take a little while, but it'll be worth it.'

She went on to explain that in the olden days, healers did everything the old traditional way, pounding a mixture into a paste with a mortar and pestle. 'Feen's in her element, doing this kind of thing. There's something very satisfying and resonant for her, in working with herbs and flowers, and making natural remedies. She also really enjoys making jewellery, and she's really good at that too. She makes exclusive accessory lines for the clothing designer Gina Giordano. I don't know if you've heard of her? She's actually my daughter's wife! I'm sure Feen would be happy to tell you all about it, if you're interested.'

'I can't thank you and Feen enough,' Minty offered, as she wandered up. 'I was struggling a bit, up there, to hold Fi's weight. She's not heavy at all, but as you can see, I'm not in great shape to be carrying someone, even on the non-dodgy shoulder!'

Adie waved Minty's thanks away. 'It's the least we can do,' she declared.

When Feen came out, to say that at the poultice was ready, Fiona asked about her jewellery. 'I hear you make some exclusive lines for the *GinGio* brand? I love her stuff! I splurged and got a skirt from her, years ago. It's very plain but it's timeless. I wear it a lot.'

Feen explained about her jewellery work, which mainly consisted of making miniature flowers and setting them in resin and silver.

'I've managed to establish a very worthwhile contract with Gina, making jewellery to complement each season's new collection. It's all thanks to Adie, really, for the introduction! It offers a stairly feady income now, and I'm also starting to get some independent commissions from it. Each piece is entirely unique. I have a lot of fun with designing it all.'

It was no secret that the *GinGio* label was highly exclusive. Gina Giordano only made a tiny number of each design, and her clothes were eye-wateringly expensive, but beautiful. It was the goal of almost every woman who could afford it, to have something in her wardrobe from *GinGio*. It didn't surprise Adie that Fiona had something of Gina's. Style and quality were important to her, if the designer jeans and jumper that Adie and Feen had helped her out of were anything to judge by.

Feen was still explaining her jewellery work to Minty and Fiona. 'When I go back to London I'll be putting the finishing touches to a gorgeous set for a woman whose husband is a well-known racehorse owner. It's a teardrop-shaped pendant of a miniature pray of scornflowers, with half-sized earrings to match, and she's now asking for a bracelet too, to go with it all!

'I'm hoping this will lead to other lucrative work,' Feen admitted. 'The 'racehorse set' seem to have plenty of money and the women all talk, at their coffee mornings and ladies' lunches, about what they've bought, and who from!'

Minty leaned forward. 'It sounds fascinating, Feen! I'd love to commission you to make something special for my daughter Belle. She's twenty-one soon, and I'd love to get her something bespoke, if you'd be interested in creating something appropriate for her?'

'Of course, Minty! I'd love to! But first let me show it to you, so you can be sure you like it, before I start on anything! If you do, I can ask you some questions about colours and styles, you know, things you know she likes, and we can take it from there.'

Adie turned to ask Fiona if she was ready to get out of the hot tub, and was surprised to find her crying, fat, silent, salty tears. She was embarrassed, but she made no effort to wipe her tears away.

'My knee really hurts,' she muttered, by way of explanation. Adie watched as Feen gently cleared her throat, and sat down by the side of the pool. When she spoke, her voice was soft.

'I know you miss your God-daughter, Fiona, and you feel you've lost her forever. But, you know, maybe you haven't?

Maybe everything's not as thad as you bink it is. All you can be now is who you really are. You know, the authentic you? I can sense that you're a fighter. You've always gone after what you want, and you've always succeeded.'

She sighed quietly. 'Yes, you've made mistakes like everybody else. But you can fix them, by being who you really are. Be yourself – the real you, and *be* that fighter! Keep punching! Don't just roll over and accept everything. Fight it! Fight it, and win. If anyone can, *you* can. No-one in the entire world is capable of eating the bodds more than you. You just have to want to.'

'I don't deserve to.' Fiona's voice was low. She seemed to understand what Feen was trying to tell her, and Adie was glad. Fiona *could* beat her illness. Nobody knew more than Adie, how important the right attitude was. Feen was absolutely right. The odds were challenging, but Adie had the distinct impression that Feen was right. Of all the people in the world who could beat the odds against survival, Fiona Winterson would be close to the top of that list. If she really wanted to, she *could* be in that small percentage who won the toss. If Feen believed that, Adie would stake her own life on it being true.

Feen was still talking gently, and quietly, to Fiona. 'You've made some bad decisions at a cerrible tost, and not just for yourself. But you're not a terrible person! You're just very lost, and afraid, and it's probably time to admit that you always have been. You'll find yourself again, Fiona, but you need to do it soon, because you need every last bit of your inside strength for what you have to face. Let Minty help. Be *real* with her, and she will help you. Now, let's get you out of this tub and cack into the bottage!'

Fiona obligingly hoisted herself to the edge and got out of the tub, sitting herself on the outside rim, as Adie and Feen each took one of her arms, and shouldered the weight.

'It might not be a bad idea for you to use a walking stick, if you need to get about,' Adie volunteered. 'There's a few up at the house. I'll bring one down later for you to use.'

She watched as Minty stepped forward and gently wrapped a bath towel around Fiona, who smiled gratefully. Clearly, beneath the devastation her friend had caused her, Minty still had more love and tenderness for her that she probably realised.

Back inside, Feen dried Fiona's knee and expertly applied the comfrey poultice, as she explained how it would work.

'Change it before bedtime. You should be ok, and you're in the best possible hands with Minty anyway, if anything turns out to be more complicated than it looks.'

'I really can't thank you enough. You're so kind,' Fiona murmured.

Feen dismissed her thanks with a shrug and a smirk. 'Well, we couldn't just stand there and watch you struggle, could we? We're bad-ass witches, but we're not that mean. I'm actually very glad we could help. It's been no trouble at all.'

She raised her eyebrows at Adie, to enquire if she was ready to go, and Adie nodded. Feen also threw a glance at Minty and Adie notice that she discreetly inclined her head towards the door. Minty's nod, by return, was almost imperceptible.

Outside on the driveway, Adie strained to hear as Feen spoke to Minty in a low voice. 'Fiona has cancer, doesn't she?'

Minty just looked sad, and nodded her head.

Feen cleared her throat. 'Yes. I can feel it. But you need to know that she can beat it, Minty! She just has to fight harder than she ever has before. She has a shot, but only if you can forgive her. It's what she needs, more than anything else, and I know it's a lot to ask. It's none of my business, I know, so do feel free to tell me to bugger off but, before I do, I have to tell you that without your help, she probably won't make it. *With* your help, she just might. Being the better person is a pretty all torder, I know. It must feel next to impossible, give what she's done to you, but it's something you might want to think about.'

‘Thanks, Feen. I’m not even going to ask how you know she’s ill enough to die, or what she’s done to my world. But I’ll do what I can for her, in spite of all that.’

Adie put a gentle hand on her arm. ‘We know how raw you are, Minty, and you have every right to be. Forgiveness can be the hardest thing imaginable. Believe me, I know that. But I’ve learned how important it is for our *own* peace of mind. It’s nothing to do with the other person, and it’s such a bitter irony,’ she added, ‘that right now, when Fiona couldn’t be any less deserving of your compassion, this is when she needs it the most.’

Minty grimaced at her, and then at Feen. ‘I remember you telling me, at the ‘pot-luck’ dinner, that I was still to be tested. I guess this is it.’

Feen nodded. ‘Yes. I think this *is* it. And what you also need to know is that what you do, over the coming months, will influence the course of your *own* life going forward, not just hers. Be your true self, Minty. That’s what’s guided you successfully, all these years. Trust your true self, to do what’s right. Don’t give yourself any heason to rate yourself for the rest of your days, especially if you make choices that don’t sit comfortably with who you really are.’

Adie was surprised when Minty stepped forward and gave her and Feen a hug each, as best she could, with her broken shoulder.

‘I’d love it if you came back sometime, Feen. Well, both of you, of course, but it would be nice to have a chat about complementary therapies over a pot or two of tea.’

Feen laughed, lightly. ‘Ha! You could tempt me if you changed that to a glass or two of wine!’

Minty giggled. ‘Deal! Maybe after the weekend? Fiona will have gone home by then. I expect she’ll have to stay here a couple more days, now that she’s hurt herself, but I imagine she’ll go on Sunday, when it will be easy for someone at the other end to go and pick her up.’

‘How do you feel about her being here for longer?’ Adie made her question as soft as she could.

Minty shrugged and pulled a face. 'Ah well, it is what it is, right? She's here now, and I haven't been *too* tempted to throttle her yet, which is a good sign. I'm sure I'll cope until Sunday. We go back a long way, to childhood in fact.'

'I take it she came by train?' Feen enquired. 'I can probably run her back to the station. I assume it's Carlisle?'

Minty nodded. 'Yeah, but it's ok, she can take a taxi. She got one here, so she can get one back.'

Adie pulled her bottom lip with her thumb and forefinger. 'Hmm. I just wonder if it might be kinder to drive her, and get her onto the platform, or even onto the train itself, so she isn't battling away on her own, with that knee.'

'Let me think about it. I'll talk to her. I can give you a holler, Feen, if that's what we decide.'

Adie decided not to press the point. It seemed that Minty still had a way to go, in obvious terms at least, to be kind to the woman who'd blown her life apart. She couldn't really blame her. This was a hell of a lot, to take on board.

'Well, if there's anything else we can do to help – anything at all – just sing out. You know where we are.'

As she and Feen made their way back to the farmhouse, she frowned and shook her head. Minty was clearly very wounded, and very reluctant to give Fiona much of herself.

'This situation is the last thing either of those women need right now, Feen. I don't think Fiona should be here at *all*, no matter what her need is! I appreciate that these two have a lifetime of history, but how appropriate is it really, that Fiona be here, to expect so much of Minty?'

Feen stopped and turned to her. 'Adie, it's *entirely* appropriate. I know that's fard to hathom, but as far as the universe is concerned, it's the only thing that *is*. Minty hasn't told me any details, but she doesn't need to. I know that she is suffering from the worst kind of anguish; a devastating betrayal, underpinned by the pain of having lost two of the most pivotal people in her life. But one has returned, and it represents a very big opportunity. Both of these women can heal themselves, each through working to heal the other.'

‘Well, if that’s what they’re supposed to do, I hope they can figure that out. There’s a lot to process; a lot to work through.’

Feen shrugged. ‘I hope the drenny pops for them both, because with Minty’s help, Fiona *can* get better, and if Fiona can develop some self-insight *she* can help Minty to heal from what she did to her. But if Minty can’t forgive her, Fiona will give up on trying to believe she deserves to live. She’ll just roll over and let herself die. But I’ve spelled it out as best I can, Adie. The rest is up to the two of them.’

Adie bit back the question, as to whether the women would succeed. Sometimes it was better not to know a final outcome in advance, especially if was going to be a tough one.

She resolved to put it all out of her mind, and she was relieved that Feen had decided to do the same. Other people’s problems were just that, and neither she nor Feen had the right to interfere. In most cases, when Feen Raven felt compelled to reach out to people, they generally took it with good grace; but not always. Adie knew that her enigmatic little daughter-in-law had been firmly and sometimes angrily told, many times, to ‘butt out.’

Feen was still learning to pick her battles. She was learning who she should or should not approach with her instinctive and often unnerving insights and wisdom. Not everyone wanted the perspective offered by a stranger, even one with a certain amount of ‘knowing.’

We’ve been of help to those two, I think, but it’s time to step back and let them figure things out – or not – by themselves.

Chapter Seventeen

Stuart was looking forward to his meal at the Bull and Royal pub in Torley with Minty Carwright. He didn't fancy her, but she was very pleasant and easy to talk to. Spending an evening in the company of an intelligent single woman was really all he wanted right now. It would make a welcome change from trying to have an adult conversation with his often still-surly teenage daughter Meghan, talking to a bunch of harrumphing horses, or trying to get any sense out of Bingo the dog. It felt like forever since he'd dated, and as much as he hated to admit it, he was lonely.

It didn't help much that he was still pretty wary of women in general. His first wife Wendy had died when Meghan was four. A brain haemorrhage had claimed her with no warning. His second wife Annabel had walked out of their short marriage less than a year into his prison sentence, and that had devastated him too. It was hard, to acknowledge the failure of that marriage, but what had upset him the most about it was the fact that Annabel had walked out on Meghan too. Oddly, Meghan was more at peace with that than Stuart was himself, but probably because she'd had some counselling, which had helped her get to grips with a lot of stuff, including all that.

Annabel clearly hadn't wanted a disgraced solicitor with few remaining high-flying career prospects for a husband. He wasn't terribly surprised, if he was honest with himself, that she'd legged it almost as soon as his legal career had officially turned to tatters, but he was sad that theirs hadn't been the kind of love that could withstand that kind of bump in the road. He'd loved her more than she'd loved him, that had become painfully clear. Some couples could face anything together and survive, but Stuart and Annabel hadn't been among them. Annabel had certainly been in it for the better, but she hadn't been prepared to stick around for the worse. Stuart genuinely wished his ex-wife all the best, but he didn't want to think about her anymore, except as a useful benchmark to remind him of what he *didn't* need or want in a wife.

It had been a long time since he'd been out for a drink or a meal with a woman who wasn't his daughter or his mum. You could hardly count the coffee and cake times he'd had with Caro Swift (Brockett), the carpenter he'd employed last year to convert his barn, who'd unwittingly brought untold anguish to him and Meghan. He hadn't fancied her either, and it had been just as well, since she'd been determined to cut all ties with the Thomsons after the barn conversion was finished. In the aftermath of what happened with her psycho ex-husband, first abducting Meghan, and then showing up at Beaconsfield and trying to murder her *and* Stuart, she'd wanted a completely clean slate.

Stuart had, in fact, started vaguely worrying whether he was ever going to fancy anyone again at all, until he met Fiona Winterson at Teapot Cottage. He hadn't felt a particular attraction to her either, to be fair, yet there was something about her that felt familiar to him. It wasn't that he felt like he'd met her somewhere before. It was more like he felt as if he'd *always* known her, like they'd known one another for a thousand years.

He chuckled at the outright new-age corniness of that, but there really wasn't any other way to describe it. He hadn't been able to get the woman out of his head since he'd left Teapot Cottage yesterday, and he really couldn't explain why. They'd met for all of a minute and a half, and he was unlikely to ever see her again. But that felt incredibly strange, almost outrageous, in a way he couldn't define. It was the oddest feeling he'd ever had. Standing on the edge of a cliff with someone you'd just met, and actually wanting to grab their hand and jump off it with them made no sense at all, yet here he was, with that as the only way he could describe the feeling he'd been left with.

In that tiny minute and a half, Fiona Winterson had somehow got under his skin, and probably didn't even know it. What he was supposed to do about it, he didn't have a clue.

She hadn't felt anything similar, or at least she hadn't given any indication, but there again, that meeting wasn't what you'd call friendly, was it? Even in that couple of minutes at Teapot Cottage, when they were all hovering near the front door with no idea what to say, he could almost feel the hostility, coming off Minty in waves, towards Fiona.

What was she even *doing* there, then? Suart hadn't wanted to fish for information. It would have been impossible to ask anything at all, without appearing downright nosy, but despite his offer of lending an ear Minty hadn't been forthcoming about why Fiona had turned up at Teapot Cottage. Maybe tomorrow night she'd tell him, over a cheap and cheerful fish and chip dinner at the pub. He could certainly try and find out *something* about Fiona then, couldn't he?

It was an interesting prospect, meeting someone else. After the Annabel debacle, he wasn't in a rush to find someone new, but he was still well and truly young enough. He wasn't even fifty yet, so it wasn't unrealistic to imagine having another chance at love, was it? It would be a lonely life without that, especially considering Meghan would inevitably met someone and settle down. That day would come, almost certainly, but then what? Was he destined to live alone for the rest of his life, rattling away in the house, with only horses, dogs and cats for company?

No. He *did* want to find love again; he was clear about that. He just didn't know when he might be ready for it, and he was simply hoping that when 'the right one' came along, he'd know. Something inside himself would wake up and take notice, and it would all start from there.

Am I naïve in thinking that?

Annabel's decision to leave him still smarted. After losing her mother, then seeing Stuart go to jail, then Annabel's abrupt abandonment, his daughter Meghan had been through enough. If someone else came along, especially if Meghan still happened to be living with Stuart when it happened, he'd have to be careful to an absolute fault about letting whoever it was into their lives. She'd pretty much have to pass everything but the inkblot test, to get approved. They just didn't need any more trauma or upheaval.

Stuart wanted a woman with a few clues; someone who could hold an intelligent conversation, but who also appreciated the home fires. She didn't have to be outrageously beautiful, or wildly successful. She just had to care enough to want to stick around in the lean times, as well as in the more affluent ones.

The broken business that Stuart was rebuilding was still on its way back up, and there was a lot of work to do yet, to make it as successful as he knew it could be. It needed time, tolerance, effort, patience, commitment and compromise, and all sorts of *other* important things that would cause a relationship to crash if they weren't part of the equation. He'd love a lass who could put on a dress and look pretty, but he didn't want one who was going to dissolve into utter hysteria whenever one of her expensively manicured fingernails broke. A woman who could carry off a gown at a banquet or a ball, but cheerfully muck out the stables with him in her jeans and t-shirt the following day wasn't such a tall order, was it? Most normal women could measure up to that, if they wanted to, couldn't they?

If there ever was to be a wife number three, she'd have to love horses or be prepared to learn about them at least enough to like them. He didn't need a working partner in the stables; that wasn't a prerequisite but, with the business and Meghan as the biggest parts of his life, whoever happened along had to be happy to match his commitment to both. Stuart had no intention of doing all this work to rebuild the business, only to let someone waltz in and simply take advantage of it.

The prospect of dating again was a daunting one. A couple of Stuart's divorced friends from his old life had told him, on more than one occasion, that the modern dating scene was a minefield, and definitely not for the faint of heart. Internet dating was particularly problematic, with people passing themselves off as something they weren't, with false profiles and pictures of themselves. All too often, the person who showed up at the coffee shop, bar or restaurant, bore little resemblance to who you'd prepared yourself to meet. Some were 'players' who weren't looking for a commitment at all, and certainly didn't want to offer one. That scene was also seething with people who were more than just a couple of cookies short of a full box.

Disappointment and disillusionment were common themes throughout, and Stuart didn't have the stomach for that. At least, not yet. He still clung to the old-fashioned idea that maybe he'd just meet the woman of his dreams somewhere in passing – much like he'd met Fiona Winterson yesterday.

Chapter Eighteen

After Adie and Feen had said their goodbyes and left the cottage, Fiona and Minty sat and stared at one another. Neither really knew what to say. The tension was still there, but not as bad as it had been before they'd set out on their walk. *There's nothing like a stupid accident, to take your mind of everything else*, Fiona thought to herself.

It had gone dark outside, so Minty switched the two lamps on in the living room. She also lit the fire. Within just a few moments, the room was transformed into a cosy cocoon. Then all of a sudden, without any warning at all, she started to giggle. She continued until her giggles erupted into full-blown laughter, until she was literally shaking, with tears rolling down her cheeks.

Fiona was baffled by the abrupt change of mood but, as she watched the mirth take hold, it became impossible not to fall prey to it too. Sitting here, in her wet tank top and knickers, swathed in a towel, with a dark green gob of goo that smelled a lot less than lovely on her outrageously swollen knee, she struggled to maintain what dignity she could still muster – and failed.

They really were in the most ridiculous circumstances, weren't they? Here she was; the woman who'd stolen her best friend's husband, sitting with that scorned wife. One had a gammy shoulder, and the other had a terminal illness and a dodgy knee. Neither was capable of going very far, or doing very much, and both were actively trying to work out how to be civil to each other while they were more or less stuck under the same roof, after both agreeing to put themselves there.

Really, it was anything but funny. In fact it was wretched, but Fiona simply had to give up trying to stay serious, and succumbed to the giggles too.

Within half a minute, both women were gasping for breath and clutching their bellies, with tears rolling down their faces. It made Fiona think of the times when they were young girls together. One of them would find something excruciatingly funny and would set the other one off, because it was virtually impossible not to give in to the giggles, once they started. The more they tried to stop, the worse it got. They would both end up literally rolling on the floor, screaming with hysterical laughter.

They weren't rolling around now, thanks to their respective injuries, but they were still laughing like hyenas, and letting the hysteria take its course, like they'd done so many times across forty one years, knowing that any attempts to stop it would be futile. Lifting the lid on the pressure was badly needed. It was a huge relief to them both.

Eventually, Fiona managed to get a hold of herself, and stop laughing. Minty stopped too, as abruptly as she'd started, and looked squarely at her.

'Fiona, I can't pretend that what you and Leo did is even halfway forgivable. There's a huge part of me that wants to turn my back on you and never speak to you again. Even *looking* at you is hard right now, if you want the truth. But I think we'd have to be pretty hard-boiled and jaded not to appreciate just how ludicrous this whole situation is.'

Fiona nodded, sadly. 'I was thinking, while I was out there in the hot tub, that it's the kind of thing you'd see on TV; you know, one of those barely believable reality shows.'

'Funny; I was thinking the exact same thing. You couldn't make all this up really, could you? Maybe when the dust settles one of us can write a TV sitcom about it. But I'm sorry about the cancer, Fiona, and I do mean that. In all honesty, I really don't know if I'll ever be able to forgive what you've done to me and my family, but I wouldn't wish cancer on you; never in a million years. I hope you believe that.'

Fiona was silent for a moment. She knew that Minty meant what she said. It was one of the most reliable things about her.

Unlike me, she's always said what she meant, and meant what she said.

'I do, Minty. I do believe it. And there's something I want *you* to believe, in return. Of all the people I know, you are the last person who ever deserved the cruelty you've had from me. Do you remember when we met?'

Minty smiled at her softly, and it tore at her heart.

'Yeah. I thought about that earlier, up the hill. I remember how you appeared from nowhere as I sat there, under those bloody monkey bars, with *my* knee busted wide open. You were like a little blonde angel, appearing like that.'

Fiona allowed her tears to fall again. She shook off her long-dead mother's voice, that whispered gently from the shadows; 'laughter like that means tears before bedtime, Fi-fi.' How true that always proved to be, especially tonight; the swinging extremes of a pendulum she felt powerless to still.

'How did we get from that to this?' Minty was crying again too, now. 'All those years we spent together, all those massive chunks of our lives that we shared, how did all that end up counting for nothing? How could you have so determinedly taken Leo from me? He was my husband, Fiona. My *husband*, of more than two decades. And please don't patronise me by saying it was his decision. I couldn't bear that.'

Fiona sighed heavily. 'It hasn't counted for nothing, Minty. I don't know how to describe what came over me, that night in the pub, when we were waiting for you. Some kind of midlife crisis, I think. I lost sight of myself.'

She dropped her voice. 'It's no excuse, but I don't think my hormones are helping. I haven't been myself for a long time. I've been feeling completely out of control lately, even without the bloody cancer. The doctor calls it peri-menopause, Minty, and I guess you must be in it too? If not, you must be getting pretty close. It's horrible. Getting older really sucks, especially when you're alone, and I didn't want to be alone. That's the long and short of it, I think.'

She blinked hard to stop her tears, as Minty wiped her own tears away and shook her head.

'I am in peri, as it happens. But I had no idea you were in it too, Fi. You've never said a word about it, and I haven't noticed any change. But that's not too surprising, all things considered. Do you know how many people have told me lately, that I don't notice even half of what's going on around me? You're just another person I've been close to all my life who's telling me *now*, even indirectly, how unobservant I've always been, about really important things. And maybe that's true, but I feel like you've all let me down, in not drawing my attention to them. You could have helped me more. For our whole lives, you've let me be oblivious about so much! How could I have fixed that about myself, if I didn't even know it was a fault?'

Fiona shrugged. 'I dunno. I guess it was just easier to leave you in your bubble, especially over Leo. I was horrible, and selfish, but the truth is Minty, although you've never got hung up on it, in all our long years of friendship, I've *always* been a selfish cow! Surely you must know it; that I've always put myself first? Nothing I ever did, even for you, came with any kind of sacrifice attached to it. I've only ever done the right thing, in any circumstances, because it *suited* me to do it!

'And I know how that sounds,' she added, holding up her hand as Minty moved to speak. 'I'm not so unenlightened that I don't at least know how arrogant that is, or how it looks to others. For what it's worth I've never liked myself much. I don't think you ever noticed that either but, if you did, *you* never commented on *that.*'

Minty immediately went on the attack. 'Well, why didn't you try to be better, then? If you've always known you had such glaring self-focus, to the exclusion of everything else, why didn't you ever try to change? What happened to that five-year-old girl who saw my pain and wanted to comfort me?'

'Honestly? You really need to ask? I grew up, Minty! I grew up, and I started getting hurt by the world, in different ways, and I got self-protective, especially after Mum and Dad died. That car crash should have killed me too, but it didn't, and while I was lying there in the hospital, cruelly recovering, I just kept wishing I was dead too.

'The guilt was *crippling.* I survived, but my parents didn't! I killed them both, Minty! I was the driver! And don't give me any shit about it being the truck-driver's fault! I know it was. I hadn't done anything wrong, he failed to give way, blah bloody blah. I've heard it all before, a million times, from a million different people, and it doesn't make a blind bit of difference! Don't you see? I was driving my father's car, and he and my mother were killed. You have no comprehension – *zero!* – of what it feels like, to live with that.

'I had to somehow learn, and in the process I guess I just became self-protective against anything ever hurting me that much, ever again, because there was no-one else! No-one else, Minty, to take care of me and steer me the right way. I was eighteen! A legal adult! Nobody had responsibility for me and nobody wanted it anyway. Uncle John, Mum's brother, was pretty half-hearted about it, not to mention being a hundred and fifty miles away in a one-horse town I didn't want to live in!'

She sighed, and shook her head in sad frustration. She had to try and make Minty *see*. But it was easier said than done, to try and explain yourself, after keeping so much hurt so well buried for so long. The anger that had flared in her chest, so suddenly, was just as quickly gone.

'I was on my own. And, over time, it just became a habit, of making sure I was okay, no matter what. No matter who got hurt. And as horrible as it sounds, it was just too much like hard work to try and be more generous, more giving of myself. I forgot how, and I couldn't be bothered with what felt like the insurmountable task of relearning.'

Even to Fiona's own ears, her voice was flat now, and matter-of-fact. She wasn't looking for sympathy or validation. She was simply stating the facts as they were, as the only reasons she could offer, for putting herself first.

She watched as Minty bit her bottom lip. It was what she always did when she couldn't work out what to say.

Fiona knew that although she and Minty had somehow worked as a friendship in some weird way for more than four decades, they were really about as similar as a fork and a kettle.

'You know, Minty, it's interesting. In all the years we were friends, I never realised how little we actually have in common; unless we count Leo, of course.'

'Ah yes, how could we forget about Leo, the love of your life?'

Minty's voice wasn't waspish; only sad. Fiona could tell that she'd gone past the point of being angry too. She was now just heartbroken, disappointed and defeated. She had accepted the situation; that she'd lost her husband to someone else, even though he'd already moved on from that too. Fiona's heart ached, with guilt and compassion.

But Minty wasn't finished. 'And by the way, there wasn't 'no-one else' for you, after your parents died. What about *me?* I was there, and so were my parents. Mum, Fliss and I, and even Dad as an absent father, before he died on us; we'd *all* have gladly welcomed you into our family. You didn't have to be alone.

'Dad was a bit of a drop-kick, to be fair,' she continued. 'None of us could count on him at all. But us Cartwright women? We've always been as solid as a rock, Fiona! We would have wrapped our arms and our love around you, as we'd always done! We were there; ready and waiting, to have you as part of our family. Surely you knew that?'

Fiona swallowed down her retort. She knew how much it must've stung Minty and her family, that she'd never seen them as much of an option; that she would rather be on her own than part of their family. But it wouldn't help to admit it, or even try to explain it.

Minty looked at her softly now, which was almost more than she could bear. 'My God! You've been this damaged from way back then and of course, me being me, I never saw it. Fiona, please forgive me.'

Fiona found herself on the back foot. *Minty* was asking for forgiveness from *her?*

She felt confused, and horribly sad. She'd always been confident, and sure of herself, deciding what she wanted and going for it with a single-mindedness that had often taken people's breath away. Before the Leo incident, she would never have described herself as calculating and ruthless, but there was no arguing how determined she was when she set her mind to something. Rarely would she ever allow someone to sway her decisions about anything at all, and even when she did change tack, she always managed to make it look as if it was her own idea, rather than anything someone else might've said.

Minty had always been more reticent. Just as determined, yes, but in a quieter and more patient way. Minty wasn't a boat-rocker. Fiona wouldn't have cared much if she'd *sunk* the bloody boat, *anyone's* boat, if it happened to be bobbing in the way of what she wanted.

Minty compressed her lips into a thin line. 'You know, Fiona, you said up at the Tor that you envied me. Well, it might surprise you to know that I have always envied *you!* There was so much about you, that I knew I could never have, or be.'

'Oh, for God's sake! Like *what?*'

'Well, where do I start? You're confident, beautiful, accomplished and independent. You're also effortlessly stylish, in a way I could never hope to be. It would never have crossed my mind, when I went shopping last week for something to wear to a dinner, to accessorise it so I looked great instead of just average. You would have known instinctively, how to dress it up.

'And while we're talking about that, apart from the time you helped me find a dress for my twentieth wedding anniversary party, at a time when my husband was already screwing you, you've never once tried to help me look any better than my very average self. Why not, Fi? Over the last few years especially, as I'm painfully aware, the pounds have quietly crept on, and I've simply adjusted. Probably peri-menopause, like you say, because that *is* where I'm at too.

'But I've taken the easy option, haven't I; the lazy one? I've started wearing slouchy comfy clothes, ignoring the fact that I'm 'spreading out,' for want of a better term, and I've gone from a size ten to an almost-fourteen. Apart from that anniversary dress, and a couple of things I bought last week, I really don't remember the last time I went shopping for anything nice.

'My white lab-coat covers a multitude of fashion sins,' she explained. 'But I don't have much that's pretty to wear underneath it, and most of what I do have no longer fits properly. Before I had my hair done last week, I'd even had the same hairstyle for over ten years! How long has it been since anyone ever looked at me as anything other than what I've somehow managed to turn into - a careless lump who's more or less given up on herself?

'You? You have the perfect figure, gorgeous blonde hair, and even at pushing bloody fifty you still make men's heads turn when you walk into a room! Me? I get more and more invisible as each year passes. Why didn't you ever care enough to say anything? Why did you never want to encourage me to make the best of myself? Did it suit you to have me looking dowdy, next to you, so that you could shine a little brighter? You know, there are two types of people in this world, Fiona.'

'Yes, I know,' Fiona muttered, rolling her eyes, and doing her downward sideways glance again. 'Illuminators and diminishers. That old chestnut! It's all you've banged on about for bloody ages, ever since you saw some video about it.'

'David Brooks, yes. But maybe there's been a subconscious reason for me 'banging on about it,' as you put it. Maybe I've been trying to tell you which you are. But I *don't* have to, do I?'

Fiona felt uncomfortable. Minty's question was a fair one. It was true that she did look after herself as well as she possibly could. She did spend hours in the gym, on the cross-trainers, and she spent roughly the same amount of time on her treadmill at home. But, in years of fitness training, at the same time as she could see what was happening to Minty, why *had* she never once asked her if she'd like to come along to the gym, or join her in a dance or yoga class, or pop over and use the treadmill? Why *had* she never once been that kind friend who tried to find a subtle way of saying; 'hey come on, chick – you need to smarten yourself up a bit, buy some clothes from the current decade, lose a few pounds and get fit, because I want you around for a few *more* decades?'

She had never been that friend. Why not? It wasn't as if she wasn't capable; she'd helped other friends make the best of themselves. In fact one time, when she'd gone shopping with Margie Bluett, Margie had told her she could have a career as a stylist if she ever got sick of quantity surveying. She was, apparently, 'so good at helping others make the best of themselves'!

But she hadn't done it with Minty. She hadn't been *any* kind of 'illuminator,' had she? Instead of treating her so-called best friend like the truly unique and special person she was; who deserved to be fully acknowledged in every way, she'd more or less ignored the goodness in her. That was passive but very real diminishment, wasn't it? And she had to face it now; it had been that way because there was more than just envy, in the mix. On some subconscious level, she had been almost violently *jealous* of her best friend, and that was far more destructive. It *had* suited her, to be the better looking one, even when she wasn't trying to gain a tangible advantage.

I did need to be the shinier one. Minty shone so brightly for Leo, on that very first night; I think on some level I've hated her for it, and I never wanted her to shine like that again.

It was the truth, and it was time to do the decent thing and be honest about it.

'I know I haven't been a good friend, Minty, even before Leo. I haven't been supportive. I think I resented you right from the very start, because it was you he wanted, and not me. I really thought I'd got over all that, and I guess I was dealing with my own shit too, for a long time. It became easier to stop really 'seeing' anyone, including you. *Especially* you.'

Minty looked at her with scorn now. 'Well you never stopped 'seeing' Leo, did you? Or your chance to swipe him from under my nose. Your vision worked when you wanted it to – when there was something in it for you.'

Fiona shrugged, accepting Minty's anger. 'You can hate me all you want. I deserve it. You'll never get an argument from me about that.'

'I don't even know you, do I? As much as it pains me to have to say it, Fiona; after more than forty fucking years, I feel like I don't even know you. There once was a time when I'd have said we knew one another inside out. But the woman I used to call my best friend, the one I'd have crawled over broken glass for? She isn't who I thought she was.

'Only now, am I finding out how much of a closed book you've always been. Only now, on reflection, can I appreciate how meaningless so many of our conversations must have been to you, over the years. You were *never* as invested in our friendship as I was. It stuns me, that I've been so wrong about you, so oblivious to who you really are, for almost my whole life.'

'That's not fair! Before we met Leo, we had a great friendship.'

'So are you saying then, that from the minute I got together with him; from the moment he 'chose me,' as you see it, I became irrelevant to you? So it's only been for *twenty* years that our friendship has been a hollow sham, not the whole forty-one? Well, how comforting.'

Fiona sighed, heavily. She felt weary to her bones. She wasn't very good at saying what she really meant, or how she really felt. This kind of heart-to-heart was a brutal lesson in how to strip your own soul, and confront the fact that you'd pretty much stripped someone else's. Being held accountable was horrible, but the time was finally upon her, and she knew it.

'Why did you never tell me how you really felt about your parents dying and leaving you, Fi? About the guilt and everything?' Minty demanded.

Fiona sighed again, and considered her response. 'I really think the words felt too hard to say. I know it was probably unfair, but I think I just relied on you to get it, the things I couldn't say without being prompted.'

'And do you feel I let you down, by not picking up on all that? By not trying to get you to talk about it?' Minty's voice was softer now. She was trying to understand, and Fiona knew it, but she simply shook her head and said nothing. She didn't try to reassure Minty that her failure to notice the agony was okay, or understandable, or anything else. She still didn't really know, even now, if it mattered at the time or since. She didn't know how much someone else's 'failure to understand her' was her own fault for being such a closed book. It was hard to know *what* to feel, about any of it.

Minty bit her bottom lip, tentatively. 'I remember when it happened. I was in my first year at medical school, and I was so distracted. I'd moved away, was living in a flat with other med students, and my head was just so *full,* of *stuff.* I remember Mum calling me, late one night, to tell me about the accident. She'd been to see you in intensive care. I'd had exams all day, and she couldn't get me until really late.

'I couldn't make it home until the day of your Mum and Dad's funeral, and I remember feeling so weird about you not being there. It felt so wrong, that you weren't. You were still in the hospital. I came to see you straight after.'

'Yes, and I don't supposed I ever thanked you for going to the funeral, but I'm glad you did.'

'We *all* went! Me, Mum and Fliss. They dropped me off at Cheltenham hospital on their way home and after I came in to see you I walked home, in the pouring rain. I cried all the way home to Charlton Kings. My heart broke for you.'

'Did it? You never told me it affected you. I always thought it didn't, much. You had your head full of Gray's Anatomy and all the different shenanigans and nights out with your student friends. You'd already gone off into another world, and left me behind.'

Minty looked sad. Fiona could see that she was trying to choose her next words carefully.

'I never wanted you to feel like that, Fi. I was so glad when you decided to study at Bath! It felt like we'd properly reconnected again, after that time apart.'

'It was only twenty minutes on the train, to Bristol, and that made things pretty easy. I wanted to move in with you, actually, but your flat was already full.'

'What?' Minty exclaimed in dismay. 'Why didn't you ever ask? I'd have happily moved out of there, and we could have got a place together! That would have been such fun!'

Fiona shook her head. 'I'd have distracted you from your studies. Back then, all I wanted to do was go out every night. Growing up in Cheltenham was lovely of course. We were happy there I suppose, weren't we? But there was never much to do at night, as I remember. Bath and Bristol were a whole new world for me. Vibrant university towns, lots of interesting pubs and clubs, and the people weren't up their own arses, like so many of the Cotswold tribe we grew up around always seemed to be. People were more *real* in Bristol, and purposeful, and I just wanted to immerse myself in all of it. I think I hassled you enough as it was, to put the books down and come out to the pub.'

Minty had to agree. 'Yeah, the two of us living together probably would have been a nightmare. My flatmates weren't too bad, that way. We were all studying medicine, and facing a longer slog than most, until we qualified. We had some good nights out, to be sure, but we were probably more serious about our studies than some of the other students were.'

Fiona knew how important it had been for Minty, be with like-minded people, so she could concentrate better. A lot of their friends did see their university years as a time to pickle their livers as much as possible before the reality of steady jobs, student loans, mortgage payments, and other heavy responsibilities wiped their social lives off the chart.

For Minty and her equally dedicated flatmates, nights out were never going to be so frequent that their studies suffered. Conversely, Fiona had enjoyed her late teens and early twenties to the absolute, liver-pickling max; she couldn't deny that.

'I'd never have kept pace with you, and I'd have driven you mad.' Minty admitted, and Fiona chuckled softly.

'You might have kept me a bit steadier. I was a party animal back then. I don't have many regrets, but the ones I do have usually involve a complete loss of control, and worrying gaps in my memory, which probably wouldn't have happened if you'd been around more.'

Minty smiled gently, and changed tack. 'Who was that guy you were seeing for a while at uni, before we meet Leo? What was his name; that blond guy – Chris something? He seemed nice. He was a few years older than us, wasn't he? And incredibly handsome, as I recall!'

Fiona nodded, remembering. 'Kris Kiehl. The Austrian guy. I wasn't actually 'seeing' him, in the romantic sense. He was kind of just *around*, you know? I liked him a lot, because he was smart. He was probably one of the most interesting people I'd ever met, at the time. He'd lived in Canada, L.A. and Paris, and he talked about all kinds of really interesting stuff. What captivated me about him was the fact that he used to really listen, when other people talked. He made you feel like your own perspective actually meant something. Few of the people we hung out with ever did that. Most of them were more interested in the sound of their *own* voices, spouting all kinds of stupid stuff. He was a bit different. At least I thought he was, for a while.'

'An illuminator?'

Fiona nodded. 'Yeah, totally, *and* an intellectual. He was fascinating to talk with and listen to, and he *was* handsome, wasn't he? Gorgeous, really. Trouble was; I think he knew it.

He fancied himself as an actor. I think he went on to RADA after uni, actually.'

'Have you kept in touch with him?'

'No. I did try, but he started ignoring me, over the summer between second and third year. There was no warning. He just suddenly became very lukewarm towards a few of us. We started getting, like, half-hearted answers to our invitations, and whenever I invited him to come and spend time with us he just kept fobbing me off with excuses. It was almost like he became too self-important to want to bother with us anymore, or *me,* at least.'

She was surprised, now, to feel a very deep pang of loss. It was random, and it prompted her to say more, about something sudden and profound that was unexpectedly stirring within her.

'He ghosted us completely, in the end; *all* of us actually, in the friendship group we had. We had no idea what changed, but it was really upsetting at the time, because I thought I'd made a meaningful connection with someone amazing, and fun to be around.'

'That must've hurt, Fi. I know you really liked him. Ghosting is such a cruel thing to do to someone, isn't it? I read an article about it recently, in a health journal. If people have invested something of themselves, even if it's just in a friendship, being ghosted really knocks them around. In fact, there's research out there now that suggests it's a form of emotional *abuse*, in how it affects people! I'd never thought about that but I guess, since that sort of behaviour is ego driven, it kind of makes sense?'

'Yeah, it's funny you should say that, Minty, because that *is* what it felt like! I *did* feel like I'd been abused; strung along, invited to place trust, then kind of abandoned; left to flounder around in my own head, trying to figure out what the fuck I should do next, you know, like should I contact him, give him space, or give him the benefit of the doubt? Should I get angry, or worry about whether or not he's okay? What if he's really ill, or something terrible has happened in his life, or his family? Do I offer help, or do I write him off and get on with grieving the loss of the friendship, or *what?*'

'That was a hard place to be in,' Minty observed.

'It was *really* hard, on the back of what seemed to be a very clear message; that we didn't matter to him, and probably never had.'

Minty mulled on that for a few seconds. 'Hmm… either that, or he was just a coward who couldn't confront whatever his own discomfort was, around the friendships. It could've been that. Either way, it's confusing, and painful, and you didn't deserve it.'

'Yeah, I don't think any of us did. We'd tried to be good friends to him. We were generous with him, you know? So we were all confused and hurt by what he did, but for some reason it really affected *me*, and it took me a long time to stop wondering what I might have done to upset him. I thought it somehow had to be my fault! It really messed with my head, for ages. It was horrible.'

It just would've been nice if he'd said something, called us out, or explained why he was distancing himself, rather than just scuttling away like a crab across the sand. I wanted to understand, but how could I?

'You'd been writing a kind of story together, but there was no full stop at the end of the last sentence,' Minty offered, quietly.

Fiona nodded. 'Yeah, that's it, exactly. Unfinished business. I went through a phase of wanting to find him and say; 'Hey, look mate, what the fuck *was* that? Why were you such an asshole to us?' But I decided that if I wasn't worth his time, I shouldn't give him any more of mine, should I? So, I disengaged from him too, and worked on letting it go. I guess he would probably say that I ghosted *him*, in the end, but I turned away because I had to find a way to stop wondering about him, and beating myself up without even really knowing what for!'

Tears sprang to her eyes again. Minty saw them before she could wipe them away, and she nodded gently.

'Fi, you did the right thing, in cutting loose from that,' she affirmed. 'If he couldn't tell you why he wanted to bail on your friendship, you had to protect yourself. If he couldn't be decent or respectful enough to offer *you* an explanation, *he* certainly didn't deserve one from you!'

Minty lapsed deep into her own thoughts for a minute, before speaking again. 'You know, I think he represented something to you that a lot of other people didn't, at the time. He seemed to take you seriously, when few other men did. I know that was a challenge for you, back then. Being so young, and blonde and beautiful, was probably as much of a curse as it was a blessing.

'I never thought about it before, but now I can appreciate how that must have felt sometimes. A lot of guys would hit on you, and a lot of girls would hate you because their boyfriends *wanted* to hit on you! Some of them were mean about it too, as I recall. A real friend, a man who you felt saw the real you; that mattered.'

'It did matter, and it's true; it *was* hard sometimes, with different guys, but Kris was one who never tried it on. He didn't fancy me, or see me as a conquest, and that was such a relief! He offered me something different; acceptance, maybe, and a genuine interest in who I was. I never realised how important that was to me, before now.'

'You felt safe with him.'

'Yes! I did, and until he slammed the door on me I thought he'd be a friend for life.'

'Maybe he *was* just really busy, or ill, or dealing with something unexpectedly awful,' Minty mused, and Fiona rolled her eyes.

'Yeah, maybe, but I doubt it. Most things get resolved eventually, don't they? If you have to dive into your foxhole for some reason, you eventually come back out and reconnect with the people you want to have around you. He never contacted us again. We had to take the hint.'

Fiona felt overwhelmingly sad now, at the memory of Kris. The anger and confusion had faded, after so many years, but the feelings of loss and disappointment were, peculiarly, still there. She still missed him! How weird was that?

Minty looked at her kindly. 'I guess there has to be a limit to how many times you can ignore someone who keeps telling you, in ways that don't involve being brave or mature, that they don't think you're worth making time for.'

'Yeah. I gave up battering on a door that didn't seem to want to open. I had to give up, didn't I? He wasn't worth the anguish, and he proved it himself.'

'It affected you though, so that's worth acknowledging, Fi.' Minty's voice was quiet, and something small but immeasurably fragile within Fiona quietly broke, at the memory, and she was surprised at what she had hidden, even from herself, and for how long.

'You know, it's funny. I'd buried all that, and its only now that we're talking about it again that I realise how much it *did* affect me. I thought I was fine about it, Minty, but I'm wondering now if I really was. It was important to me, that he was in my world, and I can't even explain why, because I never had any romantic ideas about him or anything. But, when he dumped us all, it was like a death to me. The *death* of something, you know? How stupid is that? It doesn't make any sense.'

Minty shook her head. 'It's not stupid at all, and it absolutely does make sense. It *was* the death of something! You were still very vulnerable after your mum and dad dying too, remember. Friendships with people you thought you could trust were important. It was a critical time for you, to make meaningful connections with people you hoped would be lifelong friends, to provide some stability for you.

'He had the potential to be one of those, but he turned out to be a dick. It was his loss, to not have *you* in *his* life, but he didn't get it, did he? The thing is, people with egos that big never understand anyone else's true value, Fi! They just bimble along in their own self-important, silly little worlds, oblivious to the havoc they wreak for others. They stay static too; completely ignorant of how much richer their lives could be if they actually gave other people a decent chance. Kiehl wasn't man enough, or kind enough, to tell you what his thoughts were. That says a lot more about him than it does about you.'

Fiona knew Minty was right. She wondered now if Kris Kiehl's rejection of her, even just in friendship, had somehow created a hole within her that she'd looked to Leo McLeod to fill; another handsome man with big ideas and charisma. Had she been hung up on Leo because of the gulf Kris Kiehl had created when he'd so casually tossed her friendship aside? If Kris had done the decent thing and been honest about why he didn't want her in his life anymore, instead of simply slinking away like a thief in the night and leaving her with so much to wonder about, would she have gone on to focus so fully on a man she couldn't have?

I'm no psychologist but I wonder if, on some strange level, I set myself up to focus on a guy I knew I couldn't have, so I wouldn't have to face the prospect of more rejection.

She told Minty what she was thinking, and Minty pulled a face. She thought about it for a long moment, before replying. When she did, her voice was very measured, as if she had taken real trouble to offer the right response.

'You know, that makes very real sense. It doesn't excuse what you did. Nothing can do that, but I can see how a fixation on an inappropriate person might head off the possibility that you'd be dumped again by someone you thought *had* invested in a relationship with you. I guess you knew Leo couldn't or wouldn't, until he actually did of course, in an opportune moment! But fixations can happen for any number of reasons. Maybe your fixation with Leo was less about him as a person than what he represented, to you; a safe fantasy, only in your head, until something triggered you to take things further.'

'And then he walked away from me too, didn't he, after all that? I do have to tell you that if he'd rejected my advances in the pub that night, I would never have taken it any further. I would have backed off, and on every level I wish now that he *had* rejected me. It would've saved so much heartache.'

‘Well you won’t get any argument from me on that score,’ Minty countered, dryly. ‘But there again, if he valued his marriage, he wouldn’t have let anything happen in the first place, would he? So I guess, at the root of it all, he wasn’t content. It would have been nice if we could have talked about it, but he never gave us that a chance. I think most men must be cowards, on some level. Even my own dad was, to some degree. He never faced up to what he should have, either.’

Fiona suddenly felt drained. ‘The Kris Kiehl thing is no excuse for the choices I made, Minty, but it may be a kind of explanation. I probably need therapy or something, to help me understand everything better. This random discussion about him has opened up all sorts of things I wasn’t prepared for. Maybe the unfinished business was a lot bigger than I thought.’

‘I really don’t think it was a random discussion, Fi. I have a feeling that it was *meant* to come up, and I think it is a lot more significant than you realised, too, even though I’m not sure how. But I think maybe digging into it a bit more with some counselling *would* help. Kris Kiehl’s treatment of you way back then, at such a vulnerable time in your life, may have more to do with what drives you than you ever gave it credit for. It would be good to understand that, if you could.’

‘You know what? I think it’s probably safe to admit it now, after all this time, but I think I loved Kris, Minty. I don’t meant romantically. It was something different, something I can’t really put into words. Cerebral, maybe? We were all so young, back then. I couldn’t have understood or said what I felt, or even tried to explain it, but there was *something*. I loved him, at least a little.’ The tears were falling again; anguished tears, of a deeply wounded soul.

‘I think you did too, and it’s okay to admit it, *and* to accept that you were affected by it. Friendships matter more than people realise. The hurt is so much more than you can ever imagine, isn’t it, when someone does something to ruin them?’

Fiona sniffed hard, and wiped her tears away with the back of her hand. 'Point taken,' she mumbled.

'Well actually Fi, I didn't mean you and me, in saying that. I meant what Kris did. It was cruel and selfish. It *was* emotionally abusive, and nobody who cares how another person feels would ever do something like that. He was an asshole, pure and simple. But, I suppose it does also apply to you and me. I guess it should be acknowledged too then, that the loss of my friendship with you has decimated *me*, and I think you deserve to know how much.

'While you're wondering about Kris Kiehl's motives for dumping you, and leaving you so bereft, maybe you can imagine what it's like to be in my shoes right now. You and Kris was what, a year or so? Try losing forty-one years of a friendship that leaves you wondering how well you knew that person, or whether they ever really cared about you, in all *that* time. And that's without even touching on the marriage that's disintegrated as well. Leo was my best friend too, or at least I thought he was.'

Minty's voice was quiet, still, but her words hammered home like nails into wood. Fiona felt wretched.

'I did care about you, Minty. I'm a terrible person, it's true, but that doesn't mean I didn't care. I always did. Please know that. Even though I've been the worst kind of friend, that didn't mean I didn't love you. I just don't think I know how to love *well*, you know? Properly, like normal people?'

Minty put her hands over her face, and rubbed her eyes. Fiona noticed now that she was crying again too. They'd both shed enough tears today to last them a lifetime.

'Well, for what it's worth, Fiona, I wish I'd better understood how things were for you back then. I *was* in my own bubble! I never noticed what losing Kris's friendship did to you. I know I was in the States on a student exchange programme that summer, and we weren't in touch much, but I wish you could have told me, after I got back. I didn't notice how deeply the loss of your parents affected you either, or how you felt about Leo. I didn't understand how many 'holes' you had, that needed to be filled. I was a shit friend back then, so I guess you being a shit friend now kind of weirdly balances the equation; I don't know.' Minty blew her nose, and dabbed at her eyes, with a tissue.

'I let you down, because it never even occurred to me how much better a friend I could and should have been. I missed really *seeing* you, Fi, and I took you for granted, for a very long time. I'm so sorry. And I'm sorry you lost your baby. I wish I'd known about that. I wish you could have let me in. That was a terrible thing to have to go through by yourself. Did you even tell George?

Fiona shook her head. She'd never said a word to *anyone*, about the miscarriage.

'It's okay. It is what it is, all that history. As to the pregnancy? Well, I'm not like you, Minty. I wasn't cut out to be a mother. I never wanted to be, actually. I did mean it, when I said it was never on my radar and I suppose, after I made a mistake, nature just stepped in and cleaned it up. It hasn't affected me, like it affects a lot of women. It's just something that happened; another part of my past.'

Minty looked at her sadly. 'Well, maybe so, but even if it wasn't a significant turning point for you, I'm pretty sure that whole Kris Kiehl thing was.'

'I think you're right. It's hard to believe how much he hurt me. I had no idea! I probably never would have, either, if we hadn't had this conversation. I'd have lived my entire life with that buried scar, and it might've influenced me for the rest of my life, however long or short that will be, in the same way it has until now. How scary is that?'

'Well, I'm glad it has come out. After the way he treated you, I think it'd be a bit weird if you *weren't* scarred by what happened with him. I think it explains a lot.'

Fiona laughed, but there wasn't any humour in it. 'Our uni days were a bit weird in general, though, weren't they? The people who came into our orbit and drifted off again? So many eccentric oddballs, not to mention the terrifyingly driven!

Some of those people scared the shit out of me, actually, in terms of what they intended to go on and do in the world.'

Minty nodded. 'Yeah, it was definitely an interesting time. So many of us, thrown together, all with big aspirations, and all hopeful that we'd find enough common ground to stay connected. Some of us did, but most of us didn't. People say that the friends you make at uni are the friends you keep for life, but I don't know if that's true.'

'I'm not sure, either. It's interesting though, because I've always stayed in touch with one of the Residential Matrons who kind of looked after me through my first year in halls. Her name was Dawn Wyckham, and she had a little flat just a few doors down the hall from my room. She helped me a lot through my first year, because I was still trying to get to grips with Mum and Dad dying. I wasn't sleeping, and I was going through that horrible first fear, you know, the one where you sit there in lectures like a rabbit in the headlights telling yourself that you're not bright enough to be there, and asking yourself what the fuck you were thinking, in imagining you were clever enough to do it?'

'Yeah, I went through that too. Imposter syndrome! It's a scary time, at the beginning. I wasn't prepared for how long it took me to get into the swing of it all. I remember writing an essay, thinking it was a pathetic pile of nonsense, but it came back with an A+ on it, and I kind of found my groove.

'And I remember Dawn Wyckham! I met her briefly at your and George's wedding, and you've mentioned her many times, over the years. I'm glad she's always been there for you, Fi. It's lovely to still be in touch, after so long, with someone who was so instrumental in shaping your confidence like that.'

'Yeah. You know, I had the worst kind of existential crisis, just after I got there, to halls, but Dawn was fantastic. She just kind of got it, you know, what I was feeling? She kept me going, and when I left I asked her if I could keep in touch, and I was so pleased when she said yes! I didn't expect her to. It's just Christmas cards, the odd catch-up by text, and the occasional coffee in town, but it means a lot to me that she's still around. Not sure what she'd make of me right now, though. I've always been selfish, but nobody would have expected me to be *this* much of a bitch – not even me!'

'I never knew how much you struggled in that first year. But I'm thankful that you had Dawn in your life, and still do.'

'You know, she retired recently Minty, and that kind of shocked me a bit, because when I was eighteen she didn't seem all that much older than me. She's a tiny woman who's always worn funky clothes and shoes, kind of new-agey, with purple hair, and she always looked amazing, and so *young!* She still does, to me, and when she said she'd had her retirement party at the university, I was stunned! She always seemed so timeless, like she'd be around forever. She's been in my life for nearly thirty years now, so maybe there's some truth in the idea that the friends you make at uni stay friends for life. Maybe they're just not always fellow students.'

Even back then, she mused, relationships were so much more complicated than they should have been. She said as much, to Minty.

'Student friendships just got to be too much like hard work, for a lot of people. I guess it was because most of us were so fragmented geographically, after the fact. We didn't have social media back then either, did we? Keeping in touch is easier now, with all that, and people from the distant past do occasionally pop up. Kris Kiehl was never one of them, though. We really were dead and forgotten, to him.'

Minty rolled her eyes. 'Well there are two sides to social media, aren't there? It's the silent stalkers that freak me out. If any of your information is public, you just never know what weirdos might be looking at it and tracking you. It's kind of spooky, and it never helps to think about it much.'

Fiona giggled. 'Speaking of stalking, I googled Kiehl a few years ago, just to see if he was doing anything interesting out in the world, but there wasn't much. Just a handful of mediocre movie reviews, and a TV series that bombed; some remake of an earlier series with different people in it, that had been successful, I think. But the critics savaged the remake. I paid to download one episode, just for a laugh, to see if it really was as bad as the critics said, and oh God; it *totally* was! Complete cringe, in fact. It was staggeringly bad. Needless to say, I wasn't going to pay any more of my hard-earned money to watch any more of that kind of drivel!'

'That's a bit of a shame for him, even though he sounds like he probably deserved to be taken down a peg or two,' Minty remarked.

'Well, to be fair, he's not the worst actor. He's a bit better than the lump of wood a lot of critics accused him of being, but that remake series performance was never going to set the world on fire. Having said that, you can only do so much with a shit script and co-actors with as much charisma as a bucket of week-dead fish. He was the best one in it. The others weren't even likeable. He might've done a bit better if he'd had something decent to work with, I suppose.'

Fiona laughed, in spite of herself. 'And get this; you want to talk about feeding ego? Media reports all quote him as being years younger than what he is! I *roared* at that! It got me wondering; did he tell them he was younger, or did they all make it up?'

'Well, even if they all do have it wrong, he doesn't seem to have been compelled to correct them,' Minty remarked. 'What does *that* tell you about him?'

'He's apparently still single, too. Never married!'

Minty laughed too, then bit her bottom lip. 'Well, I guess there's still time, isn't there, for anyone who could live with that ego? Maybe you could track him down?'

'What, are you kidding me? No chance! Single men of his age are usually still single for a very good reason, Minty – make no mistake about *that!* No, I think Kiehl had a ton of issues, and probably still has them.'

'Maybe he's gay, and still lurking in the back of his own closet!'

Fiona laughed at that. 'It was suggested once, and he hotly denied it, but maybe the man 'dideth' protest too much! Who knows? Anyway, it was all a long time ago now. He's history but, as I'm now discovering, it is a little *unfinished,* so I suppose I have some work to do on putting that to bed. But, enough of Kiehl the 'Austrian Thespian! Tell me about the man who was here this morning. What was *his* name? Stuart? He seemed nice.'

'Yes, Stuart Thomson.' Minty briefly explained about Stuart owning the stables and that she'd had her accident there while she'd been staying in the holiday home while Teapot Cottage had been occupied.

'I just wasn't ready to come back to Bristol,' she explained. 'As it turned out, I probably should have faced the music and gone back when I was originally supposed to. I wouldn't have this damned shoulder to deal with and you wouldn't be up here, hobbling around with a banged-up knee, on top of everything else.'

'Well, for what it's worth, I don't blame you for not wanting to go home. And I know how horrible I've been to you, so that must've been a big part of why. Everything I touch seems to turn to shit.'

'Look, Fi; I know you've had the worst news possible, but please stop playing the victim about everything else. You *have* ben horrible, and I'm glad you at least have something of a conscience about everything that's happened, but if you think I'm going to sit here feeling sorry for you about anything else but the cancer, you can forget it.

'There might be some kind of truce here, while we're sharing remnants of the past, but we're not friends anymore. After what you did to my life, I don't owe you a single thing. A lot of what you touch *does* turn to shit, but maybe it's time to start thinking about how much of it has been your own bloody fault.'

Fiona knew Minty was right about that too. Her marriage to George hadn't worked out. Three other engagements had all hit the deck, and her friendships with other women weren't what she could really call close. She'd fallen out with more people than she could count, over the years. Her job as a quantity surveyor was secure enough and her house was paid for, which was no small achievement in Bristol, but as for personal relationships, there wasn't much that mattered. She'd systematically squandered friendships like water. She had a lot of acquaintances, but very few real friends.

Minty had made a few astute observations about her tonight. Suggesting that it might be time to take responsibility for her own situation, was probably the most important, but it was also the most painful. The accusation stung.

'Ouch, Minty. Don't hold back with your opinions, will you?'

Minty shook her head with frustration. 'Look, I'm done with playing nice, okay? You know, I was always loyal to you. I've always been protective, standing up for you, and telling people they were stupid or mean for turning their backs on you. I never once questioned why they did it. I always just told myself that you were just an unusual character; a bit of a 'marmite' person, for want of a better phrase, who people either loved or hated with nothing much in between.

'I never once considered how many of them might have been right in being upset or offended, and deciding to keep their distance from you. A lot of things weren't clear to me, for far too long. Just because they are clearer to me now, like why you don't trust friendships enough to fully commit to them, that doesn't mean I'm willing to mend any fences.'

'Fair enough, Minty. At least in this discussion I've had a glimpse into my own psyche too, for once. I think the Kris thing is what started me off, mistrusting friendships. I think I test people, and I do it too far.'

Minty nodded, curtly. 'Yes, you do, but I get it. I understand a lot more than I did, and I'm sorry about how much past hurts have driven your behaviour. If I could turn back the clock for all of us, I would. But we are where we are, Fi. All I can do now is let the dust settle on all this implosion, and figure out how to rebuild my life.'

Minty visibly shook herself and carried on with her explanation. 'So anyway, as I was saying about Stuart; I lost my earrings, which I thought were probably at the bottom of the stream where I fell off the horse, but they must have got caught up in the bedding at the barn before that, because Stuart found them while he was hoovering.'

'So, he's a man who hoovers! I saw you hug him outside. Are you interested in him?'

'What? God, no! Of course not! What kind of stupid question is that? Bit soon, wouldn't it be, since I'm still trying to piece myself back together after you and Leo destroyed my world as I knew it? Stuart and I are friends, Fiona, and I hope we'll continue to be. As a matter of fact, I'm meeting him in town on Friday night for a quick bite at one of the local pubs while his daughter's at youth club. Don't look like that,' she snapped angrily as Fiona smirked.

'Are you for real? It's barely two bloody minutes since my marriage blew apart, thanks to you! I'm not even halfway to a point where I can even *start* grieving properly for *that*, let alone look at anybody else. The shock has been immense, Fiona. Fucking *immense*. Maybe you can move on at the drop of a hat, but then you've never loved someone with all you heart and soul for more than twenty years, have you? You wouldn't know what it's like, how disembowelling it is, when the person you love most in the entire world, who you've spent more than half your life loving and trusting, just walks away from you without any warning, would you?'

'Well, like I said, Minty, I fell in love with Leo more than twenty years ago too, even before you did, actually, so I *do* know what it's like, thanks very much. And when it comes to feeling disembowelled, *you* try watching the only man you've ever loved shacking up with someone else.'

'Oh, believe me, I have a ringside seat for that, in case you'd forgotten! What are you, if not the 'someone else' he's 'shacking up' with now, to borrow your crass turn of phrase in describing my busted marriage? Stop fishing, Fiona. I know how well it would suit you, if I was already 'over' you destroying my life, and thinking about someone else. That way you could feel less guilty about what you've done.

Clearly, whether you actually did love Leo or were in fact just a bit obsessed with him, you have no idea what you've ruined.'

Minty was angry again now. Fiona knew she'd wound her up again, just when they seemed to be on more solid ground; reminiscing about important parts of the past. She berated herself.

Christ! I just can't help myself, can I? Why can't I just leave her to lick her own wounds – the ones I inflicted on her? Of course she isn't interested in anyone else! It's been barely a month, since all this blew up. Why do I have to be so bitchy? I have to stop trying to antagonise her. I don't even know why I'm doing it!

She turned away from her own thoughts. Minty was still talking to her.

'It's a shame the lily-livered Leo doesn't have the stomach to see you through your cancer journey. You two were bloody made for each other. Forgive me, but it's pretty hard not to feel bitter about everything, let alone what you're insinuating. You don't get to play with me anymore Fi, or judge me, or even make comment on how I choose to live my life now. Stuart's just a friend, but I really don't care if anyone thinks otherwise. I certainly don't care what *you* think anymore.'

Fiona pressed her lips into a thin line and looked down at her hands. She allowed her shoulders to sag, in defeat.

'Look, Minty, I don't want to fight with you. I don't have the energy, and neither do you. It's a waste of what strength we do have, to spend it tearing lumps out of each other. I'm going to leave first thing in the morning. I should never have come here. It's still too raw, and I'm just as selfish as ever, in thinking I could get some help here. You've said you would support me through the cancer journey, to whatever end it takes me, but I think that's too much to promise, under the circumstances. It's too much of me to expect, as well. And that's okay. Really, it is.'

Minty shook her head. She had regained her composure and was calm again. 'You don't have to leave, and when I said

I would support you I meant it. But it has to be on my terms, Fiona, not yours. I don't want to be goaded into responding to you or left trying to hold my resentment in check while you sadistically poke me like a wounded bear. Like I said, you don't get to mess around with me anymore. You gave up your entitlement to test me in any way whatsoever when you helped yourself to what was mine. There are certain things you need to accept, just like you told me I needed to accept you and Leo, as was, before he showed *his* true colours.

'So you can stay if you want, but we need to call a decent truce. We can't just keep going through the peaks and troughs of conversations that hurt us both so much. You can modify your behaviour, or you can go. It's your choice.'

Chapter Nineteen

The silence lengthened. Fiona stared at the wall. Minty, ever the peacemaker, felt a compelling need to restore peace to this beautiful little cottage. The turbulence in here now made her feel physically sick. The air seemed brittle, somehow, like something was about to shatter. It was like the cottage itself was trying to reject the discord within its walls. The hard truths were necessary, but she wondered if she had been unduly harsh in her own defensiveness. She decided to extend an olive branch.

'I tell you what, why don't you come with me on Friday night? Come and have a drink and a bite to eat with me and Stuart. You can see for yourself, how boring and platonic it all is. If you want to, come. If you don't, don't. I really don't care one way or the other,' she added with a shrug.

'I was meant to be going home on Friday morning anyway,' Fiona mumbled. She looked wretched.

'Well it's fairly clear to me that you'll need a couple more days. You should probably stay until Sunday. Your knee will have healed up a bit more by then, enough to travel by yourself anyway.'

Are you sure that'll be okay? I mean, me being here is obviously very difficult for you. I don't want to stay if it will be too much. Maybe we were both kidding ourselves that we could make this work.'

There was no trace of antagonism in Fiona's voice. She sounded defeated, in fact; more or less resigned to whatever might happen next. Minty supposed it might be because she'd managed to convince herself that she didn't have much of a future. Maybe she no longer felt there was anything to fight for, or achieve, and it was time to go with the flow.

Then she remembered Feen Raven's word, just a few hours earlier.

She can beat her illness. She just has to fight harder than she ever has before. If you can forgive her, she has a shot. Without your help, she won't make it.

'It's fine. Feen Raven has offered to drive you to the station on Sunday, so we can see you safely onto the train.'

'Has she? That's incredibly kind of her.'

Yes, it is, and it's more than you deserve, Minty wanted to retort, but she bit it back, suddenly remembering what Adie Raven had said.

Right now, when Fiona couldn't be any less deserving of your compassion, this is when she needs it the most.

Minty's head felt as if it were about to explode. Her body was cold tonight, and although she was fairly sure it was peri, tapping her on the shoulder, she wondered if the emotional rollercoaster she was on with Fiona was making her symptoms worse. It was hardly surprising that Fiona was in peri too, and maybe it was her pinging hormones that had compelled her to seduce Leo. Even if they only played a small part, it begged the question; would she have gone ahead and done it if her hormones had been stable? Was she experiencing changes in her own behaviour that she wasn't even fully aware of? Medically, Minty knew how much hormonal imbalance can be responsible for, often without the 'victim' being fully aware of the interplay. Maybe Fiona's decisions had been driven by something scientific, and a little more complicated than she might understand on a conscious level. With peri-menopause, and the complex interplay of biology and emotion, almost anything was possible.

She wondered if that might be worth a conversation, and decided that it probably was, but not right now. Enough had been said already, for tonight. It had been an intense few hours, with a lot of revelations and a very full spectrum of emotions. She and Fiona were both exhausted, and they were injured. It was time to step back, at least for now.

She decided to read, and try to immerse her head in something different and distracting. She picked up her book, and settled into the window seat to read it. It was a pointed gesture, wordless, designed to inform her only-half-wanted guest to amuse herself with something else for a while. Fiona took the hint and went upstairs, presumably to lie down.

Minty woke with a jolt, two hours later, to find the room almost in darkness. She'd fallen asleep! Her book had hit the floor and the front cover had bent backwards, leaving a deep diagonal crease from top to bottom. The fire had gone out too. She sighed with irritation.

Everything was quiet in the cottage. Her shoulder throbbed dully. She couldn't hear a thing from upstairs. *Maybe she left, while I was asleep. How would that make me feel? Relieved? Panicked?*

Fiona's coat was still hanging up behind the front door though, so she clearly hadn't left. Minty decided to make a dinner of pasta with pesto, cherry tomatoes and goat's cheese. She was still in the process of throwing it all together when Fiona came back downstairs, rubbing her eyes. She'd been crying again – another thing Minty hadn't known her do very often, before today. But who wouldn't grieve for the mess they'd made of their own life, and for the impending loss of it? Fiona smiled wanly at her and limped across to the freezer, where she pulled out a fresh poultice.

'Do you want to get back in the hot tub for a while? It might help?'

Fiona shook her head. 'No. It's pitch dark out there now, and to be honest, I'm so stiff I don't think I could get in it, let alone back out of it. The poultice will be fine, and a couple of painkillers will help. I think I have some more in my handbag.'

She unwrapped the cling film from around her swollen knee and gently pulled it off. The skin was a dark, shiny purple, but the bruising hadn't spread anything like as far as Minty had expected it to.

'Wow! That looks a lot better already! The first poultice seems to have done an excellent job. D'you want me to put the new one on?'

'No thanks, I think I can do it. It's stiff but it's not as sore as before. It might be even better by morning.' She laughed, lightly. 'It's funny, really. I was googling the use of comfrey and I think your friend Feen is right, as there's a lot of information out there about how good it is for bruising and sprains and stuff. But it's been banned in the USA, apparently, because it causes cancer. Boom-boom-*tish.*'

Minty didn't know whether to laugh or cry. 'Well, I know you're not supposed to ingest it, because it can cause liver failure and other problems if it's used for prolonged periods. Even as a skin poultice, it's only fine just for a few applications, but that's all Feen has provided. I'm sure any risk is minimal.' She handed Fiona a bandage. 'Here. This will be better than cling film, for overnight.'

'Ok, thanks. I'll wrap it in the cling film after though, as well, so it won't leak through and stain the lovely sheets. It really is the most evil colour. It doesn't smell very nice either,' Fiona added, and wrinkled her nose. Minty laughed in spite of herself.

After dinner, Fiona did the washing up, and Minty chose a movie from the DVDs in the rack by the side of the TV.

'Pretty Woman - what do you think? A bit of an old cliché girly movie, but it's still a goodie, and worth another watch?'

Fiona smirked. 'Are you picking that one because Julia Roberts is a whore?'

'No, I'm picking it because Richard Gere is a hunk, and a happy ending is always welcome, however implausible it might be.' Minty pulled a bottle of wine from the fridge, poured a couple of glasses, and handed one to Fiona. They settled down to watch the film.

'My favourite bit is when she goes back to those shops that wouldn't serve her,' Fiona chuckled. 'It must've felt so good, to rub their faces in all that lost commission and remind them what assholes they were to her when they thought she didn't have a bean to her name.'

Minty nodded. 'It's a good story. It makes you hope there's a way out for some of them at least.'

You can never judge a book by its cover, can you? And I bet most women who are prostitutes don't want to be, and I bet a lot of them cry themselves to sleep at night.

When the movie came to a close, Minty got up to make a cup of tea. 'How are you feeling about starting the chemo next week? I guess you haven't had a lot of time to come to terms with that.'

Fiona shrugged lightly. 'Well, I've had a bit, and if it helps me live a little longer, I'm all for it. I'm at peace with the mastectomy too, even if it does turn out to be a double. I've come to the decision that being alive is more important than having good looking tits. Not that Leo feels the same,' she added bitterly.

'Clearly, he was far more interested in how I looked than what I was like as a person, or the fact that I'm scared to death. No, Minty. I can't rail against any of the treatment; not if it increases my time. I'm completely in their hands. Whatever they can do to help me, I just have to trust them to do it.'

She sounded sad. Resigned, pragmatic, but sad. Minty felt sad too. 'Will you have reconstructive surgery?'

Fiona shrugged and shook her head. 'I'm not sure. I think the main objective at first is survival, for however long. I've no idea what I'll feel like with no breasts or nipples. A decision on that will have to come later. They wouldn't do it for at least six months anyway, so there's time to adjust and decide.'

'Yep. You can choose whenever you feel the time is right. There's no rush. A lot of women wear prosthetics, and they find that's enough.'

'I guess it is, if you care more about how you look in your clothes than what you look like naked. Me? I've always enjoyed sex, and men appreciating my body. It's always been a good body, even though I've had to work at it, but I've taken it for granted, for my whole life. It won't be the same body after this process. I'll be horribly scarred and disfigured. I can't imagine any bloke wanting to get near me after that. Having two horizontal slashes where your tits used to be, well, it's not exactly sexy, is it?'

'On the face of it, no,' Minty admitted. 'But there are a hell of a lot of men out there who love a woman for who she is, and the fact that her scars are a part of her. It's not just breasts that make a woman who she is. A lot of men find other things sexy, you know, in fact some aren't boob-men at all! A lot are turned on by other things more, like a great pair of legs, or a pert bum, or even a 'fine mind,' and you do have all that too.'

'Since when did you become such an expert on men?'

Minty shrugged. 'Oh, I dunno. You pick up a lot of info from them, and from women too, in a hospital setting. While you're getting them sorted they start confiding in you about all sorts of stuff. It's like the floodgates open, especially when they think they or a loved one might die. You'd be amazed at what comes out of their mouths. It's been incredibly enlightening, over the years.'

'Tell me some stories. You know, about your patients. You must have some doozies.'

'Yeah, some are funny, but a lot are just sad. You know, people losing loved ones or praying and promising all kinds of things to Gods they probably don't even fully believe in, if only their 'person' will survive. Mothers having to make decisions to switch off life-support machines and donate the organs of their fatally injured children. Besotted girlfriends keeping vigil by their boyfriends' bedside until an unknown wife and kids show up out of the blue. That sort of thing. We do try, but some days it's even hard to find enough gallows humour, to balance the heartbreak.'

Fiona was thoughtful. 'Yeah, I guess you must need some guts, to show up for that every day. Why do you love your work so much?'

Minty considered her response. 'I guess I respond well to the urgency of it, the challenge of getting people sorted quickly. I'm on my toes all day, every hour is different, so I don't get time to be bored or complacent. I thrive on finding quick solutions, and seeing the team pulling together to make a positive difference, wherever possible, to what comes through the door.'

'Have you ever wanted to do anything else?'

'Nope. I dunno how long I'll keep up the pace for, and I'm getting to that time in my life where I'm willing to consider less demanding options for the future, but nothing's popped up so far, to sway me away from what I'm doing now.' She uncurled her legs from beneath her, aware that her left leg was falling asleep. She yawned and stretched.

'I think I'll take a couple of painkillers and head to bed. The shoulder is singing a bit, tonight, and I need to do my exercises with it so I'll do those upstairs. Stay up if you want, there's more DVDs and books dotted about, and probably another glass of wine in that bottle. I'll see you in the morning.'

Chapter Twenty

As he clicked off Minty's call, Stuart suddenly found himself feeling incredibly nervous. She'd rung to ask him if he minded her houseguest tagging along for dinner at the pub tonight. Apparently Fiona Winterson had injured herself on a walk, the day before yesterday, and would now be staying until Sunday.

Of course he didn't mind! Having resigned himself to the fact that he would probably never see her again (and pushing to one side as far as possible the peculiar hollowness he felt at the thought), he'd been over the moon to learn that she'd be accompanying Minty to dinner. He'd tried to sound nonchalant about it, along the lines of; 'yeah, it's fine. I don't mind, if you don't either.'

But he was excited. And he resolved to take more care with his appearance tonight than he otherwise might; not that Minty didn't deserve him to dress decently! But he thought he might wear one of his newer shirts now, maybe the one Meghan liked that she always said made his grey eyes look a little blue, and he could even splash on a bit of aftershave for a change! He fretted a bit about his hair, whether or not it might need cutting. It was a little on the long side, since he'd given up on the clean, clipped corporate look a long time ago and had gone for a more casual appearance befitting his new career as a stables owner and riding trainer. He wondered if he could get a cut at short notice in Carlisle, but decided against trying. Instead, he thought he'd ask Meghan if she could do something with it, with some gel or mousse, or whatever she had in the big basket of hair products that sat on her dressing table.

So, blue shirt, and clean jeans. He was sure he had at least one decent pair of Levis tucked away in a drawer that hadn't fallen prey to indelible horse poo or grass stains. Teamed with casual boots, and maybe that lovely red cashmere jumper his Mum had given him last Christmas, slung around his shoulders, he'd hopefully look smart but not overdressed.

When he'd unwrapped the fire engine red jumper, he'd been startled by how bright it was. It had been a bold choice from his 'ageing hippy' mother, given how conservative he was by comparison, and at first he wasn't sure it was really appropriate for someone of his age. But Meghan had hastened to reassure him it was perfect. He generally deferred to his daughter, because he knew that she simply wouldn't allow him to go *anywhere* looking ridiculous. He trusted her judgement and had in fact allowed her to take him shopping after realising how woeful his wardrobe actually was, just after they moved up here. He had a few things that he'd bought just after his release, but they were starting to look a little scruffy now, after untold washes, and the rest of his stuff was pretty awful.

His disdainful daughter had taken one look at his outdated clothes, most of which had been salvaged from suitcases stored for the six years he'd been in prison, and almost cried. Clearly he needed to be 'dragged into the twenty-first century,' as Meghan had plainly put it, and they paid a visit to the more upmarket chain stores in Carlisle. He'd given his credit card a hefty hiding, stocking up on decent jeans and trousers, a few good shirts, several pairs of much-needed shoes (Meghan would not permit him to buy any 'old-fart' slippers), a handful of good jumpers to get him through the winter, and a couple of go-anywhere type jackets. Satisfied that he had indeed been fully made-over, he was so chuffed he'd treated Meghan to a lovely lunch in a little Italian place just off the High Street.

They'd laughed a lot, that day, especially when Meghan had insisted he try on a truly hideous Hawaiian-style shirt; bright yellow with green and red parrots all over it. He'd indulged her, and then had actually threatened to buy it. By putting on a serious face, and appearing determined to take it to the counter and add it to the rest of his purchases, he'd had her in a panic and actively trying to restrain him from doing it.

They'd fallen about laughing, and the shop assistant had realised what was going on and had joined in, to the chagrin of a truly horrified Meghan, by gushing and complimenting Stuart most enthusiastically on his impeccable taste. The icing on the cake had come a few months later, on his birthday, when Darren and Debby had presented him with a gift; the horrible Hawaiian shirt.

Meghan had told Debby, who'd decided on a bit of mischief. They'd all laughed until they cried. 'Just for that, I'm going to wear this bloody thing *everywhere*, especially when I'm out with *you!*'

Should he tease Meghan and threaten to wear it tonight night? He could make a point of escorting her into the youth club so everyone would see it. He toyed with the idea, then decided against it. That particular joke had probably run its course. One day the shirt would end up in a bag destined for the charity shop, but for now, every time he saw it hanging in his wardrobe, he remembered that lovely bonding day. He wasn't ready to give the shirt away just yet. Besides, you never knew when there might be a fancy dress party to go to somewhere, and if he ever did make it to Hawaii (which had been on his bucket list for a long time), he'd fit right in, wearing it there. He laughed again to himself as he also recalled his threat of picking Meghan up from youth club, one random night, in his pyjamas. He said he'd come inside looking for her, with old-fart slippers on the wrong feet, messed up hair and a mad look on his face. The look on hers had kept him laughing for a week.

As he went about the business of exercising the horses, tidying the yard and confirming the bookings that had come in overnight, he found himself looking at his watch every five minutes. He laughed at himself. *Get a grip, you silly bastard!*

You're not fifteen, and it's not even a bloody date! It's just a cheap pub dinner with a couple of women.

But there was no denying how much he was looking forward to meeting Fiona Winterson again, and after he'd dropped Meghan off at youth club, and pulled into the car park at the Bull and Royal, he suddenly realised that he'd been so distracted by the thought of meeting her again, he had completely forgotten that Minty had asked him to collect her and Fiona from Teapot Cottage! Quickly he rang her number.

'Hey! You guys need a ride, don't you? I completely forgot, but sit tight. I'm on my way!'

Minty laughed. 'We're already here. Feen gave us a lift down, but it would be great if you could take us back later? That would be a big help. Fi has injured her knee and it's not possible to walk back.'

Stuart quickly made his way inside. He spotted Minty and Fiona immediately, and they waved him over. They already had a drink each. Fiona appeared to be drinking lime and soda, and Minty had a half-drunk glass of white wine and was clutching a menu.

'Oh, God, am I late? I'm so sorry if I am. I thought I was in plenty of time, partly because I'd forgotten I was meant to come and get you. Hi, anyway.'

Minty grinned at him. 'Hi to you too and no, you're not late. I should have called *you*, and *I* forgot! We got here early, in time for the last bit of happy hour. Feen and Gavin Raven were heading to his grandparents for dinner, so I waved them down, and they very kindly dropped us off. It's all good, Stuart. Can I get you a drink?'

'No, let me get the next round in. What are you having?'

As he went to the bar, Stuart forced himself to relax. *I can't keep twitching like a cat on a hot tin roof! They'll wonder what the hell is wrong with me!*

As he laid the drinks on the table, Fiona smiled up at him. He noticed, for the first time, that she had lovely brown eyes, but they were puffy, with dark rings beneath them. She looked like she hadn't slept very well.

‘How are you finding Teapot Cottage? Are you enjoying your stay? I’m sorry to hear you’ve injured yourself walking. What a bloody nuisance!’

Fiona looked a little sheepish. ‘Yes, a bit unfortunate, to say the least, given that I was supposed to have left this morning.’ She coughed, and cleared her throat. ‘The cottage is lovely, and the views from the windows are stunning. But I’m not really here under the happiest of circumstances, I’m afraid.’ She cast a downward, sidelong glance at Minty, who was studiously looking at her menu, clearly reluctant to chip in.

‘Oh? Well, I’m sorry to hear that too.’ Stuart felt a bit back-footed. *What am I supposed to say to that, then?*

He waited to see if either woman would be more forthcoming, since it wasn’t easy to continue the train of conversation, given what Fiona had just said. It wasn’t like he could just ask her why she *was* here, then, was it? That would have seemed nosy and rude, even though he was dying to know! Minty was still avoiding looking at either of them, and Fiona seemed reticent too.

Well, this is going to be a barrel of bloody laughs, isn’t it?

Fiona sighed and shifted uncomfortably in her seat then met his gaze. ‘Well, are you ready for the landslide? Brace yourself, and let’s get it out of the way.’

Stuart didn’t even have time to interrupt her and tell her that it was none of his business and she didn’t have to tell him anything if she didn’t really want to. Fiona simply launched straight into her speech.

‘I’m Minty’s friend of more than forty years, but I recently stole her husband, who’s left her, to come and live with me, but he’s left me too, because I’ve just popped up with what looks like terminal breast cancer, and apparently he can’t face it, which is the worst sort of payback I think, but probably well-deserved, and I’m not even sure why I’m here, or why Minty has even allowed me to be, but we’re trying to figure things out so I can die in peace when the time comes, having hopefully mended a few fences along the way.’

Well, that was quite a sentence!

Fiona caught a breath, finally, and shrugged lightly before continuing. 'That's basically it, in a nutshell, and I was meant to be gone by now but my clumsiness got in the way of that, so here I am, in a pub in the middle of nowhere, sitting next to the woman who has the best reason in the world to be glad that I'm dying, even though she says she isn't, and telling my wretched tale of woe to a complete stranger. How's all that, Stuart, for home-wrecking napalm? I bet you're glad you asked.'

She spoke quietly, matter-of-factly, and clearly defying any overture of sympathy or reproach. Stuart hadn't a clue what to say, particularly since he hadn't asked at all, in fact! Baffled, and this time *definitely* back-footed, he stared at her for a moment, dumbstruck, and then managed to clear his head, and then (regrettably?) he spontaneously blurted out the first thing that came into his head.

'Well, not that it's any kind of competition or anything, but I'm a home-wrecker too, and I nearly died last year myself.'

Oh God, did I actually just say that out loud?

Fiona's mouth twitched. Was she trying not to laugh, or was she just trying to stop herself from hurling a well-deserved insult at him? He felt the need to quantify what he'd just said so he jumped in, headfirst, *and to hell with the consequences!*

'I used to be a solicitor but I drove drunk and killed a woman and her unborn baby, went to jail for six years and almost got myself murdered last winter by a deranged head-case abuser who showed up at my stables looking for his ex-wife who I'd employed as a carpenter.'

'Napalm snap,' Fiona murmured.

The silence was deafening. Nobody spoke. Nobody had the slightest idea of what to say next, until Minty lifted her head.

'Well, I guess I can't compete with either of those particular life-changing or life-limiting 'napalms,' as you call them, but in the spirit of airing dirty laundry, I've recently been shit on from the greatest height imaginable by the two people I've loved and trusted the most in the entire world, for the longest time. I'm reeling, injured, off work, wondering why I've never even noticed so much of what's gone on under my nose all my life, and why the people closest to me never drew my attention to it when they fucking well should have. My husband is the asshole of the century, and I'm not dying but the woman I love and hate in the highest possible equal measure is. And I'm officially homeless. Does any of that compete?'

Great, thought Stuart. *Tonight is going to go swimmingly. Maybe I should have brought a bloody crash helmet.*

But curiously, neither woman seemed to be particularly keen on having a go at each other. They both simply stated their positions, and everything was distinctly and quite bizarrely civilized, if a little stilted now, with nobody having the faintest clue what to say next. He decided that he'd have a go at getting the evening onto more of an even keel despite feeling sucker-punched at the news that the captivating woman he'd been dreaming about for days now was evidently going to die. The brutality of that was hard to stomach.

'Is that why you're only on soft drinks, Fiona? Because of the cancer?'

She nodded grimly, her mouth set in a straight line. 'Yep. Not that it matters, really, since I've pretty much got my one way ticket out of here anyway, and pickling my liver wouldn't change the outcome one way or the other. But I'm starting chemo next week, so I'm trying to behave myself. I had a few glasses of wine a couple of nights ago, but they were my last for a while. It seems to be one of the few choices I have left, about anything at all, so I may as well use it wisely. Not much else that I've done has been wise lately, has it, Minty?'

Minty smiled at her tentatively, then turned her attention to Stuart. 'Fiona's here to try and mend fences, as she said, and I've offered to support her through what could well be a terminal illness. She doesn't have anyone else, and despite everything that's happened I don't want her to go through this alone.'

Stuart thought that Minty had to be some kind of saint, to want to do that for the woman who'd blown her world apart, but there again, they'd known one another all their lives, hadn't they? He supposed that still counted for something. Who was he, to make assumptions or cast aspersions about other people's actions, especially when they came straight from the heart? Women were a complete mystery to him, and doubtless always would be, but the situation these two found themselves in was extraordinary, to say the least, and probably unprecedented. How they dealt with it was really up to them, and it very much looked as if they were flying by the seat of their pants, feeling their way as they went along. Well, he supposed, what else could they do?

It was awkward. He wanted to commiserate with Fiona, over her devastating diagnosis, but he wasn't sure if doing so would seem patronising to her, or offensive to Minty. On the other hand, if he didn't say *something* at least, it would seem to Fiona like he didn't care, and that was the very last impression he wanted to give. As he was trying to think of something to say, Minty piped up again.

'None of this is to say that I forgive her, because I don't, and she knows it. However, we have to focus now on what pieces we *can* pick up.'

Her voice was cool, pragmatic, much like Stuart imagined her to be in her normal day-to-day hospital setting where decisions were made clinically about what was to be done about people's injuries. As invested as she clearly was, in assisting Fiona to die with some dignity, the approach was somewhat clinical. Stuart supposed it was probably the only way she could manage it. To show too much of what was left of her heart was probably beyond her. He understood it completely. But it did little to dispel the awkwardness of the meeting. Out of the corner of his eye he could see a waitress hovering.

'Look, ladies, if either of you would rather we didn't do this, I fully understand. I can run you both back to Teapot Cottage, and we can meet up another night, Minty? Don't get me wrong. I'm happy to be here, but if you're not, I won't take offence at all if you want to pull the plug. We should decide before we order any food.'

Fiona and Minty looked at one another. Fiona spoke first. 'Well I'm actually hungry, for a change. I want a fat-trimmed sirloin steak with all the trimmings.'

Minty nodded. 'I fancy the mushroom tagliatelle with cheesy garlic bread and salad on the side.' She smiled tentatively at Stuart. 'There's no need to go home. It is what it is, all this, and we decided before you got here I think, even though we didn't actually talk about it, that we'd just get our cards out on the table straightaway so there wouldn't be any awkward conversations or pauses that you'd struggle to understand. That would be even more uncomfortable, not to mention unfair.'

Fiona giggled lightly. 'And thank you for doing the same, Stuart. There are a number of elephants in the room, and you've brought a few of your own, so none of us spoils another zoo, do we?'

Stuart laughed, in spite of himself. 'My mother used to say that all the time, about horrible or ugly couples. 'Ah well, best they're together so they don't spoil another pair.' In fact, after I got thrown in the can, she probably said it about me plenty of times to anyone who'd listen. At least in there he won't spoil a pair!' He made his voice slightly falsetto, to imitate his mother, and Minty grinned.

'Was she pretty mad with you, back then?' Fiona probed.

He thought for a moment and nodded. 'Yeah, she really was. I expected her to be disappointed, and of course she was, but I didn't expect her to be as bloody *angry* as she was, and it was only made worse when my second wife decided within a year to divorce me and abandon my daughter, and Meghan had to go and live with her Nan. Poor old Mum suddenly ended up with a very full plate, thanks to me, so she had every right to be upset, but we somehow got through it all, and we're still each other's biggest allies. I let her down as badly as any son could, but she never did the same to me. She's great, actually.'

'My parents died in a car crash when I was eighteen. A trucker failed to give way, and I was driving the car. I don't have brothers or sisters, and no relatives I'm connected to, so I'm on my own. But my Mum and Dad were great too. Good people.'

The waitress came to take their order, so Stuart ordered for the two women and decided to have the steak too.

'How old is your daughter?' Fiona enquired.

'Almost sixteen. She's preparing for her A levels next year. She's working her arse off, hoping for good enough grades for Lancaster, to do a science degree. She has her heart set on Psychology and Zoology.'

Stuart went on to explain how his daughter had developed a passion for horses and wanted to establish a career in Equine Therapy, focussing on healing people from trauma. 'She was a bit of a brat when we first moved up here, about a year ago. She had a few behavioural issues. Nothing too serious, but enough to give me a few sleepless nights. She'd been through a lot, though, so I made a lot of allowances for that. I was wondering what I could get her involved in, to try and settle her down, when I first came out of prison. I wasn't sure what I wanted to do, myself, but things just naturally evolved. It was a stay at Teapot Cottage actually, of all things, that led to everything falling into place.'

He described the pivotal point in their stay in Torley, where Meghan had met and bonded with a horse in the adjacent field to Teapot Cottage, and how he'd witnessed something so profound it had stopped him in his tracks and forced him to re-evaluate everything he thought he knew about relationships between animals and humans.

'And here we are; running a horse trekking and riding school business in the Lake District, which is about as far removed from my old corporate life as you could ever imagine. If someone had told me, two years ago, that this is where we'd have ended up, I don't think I'd have believed them.'

Minty leaned forward. 'But are you happy?'

He thought for a moment. 'You know something, Minty? Nobody's actually asked me that! And it's a good question, one I haven't even asked myself until now, in what's been a pretty crazy year. But I think I really am, yes. I have good friends here who don't judge me on the past, I'm enjoying slowly renovating the house, the business is turning a corner, and my daughter is settled and is apparently mapping out a very solid future for herself. So yeah, things are pretty good. Of course we could always do with more business, and for it all to not be so seasonal, but it is what it is, and we manage okay.'

I just wish I had someone special to share it with, that's all. There's a piece of the jigsaw missing, and I'm pretty sure that's what it is.

He was aware that Fiona Winterson was watching him keenly, hanging on his every word, and he felt vastly relieved that his runaway tongue hadn't actually said that last bit! She piped up; 'Well if it's so seasonal, maybe you should be looking at something else that's seasonal, only in counter-balance. You know, a winter thing, as presumably the horse riding is a summer thing?'

Stuart nodded. 'Yeah, We do get some bookings through the winter, at school half-term times and such like, but it's not consistent, and it doesn't pay the bills too well. I've been thinking about what to do though the off-season months, but I haven't managed to come up with anything yet.'

As the evening progressed, they finished their meals. When Fiona declined dessert, saying she was avoiding sugar, Minty and Stuart decided to show solidarity by doing the same, even though Stuart would secretly have loved the sticky toffee pudding and custard. He found out a lot more about both women, but he was particularly fascinated to hear about Fiona. She was very forthcoming, and when he told her about his first wife, Wendy, dying of a brain haemorrhage, she opened up more about her own illness. He was devastated to hear that she had IBC, a particularly virulent form of breast cancer that had a very challenging survival rate. If she was lucky, she said, she might have a few years left, and his heart secretly ached when she told him she was having what would probably be a double mastectomy in a few weeks' time. She also talked about her work as a quantity surveyor, and he was fascinated to learn that her favourite jobs were the restoration of historic and derelict buildings, which he also was in full favour of being restored rather than demolished.

'I'm usually involved right from the start of a project, whether it's a planned construction or a renovation,' she explained. 'I check the feasibility and the process and costs, and I keep a close eye on the budget as things move along, as well as problem solving, spec changes with revised costs and feasibility reviews, that sort of thing. I spend quite a bit of time on site, and will typically still be there at the end of the job.'

'D'you enjoy it? I presume you get to wander around in a hard hat and boss people about?' Stuart smirked in spite of himself, and so did Fiona.

'I'm going to overlook the inverted sexism there, and say yes, I do enjoy my job. It's great seeing a project through to completion.'

She took a sip of her lime and soda, and Stuart noted that the ice in it had melted.

'We cover a lot of projects, of all sizes,' she continued. 'But I like the smaller ones better. One of my favourites was the restoration of an old Victorian workhouse that had been derelict for more than fifty years. It had been bought by some Arab, for a paltry amount, and he never did anything with it so it gradually just became more and more of a crumbling eyesore in the local community. It represented a very unwelcome reminder of a horrible time in our history too, of course. Everyone in the local area hated it, but it was a listed building so it couldn't be pulled down.

'Then a property developer with the gift of the gab managed to wrestle it back off the Arab, and he had the whole thing restored, at mind-boggling cost, and converted into lovely flats. They sold for an absolute fortune; people buying an important slice of history. It looks a lot different now, all sandblasted clean, with landscaped gardens and everything.'

Minty chipped in at this point. 'Fiona's taken me around to see a few of the projects she's done, over the years. Some of them are beautiful, like that old stone gatehouse on the road at the entrance to that stately home. It was a wreck too, wasn't it, before it was renovated?'

'Borrellwood Gatehouse, yes. Tiny little place, only one decent bedroom, but it still sold for a staggering price when it was finished. People do love romantic-looking buildings, whatever their size. A piece of history, particularly if it's linked to the aristocracy, is always compelling to a buyer.'

At quarter to ten, Stuart realised with a jolt that he only had fifteen minutes to get Minty and Fiona home to Teapot Cottage, and be back at the youth club in time to pick up Meghan. Apologising profusely for having to cut such a nice evening short – for it *had* turned into a nice evening after all – Stuart asked Fiona if she would like to come over the following day to see the stables. She gave him a small smile and confirmed that she would, so as the car pulled up at the door of the cottage and Minty and Fiona got out, he told her he would collect her at eleven the following morning, take her over, have a spot of lunch, and bring her back whenever she wanted. He added that of course Minty was also included in the invitation, although he suspected that she might be glad of a few hours' break from her houseguest, and he was right.

'That's awfully sweet of you, Stuart, thank you, but I have some chores to do, and I want to visit the Farmer's Market for a few things. I'm sure I can get a ride in with Adie, and I can easily walk back, since the weather's meant to be halfway decent tomorrow, from what I remember. She'll bring my groceries home for me when she comes back.'

Stuart had got out of the car and was walking the two women to the front door, which Fiona seemed to find amusing. 'So chivalry isn't quite dead, then?'

He gave her a mock bow. 'Gentlemen who've been taught to be gentlemen don't tend to change their spots. Or something like that.' He realised his own mixed metaphor, and laughed, and Minty and Fiona did too. 'Thank you for a most delightful evening, ladies.'

Minty grinned. 'It ended better than it started, didn't it? Thanks so much Stuart, I've had a nice time.'

'Me too,' chimed Fiona. She looked so lovely in the lamp-light, Stuart suddenly had an insane urge to kiss her. Inappropriate wasn't the word, but he couldn't shake the speculation of what it might be like. He blinked a few times and checked his watch again.

'Right, gotta go. I can't leave my kid standing around on a street corner.'

He watched Minty and Fiona go inside and got back into his car. On the way down the hill, he decided he'd probably only be a few minutes late, and a lot of the kids hung around outside the doors anyway for parents who were sometimes a bit tardy on pick-ups. The ones that walked home tended to hang around a little longer and Ian Handlett, their leader, would never leave until all of the kids had gone anyway, so Meghan would be fine for five minutes.

Wow! What a doozy of a night! They'd all certainly got the warts-and-all versions of each other tonight, hadn't they? Good grief! Minty had already known about his past, of course, but he'd had no idea what a mess *she* was dealing with! She had broad shoulders, and he'd been pleased to hear that her broken one was healing nicely, but did the poor woman not have enough to contend with? Was she really up to dealing with the terminal cancer of the woman who'd shattered her world?

He sighed heavily. It was really none of his business, but they'd let him into their lives a little bit, so he couldn't help but think about it, could he?

Meghan bounced into the car. 'Hi Dad, how was your night?' She didn't wait for his reply before launching in to describe her own evening at the youth club

'I was going to stop coming to the youth club, as they're all a bit young there now, and the friends I've made there don't always go anymore. Maybe I'm getting too old for it Dad, the stuff they want to do there, but tonight some of us older ones had an impromptu debate, about the good and bad bits of artificial intelligence, and it was really interesting. So I might keep going for a bit longer.'

On the journey home, Stuart was able to tell her a bit about Fiona Winterson, and she seemed interested, particularly since Fiona was coming over in the morning to see the stables and have lunch.

'Hmm. It'll be interesting to see how the horses react to her, since she's got invasive cancer.'

Stuart agreed that perhaps it would. He added that they probably needed to do some cleaning in the house in the morning, so their guest wouldn't end up thinking they were complete slobs.

Later, and quite predictably, sleep didn't come as easily as it usually did. He found himself tossing and turning, hoping his interest in Fiona Winterson hadn't been overt enough for anyone to wonder at his motives for bringing her over here. He wondered himself, what they were. Yes, he wanted to show off his business a little, and he was definitely interested to hear her professional opinion of the barn renovations, but none of that mattered half as much as the fact that he simply wanted to see her again, and that was the best excuse he could come up with. She hadn't turned down his invitation; in fact, she seemed to enjoy their conversation, and was more than just polite to him. That was a good sign.

* * * * *

'Hi,' Meghan said shyly, when Stuart introduced Fiona. 'Did you have a good trip over?'

She and Stuart had been up early, cleaning the house, in preparation for their guest. He was pleased to see that while he'd been gone to pick up Fiona Meghan had started making a large cheese, tomato and herb omelette. It was one of her specialities, made in a huge skillet that was then placed in the oven so the top would puff up. It was virtually like a pizza when it came out, and it was always delicious. She'd already tossed a vinaigrette salad and done some jacket potatoes to have with it, too, and had prepared a large cafetiere of fresh coffee.

When Stuart had told her about Fiona coming for lunch, he'd half expected a bit of a tantrum. After the episode with Caroline Brockett last year he had no idea how she'd react to another woman coming into their well-protected bubble. It might have been a different story if Fiona hadn't been ill, but Meghan was keen for her to come. The fact that she'd created such a lovely lunch for them all reinforced his feeling that she would make Fiona welcome. It somehow seemed important that the two would get along.

Fiona was smiling gently at Meghan. 'I did, thanks. Your Dad's a more careful driver than he used to be, from what he tells me!'

Meghan grimaced briefly. 'Yeah, I guess you've been filled in on the history of that. But no, he's not quite beyond redemption. I've managed to teach him a few things.'

'I'll bet you have! Well, this lunch looks delicious, an omelette, is it? I can't wait to taste that.'

'I forgot to ask Dad if you were a vegetarian, so I've left out the smoked ham, just in case, but it's not too late to add it, as I haven't started cooking it yet.'

'Ooh yes, ham would be lovely, if it's not too late! I'm not a vegetarian. I had steak for dinner last night. But there's no rush. We don't have to eat straight away, do we? Why don't you two show me around first?'

Stuart led the way, with Meghan and Fiona trailing along behind him. They'd dropped back a little bit, and he could only vaguely hear the conversation, but they seemed to be talking about university. Fiona was telling Meghan that she'd done her engineering degree at Bristol, and Meghan was talking about the courses she wanted to do at Lancaster.

‘I might end up taking a gap year though, after A levels. I’m not sure yet. Part of me wants to get going on it all, but another part of me wants to just breathe for a while and enjoy all this, before knuckling down again.’

She extended her arm around the property to show Fiona what she meant. ‘The subjects I’ll be taking are heavy, and my feet haven’t touched the ground with one thing and another since Dad got out of jail. I decided what I wanted to do quite late into the last academic year, so I’ll have to work my butt off all through the run-up to A levels, to get the grades I have to achieve. I’m already knackered. I might be better off taking some breathing space at the end of the exams.’

That sounds sensible,’ Fiona offered. ‘And of course you don’t have to decide straight away, do you? You can see how you feel about it all when the time comes. So what will you do if you end up taking a gap year?’

‘Well, we have a really good friend, a guy called Darren Davies. He’s the local vet, and he’s like a big brother to me, really. I could learn a lot by shadowing him a bit, especially with the horse work he does on the various farms, and so on, and I still have a lot of work to do with my own horse, who’s still being rehabilitated, after being rescued. There’ll be plenty to do around here, mucking out, leading some horse treks, and keeping the website up to date for Dad.’

Fiona laughed. ‘Well that sounds like it’d be enough to be getting on with! But at least you can do it at your own pace. Tertiary study rolls along regardless. It will leave you behind if you don’t keep up. You do have to be ready for it.’

They approached the main ring, where the horses were congregating. Meghan’s horse stepped forward, as she always did.

‘This is Astro,’ Meghan said proudly. ‘She was a rescue horse, owned by Darren. I fell in love with her while we were staying over in Torley, at Teapot Cottage. He was keeping her in the field next to the house, and he let me work with her for a while. We bonded pretty well and he gave her to me for my birthday. She’s the best, aren’t you, gorgeous girl?’

Fiona seemed fearless, faced with the horses. She stood quietly, looking at them, and they all stood stock still and stared back, benignly. Stuart put his hand lightly on her right shoulder. 'Why don't you go into the ring, and let them say hello to you?'

Fiona looked up at him, her teeth catching her lower lip. He found her tentativeness quite sexy, but of course he wasn't about to let her know that!

'D'you think it'll be ok? They don't seem threatening, but they are enormous!'

'No, they're fine. They won't hurt you. Just avoid sudden movements as one or two of them are a little highly strung, which is quite common in horses. But they'll be fine. Go on, see how they greet you.'

Fiona limped into the ring and stood stock still. 'It's ok to talk to them, if you want,' Stuart suggested, so she started murmuring to them gently. One by one they came over to her and all but one put its nose directly on her body, ever so gently. One or two of them snorted gently, and they shuffled about a bit, but they didn't take their noses off her. Finnegan gently blew into her face, and she gasped, lightly. She carried on murmuring to them, and they continued to give her their full attention. When Stuart looked over at Meghan, her eyes were glistening with unshed tears.

'This is what I was talking about,' she whispered. 'They can sense her illness. They're giving her healing, Dad. Look!'

Fiona's eyes were closed now, and she had stopped talking. The horses continued to touch her with their noses, and Finnegan again blew gently into her face. They were all snorting and making light snicking noises to one another, communicating among themselves in a language only they really understood. After a few more minutes a couple of them stepped back and the others followed. Fiona opened her eyes and was weeping quietly, and Meghan stepped forward into the ring and put both hands on her shoulders. 'You ok?'

Fiona nodded. 'Yeah, I'm ok. But what was that? It felt like they were trying to talk to me, like they had something important to tell me, but I didn't get it! I didn't get it. I'm sorry!' She seemed genuinely upset that she'd somehow messed up. Meghan reassured her it wasn't the case.

'No! It's ok! You didn't *need* to get it! They were just offering you their healing energy. Horses are very spiritual animals. They can sense when something's wrong, either physically or emotionally, and when they know they can trust someone they step forward and make the healing connection. It doesn't always happen, but when it does it's something special.'

Stuart was astounded, as Meghan gently led Fiona back out of the ring. Fiona seemed infinitely vulnerable in that moment, and Meghan was taking the most wonderful care of her. Never had he seen his daughter act with so much compassion, towards someone she hadn't met before. It typically took her a long time to trust people, but here she was, having barely met Fiona ten minutes ago, acting as if she'd been a close friend for years. He had a lump in his throat, and fought to swallow it down.

'Would you like to see the barn, Fiona? It's the jewel in our crown here, and there's quite a story attached to it. We can wander through Block two, so you can see the stables, and the horse hospital, and we can go out through the doors at the bottom and over to the barn.' He placed his hand beneath Fiona's elbow.

Fiona thought the hospital was wonderful, and the barn even more so. Stuart confided that he was quite proud of the achievements, and she affirmed that he had every right to be.

'It's absolutely lovely here. You've achieved such a lot, in such a short space of time, haven't you? Wow. The whole place is fabulous. Tell me, does *everyone* in this part of the world have a hot tub?'

Stuart laughed. 'I'm not sure, but we wouldn't be without this. I can't tell you what a help it is, after being out on a horse all day and coming back with an aching back and shoulders.'

Meghan excused herself, saying she wanted to get back and start lunch. Fiona asked her if she needed any help but she declined, grinning, and left them in the field. Stuart watched her retreating back. 'Well I'm gobsmacked,' he murmured. 'That girl never fails to surprise me.'

'Really? Why's that?'

'Oh, you know, typical stroppy teenager. She's a lot better than she used to be, that's for sure, but she doesn't usually take to people as well as she's clearly taken to you. Maybe you should stick around.'

He hadn't meant to say that last bit! What was it with this woman? Why did he seem to be floundering around like an adolescent schoolboy, whenever he was around her, anxious about saying things he shouldn't, and probably not saying the things he should? Where had the self-assured corporate lawyer gone, who could hold his own in a conversation with anyone, from any walk of life? Who was this bumbling idiot who couldn't stop making a fool of himself with everything that came out of his mouth?

But Fiona just smiled. 'Well, I'm sure there are worse places to hang out. It is lovely here. Maybe I could come and convalesce here, you know, after the chemo and everything. I could rent your barn, maybe.'

She blinked suddenly, a few times, as if she too had said something unintended. She turned to look at him. 'It's funny. I just met you, but I feel like I've known you longer. And I don't mean in a past-acquaintance kind of way, it's almost like an old-soul thing, for want of a better term. Like we've been here before, here in this place. In another time, not this one. Do I sound mad?' She chuckled.

'No you don't sound even remotely mad. For what it's worth, I felt that too, at our first meeting. I drove away from Teapot Cottage wondering what had happened to my head.' He laughed out loud. 'Now it's *me* who sounds mad! Anyway, let's go and have some lunch.'

Chapter Twenty-one

Stuart and Meghan brought Fiona home hours later than expected, and just in time for a late supper. Minty invited them to stay. She had cooked a simple butternut, spring onion and spinach risotto with crusty fresh bread, and there was plenty to go around. She'd made enough to set aside a hefty portion in the ice box of the fridge, with the intention of having it later in the week, but when everyone turned up, it seemed a bit mean not to invite them to join in, especially after Meghan had remarked on how good the risotto smelled. Minty knew she was learning to cook, so she offered the recipe and Meghan was enthusiastic. 'Ooh, yes please! This is so yummy.'

After they left, Fiona asked her if she'd made it to the Farmer's Market as planned.

'Yeah, and I'd have asked you to join me if you hadn't had other plans. The market's quite the hub of the town on a Saturday morning, and it's not just food that they have there. There's arts and crafts and stuff too, and a bric-a-brac stand.'

'I'd love to have come. I would have, if I'd been able. I can't resist a bric-a-brac stand. I should have asked Stuart to stop there on the way through this morning. Ah well, maybe another time.' Neither woman had the heart to wonder aloud how much time there might actually be.

She seems very much at peace tonight, Minty thought to herself. 'Did you have a nice time? You seemed to get along well with Meghan?'

'Yeah, it was nice, thanks. She's a good kid. She has a big heart, and big plans too, for one so young! Do you remember when we were that age, with the whole world in front of us, trying to decide what to do?'

Minty pulled a face. 'Yes I do. I always knew I wanted to be a doctor, though. Nothing else ever occurred to me, so I totally get how focussed she is. I see a bit of myself in her, as I was at her age. What did you think of their barn?'

'Oh, I loved that! Haven't they done a good job, there?'

'Did Stuart tell you how much he shaved off the cost of it, by ferreting around?'

Fiona laughed. 'He did! Quite the bargain-boy, isn't he? You know something? I like him. He's so genuine, much nicer than the guy he used to be, if what he said about himself was true. What you see is what you get, I think. Are you sure you're not interested in him?' Her voice was light, almost nonchalant.

A faint alarm bell rang in the back of Minty's mind. *Why are you asking me that, again? And asking so lightly, as if my answer doesn't really matter? If I know you, missus, it's because the answer matters more than you want me to know.*

'No, I've told you before, he's not my type. Yes, he's nice looking, and fun to be with, and he's certainly what you'd call an eligible catch, but there's no spark. I'm not attracted to him.'

I still miss my husband. You know? The one you stole, about five minutes ago? Some of us do need time to grieve for what we've lost, strange as that may seem to you.

'Are *you* attracted to him?' *Please tell me you're not, because that would be obscene.*

Fiona shook her head. 'Attracted? No, I don't think I am, at least not in the traditional sense. But I am drawn to him.'

Her voice was thoughtful. 'I don't know why, but there's something about him that just feels like, I dunno, *home*? Sounds stupid I guess, but I really don't know how else to describe it, Minty. Spending time with him just feels comfortable, safe, like I don't want it to end? And not like a dependency, or a fizz, or anything concrete, just a kind of settled feeling. An old-soul kind of thing, like he's been a trusted part of my family for aeons.'

Nobody could have been more astonished than Minty at that revelation. It wasn't the kind of thing she ever thought she'd hear coming out of Fiona Winterson's mouth! Fiona went on to say that it wasn't a boy-meets-girl attraction at all, that she felt. She seemed as baffled by it as Minty was herself.

She went to bed, and decided to read for a while, after telling Fiona they would talk in the morning, before she left, and thrash out the logistics of how she could provide the support Fiona would need in the coming weeks and months. Minty was due to go home herself in another couple of weeks. She toyed with the idea of cutting her own stay short, and being back in Bristol in time for Fiona's chemo, but decided against it. She felt she now needed time on her own, to digest the events of the past few days and get ready for what was coming.

It wasn't going to be an easy time. She needed to be fully prepared. Fiona's train wasn't leaving until eleven tomorrow. Perhaps they could have brunch in a nice cafe in Carlisle, somewhere near the train station maybe, before saying goodbye. Feen would no doubt be up for that, so Minty sent her a quick text. It wouldn't matter if she didn't reply until morning. She turned out the light, glad that Fiona had had a nice day with the Thomsons, more than a little bemused at her apparent 'old-soul' connection with Stuart, and relishing the thought that tomorrow night she would be on her own again in this lovely tranquil space.

Things didn't go quite the way she planned, however. Just as Feen's text pinged through on Sunday morning, turning down the offer of bunch because Gavin's family were all coming to Ravensdown for a big roast lunch at one o'clock, there was an insistent knock at the front door.

Minty checked her watch. It was only half past seven! Who would be pounding on the door at this hour? She went downstairs and opened it to find Stuart and Meghan standing there, declaring that they wanted to see Fiona straight away if possible. Minty obediently padded to the foot of the stairs and called her down.

Stuart and Meghan's mission stunned her. They wanted to take Fiona back with them to Beaconsfield, and said that if she was amenable, she could stay with them until Tuesday and Stuart would drive her back to Bristol himself, in time for her first chemo on Wednesday.

'W-well,' Minty stuttered. 'We haven't had time to agree on any details ourselves yet, about what happens after that. I was going to sit down with her this morning.'

'You can still do that,' Meghan said cheerfully. 'We don't want to get in the way of anything, but we thought she might enjoy a couple of days with us before everything changes.' She lowered her voice. 'Look, we get it, that she's kind of outstayed her welcome here. Let us take her off your hands for a day or two so she doesn't have to go home just yet.'

'Unless she really wants to, of course,' Stuart added. 'If she's keen to head home, that's fine.' He looked up as Fiona came limping down the stairs, holding tightly to the banister with one hand and trying to fasten her dressing gown with the other. Her hair was in a complete rumpled mess and she looked half-dazed.

'My God, Minty, what do you want at this hour? I was fast asleep! Oh! Hi guys! Sorry, did I forget you were coming over?' She looked confused.

Stuart stepped forward. 'No, this is part of a plan we hatched last night after we'd brought you home.' He went on to tell her about his and Meghan's offer.

'Wow! Well, that is so kind! Let's all sit at the table, shall we? Minty and I were going to talk about a few things before Feen picks me up, to run me to Carlisle station. We should still do that, but if you don't mind, I would *love* to spend a couple of days with you! To be honest,' she added, 'I know I can't stay here any longer but I've been dreading going home. It just brings everything that much closer, if you know what I mean?' She laughed lightly. 'The longer I can put off thinking about the chemo and surgery and everything, the better. I can't escape it, sitting at home by myself.'

Meghan nodded. Minty had nothing to contribute at this point so she busied herself making a pot of coffee for everyone. She didn't feel inclined to offer breakfast, since she'd already fed them all once, in the last twelve hours!

As they all sat around, talking about Fiona's cancer journey and the time it would take to recover, she couldn't help but notice how easy Stuart and Fiona were with one another. Both were perfectly relaxed, without being in one another's thrall, as if they'd been good friends for a long time, not just a couple of days. It was fascinating to see them acting as if they'd always been in one another's lives. Never before had she seen Fiona so at ease with a man. With every other one, for as long as Minty had known her, Fiona had always tried to get a rise out of them, flirt with them, or be downright condescending. Rarely was she ever so at ease with someone that she didn't feel compelled to make *something* of his presence. Here, it was like she and Stuart were almost some kind of weird extension of one another, with neither making an effort to impress or be anything other than who they really were.

Stuart himself wasn't bashful, tongue-tied, falling over himself to apologise, or doing anything else to try to make an impression or pretend he wasn't there. He was as relaxed in Fiona's company as she was in his.

And, as for Meghan, what an interesting study she was! The girl had clearly taken a shine to Fiona, which was ironic as the other woman didn't generally endear herself to adolescent girls. Even Belle, Minty's own daughter, had found her relationship with her godmother more than a little abrasive throughout the teenage years, with Fiona barely being able to tolerate the egocentricities of the average teenager's mind and how self-obsessed they all were. *Too similar*, Minty supposed. Fiona had never had a lot of patience with Belle's adolescent moods and self-absorption. The fact had clearly escaped her, more than a few times, that she'd once been there herself.

Meghan Thomson wasn't the kind of girl who could ever pretend to like someone if she really didn't, but there was a real tenderness there, as if she truly appreciated Fiona's unspoken fragility and wanted to protect her. Minty had fully expected Meghan to have revealed some kind of brat-ness while Fiona was about, but that didn't seem to be the case, and even if it had been, the two seemed to have got past it. It was as if *they'd* known one another all their lives as well!

Well, good. She'll be a far better friend to Fiona than I'm capable of being right now.

They quickly came to an agreement about Minty's role in Fiona's recovery from chemo and surgery, organising a cleaner to come in once a week, arranging either at-home or clinical care as Fiona would decide when appropriate, doing chores as necessary and taking her to appointments as and when she was available to (or finding someone who could when she couldn't). When Fiona asked her if she would act as power of attorney over her affairs when the time came, Minty felt a lump forming in her throat.

Despite everything, I don't want to lose her!

'I'll phone you on Wednesday night, to see how it went. Do you want Belle to know about this?'

Fiona winced. 'I dunno, Minty. Can I think about that? I know how much she hates me right now, and of course she has every right to. I don't want her to think this changes anything, you know, that I have any expectations of her or anything. Let me think about it for a few days. By the time you get back, I'll have made a decision about that, and a few other things besides.'

She looked sad. Minty knew that she and Belle had always been close. Belle had always treated her Godmother like a second Mum. Finally, it seemed that the full consequences of Fiona's burning bridges were coming home to roost. Minty found it interesting that she hadn't mentioned Leo once, in the last twenty four hours. Minty had the absurd notion that if she mentioned him Fiona might well just say, 'Leo who?'

It didn't take Fiona more than a couple of minutes to pack up her stuff, and as she was limping out the door she gave Minty a wobbly smile. 'Thank you for having me. I hope it wasn't too horrible, letting me stay. When I said I was sorry I really meant it, Minty, and while I don't expect you to forgive me, I hope one day you can, for yourself. Not for me. I'll never deserve it, but I want you to be happy, and letting go of all the horrible stuff that I've been the cause of, well, I think it will help you be that.'

Minty suddenly felt a rush of compassion for her. 'Fiona, Leo is a first class bastard. You've shown me that. If it hadn't been you, it would have been someone else, eventually. If he'd been truly happy with me, he wouldn't have fallen for you. He was unhappy, and he never talked about it, so it was only ever going to be a matter of time before he went off with someone. That could have been later rather than sooner, too, and by then I might have been too old to start again. As heartbreaking as this all is, and as long as it's going to take me to put it all behind me as best I ever can, you've actually done me a favour.'

Fiona compressed her lips into a thin line. 'You're a better person than me, for even thinking that, let alone saying it.'

Minty shook her head. 'It's the practical way to look at it. It's the *only* way. There's no room for him in my life anymore. He's not worth the pain. He's proved that to us both. I have to move on, and I will. I'll figure everything out.'

Fiona smirked. 'I'm glad now, that you butchered all his clothes and wreaked havoc on his stuff. I'm only sorry I paid for all the new stuff, although he did pay me back, the week he got paid. And I'm sorry I gave you such a hard time. You were right. I *was* just trying to make myself feel less guilty, but when death stares you in the face it makes you think again about how you want to be remembered. I don't want to be remembered just as the harridan who destroyed your family and harangued you for weeks because I didn't have the guts to face up to what I'd done. I hope I still mean something more than that to you, but it's okay if I don't.'

'You do,' Minty mumbled. She was determined not to cry, but knew it depended very much on Fiona leaving right this very minute. 'Now, go! Enjoy your stay with Stuart and Meghan. And good luck on Wednesday. I'll see you back in Bristol in a couple of weeks.'

She suddenly felt awkward and torn, half wanting to hug Fiona, yet still half-feeling like it was the last thing she wanted to do. She settled instead for squeezing Fiona's shoulder. Fiona looked at her and nodded, almost imperceptibly, understanding the awkwardness that still lay between them. Meghan picked up Fiona's bag and, after making sure Minty knew she had an open invitation to come over, they all left.

An immediate peace settled over Teapot Cottage again. Minty felt it like a warm embrace.

Chapter Twenty-two

Shaking out the duvets and pillows, and putting them out on the clothesline, was an important part of the ritual of cleaning Teapot Cottage once guests had left. Adie was glad of the blustery morning, with plenty of wind, and thankfully no rain for a change. December was always hit-and-miss, for getting those kind of jobs done, but she had a few days now, before Miranda and Max were arriving for Christmas. There was time, to ensure that everything would be fresh and lovely, well before Christmas Eve.

Minty Cartwright had decided to leave almost a week early, and that had been an absolute godsend. It gave Adie the chance to clean the cottage herself, instead of getting Peg to do it as originally planned. Minty's decision had come off the back of managing to reconcile, at least a degree, with Fiona. That terrible wound had started to heal, and it meant that she'd felt a lot more comfortable about heading back to Bristol. She felt ready, to go back and deal with her ex-husband, the house sale, and start making onward plans. Her daughter Belle and her son Ethan had driven up to collect her and, after meeting them, Adie had been left with the conviction that all three of them were going to cope just fine with supporting one another through the upcoming changes to their lives.

Minty was stronger, and more focussed on getting through everything, and going back to work, initially part time, and without doing any hands-on work. As a consultant, she could just 'consult,' at least for a while. Significantly, she was no longer afraid of the future. Much of it was still uncertain, but she genuinely felt that a lot of the turbulence was behind her, and she was able to start getting mentally prepared for whatever came next. Her peri-menopause was still a big distraction but, once a few other things were resolved, she was determined to meet that head-on too, and get whatever support she needed, as her transition got fully underway.

Adie knew that there Minty still had a long way to go, and that she'd have her ups and downs for a long time yet, on lots of levels. But it was always wonderful to see people emerging from a time of terrible trauma, with a new sense of resolve, and lifting their heads to look forward. Life would certainly be very different for Minty than what she was used to, but she seemed to be the kind of woman who made the best of things. Fiona's battle with cancer would be an ongoing challenge for her too, but at least the two women had salvaged something of their friendship. It could never again be what it was, and they both knew it, but both seemed to be hopeful of re-establishing some kind of meaningful ongoing contact. Minty had forgiven Fiona, and that was pretty big, as human triumphs went. Adie had no doubt that eventually, when the dust had fully settled on all of the things that had hurt her, Minty Cartwright's future would be a very bright one.

Cleaning and preparing Teapot Cottage was a job Adie always enjoyed, especially when friends or family were coming to stay. Her dearest friend Miranda was coming for Christmas this year, with her new beau Max, and Adie planned to add a few special touches, like a bottle of bubbly for the fridge, a box of luxury chocolates for Miranda's pillow, and a huge bouquet of festive flowers, which she'd ordered from Heavenly Blooms.

She also planned to hang a holly wreath on the front door, dot a few Christmas snow-globes around, and put a little Christmas tree in one of the bay windows, much like the one she'd been lent, a few years ago when she was merely a house sitter at the cottage. Maddie Murphy from Torley Tresses had dropped it off early on Christmas morning for her to enjoy, and she grinned to herself now, remembering how touched she'd been by that small but important act of kindness from a woman who was virtually a stranger.

It was lovely to be back in tune with her lovely little cottage, the place where her own life had changed so much after arriving in utter emotional turmoil, and eventually getting married to the owner of the neighbouring farm. She'd never for one moment regretted buying this gorgeous place. Its peculiar, almost magical energy had soothed many a troubled soul since, after she'd started renting it out as a holiday let, and that had brought into her and Mark's lives some of the most interesting people they could ever have hoped to meet.

Adie wondered where Minty Cartwright's journey would take her. It was an interesting development that Minty's friend Fiona, the one who had created all the havoc in her life, was the one who'd come more into focus here in Torley, thanks to her quickly developing relationship with Stuart Thomson, of all people! But, like a lot of the other quirky and random outcomes that always seemed to occur around here, Adie had long-since stopped questioning why they happened. The 'little bit of magic' that always seemed to prevail here had struck once again, bending broken lives in a completely different direction from where people imagined they would go. It was always a gentle process, but sometimes surprisingly swift.

As she cleaned down the kitchen surfaces, she heard the back door open, and she smiled as Feen came in. She had her gorgeous coat on; a bright red 1940's style fit-and-flare wool and cashmere number, that almost reached her ankles. It was a GinGio designer piece that she'd had specifically commissioned. It had cost an absolute eye-watering fortune, but she had got a generous 'staff and family' discount on it, and there was no denying how beautiful it was. With that, her green silk scarf, and her black-buttoned ankle boots, she looked very 'Christmassy' herself!

'I'm off, Adie. If I leave now, I can be home in dime for tinner. I think I'll pick up a tinese chakeaway so Gavin won't need to cook, and I can get the twins to bed and read them a story, and have a nice evening with my husband. I've meally rissed him.' Her eyes were twinkling. Adie laughed.

'Yes, I know you have. It must be a bit strange to have had all this time up here without him. You've never done this before, have you? A takeaway and a snuggly night sounds like a good plan.'

'He's missed us too! Said the house has been far too quiet. Reckons he works better with at least one of the twins having a tantrum close by. He's off his head, in saying that, but I think that was just his way of telling me it's time to head home!'

'You're ready to go, anyway, I think.'

'Yes, I am,' Feen nodded emphatically. 'We all are. Alder and Willow have officially had enough. They just want their Daddy now. It would have made more sense to have stayed here and waited for him to get here, since Christmas is literally around the corner, but I do think I need a new fights in London. I have some important things to pick up from the sherb hop over in the Elephant and Castle, not to mention having a ton of last-minute Christmas shopping to do. Gavin can watch the kids, while I do the department stores. I'll bring back a nice box of crosh packers for the table, and a few bottles of decent champagne.'

She looked around the cottage. 'So you're getting everything ready for Mand and Max! It'll be nice to see Mand again, and to mee her new man. You realise, of course, that we can't Spoonerize them? Two M's! It gives me no room to move, Adie. I suppose we'll have to be content to just call them M and M. It's been a while for you, hasn't it, since you've seen her? It's exciting for you both.'

She paused for breath, before continuing. 'Minty Cartwright was an interesting study, by the way, wasn't she?'

Adie grinned. 'Yeah, she was. Nice, but a bit dreamy, and at first I wondered what she was like at work, as an A & E Consultant, which is a job that needs a lot of focus. I didn't really see much evidence of that, to start with. But then I understood what her distractions were, and then there were glimpses of real resolve in the conversations we had, so I got to appreciate she'd probably be quite formidable in her job.'

'I liked her, Adie. She still has a lot to contend with, but I think she'll get there. I'm glad she managed to resolve things with Fiona, at least to some extent.' Feen chewed her bottom lip.

'I liked Fiona too and I think she has learned a few important lessons, in all this. She has a decent chance of survival now, since forgiveness and love have both touched her. She has something to fight for now. I think she has a really good chance at caving off this stancer for a good while, because of that.'

Adie was pensive. 'Yes, I remember you saying that she didn't have much of a chance when she thought she had nothing left to live for. Doesn't love make a difference!'

'It certainly does! Nothing makes any sense without it. And on that happy note, I'm going to go and fly to my morgeous gan. I'm sorry I don't have time to help you in here, but I'll be six hours on the road, and I want to be home before dark.'

Adie knew Feen was more anxious than usual because it was raining further south. The young woman was still very mindful of the accident she'd had a couple of years ago, when she'd been pregnant and driving Gavin's car. She'd gone out on a quick errand into the town on a rainy night and the car had gone over the bank after she'd been hit by an oncoming car that had been driving on the wrong side of the main road, just a few hundred metres from Ravensdown. She'd been lucky to survive that. Only a large rock had stopped the car from plunging a hundred metres further into a ravine. The twins had been born prematurely as a result, and they'd fought for their lives too. Adie understood entirely why Feen wanted to get home as quickly as she could.

'I hope you'll get there well before dark. You should, if you set off now, but if there are any delays, just take your time, and don't try to rush.'

'The par's all cacked, I just have to get the twins buckled in. They're having a last bounce on Daddy's knees!'

Adie closed her eyes and smiled to herself. She could instantly picture Mark, with a toddler on each knee, making silly noises and blowing bubbles at them. The twins could already both blow a fairly protracted raspberry, much to

Feen's disgust and Gavin's delight, and thanks to Mark's patient teachings.

She gave Feen a big, warm hug, which was readily returned. 'It's been lovely to have you! It'll be Christmas Eve, when we see you next.'

Feen grinned ruefully. 'At worst, yes; just in time for your birthday, but Gavin plans to stop work a day early if he can, so I'm hoping we can get here the day before. And we're here until the week after New Years. Two weeks in total, I guess. It'll be like I never left!'

'Have a safe trip, and don't forget that tin of cookies I left on the kitchen table. They're Gavin's favourites. Tell him we've missed him this time, and will look forward to seeing him at Christmas. Let me know when you're safely home!' she called out to Feen's retreating back. Minutes later, she heard a cheerful double-toot as Feen drove her car past the cottage and down to the main road.

Christmas *was* right around the corner, and Adie was glad that she already had a lot prepared in advance. The Christmas cake had been made since the end of October, the turkey was ordered, and her list was in with the other traders at the Farmers Market for everything else she would need for the Christmas table.

Matty, Marie and their kids wouldn't be coming this year. They were headed to Marie's family, instead. Theresa would be here of course, and with Gavin, Feen and the twins, Ruth, Gina and Chiara, *and* Miranda and Max, they'd have a full enough table. Christmas Eve was her birthday, and the party on Christmas night would no doubt be the usual jolly affair, with all of their friends coming. Sheila, bless her, always organised that. She and Peg Tripper were doing the bulk of the catering too, as usual. Adie felt a warm glow inside her at the memory of her first Christmas party at Ravensdown, and how completely her life had changed because of it.

Adie's mind drifted back now, to Minty Cartwright, and she realised how much she admired her. It had to take a lot of guts for Minty to allow her primary antagonist into her personal space and confront all the demons laid bare because of it. But, as Feen had pointed out (and many, many times, in different contexts), love is the basis for everything that matters, and the love that existed between the two women for virtually their whole lives had turned out to be stronger than anything that threatened to break it. That love had got them through the worst possible storm, and it was love that allowed them both to make sense of their lives that were going in different directions.

If Feen was right, Fiona Winterson would gain at least few years on her initial prognosis, and she may even at some stage go into remission. Adie hoped so, not just for Fiona's own sake but also for Stuart and Meghan Thomson's. Those two had already run a few mental marathons and overcome a lot of adversity. But Stuart had found love again, which he fully deserved, and Meghan had found someone she could relate to as a mother figure at a really important time in her life. It would be nice if they all got a clear run for a while without any more drama showing up. Fiona's death may not be inevitable, and at least now she had every reason in the world to keep fighting, for as long as she was able. So many unusual, unpredictable and profound things happened in this little corner of the world that it made Adie almost confident to imagine the best possible outcome.

Whatever the future held for any of them, she had no doubt that they would all face and deal with it well. The only apparent loser would be that cheating, cowardly husband of Minty's Cartwright's, and Adie didn't have a single scrap of sympathy for him!

Chapter Twenty-three

Fiona asked Stuart, for what felt like the thousandth time; did he have rocks in his head? Was he sure? Was this the right thing for him to be doing? They were driving back towards Carlisle, with the sun finally setting on a typically rainy April day. Fiona had been sound asleep beside him, but now she was awake. Her belongings were all piled in the back of the hired van. As he drove, Stuart patiently answered the question in exactly the same way he already had, countless times.

'Yes, sweetheart. On a very visceral level, it does feel right. Absolutely. It also feels right for Meghan, and I know it does for you too. So it *is* right. Okay?'

Fiona pinched herself again; not just for the fact that Stuart had chosen to get involved with her as a 'cancer victim' who maybe had limited time left on the planet. It was also the fact that his daughter had also taken to her like a duck to water. It had been the most extraordinary sequence of events that had led Stuart and Meghan to know absolutely, before they had even sat down at the kitchen table and had the critical discussion, that they both wanted Fiona in their lives.

Stuart had said, many times, that he wasn't able to put his finger on exactly what it was that had drawn him to her. It wasn't a huge or powerful attraction or a passion of any kind, like you'd usually get with someone you meet who you just can't seem to get enough of, physically or intellectually. It hadn't been like that at all. Stuart had said that for him, as well as for Meghan, it was as if a small but important piece of their puzzle they didn't even really know was missing just quietly slipped into place without them noticing until it was there and the picture was somehow complete.

There hadn't been a 'wow' moment, or even a sharp shift. It was more like a subtle and gentle push towards her, he'd explained, as if the universe had quietly whispered *'yes, this is your destiny, this is where you need to go next.'*

Fiona understood it because she felt the same way. Being with Stuart and Meghan somehow felt like coming 'home,' after a long time away, and the speed at which it had happened hadn't fazed any of them at all. The fact that Meghan was fully committed too had left Stuart in no doubt whatsoever that 'the universe had spoken' – yet again – and steered his and Meghan's lives in a certain direction. He was certain that he was doing the right thing, that *they* were, in moving Fiona into Beaconsfield. This last trip to Bristol, to put her furniture into storage and bring back everything she wanted to have with her, meant that she was moving in with him and Meghan, lock, stock and barrel. She'd rented out her house, and instead of feeling uncertain or afraid about the future, and how difficult or long, or short it might be, she felt quietly *settled* in a way she couldn't define.

Was she disappointed in the lack of fireworks, the instant fizzing attraction that would make them want to rip one another's clothes off or climb inside each other's heads? If she was honest, no. She'd had the great sex, the passionate, lust-filled nights where the last thing that ever happened in bed was sleep. She knew all about those, and so did Stuart. He'd never said no in the past, to a bit of stray sex when it was offered, by either his first or second wife or in the casual relationships he'd had in between that were usually little more than one night stands. They both felt the same way; all that 'fizz and bang' had been brilliant while it lasted, but it wasn't what they wanted anymore, now that they had found one another.

Fiona and Minty Cartwright had insisted on the transfer of Fiona's cancer care from Bristol. As a medical heavyweight, Minty had successfully lent real muscle to making the process seamless. As she'd said; sometimes, using whatever influence you have is appropriate. She didn't pull strings very often, but she'd been glad she could when it mattered.

Debby Davies had caught the ball from Minty and talked to the right people at Cumberland hospital, who had facilitated Fiona's transition to the radiation and chemo departments, as the final push to ensure that her transfer from Bristol would go without a hitch. Stuart was glad that Fiona had been able to have the rest of her chemo locally. Arrangements had quickly been made for her double mastectomy to be done at Cumberland too, and she was profoundly glad that that Stuart was on hand to help with her recovery process.

Fiona knew that what Stuart felt for her went well beyond the physical. She knew he was attracted to her, but she wasn't ready for anything yet. She still had a lot of battles to fight, and she'd explained that, as best she could. Thankfully, he'd understood her initial reticence about intimacy, saying that on some level he knew that he wasn't quite ready for it either! It was the sweetest thing to say, and she loved him for it.

But, after the operation, he had made a point of reverently kissing her angry red and purple chest scars that were still all covered in stitches, and telling her it didn't matter to him that the fulsome breasts were gone.

He'd meant it. It really *didn't* seem to make a difference to how he felt. She'd been shaking with shame and fear, that first night when they'd shared a bed for the first time, but he'd simply kissed it all away, held her in his arms, and told her the truth; that she was still the most incredible woman he'd met in many years and it didn't matter a bloody jot what she looked like. She was beautiful just the way she was. He just loved her, pure and simple, and he wanted to be with her for whatever time they might have together, and that was that. How wonderful it was, that she could trust him to tell her the truth.

She knew that he'd been dreading telling some of his friends about his new relationship, but they'd been nothing but happy for them both. Debby and Darren Davies had been quick to invite the new little family over for dinner. They hadn't hesitated for a heartbeat, about making Fiona welcome.

As a theatre nurse, Debby was great at checking Fiona's healing progress too. She'd swung by most days, either before or after her shifts at the hospital, to see how things were going, and the Home Care team had been set up to also check in daily, to make sure things were going in the right direction. Fiona felt pretty well looked after. She was a long way now, from the fear she'd first felt, immediately after Leo had left, and she was facing a bleak battle alone with no certainty of survival at the end of it.

Stuart's mum was lovely too. She was still somewhat bemused about the turn of events in her son and granddaughter's lives, but she'd come up for Christmas, as arranged, and it had been a quiet but lovely few days. Fiona had already met her on a Messenger call beforehand, and both women had decided they liked one another, especially after Meghan had told her Nan how easily and gently their relationship was developing. Nan had proclaimed that if her prickly granddaughter liked someone, she should make the effort to like them, too. And she did, and Christmas had been quiet, and a little surreal, but lovely.

The Ravens had been on the phone a few times, with Feen offering to come up to Beaconsfield whenever she was up from London and take Fiona shopping for whatever she might want or need, pick things up for her as required, or just take her for a girly coffee and cake if she felt like doing that. A couple of Stuart's friends and their wives from Taunton had been on a Zoom call with them both, a few nights after she'd come home from hospital post-surgery, and that call had been a bit of a laugh. Fiona made the effort to respond well to their gentle banter, giving as good as she got, and offering to show them her terrible scars, and be a good sport and 'get what's left of her tits out for the boys.'

Stuart's friends seemed to love her, and the general consensus was that he'd vastly raised his game in the wake of the catastrophic Annabel, who it seemed nobody had liked. It was always hilarious how, after a relationship ended, people suddenly felt entitled to be honest. Stuart had admitted that he wasn't sure if his friends' simultaneous need to openly denigrate Annabel was the truth or a simple show of solidarity, but he decide he'd take it, either way. It seemed to Fiona that the hurt of his past relationship, and the pain it had inflicted on Meghan, was well behind them both now.

Adie Raven, whose kindness knew no bounds, had commissioned her daughter in law, the acclaimed dress designer Gina Giordano, to quickly make Fiona three utterly stunning headpieces to wear, to prepare her for her hair falling out as the chemo got underway. She'd arranged for them to be delivered directly to the hospital when Fiona was having one of her sessions. One was a rather exotic-looking turban in a gorgeous cream satiny fabric covered in pink and lavender peonies, to which tiny diamantes had been affixed to look like raindrops, with a larger one at front and centre. Another was a cap-like affair in tie-dyed green and blue silk, with gorgeous wide ties that fastened and hung down the back, and the last was a simple turquoise silk scarf with scalloped fine lace edging that came with instructions for various ways to tie it. They'd arrived by express courier directly from the Giordano Fashion House, in a very beautiful black box, lined in gold satin, and monogrammed on the outside with the gold embossed GinGio logo. Inside was a hand-written note from Gina;

'Fiona, cara... Be bald and beautiful with pride! But on the days when you feel like you need more eleganza, if there is such an eleganza greater than the magnificosa shape of a woman's head, maybe these will help. Buona fortuna, donna coraggiosa – Gina Giordano.'

Fiona had burst into tears. She was beyond thrilled with the beautiful pieces. Each was a carefully crafted masterpiece in its own right, with the exquisite GinGio label on the inside, complete with a serial number to depict it's exclusivity as part of a strictly limited line. Apparently, since it was every woman's dream to own a GinGio item of clothing, no matter what it was, Fiona found it almost unbelievable that she actually now had three (aside from her lovely old skirt)! She cried like a baby when she saw them, and she immediately put a call through to GinGio's offices and was able to leave a message with Gina's PA to convey her gratitude. To her amazement, the PA asked for her phone number, and later that day, when Fiona's mobile phone rang showing that same London number, she had no idea she would be talking to the woman herself!

Gina had rung to say she was glad the headgear had arrived safely, and to express her *own* gratitude, because Adie's commission had given her the idea to approach the country's biggest cancer charity with the offer of producing an exclusive line of headgear for women fighting cancer. The charity had embraced the concept with open arms and it meant GinGio could employ a fashion design graduate, on a government-subsidized scheme, to produce a small range that would only be available through the cancer charity's website link to a hidden page on GinGio's with 50% of the cost of each piece being donated to it.

It was a whole new line; an important one, and Gina was excited about it. She told Fiona she imagined many women who still had their hair, who weren't even cancer sufferers, would be interested too, and would no doubt purchase the head pieces also, but Gina wasn't bothered by that because it was all helping the charity and raising her profile to boot.

The head pieces were still likely to be quite costly, like everything else in the GinGio line, because Gina only ever made a very limited number of items each season in each style or fabric, and never did discounts, never had a sale, and never devalued her product in any shape or form. But the cost of these particular items wasn't going to be as eye-wateringly expensive as everything else in her lines and with half of the proceeds going to the charity, few would quibble too much about the cost. Each piece would still be, after all, a limited edition-fabric designer product.

Fiona had also contacted Adie to give her effusive thanks, saying how thrilling it was, to not only have the pieces but to also have had an incredibly kind personal call from the designer herself, and declaring she'd probably be pinching herself for at least a week. She asked Adie if she could pay her for the headpieces.

Adie had laughed off the suggestion, saying that there *were* some perks within the family, and that Gina had agreed to make them from fabric off-cuts that would probably only have gone in the bin anyway. But, as prototypes, they had inspired Gina to work with the cancer charity, and that kind of win-win scenario was the best possible outcome for all involved, so Fiona could happily have them with everyone's blessing.

Kindness on that scale was everywhere. From the minute Stuart had got Fiona home to Beaconsfield, everyone rallied round, as if she had always been there, as if she'd always been in Stuart and Meghan's lives and had only now developed an illness. Adie's friend Maddie Murphy, who owned the hairdressing shop over in Torley, came by one day after the salon closed, and manicured and polished Fiona's nails, and given her a trial-sized range of beauty products, all for free. Meghan's friend Jayde, who ran the jewellery stand at the Torley Farmer's Market, had made a bracelet laden with healing semi-precious stones for Fiona to wear. It was a curious thing, how humbled she was by all the support she received. One night, feeling a little overwhelmed, she confessed to Stuart, how she really felt.

'I feel like such a fraud, accepting all this kindness from virtual strangers. I feel I don't deserve it, because I really have been the most horrible, self-centred person for most of my life. I've been especially cruel to the person I've always loved most in this whole world – no offence – poor Minty! If people knew what I was really like, they wouldn't be this nice to me. They'd hate me. They'd avoid me like the plague, and I wouldn't blame them one bit.'

Stuart had hastened to assure her that she shouldn't feel guilty, but instead be accepting of people's heart-centred attempts to ease her burdens, with the kind of grace he knew she was capable of. The past was the past and needed to be left there. Fiona had simply evolved as she'd needed to, like everyone else has to do, when their circumstances change. She also needed to recognise that people's kindness was often driven by the need to feel like they were making a positive difference to the life of someone in a far worse place than they were in themselves. They contributed for *themselves,* as much as for her, if not more so. And, he pointed out, even though she might be dying, Fiona really *was* happier within herself, at who she was now. He told her she just had to believe that most people were inherently good, *including her*, and hold fast to that.

He seemed to understand everything, and he took great care to point out to her too, that her goodness had been buried by grief and self-defence, after finding herself alone, brutally orphaned at the very time when she needed the reassurance of the solid backstop of her family as she started to make her way in the adult world. There was never a good time to lose your parents, but on the cusp of adulthood, to find herself completely adrift without the anchors she'd always assumed would be there, it was little wonder Fiona had become so insular and self-protective.

When he'd questioned her about why she'd never adopted Minty's family as her own, she'd admitted that she hadn't wanted to be a burden. She couldn't imagine anyone else loving her the way her parents had, and she felt she would have been a dead weight to Minty's family. She also confessed to not liking Minty's dad, who was often drunk and sometimes quite belligerent with it. Living with that was more than she'd felt able to take on, at the time. It was one thing, to live with your best friend and her mum and sister, but quite another to be sharing that space, even if it was only occasionally, with a 'father figure' who was unpredictable and difficult on the rare occasions when he did make an appearance. It would have been like waiting for an axe to fall, every time the back door opened. She'd just lost her own father; the rock of her life, who she'd never had to worry about, distrust or be afraid of.

She did realise now of course, with the benefit of years of wisdom and a newly developing empathy, that Christine Cartwright and her daughters would have welcomed with open arms the chance to have adopted her – if not in the legal sense, then at least in all the other ways that mattered. Together, as a united front, they would *all* have managed to cope with Frank Cartwright's intermittent presence and the belligerence that usually came with it. Christine would never have allowed Fiona to be scared of him.

Fiona was riddled with regrets, and she wondered if everyone facing the prospect of their own death reacted the same way. She supposed they probably did. After all, when you know you have few opportunities left, wouldn't it be entirely natural to rue the ones you'd squandered, before you were brought to realise in the worst possible way how precious life and love were?

Minty was still in touch fairly regularly, but of course their friendship could never go back to being what it was. Fiona has already accepted that, and it seemed that Minty had too. Their conversations were generally quite light, and confined to matters of Fiona's recovery and superficial things. They never strayed into serious territory, like talking about Leo or Belle, ruminating on the past, or even discussing the future.

The only 'weighty' thing Minty had mentioned was that she was considering moving to France. Fiona knew she didn't have a right anymore, to make any observations about that. All she could do now was hope that Minty's decisions, whatever they were about her future, would put her in a happy place. She deserved that, and it was nobody's place to judge how she made it happen.

Only now could she see how much she had lost, in snatching Leo away from Minty. Only now could she appreciate how much that forty years of friendship had meant, even as she was blowing it apart. But Minty had been right when she'd said, in one of the many discussions they'd had while Fiona was with her at Teapot Cottage, that some things got so badly broken that they really couldn't be fixed, and it wasn't realistic to imagine that they could.

Fiona knew what she meant. It was like a favourite old vase that you'd had forever. One day, you were careless with it, and it slipped from your hands and broke. You could only ever glue it back together into some semblance of what it used to be. It would never again be what it was. The cracks would forever still show. It wouldn't hold water as well as it used to but, even in its broken and reconstituted form, you could still appreciate what beauty it still had. You just had to *want* to. You had to want to still see its value, and remember what it had meant to you once. In certain cases, a broken vase was still better than no vase at all.

That's where they were at now, she and Minty. They had some semblance of a friendship, and that was only because both women could appreciate the value of what they'd had before it was lost. Fiona was hopeful that with time, they may move forward onto a slightly closer footing. She still missed her old friend. Just like a broken and glued-back-together vase, their relationship could never again be what it was, back in the days where they didn't know half as much as they should have, about each other, and where respect had been lost because of it. But maybe with the gift of hindsight, and new understanding, they could make something better in the future.

Fiona had hope now, for a future. She had hope for her own survival, but she also had hope for the survival of her and Minty's friendship, as part of that future. If Minty felt the same, maybe they could make something work.

Chapter Twenty-four

Stuart finally managed a rare late-afternoon catch-up with Darren for a quiet drink in town. They didn't very often get to do it. One or the other was usually too busy, with different things, and the women usually wanted to be involved with anything social, which wasn't a problem of course, but a bit of 'guy-time' was always very welcome. Stuart took advantage of the chance to ask Darren a burning question; what he *really* thought of Stuart's new relationship.

'I know you've said and done all the right and best things, you and Debby, but I do wonder what you really think. I'm pretty sure I know the answer, but tell me, honestly; have I done the right thing, or am I just setting Meghan and myself up for a whole new world of pain? I adore this woman, Darren. I love the bloody bones of her, and so does Meghan, but I am a bit scared about the future, you know...' he trailed off, not being able to find quite the right words to finish the sentence.

Darren nodded. 'Yeah, I know what you're trying to say.'

He sat back and regarded Stuart speculatively, for a moment or two, clearly weighing up his words before he uttered them. Stuart momentarily experienced a horrible sinking feeling in the pit of his stomach. It wasn't that he cared much what most people thought, if he was honest, but he valued Darren's perspective more than any other, since the vet had enough life experience to have his feet firmly on the ground. Darren wasn't under any illusions about much in life at all, and he very much called a spade a spade. But he was unexpectedly positive.

'Mate, you're a bloke with a penchant for ending up with troublesome women, aren't you? Your first wife was hell-bent on being a robotic Stepford version, until she died of a brain bleed. Your second one turned out to be the flake of the century who walked out on you and Meghan while you were banged up, then you had that mad carpenter-woman who nearly killed you. To be honest, I wouldn't have expected anything less than another chick with complications, but it's obvious that you love her and she loves you. Okay, it might not be a long-haul thing, because of her condition, but you know that already. It's been a few months now, and if you and Meghan are both still over the moon with the new family unit, who the hell am I to judge you for that?'

Stuart gave him a light punch on the arm. 'I don't suppose it's worth pointing out – *yet* again – that it wasn't the so-called 'mad carpenter-woman,' but her ex-husband, who was mad and tried to kill me? Oh, and that Caro Swift was only ever just my carpenter and nothing more?'

Darren just grinned. 'If you think I'm ever going to let you forget that one, you'll have a long wait. I'll be dining out on that story for the rest of my bloody life, especially the really interesting bit where Keith Brockett died after I smacked him!'

He looked sideways at Stuart, and smirked. 'Nah. Fiona's a sweetheart, Stu. For whatever time you've got together, me and Debs wish you nothing but the best. And you know we'll be here for you both, you and Meghan, if and when, well, you know. . .'

Darren hadn't finished his sentence either. He hadn't needed to. Everyone knew what could still be coming, and how hard it was, to put it into words. They just didn't know if or when Fiona's time would be up. That in itself was hard, but it had encouraged Stuart to live more in the moment, cherishing each day, without getting too hung up on the future and what it would bring.

'How I'll manage Meghan's grief is another story, if the worst happens. But we've already talked about the very real possibility that Fiona might die, and Meghan's old enough now to be able to discuss and manage her emotions. She's already said that if she felt she needed grief counselling, either before or after, she wouldn't hesitate to get some.'

'I know, and that's good. She's already asked if she can talk to me and Deb about it too, and we've both said yes, of course. Counselling helped her before, after the abduction and everything. It's good that she understands the value of good therapy, and wouldn't hesitate to take it again, if she felt the need.'

Stuart nodded. 'We've got everything in place; with Fi's affairs, I mean. Minty Cartwright's a good support, and very practical. I'll be a basket case probably, but she'll be a tower of strength if and when the time comes, I'm sure. But it's better to have loved and lost, and all that, right?'

Darren stared into his pint for a moment, then nodded sagely. 'Yeah, that's an interesting one, isn't it, that theory? But after everything me and Debs went through, you know, with the IVF and everything, when it looked like we were going to split up because nothing was working, to get pregnant, I thought about that old saying quite a lot. I wondered what my life would be like if I was on my own again, and whether I'd think it hadn't been worth it, but I decided that it probably *is* better to have had love and lost it than to have never experienced it at all. I really do. What in the world means anything, without love?'

Stuart punched him again, playfully. 'Soppy bastard,' he chuckled.

'Yeah, back at ya, tosser! You're a sucker for punishment, I'll give you that, but love's just love, isn't it? No arguing with that. And you know, she could still beat this cancer. With you guys in her life, she's got the best shot possible. So let's drink to that! To the best shot possible!'

And Darren raised his pint, Stuart raised his glass of coke, and they then went on to talk about other things.

Stuart wanted to marry Fiona but he hadn't formally proposed yet. He didn't want to overwhelm her. She had enough to be dealing with. The chemo and radiation had been brutal, and the mastectomy had been agonising. But the two of them had talked about marriage, and she had been open to the idea, provided her health could be stabilized. They'd agreed to leave things as they were until after the results of her treatment could be fully assessed, but Stuart felt it was important to make that declaration of intent, just so Fiona knew he was serious about wanting whatever kind of future they could have together as husband and wife. He'd told her it was about time someone made an honest woman of her, and he'd be thrilled if she'd consider him as prime candidate. She'd replied with her customary smirk that he was – so far – the best of a bad bunch who'd offered to take her hand. And that had been enough. They weren't formally engaged, but the intention to get married was very real.

If they managed to make it happen, it would be a small, understated affair, more about the two of them than any kind of attempt to impress friends and family. They'd already decided to take Adie and Mark Raven up on their generous offer of using the lovely lavender garden at Ravensdown House, for a quiet garden wedding, in a pretty marquee if the weather was bad, and with just a few friends and family in attendance. A nice catered buffet and a wedding night at Teapot Cottage would make it the perfect event. Adie promised that, come hell or high water, she would make sure the cottage was free for whatever night they might choose.

Stuart couldn't have been happier with that, and the smile on Fiona's face had told him all he needed to know about it being the right thing to do.

'I still feel so lucky to have meet her, Darren,' he said, swinging the conversation back. 'It's not just a pay-it-forward thing, like we're always talking about. I genuinely love her, and I want to have a long, and happy life with her, and as you and God are my witnesses, I'm going to help her do everything in our doubled-up power, to make that happen.'

Darren blinked back a tear, but not before Stuart saw it. 'I hope you have a good long time together, mate. I really hope you do. You both deserve it.' His voice was husky, and Stuart was humbled all over again, by how much his new friends cared.

It would be what it would be, for however long or short it would be. But he made a promise to himself, and to Meghan, and to Fiona too, that they would make the most of every second of every minute of every day, for however long they could.

One Year Later

The sun was a little watery, which was to be expected at this time of year, Minty supposed, as she sat in the white cane swing chair that hung from a heavy hook embedded in the patio rafters, just outside her front door. She had a light cotton throw over her knees this morning. Summer was on its way, but this was a typical crisp, cool spring day. People often mistakenly assumed that it never got cold in the south of France. She'd been surprised herself at how chilly it was, especially at night, once the autumn had officially ended and winter had set in.

L'Aquitaine was a truly lovely area of the country, with its endless rolling fields of vines, and she was just over half an hour away from Fliss and Filipe. From the minute Minty had said 'yes' to the house, she felt like something critically out of balance had righted itself in her head. She'd been so lucky with the place, thanks to Fliss' eagle eye for what was coming on the market. Fliss had offered the asking price on her behalf on the very same day it had come up for sale, without even asking Minty. She'd known what the budget was, and she'd landed very safely within it. She'd even managed to wrangle the whiteware as part of the sale!

She'd known instinctively that Minty would adore the place, with its whitewashed walls and sage green shutters. It had lovely tiled floors and, incredibly, it also had a little fenced-off heated swimming pool with a canopy above it, and a small walnut orchard! There were two generous bedrooms and one smaller one that served as an office, befitting Minty's new role writing training programs for A & E staff in several different countries. She also had a part time job at the local medical centre, just 15 hours a week spread over three days, as a job share with another doctor who'd had a baby and wanted to reduce her hours a bit.

So she was still as busy as she'd been before the apocalypse that had torn her life apart, but she was very much getting to like her new one. Who *wouldn't* want to live in the South of France with its gorgeous climate, world-class wines, and opportunities to pop across the border in a heartbeat, into even sunnier Spain?

Filipe had helped her buy a car, and with the assistance of one of his own friends in the distribution trade, he'd organised affordable transportation of Minty's furniture and personal effects from England. She'd had to downsize a lot, but she'd been astonished at how much money she'd made from the sale of some of the surplus furniture. That extra money had helped massively with the move.

The legal side of buying the house had been frustrating, but Stuart Thomson had friends who'd helped a lot to get things moved along. He had a solicitor friend who had moved to Paris after marrying a French girl, and although the guy wasn't a conveyancing solicitor, others in his firm were. He'd put Minty in touch with a well-experienced guy called Marcel Junot, who eased her through the final stages of the purchase. Marcel's bill had been high, but worth every cent.

He had since become a close friend, and while Minty wasn't really ready for romance just yet, there was an unspoken, tacit agreement that when she was, Marcel would be waiting. That suited her just fine. He was lovely, good company, respectful, and handsome to boot! They had a lot in common, and she could definitely imagine a quiet, gentle future with him, when the time felt right.

Virtually every day, she thanked her lucky stars for taking French all those years ago at school. She never thought she'd need her second language, but she was amazed at how quickly certain words she thought she'd forgotten just randomly came back to her. She'd been wandering along the main street of a local town, when she'd suddenly remembered the French word for ice-cream! A few sessions with a local tutor had refreshed her memory of French grammar, and Fliss and Filipe unfailingly corrected her whenever she got something wrong. In the time since she'd moved here, her language skills had exponentially improved. After all, when you're trying to enquire about the availability and price of something you needed, or explain to a patient why they needed to have an operation, you had to be able to speak to them properly in their own language!

It had taken quite a while for the dust to settle back in Bristol. The sale of the marital home had been as painless as predicted – in practical terms, at least – but Minty had been surprised at how deep the grief was, in the end, after saying goodbye to the house she and Leo had poured so much heart and soul into for more than twenty years. The death of any relationship is hard, even when you know it's the right thing, but there is always more of an investment than simply what goes into the relationship itself. You don't just end up mourning the relationship. You end up mourning the history, the memories you made, the bits of yourself you gave away in the interests of compromise, and the solidness of a home you saw so much of life in, together. Minty had conceived both of her children in that house, and brought them home to it as new babies. They'd grown there, experienced highs and lows of life there, and the walls could say so much, if only they could have talked. Just because selling the place was the right thing to do, that didn't cancel out the visceral grief and pain of doing it.

Even saying goodbye to the furniture had been a tricky task. An occasional table that has been found at a flea market; a big bottle they'd picked up on a holiday in Cornwall that they'd filled with corks and turned into a lamp; artwork they'd fallen in love with abroad, and had shipped home. Every item told a story, and letting some of that go had been harder than expected. Sentimentality had to give way to practicality, but there'd been many a night when Minty had fallen into bed weeping, at what it all meant.

Getting here to France had been a process too! It hadn't been as straightforward as Minty had hoped. The immigration process had changed a lot in recent years, and getting her sponsorship visa was taking its sweet time, but she had thankfully got to the end of that marathon with the help of another solicitor Marcel knew pretty well.

The management of Fiona's chemo and her recovery from her double mastectomy were things that she hadn't needed to worry about, thank goodness. Fiona's relationship with Stuart Thomson had developed very quickly, and he had happily stepped in to be the rock she sorely needed. He and Meghan adored her, and because she'd moved in with them, they were right there on hand, to deal with any problems she might have while she battled her way forward from it all. Minty had been in regular contact, with all three of them, and had always been reassured that things were working out as well as they possibly could, under the circumstances.

Minty was amazed at the change in her old friend. Taking up with Stuart had encouraged her to stop playing the victim and start fighting for her life, and she was doing exactly that. A year on, the cancer appeared to have stopped spreading (for now at least), and her hair was growing back. Fiona insisted that it was a combination of her love for Stuart, and his for her, and the equine therapy Meghan had been giving her, in her as-yet unqualified way, that had turned everything around. Fiona said she felt settled, in a way she'd never felt before.

From a place where time and distance had allowed the growth of a kinder perspective, Minty was glad that her friend had found real love. Fiona hadn't loved her first husband George at all, and she came to understand that what she'd felt for Leo was the remnants of an age-old crush she hadn't known how to let go of. At eighteen, she'd fallen in love with the *ideal* of a man. Finding out that the reality fell a long way short of that ideal had been a brutal lesson for her, and a tragedy for all concerned, that she'd wasted half her life carrying a torch for a man she didn't even really know, in the true sense of the word.

Fiona had *never* experienced true, deep, meaningful love until Stuart Thomson had innocuously wandered into her life and turned it on its head. She was a very different person now, much more grateful for what she had in her life, and a lot more respectful of others. She had been through a fire, and she wasn't out of it yet. Nobody could say whether she was going to survive for two years or ten, and although it must feel like having the Sword of Damocles hanging over her, Fiona had resolved to do all she could, strive to stay as healthy as possible, and enjoy life to the full for however long or short a time it turned out to be.

She'd had some counselling, as part of her treatment regimen, and that had enabled her to examine other issues too, like her long-buried heartbreak over how her 'friend' Kris Kiehl had treated her, when she was a fragile teenager. She'd said herself how 'heavy' that unidentified grief had been, until she was encouraged to let go of it. Buried grief and guilt over the death of her parents had surfaced too, and been addressed. It all left her feeling pretty battered, but not in a way that was harmful, like carrying around all that deeply-buried poison had been. She said she was able to think about those sad events without being adversely affected by them anymore, and she felt stronger now, in dealing with her cancer.

Stuart and she had started renovating old cottages too, buying derelict and abandoned properties dotted across the Lake District and turning them into holiday homes to rent out to tourists. They'd started their first one with the profit from the sale of Fiona's house in Bristol. In the past five months they'd done up two cottages, and more were in the pipeline. Fiona was in her element, happily project-managing all the contractors involved in the work, and Stuart was happy too, doing what he did best – sourcing the materials, fixtures and fittings from far and wide, for a fraction of their normal cost. If the photos were anything to judge by, they'd done an excellent job both times, and the cottages were beautiful. Stuart said that although they'd tried hard to recreate the atmosphere at Teapot Cottage in their own houses, they'd never really managed it. They'd come to the inevitable conclusion that Teapot Cottage was uniquely magical, and no amount of effort or insight could ever replicate the peculiar healing, nurturing energy that lived within its walls. Minty had laughed, saying they'd get no argument from her about that!

She often wondered about the energy at Teapot Cottage. If she hadn't been there, and invited Fiona up to stay for that fateful few days that changed both their lives, would they have got to where they were now? She doubted it. She was certain she would still have moved to France, but she wasn't at all sure she'd have ended up in a place where she felt any kindness towards the woman who'd wrecked her marriage. And, of course, Fiona would never have met Stuart.

Minty had managed to maintain a friendship, with her former friend, but it was looser now. It didn't feel appropriate to be really close anymore, like they used to be, and after a period of deep reflection she realised that it was okay to feel that way. It was a curious thing, but it had become an entirely acceptable one, how you could love someone enough to want every good thing for them, and yet not want to have them in your life in the same way they'd been in it before they hurt you. Forgiveness was important, but so was protecting your own heart. A balance between the two was possible, and Minty had managed to achieve it for herself.

She though back, now, to what Adie Raven's stepdaughter Feen had said, over a year ago now; *Fiona can beat her illness. She just has to fight harder than she ever has before. If you can forgive her, she has a shot. Without your help, she won't make it, Minty. With your help, she just might. It's something to think about.*

It had taken Minty a while to realise that she *had* forgiven Fiona, and without much conscious effort at all. Fiona had said to her, as she was leaving Teapot Cottage, that forgiveness was important for Minty herself, if she could manage it, and Minty realised she'd been right.

It hadn't been a conscious process. In fact, it simply reached a quiet, unheralded point where all of the anger and resentment she'd had towards her old friend had simply just dissolved without warning. It was probably because the love she'd always had for her, that bubbled beneath it all, had never gone away. Minty had felt mortally wounded, but she was strong enough to recover without bitterness or rancour, and that was something worth celebrating.

Knowing that Fiona would go through the unimaginable brutality of chemo, having her beautiful breasts removed, and then the misery of ongoing radiation was hard. It had been a truly wonderful thing, to witness how much courage the poor woman had managed to find, to endure all of that, thanks to the love she'd found with Stuart, and thanks to Minty's forgiveness. Minty was proud of her in a way she once would never have believed she could be.

What she'd said to Fiona when she left had been right too. In a perverse way, in the most painful way possible in fact, Fiona *had* done her a blinder of a favour, in bringing Leo's true colours to light.

Poor Leo. His swansong had been pathetic. Not realising that Minty and Fiona had mended fences, he'd first approached Fiona and begged her to take him back. He said that he was sorry he'd overreacted, he didn't mean it, he loved her and wanted to be beside her to support her, and if she gave him another chance he would be with her until the bitter end. What he didn't know was that by the time he'd finally got around to saying that, she had already mended her fences with Minty and discovered her soul-mate in Stuart. In the face of that, what she'd felt for Leo had quietly withered and died. It was gone; evaporated into the ether; replaced by something a lot more solid, reliable and real, and she'd taken great delight in telling him so.

Leo had then quickly contacted Minty, saying he realised what a huge mistake he'd made, he still loved her more than she could ever imagine, and pleading with *her* to take him back. She had *also* taken great delight in informing him that she had moved on too, in ways that could no longer be disrupted by the likes of a monumentally shallow, two-faced and self-serving coward who'd chosen to hedge his bets so shamelessly in his own self-interests.

So Leo Carleon McLeod, that despicable man of three lions, had found himself unexpectedly alone with both of the doors he'd hung his hopes on slammed firmly in his face. It would be hilarious if it hadn't all been so ironic. The wrecking ball he'd unleashed upon the women in his life had swung back and crushed him the hardest, in the end. Even Belle was still struggling to give him much more than the time of day. She was also struggling to have much time for Fiona, despite her Godmother's gruelling challenges. Belle truly felt for her, and hoped she'd have as good an innings as possible, but they weren't at ease with one another anymore. Minty hoped that Belle's full forgiveness would come in time, before poor Fiona might run out of it. So much damage, to so many relationships; life would never be the same again for any of them.

Minty and Fiona's friendship had proved strong enough, in a certain way, to weather the terrible storm. Even though they both accepted that they could never go back to the way they'd been before, they were on pretty good terms, all things considered. They loved one another, pure and simple, with a love that went back to the earliest of times, and they encouraged one another to continue to triumph over the adversity that had very nearly destroyed them. Minty was genuinely overjoyed that her friend had finally found true love, and she knew Fiona was glad that Minty had found her feet.

It was too late for Fiona to have her own children, but her relationship with Meghan was warm and nurturing. The two women genuinely loved and respected one another. There was talk of a quiet wedding for Fiona and Stuart, provided Fiona's health continued to remain stable, and Minty hoped with all her heart that it would happen.

She'd told Fiona about Marcel, and had giggled at her reaction.

'Wow! Financially independent, good looking French lawyer with an uncomplicated divorce, sane grown-up children, no residual baggage, and he's waiting in the wings until you're ready for him? He sounds like a keeper, Minty. I like the sound of him,' Fiona had said on the phone.

'You keep your hands to yourself!' Minty had warned her with a chuckle, and Fiona had laughed back.

'Oh don't worry! I already have the man of my dreams. I'm not interested in the man of yours. But I have to tell you, if you loved Leo half as much as I love Stuart, what I did to you was truly despicable, and a monumental thing to forgive. I don't know what I'd do without Stuart. I truly love him Minty, in a way I once never imagined I could love someone, and that makes what I did to you so much worse, in my own eyes. I don't know how you forgave me, now that I can imagine the pain of losing half of my heart. But I'm so glad you managed it. It's a privilege I don't deserve.'

'Life's too short, Fi, as you already know. We all just have to make the best of things, and for my own part I'm trying to be more appreciative too, of the people around me. Maybe I took Leo for granted. The reasons why he was unhappy couldn't have been all his fault, could they? I just wish he'd talked to me about it all. Attention to the minutiae of what goes on around me has never been my strong suit, outside of work of course, and I've missed so much of what was going on right under my nose,' Minty had confessed.

'I'm going to try to pay more attention to what's important to others, as well as just to myself. I've been selfish too. I probably didn't pay enough attention to Leo's wants and needs. It's not enough to simply blame him for not hitting me over the head when he should have, about things I ought to have seen. None of us is without fault, are we?'

'I suppose not. I guess we all make the beds we go on to lie in.'

They'd had a few such conversations since Minty had moved to France. Initially, their communication had been confined to dealing with Fiona's cancer, and superficial things, like the weather and the general state of the nation. They'd been at great pains, initially, to avoid a lot of in-depth discussion about the events that had torn them apart. When it became apparent that Stuart had become significant in Fiona's life to the point where he was then going to do all of the things for her that Minty had initially agreed to do, there was a huge sense of relief at being let off the hook.

Stuart had asked her if she would be joint power of attorney with him, because he didn't want to assume sole responsibility for Fiona's affairs, having only known her for a short time, and Minty readily agreed. It simply underscored what a thoroughly decent person he was, that he would do that to ensure Fiona's rights were protected with accountability. He was determined that nobody would take advantage of her, least of all himself, not that he intended to do that. Minty understood how precious Fiona had become to him, and how quickly. He adored her. They were quiet soul mates, in the truest sense, and it was so interesting that they'd met at Teapot Cottage. It was as if that magical little place had somehow dawn them both there, just so it could fuse their futures.

Minty cared deeply about Fiona, but the relief that she didn't have to stick around to see to all the practicalities of her cancer journey was immense. It wasn't because she hadn't *wanted* to be to Fiona what she'd promised. She did, and a promise was a promise, and she'd have seen it through to the very end, no matter how long it took. But Leo was still in Bristol of course, because of his job, and the last thing Minty really wanted was to be continually running into him or having to deal with him in any shape or form as he fought for his own recovery from the fallout of his actions. Fiona moving to the Lake District had neatly put paid to all that so, as it turned out, Minty needn't have worried, on that score, but it still felt good to have been able to take a step back.

Before leaving Torley, she had gone back to GladRagz boutique, and thrown herself on the mercy of Trudie Sangster. She'd made a proper appointment for it, after deciding that her days of being dowdy and dishevelled were gone.

Trudie had helped her pick a whole new wardrobe, in a full afternoon of girly giggles, delightful dress-ups, and plenty of coffee and cake. Trudie had invited Adie to come down, and she'd made a big pot of coffee and arranged for Peg Tripper to come over with a jelly-cake. The four women had ended up having a wonderful time together, and Minty had left Trudie's boutique with no less than nine bags of new clothes, shoes and accessories. It had cost her an eye-watering fortune and left poor Trudie with virtually no stock in her shop at all, for anyone else in a size twelve-to-fourteen, but life was for living, and Minty didn't want to waste another minute of it looking or feeling like anything less than her best. Both Trudie and Peg were now firm friends too, and they regularly caught up with emails and phone calls.

As soon as she'd got back to Bristol, Minty had thrown out every last stitch of what she'd previously worn, right down to the underwear and shoes. It was the best feeling in the world. She also booked a full-day appointment with one of Bristol's better-known personal trainers, to help her improve on the fitness she'd attained while walking on the fells around Torley and then partially lost thanks to the broken shoulder. She had gone to the city's top salon and had her hair properly restyled and coloured to ward off the approaching grey. She spent a week at a health spa with Belle, where they both had the full range of treatments, ate fabulous healthy food, and indulged in lots of pampering.

The entire make-over process had run into five figures, cost-wise, but it had produced a reinvented Minty Cartwright, who looked and felt amazing, and who wasn't going to stand in anybody's shadow anymore. All people could say was 'wow!' and that was exactly how she liked it.

Minty definitely had a lot of blessings to count, and Fliss had been one of the greatest. Her sister had been an absolute rock from start to finish. They'd never been as close as they could have been, growing up, and after Fliss moved to France it was even harder, but that was changing too. Living close to one another now meant they spent a lot more time together, and their relationship was deepening as the months wore on. Fliss was in the throes of menopause, and she was a massive support to Minty as she battled with her own symptoms of peri that were still plaguing her.

It was easier to manage, though, now that the rest of her life wasn't so turbulent, but the fact that Menopause 'proper' was right around the corner still had her worried, from time to time. Having Fliss to confide in (and occasionally rant at, when the frustration got the better of her) helped enormously. So did her communications about it all with Adie, Peg and Trudie.

Fliss had also introduced her to an online social media group for women in peri, where they could talk about their journeys and share their experiences and frustrations. She had been able to contribute herself, from a medical angle, in explaining why certain symptoms happened for some women and not for others. Knowledge meant power, as the saying went, and ignorance meant confusion. She firmly believed that understand *why* something was happening made it a little more bearable for many.

Fiona was in that group too now, at Minty's insistence. She was managing her peri better too, and she'd made Minty laugh when she said that she'd done plenty of research and she'd insisted on sharing it with a terrified but mostly-willing Stuart, so they could *both* understand why she sometimes felt like climbing the walls, or shoving him violently out of bed when he snored. Minty fully understood that it was part of Fiona's new strategy of ensuring she didn't have to be alone with *anything* anymore, especially something as important and potentially turbulent as the change of life. She decreed that for their mutual benefit, Stuart had to understand; it was as simple as that.

And Minty had a new companion in her lovely little French house! Sully the dog had been an unexpected gift from Marcel, 'to keep you company and help keep you fit.' Minty had been so thankful to have received him, because she still missed the family cat, Gizzard, who had eventually gone to live with Belle and Tim after Minty and Leo's marriage had ended. A home without a pet was a sad place indeed, and when

Marcel had turned up on her front porch with Sully, she had literally wept with joy.

Sully was a dog of indeterminate breed, a rescued dog whose first home hadn't worked out, but he was a lovely, loyal soft creature with floppy ears, soulful brown eyes and a very waggy tail. Minty imagined there was a bit of beagle in there, and maybe a little bit of labrador too, and a random assortment of other contributing genes. He was protective, and great fun. He was also a loving, sensitive animal, and even though he'd only been with her for a few months, they'd already formed a strong bond. He intuitively snuggled closer on the days when she still struggled to deal with her sadness, which were admittedly fewer these days, but sometimes quite random and unexpected. There was still quite a lot to grieve for, and that didn't go away overnight. Minty knew that she was still in a process, and most of the time it was fine, but occasionally it wasn't, and that was all part of adjusting to a very different life from the one she always thought she'd have.

Marcel had also given her a book on dog training and since Sully was still only a year old, it wasn't too late to start teaching him obedience and tricks. He was a fast learner, which was just as well, since one of the first lessons he'd had to learn was not to chase the chickens!

Minty had very quickly given in to her desire to have a few hens. Her time at Teapot Cottage had been made all the more special by the feathered little friends she'd made there, and as soon as she was settled in L'Aquitaine she'd commissioned a local carpenter to make a rather splendid-looking hen-house. Fliss had proclaimed it to be the epitome of luxury. Four laying hens had come to live in it, and Minty was now enjoying free range eggs again similar to those she'd fallen in love with at Teapot Cottage.

Sully had accepted his place at the bottom of the pecking order, and had stopped trying to continually engage the chickens in round-up, which had initially been exhausting for them until they'd staged a mutiny and decided one day to simply stand their ground and not be intimidated by him anymore. It had been a hilarious turn of events. The confusion on his face had been priceless as they'd stood there with their heads on one side, just staring him down. She'd told Marcel and he'd roared with laughter.

There was also a reasonable Farmers Market about twenty minutes away, and she would usually meet Fliss there on Saturday mornings to get the week's produce before heading to a nice little sidewalk cafe for a late *petit déjeuner*, which usually consisted of *un croissant et du café* and the two of them would catch up on their week. The little places weren't a patch on Adie Raven's locally famous Farmers Market in Torley, or Peg Tripper's café in the town, but they offered the basics, and one thing the French did really well was *l'épicerie fine*, the delicatessen, with each decent-sized town having at least two good ones. *Boulangeries* were everywhere too, selling gorgeous fresh bread in various shapes and flavours, and of course the most adorable cakes, so there was no way Minty was going to run out of food. Wandering down to the local bakery in a morning to buy delicious fresh bread every day was a much nicer experience than stocking up once a week on the doughy, tasteless stuff that passed for bread in English supermarkets, and she could buy wine locally by the litre if she took her own container to the corner shop. It was good stuff too; fit for export.

It certainly wasn't the life she imagined ending up in but, all in all, it hadn't been a bad exchange. Part of her still occasionally wondered if the move to France hadn't been just a little reactive and rash in response to everything, but what was there back in Bristol for her now? A job? Her daughter? Important things yes, but not the be-all and end-all. Belle was creating her own independent life, and Tim had suggested moving out of the city anyway, so there was no guarantee she'd be around for long even if Minty had stayed put. London beckoned, for Tim's career as an airline pilot, and while Minty couldn't think of anything worse, they were young and just starting out, and London was an exciting prospect to them. She couldn't blame them for considering it. Tim's question had been a good one; what's the point in paying London prices but not having the advantages that London has to offer? Bristol *was* nearly as expensive as London, as the cost of living went, and Tim was sure it would all even out with the higher wages he could command there.

If that did happen, and if Ethan stayed in Swindon (which seemed likely, as his relationship with Kal appeared to be rock solid and Kal had invited Ethan to move in with him), Leo would be well and truly on his own. In spite of everything, Minty did feel slightly sorry for him. She'd loved him so much, once. The love was still there, but it had changed now. It was no longer the kind of love that wanted to turn back the clock, even to before things started going awry, whenever that had been.

Minty still wasn't sure when the rot had set in, not that it mattered anymore. No; what she felt for Leo now was the kind of love that hopes for the best, the kind that accepts that what's lost is lost, and you can never go back, but you still want the other person to be happy, even if it isn't with you. Forgiveness had stolen up unannounced on that front too. Minty simply woke up one morning, in her new home, and realised she no longer bore any bitterness towards Leo. She thought back to what Adie Raven had said to her in the kitchen at the pot-luck dinner at Ravensdown House, so many moons ago, when they'd been talking about the way people's lives evolved the way they were supposed to, after a seismic shift, if they could simply let themselves go through the process without trying to control it too much or let the sadness of it overwhelm them.

'Finding the balance between being sad and being hopeful is enough. Taking it day by day until you feel more confident in considering a bigger picture will enable you to nurture yourself through the grief process without falling into a bloody big hole you can't haul yourself back out of.'

Minty smiled to herself now, as she recalled Adie's words. She hadn't consciously applied herself to trying to forgive her ex-husband, just as she hadn't done so with Fiona, but she had refused to devote any real energy to trying to maintain her anger or bitterness towards them either. Within her day to day life she'd found that all-important balance between being sad and being hopeful.

Adie had said that taking things day by day, just dealing with the normal stuff that came along, and being practical about it all, was the key to getting through it. And she'd been right. Applying herself to dealing with the daily realities of healing from her broken shoulder, her transition back to work, seeing the house sale through, supporting Fiona, and keeping her communication open with Belle and Ethan, and some of her friends that had still hung around after the split (and it was surprising how many hadn't), Minty had little time left over for anger, bitterness or depression. As she'd said to Fiona, life really was too short.

Feen Raven had told her too, that she'd be tested to the limit, and she *had* been. But, just as Feen had *also* said, everything had turned out pretty well.

So, while Minty had no desire to reconnect with Leo, she did wish him all the best. She vowed to learn from the mistakes she'd made, in failing to notice what was going on around the edges of her life, or what had started eating away at its very foundations. She knew Fiona had learned important things too, after being confronted with her own mortality and realising how important honesty and real love were, to everything that really mattered.

All that was left to hope for now was that Leo would learn some lessons too. He'd let Minty down, in the latter years of their marriage, by not drawing her attention to the fact that he hadn't been happy. Minty had let him down too, in her failure to see it, but his response had been to exploit her distraction and go on to make decisions that ultimately devastated them both. He'd been a self-serving coward, and it had cost him everything.

Minty also knew that she'd let Fiona down too, for their whole lives, by failing to notice how much her friend had always needed her. Fiona's aloof self-centredness and detachment from virtually everything that was meaningful, while they were growing up had hidden deep, decimating wounds that Minty had failed to see.

And Fiona had let *her* down by failing to fully appreciate her, and ultimately stealing her husband. Leo clearly had demons he was wrestling with, and he'd walked out on both of the women who loved him, but neither had fought very hard for him, or made him think he was even worth fighting *for*. So maybe they'd let him down too.

They'd all disappointed and neglected each other, in some fundamental way but, as hurtful and horrible as that all was, it was a lot less important than what it had taught them. Minty did hope that Leo would learn, and find happiness. The rest of his life was going to be a long time to be alone, otherwise, wasn't it? If he found someone, Minty hoped he'd recognise and appreciate what he had. Only time would tell, as to whether he pulled it all together or continued to lurch from one crisis of his own making, to the next. She'd only spoken to him once on the phone since the house sale had gone through; to ask him to come and collect the last of his things after she'd moved all her stuff out, and then drop the keys she'd left for him off at the agent. He'd told her he'd seen her crossing a road in Bristol one afternoon, after her make-over, and said she looked utterly amazing. She thanked him graciously for the compliment, wished him good luck, and never spoke to him again.

That part of her life was over. She'd moved on, and yes it still hurt, and yes she still wished that none of it had happened, but it was easier to be physically removed from the places and the memories they'd all shared. It was less painful, to be dealing with it all from a distance. She still missed Ethan and Belle like fire, but technology allowed them to talk often, and England was only a short flight away if she ever had to get back in a hurry. Both kids had given their full blessing to Minty's move to France, and Belle, Tim, Ethan and Kal had all come over for Minty's first French Christmas. They'd stayed in a local hotel, and had Christmas dinner there, as a family. It had been a fun few days, especially since Marcel had also made it down on Boxing Day. He'd come on a flying visit, to meet everyone, before heading back to Paris. The poor man had drawn the short straw, to man the office, over Christmas and New Year.

Minty had received a lovely card and a gorgeous lime green plastic Art deco style vase from Adie and Mark Raven, as a housewarming gift. The vase turned out to be perfect for the porch window. Adie's note said she'd got her new address from Fiona and Stuart. The card had read;

'Keep this full of French flowers, and whenever you look at them, remember <u>*you're*</u> *remembered, from our little corner of paradise. Bonne chance dans ta nouvelle maison!'*

She'd emailed to thank them, and they'd kept in touch since. Minty wasn't sure when she'd ever be back in the Lake District. She suspected it might be for Fiona's funeral, but who knew when that might be? It could be years away. There might even be a wedding first! It was enough to know, for now, that her friendships there would still hold good if the time ever came to return.

Her memories of her time in Torley, and the unusual and incredibly special Teapot Cottage, would always be with her. It had been a bright beacon in the darkest of times, and the path it had set her on was one she would once never have imagined taking. But she was happy. In spite of the fires she'd walked through, there was a certain contentedness within her now that hadn't been there even *before* everything had blown up and ruined her previous life.

As the saying went; 'life pushes you forward whether you want it to or not, and it's only when you kick against the process that you start having problems.' Maybe Minty was *always* meant to end up here; divorced, and rebuilding a whole new life in a brand new place. Adie and Feen Raven would both have insisted it to be true, and Minty had to concede that through relinquishing full control of every little thing, she'd ended up in a place of real contentment. And rather than dreading the future, as she'd done at the time of her arrival at Teapot Cottage, she was now quite excited about what might lie ahead. Going with the flow was still a new concept, and not as comfortable yet as she'd hoped it would be when she started out, but she was getting there. She knew the time was coming when she would be fully at ease with letting things take their course.

To quote another time-worn phrase; 'the longest journey starts with a single step.' Whoever said that was absolutely right, and whoever followed it up by saying that the destination isn't as important as the journey was right too. Most clichés did have a foot planted firmly in reality, and Minty's reality was that she still had a lot of journey left to take, and she wanted to be more open to enjoying where it took her. She was excited, about who might come into her life, and what opportunities might present themselves. And vowing to notice the little things more, the meaningful small occurrences and nuances that punctuated her life, would make it all the more rich and interesting.

She stood up and wandered over to the edge of the patio. Sully was sleeping quietly under a vertical raft of raspberry canes, his tail twitching as he chased an imaginary rabbit. The early-morning sun threw long shadows across the little courtyard. Even though the air was a cooler than she would have liked, she thought she might just have a quick swim before getting ready for work. Tonight, she would fix a light supper of bread, fruit and cheese, and of course have the almost obligatory nightly glass of beautiful Bordeaux. Then she would have a lovely long Zoom chat with Marcel.

'My new life? Bring it on,' she said softly to Sully, who woke up and thumped his tail.

'Bring every single slice of it on.'

In a Chat With Annie Cook...

1. What was the moment you decided to write your first book? What prompted you?
I had a story I wanted to tell, so I simply sat down and started to write it. It felt important to get it out of my head and onto paper, and I wasn't sure why, only that I had to do it.

2. Do your stories unfold as you write or do you plan out a whole script then start writing?
I never start with a full script in my head. For me, a story is always better when it evolves organically, rather than trying to stick to a pre-conceived idea. That kind of rigidity doesn't work for me, as a storyteller. I start with a character or two, and an idea of where I want them to go, but I've had to learn to be flexible with that because things usually find their own direction and that becomes part of what makes the story believable.

3. Have you ever completely changed the plot or outcome part way through writing if you've had a new idea?
That happens all the time! Normally, when I create my characters, they evolve as we go along, and sometimes they just dart off in a direction I wasn't anticipating. It's always fun, and in an upcoming story in the Teapot Cottage Tales, one of the characters suddenly evolved career-wise, which was a huge surprise for me! But it was where she seemed to want to go, so I went with her on it, and I think the book is better for that element having evolved. It gave the story a little more depth. Odd as it sounds, sometimes the characters know best.

4. Where does your inspiration come from?
Much comes from my previous work as a Family and Forensic Psychologist. I've worked with a lot of people who were

dealing with trauma, crises or life-challenges of various kinds. Just as much has come from simply observing life as it goes on around me, and from my own experiences, and listening to the conversations, perspectives and experiences of others.

5. What advice would you give to someone who is thinking about writing a book?
Just start, really. Whatever your thoughts are, get them out of your head and onto the screen (or into a notebook), and see where it takes you. You don't need much at all, for a beginning. People wrongly imagine they have to have the whole thing in their head when they start, and that's a lot of pressure. Making a start and seeing how things unfold, that's what allows a writer to find their 'flow' and things tend to follow from there. If it's non-fiction, do you research and make sure what you're reporting as fact actually is, and with fiction (unless its fantasy) it still needs to ring true for the reader.

6. As a writer: how do you make yourself write, and write consistently?
That's never been a problem for me. I've never had to 'make' myself write, because it never feels like work. My biggest problem, actually, is knowing when to stop.

7. How did you get published initially?
Perfectly good literature from amazing writers that deserves to be published is consistently being rejected instead because traditional publishing houses now have such narrow criteria that most writers don't tick enough of their boxes. I decided to take the self-publishing route. More and more writers are doing this now because it has become a lot easier to do, with increasingly good support, and it gives us greater control of all aspects of the writing, design and publication process.

Annie Cook's Debut novel is available now...

No Small Change

A Teapot Cottage Tale (#1)

The 'change of life' means menopause.
But what if it also means reinvention,
with the help of a little bit of magic?

Adie Bostock is a self-confessed 'basket-case.' She's fifty-two, at the mercy of her haphazard hormones, and struggling to face the end of her marriage. Alone for Christmas and fed up with family drama, she lands at Teapot Cottage where she plans to wallow in guilt and self-pity in private.

But the cottage, with its mysterious healing energy, has other plans for Adie and she soon finds out that it takes more than one person to make things fall apart, and more than one to put them back together.

Confirmed widower Mark Raven is a rough-edged farmer determined to hide his heart. He's battling with grief and ageing, and keeping his rather dreamy daughter at least partly in the real world. Romance is not on his radar.

Adie and Mark want to keep things purely platonic, but an unseen influence is nudging them in a different direction. Then Adie's husband decides he wants her back. It's what she's been praying for, but is it still what she really wants?

Escape to the Lake District with this magical,
life-affirming story about overcoming adversity
and finding love again later in life.

The Power of Notes and Spells

A Teapot Cottage Tale (#2)

Every woman dreams of finding the love of her life. But what do you do when yours brings baggage that can hurt you and your family?

Feen Raven is often described as more than just a little bit barmy. The young 'white witch' has finally found her soulmate, but old family wounds are opened again when she finds out who he's involved with.

Gavin Black is on an unhappy errand that forces him to reconnect with his estranged mother. All he wants is to claim what's his and go home again, without any complications.

Carla Walton can't let go of a grudge. After a lifetime of pushing everyone away, she is isolated, bitter, and blaming everyone else for her problems. She wants to be left alone so she can keep ignoring her demons.

But Teapot Cottage, with its mysterious ability to heal the broken-hearted, always has a more complicated agenda for people who don't want to rake up the past. Pretty soon, Gavin, Feen and Carla come to question everything they think they do and don't want in life.

Will love and a little bit of magic help them find a way forward? Or will old family fractures be too hard to heal?

Come to the Lake District, to a gentle place where a beautiful blend of music and magic can heal the hardest hearts.

A Moral Swerve

Nobody comes home expecting to find intruders -
But what would you do if you did?

Alison Jones is single, lives alone, and doesn't have a lot of self-awareness. But, after coming home to find burglars in her house, she does a terrible thing without thinking, and is forced to confront some ugly truths about herself.

Darren Davies is a petty thief, stuck in the revolving door between small-time crime and prison. After he makes the biggest mistake of his life, he is compelled to re-evaluate the path his life is taking, and deal with the demons that drive him.

When Darren and Alison's lives intersect, they each find themselves on a soul-searing journey, as they struggle to come to terms with the catastrophic impact of their acts and omissions. After stumbling through the wreckage, the future for them both becomes crystal clear, but it's not what either of them expected.

As one door opens and another slams shut, choices expand and diminish.

At the crossroads of Beginnings and Endings,
who decides to go where?

When It's Meant To Happen

A Teapot Cottage Tale (#3)

Having a baby is something most women dream of and plan for. But what does it mean if you can't make it happen, no matter how hard you try?

Debby Davies longs for a family of her own. She is desperate to have a baby with the husband she adores, but fruitless years of trying to conceive have left her feeling like a failure. It's starting to make her crazy, that she can't seem to achieve the one thing she always felt destined to do.

Darren Davies is at his wits' end with his wife. Her simmering resentment is changing her in ways that really scare him, and the horrible way her parents treat him is starting to take its toll. He's beginning to question whether their marriage can survive what feels like a never-ending series of storms.

As their doubts take hold, that their love can survive, they know they're in the last chance saloon. But Teapot Cottage, with its mystical ability to pour balm on battered souls, has plans for
Debby and Darren that show them what's possible in ways they could never have imagined.

Can they stay together and face a very different future from the one they had planned, or will they find the challenges too great, and go their separate ways?

Run away from home for a while! Come to the Lake District, to a place where miracles can happen, with the help of a little bit of magic!

Ruin, Reins and Redemption

A Teapot Cottage Tale (#4)

Everyone makes mistakes, and some of them are hard to come back from. When you've taken someone else's life, and destroyed your family in the process, where do you begin, to pull things back together?

Stuart Thomson is a disgraced lawyer whose catastrophic error of judgement has all but ruined his life. By the time he leaves prison, after six years, he no longer has a career, a home or a marriage, and his troubled teenage daughter is barely speaking to him.

Meghan Thomson is almost fifteen. She's a mixed-up mess of anger and confusion, and she has no idea how she feels about anything at all, especially her father. When he books a holiday to the Lake District together, to reconnect, it's the last thing she really wants to do with a man she doesn't trust.

On holiday, father and daughter both struggle to understand each other. But Teapot Cottage, with its enigmatic way of turning troubled lives around, reveals an amazing opportunity they once could never have imagined. The future on offer means a whole new level of faith and commitment from them both, to make it happen.

Stuart and Meghan desperately need a new start. Can they trust themselves and each other enough to make it happen? Or does the heartbreak of the past make the leap of faith too tough?

In Torley town, in a very special cottage, lives are often transformed with the help of 'a little bit of love and magic.'

THICKER THAN WATER

Earth-shattering secrets will always come out, and the truth doesn't care about the cost.

Adie Bostock has finally found the baby she was forced to give up at fifteen – the one her husband and grown-up children don't know about – and she intends to keep her secrets. But, in the wake of a shocking crime, her tightly-woven web of deceit starts unravelling and she doesn't have a clue how to stop it.

Matty Bostock boosts his graduate income with sex work. Everything ticks along nicely in his smug, self-satisfied world, until one of his clients is murdered. With another refusing to give him the alibi he needs, he can't prove his innocence, and he faces going down for a crime he didn't commit.

Ruth Stenton has a happy, settled life with her wife Gina Giordano, and she is blissfully unaware of just how big a lie she's been living. When she discovers who has been hiding a terrible truth from her, and for how long, the impact is profound and far-reaching.

Ruth is forced to face demons she didn't know she had, and Gina has to find a way to help her. Adie can't protect one of her children without destroying another, and Matty must confront the consequences of the way he has chosen to live.

As moral dilemmas start to crush a family that's been buckled by betrayal, everyone has to decide; how much does 'blood' really matter, and what can or can't be forgiven?

Coming Soon .....

The Choice Between Safe and Brave

A Teapot Cottage Tale (#6)

When the woman you love is ripped from your life without warning, how do you pick up the pieces if you think it's all your fault?

Chris Darcy is a mountaineer on a mission to scale the world's summits, but when his world is shattered on a climbing trip with his fiancée Daisy, he is crippled by guilt, and dealing with demons that have plagued him all his life. Bereft and broken, he goes back to Teapot Cottage, where he'd been once before, with Daisy.

Tezzie Bostock is finally home from travelling. She is reeling from a badly broken heart and reluctantly drifting towards a career she doesn't want. When epiphany strikes, she decides to do something different. She knows she has to regain her self-esteem to make it happen, but she doesn't know where to start.

As Chris and Tezzie's lives intersect, they realize they've met before. Reeling from heartbreak of different kinds, they forge a solid friendship, and form an alliance that helps to push them both forward, towards an exciting future.

But, even as they find themselves edging towards romance, Tezzie has plans to be somewhere else, where her own life will be at risk. Can Chris even contemplate losing another love? Can Tezzie make a compromise that can still let her have her chosen career? Or is it all too much of a challenge for two lost souls who seem to want different things?

Come and spend some quiet time in a little house of healing in the Lake District, where lives get reinvented, with the help of a little bit of magic!

www.ingramcontent.com/pod-product-compliance
Lightning Source LLC
Chambersburg PA
CBHW070418170726
48291CB00002B/254

* 9 7 8 1 9 1 7 6 0 1 0 7 8 *